# THE REBORN

# THE REBORN

## Lin Anderson

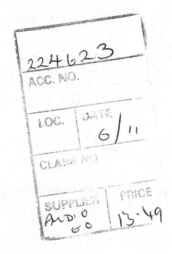

**WINDSOR**
**PARAGON**

First published 2010
by Hodder & Stoughton
This Large Print edition published 2011
by AudioGO Ltd
by arrangement with
Hodder & Stoughton Ltd

Hardcover  ISBN: 978 1 445 85425 0
Softcover   ISBN: 978 1 445 85426 7

British Library Cataloguing in Publication Data available

Printed and bound in Great Britain by
CPI Antony Rowe, Chippenham and Eastbourne

# ACKNOWLEDGEMENTS

Thanks to Dr Jennifer Miller of GUARD, DCI Kenny Bailey (retired), Andy Rolph, R2S CRIME Forensic Services Manager, Scottish people's tenor John Innes and Sharon Mitchell, Scottish artist (www.sharonmitchellartist.co.uk).

To Detective Inspector Bill Mitchell

# CHAPTER ONE

It was fear of the clown that drove Kira inside.

He appeared suddenly beside a group of kids at the candyfloss van, bringing her to an abrupt halt. Then it began. The rapid heartbeat, the burst of perspiration, the shortness of breath. The baby lurched inside her, as though sharing her panic.

The clown looked up, catching her eye. There was nothing funny about the mask it was wearing. Its deformity terrified her. She imagined her unborn child emerging from the womb, clown face grinning up at her, hands and feet unnaturally large.

Kira dragged her gaze away and forced her frozen limbs to walk to the nearest booth. The young male attendant pushed a ticket and her change under the glass and she grabbed it, her hand trembling, imagining the clown's gaze fastened on her back.

She pulled aside the thick black entrance curtain and let it fall behind her. Now that the clown was out of sight, her fear began to subside. Kira closed her eyes and took slow, deep breaths, mimicking the pre-natal classes her mother had persuaded her to attend. Gradually her heartbeat slowed and she began to feel foolish. Thank God she hadn't been with David—or even worse, Sandie—when it happened. She would never have lived it down.

Calmer now, she took a look around her. She was in a narrow corridor lit by an orange lamp. God, she hoped this wouldn't turn out to be some fright trip. The clown had been scary enough. The

1

baby was due in ten days and she didn't fancy an early delivery, not that she was looking forward to any delivery if she was honest.

She glanced back at the curtain. Should she leave? The clown might have moved on. Then she decided no fairground attraction could be as terrifying as seeing that face again.

The corridor terminated in another black curtain. Kira pulled it aside and stepped through, and was immediately confronted by herself—swollen beyond all recognition.

The image was every pregnant woman's worst nightmare. Short, squat, a ball on thick legs. Only her face remained normal in size, its gaze startled. Her initial shock gave way to amusement and she smiled at this version of herself. Her reflection smiled back, the grin flat and wide like the Cheshire Cat's. She giggled and stepped sideways to see what the next mirror would offer.

This time she was as thin as a rake, the bump a funny nodule in the middle, yet her face was fatter than ever. A big round Humpty Dumpty face.

Laughter bubbled up inside her. No longer a seventeen-year-old expectant mother 'whose life had been ruined', Kira was, for a moment, a child again. The baby jerked into life, stretching her skin with its kicking. She turned sideways to watch the effects of its movement in the mirror.

It was then she became aware that there was someone else in the tent. She waited, expecting voices or laughter, hearing only footsteps on the wooden flooring. Turning towards the sound, she was horrified to see the hideous white face with its obscenely large red mouth and tiny black eyes. Not just one clown this time, but multiple versions

2

reflected in the maze of mirrors.

Then the whispering began, an eerie cacophony that rose and fell like a wave about her. Shrieks from the nearby rides drowned her own scream as she took off, darting down paths between the mirrors, desperate to find the exit, imagining the clown following, getting ever closer.

A sudden pain tore at her belly and she bent double, sending a rush of hot water streaming down her inner thighs to pool between her feet. She smelt the cloying scent of sweat and plastic and knew he was there, right behind her. *Help me*, she whispered as she sunk to her knees.

Hands gripped her head and tipped it up. The rubbery gargoyle face was inches from her own now. Kira moaned as another spasm caught her in its grip, and the hands suddenly released her. She slumped to the floor and rolled onto her side, drawing up her knees. As the contraction built to its peak, she closed her eyes and concentrated on the pain, then something soft and ice-cold covered her nose and mouth, smothering her cry.

She fought against breathing in the acrid fumes, but failed. As the sounds of the funfair began to fade, the image before her began to blur. Now the clown became a doctor who had come to help her. As the pain subsided, Kira gave a little whimper of relief.


## CHAPTER TWO

David checked his hair in the ticket booth glass, smoothing it into shape.

'This isn't a hairdresser's, mate.'

He grinned and passed the money for two tickets under the glass, then gestured to Owen to follow and made his way nonchalantly across the floor towards a red dodgem car.

'I'm driving,' he said as they got in.

Sandie was already climbing into a blue model nearby. She threw him a look, daring him. He had every intention of ramming her—again and again. He was looking forward to hearing her scream.

She had been playing up to him all night when Kira wasn't looking, thinking she would soon be out of the picture. She had no idea what he and Kira had together. How they understood one another perfectly. Yin and Yang. Joined at the hip, although the bump got in the way at the moment.

The buzzer sounded and he took off, wrenching the wheel immediately to the left, slamming the blue dodgem side-on. Sandie jerked forward, then back, screeching in fright.

'Bastard!'

She even swore in a posh voice. Weird. He swung full circle and rammed her again. The blue car was going nowhere.

When the hooter sounded Sandie had barely moved from her starting point. David jumped out, elated, and strode towards the side. 'Waltzers next,' he called to Owen. He scanned the crowds waiting to take their place on the cars. No sign of Kira. How long did it take to buy candyfloss?

Maybe she'd headed for the toilets set up in a row outside the circle of motor homes. These days she needed the toilet all the time. He shrugged and set off towards the Waltzers.

A young guy with a shaved head took their

money, eyeing up Sandie, who'd made a point of sitting between himself and Owen. She gave him a flirty look, and as soon as the ride started up he made a beeline for their carriage and began to twirl them mercilessly.

Now Sandie's screams were much too close for comfort. David wanted to take her striped scarf and shove it down her throat. As they swept round, he thought he spotted Kira in the crowd, but the next time round she had disappeared.

The bald guy's antics with their car were threatening to bring up the three bottles of Becks he'd drunk. He'd seen that happen once before, a guy projectile-vomiting on a Waltzer. Mad panic had ensued as the occupants of neighbouring cars ducked and dived and the crowds lining the barrier jumped out of the way.

What an arse the sick guy had looked as he climbed off, jacket streaked with vomit, half the surrounding throng out to get him. He didn't want that to happen to him.

David focused on keeping the beer where it belonged, although Sandie didn't help matters, clinging to his arm, her face buried in his shoulder. She stunk of strong perfume or hairspray. Not like Kira, whose skin had recently developed a milky smell like white chocolate.

They were slowing down, and Sandie's screams had quietened to a relieved whimper. Making a point of ignoring David, Baldy slipped her a piece of paper, doubtless with his number on it, then gave them a final twirl. The bar was released and David stood up, not making any attempt to assist Sandie, even though she pouted at him.

The truth was, he was fed up with her and

5

wanted only to locate Kira. He turned on his heel and walked away without explanation. Sandie was already putting Baldy's number in her phone.

There was a queue at the candyfloss van but Kira wasn't part of it. He thought about asking the woman serving if she'd seen her, but decided against it and headed instead for the toilets. There was a queue there too. He stood watching until he'd seen each cubicle door open and someone emerge. None of them was Kira.

Finally he pulled out his phone and called her, wondering if she would be able to hear it above the noise of the fairground.

*Hi, this is Kira. Leave a message.*

'Where are you? Call me back.'

He hung around the toilets for a while, getting some funny looks. Half an hour later he decided she must have gone home. But why do that without telling him? He had a sudden thought that she might have seen Sandie drape herself round him on the Waltzers and taken umbrage. But Kira knew what Sandie was like and she also knew he didn't fancy her. Still, pregnancy had made her a bit weird and emotional.

He contemplated calling her home number, but that was strictly against the rules. Her parents didn't know about him, and Kira had forbidden him to call her there.

His next thought was the hospital. She was booked into the Maternity Unit on Alexandra Parade. Should he call up and ask if she'd been admitted? He could say he was the baby's father, although if her parents were there, that wouldn't go down too well.

He decided to check the area around the

6

candyfloss van again, in case Kira had decided to wander about the nearby stalls. She wouldn't go on a fast ride, but there was no reason she couldn't try out the other amusements.

The nearest one was a ghost train. He checked at the ticket booth, although he didn't hold out much hope. When he described Kira, the man pointed to a health and safety notice too small to decipher.

'Nae pregnant lassies allowed in here,' he rasped.

Next to the ghost train was a large black tent housing the Hall of Mirrors, which promised entrants a 'Fabulous Freaky Time'. David approached the booth.

'Did a pregnant girl with long blonde hair come in here?'

The young male behind the glass didn't answer immediately, but his smirk said plenty.

'What's it to you?'

'Did she or didn't she?'

'Aye.'

'Is she still in there?'

The guy shrugged. 'No idea.'

'Can I check?'

'Two quid.'

David handed over a fiver and took his change. As he pushed through the curtain, the guy shouted after him, 'We're closing in five minutes.'

David walked the orange lit corridor, cursing the attendant for conning him and fighting the urge to go out and demand his money back.

When the second curtain fell shut behind him, he was suddenly struck by the intense stillness, the way the sounds of the outside world were muffled.

He knew instinctively that he was the only one in there, but he called Kira's name all the same. When there was no answer he called again, but his voice was swallowed by silence.

'Shit.'

On entry, he'd ignored the reflection of himself, now he peered at the squat body and stumpy legs the mirror showed him. Only his head was normal size. He consoled himself that at least his hair looked OK.

He wondered how Kira had reacted when confronted with a similar image of herself. She didn't like being 'fat', as she called the last stage of pregnancy, although he loved to hug her rounded body and feel life jump against him.

Kira wasn't in here, that much was obvious. He thought about turning and going out the way he'd come in, but decided if he saw that smirk again, he might just hit the guy.

He looked for the exit, and realised the mirrors were set out in a maze. It might take him longer than the threatened five minutes to find his way out. As if on cue, the drone of the generator faltered and the dim overhead lights flickered off and on again.

The guy in the booth must be doing it on purpose just to scare him. He swore under his breath and started running through the maze, darting down one path, then turning and trying another. After a few turns he stopped, ashamed of himself.

Thank God Kira wasn't here to see him act like a big girl's blouse.

As he turned his head, he caught a glimpse of something familiar in a nearby mirror, and as he swivelled for a better look, the image multiplied. Now it was reflected in three mirrors.

His breath caught in his throat as he recognised the object as a small blue shoe. Like the ones Kira was wearing.

His stomach twisted in a knot. He followed its reflection and picked it up, trying to convince himself that he was wrong. But he knew he wasn't. This was Kira's shoe.

Had she taken fright like him while looking for the way out? He stuffed the shoe in his pocket and set off again, following a cold draught which he hoped would lead to the exit.

When he turned the final corner, he saw her.

She was lying on her back, and his first thought was she had gone into labour. He ran towards her, shouting her name, then slipped on something and went down hard, his head slamming against the wood.

He came to moments later, his vision blurred, his ears ringing. When he lifted his hand it was covered in blood. He staggered to his feet, slithering on a mess of blood and other stuff he didn't dare give a name to. He hesitated before getting any closer, not wanting to register what he was looking at.


CHAPTER THREE

Rhona was surrounded by shadows. In the firelight they seemed to advance and retreat, dancing about her. She liked the room this way. No lamps, the only light coming from the flames licking the coals.

9

She could hear the distant sounds of the funfair in Kelvingrove Park. In years gone by it had been housed in the Kelvin Hall, now a sports arena. She had gone there as a child with her father and now the carnival sounds conjured up memories of his warm hand enveloping hers, the scent of tobacco from his coat and the sweet crunch of candyfloss.

Her father's ghost wasn't the only one haunting her tonight. Detective Sergeant Michael McNab had been dead for six weeks, and the realisation that she would never see him again had only started to sink in.

For months after her father's death, she had imagined him still resident in the cottage on Skye. She'd tried to convince herself that if she called he would answer, just as always. She'd never dialled the number, never dared. She couldn't bear to hear it ring into the emptiness.

As for McNab, she felt his presence constantly, even now among the shadows. She imagined she saw his tall figure in every crowd, his distinctive auburn hair, that quizzical look he used to give her, his infectious laugh. She even heard his voice, and sometimes she forgot herself and answered. She'd fooled herself for a while by imagining he had been posted away somewhere—the police college, perhaps, or helping on a case somewhere rural. It amused her to think how McNab would have hated that. He'd never liked the wilds of Scotland, preferring the mean streets of Glasgow.

She had dreamt about him constantly, reliving his last moments over and over again. Eventually she could bear sleep no longer and had taken to spending the night sitting here dozing and waiting for a call-out, because concentrating on other deaths helped her to briefly forget McNab's.

There had been no family members present at the funeral at Glasgow Cathedral, the only mourners his friends and colleagues. That was another thing they'd had in common: no family left alive. It had been her assistant, Chrissy, who told her that McNab's mother was dead and he'd never known his father. All the time they'd been colleagues—and occasionally lovers—he had never told Rhona that.

*You never really know someone. Not truly.*

She couldn't blame him for not confiding in her. They had briefly played at being together, but it felt more like a game than a relationship. Nevertheless, when she'd ended it, he had reacted badly and it had taken DI Bill Wilson, his superior officer, to sort things out. Bill had dispatched McNab on a police training course to break his obsession with Rhona.

Bill had never chastised her about that unfortunate liaison. It was never wise to get involved with colleagues, and it was a particularly bad idea for the area's Chief Forensic to sleep with a Detective Sergeant, as they had to work so closely together; but the habit was widespread. You were constantly in one another's company, inhabiting a strange world that only those who were part of could possibly understand. Violent death drew people together, and sex was a good way to celebrate being alive.

When McNab had reappeared, she'd already moved on to Sean Maguire, an Irish charmer who played the saxophone in a local bar. She'd even gone so far as to allow him to move in with her—delightful at first, but inevitably a disaster. He had figured out her notes and learned how to play them, but she'd grown suspicious that she might not be the only tune he was playing. She had no proof, but the time she spent thinking about it disturbed her. So Sean had gone the way of the others and solitude had returned.

*I can't count on anything or anyone. I am better off alone.*

If McNab could hear her he would have mocked her self-pity and then made a pass at her, fully expecting the usual knock-back.

But McNab was dead.

An officer killed in the line of duty. It could happen to any one of them, which was why so many of his colleagues had been at the funeral, a hundred at least. McNab's real family, the people he had worked with day after day. The people who would seek his killer, however long it took.

Chrissy had given the reading, and it was she and Bill who'd organised the funeral. Rhona hadn't known McNab was a Catholic, although she'd seen him rub both sides up the wrong way by humming the wrong tune in the wrong bar. *It takes one to know one*, Chrissy had said. *And it's easier to do it this way. The priest takes care of everything.*

It was more than that. McNab had saved Chrissy's life and that of her then-unborn child, a little boy she'd named Michael in tribute. She might profess to be a lapsed Catholic, but she'd preferred to hedge her bets where McNab was concerned. *If it's not true, it won't matter. If it is, then I've seen him right.*

Chrissy's voice had been strong as she'd recited Corinthians, Chapter 13. Rhona had heard a muffled sob beside her as DS Janice Clark had striven to contain herself. Rhona would have put her hand on Janice's arm had she been able to control her own trembling. Most people there that day wouldn't have been inside a church for years, but you didn't need to be religious for the final proclamation to ring true.

*As it is, these remain: faith, hope and love, the three of them; and the greatest of them is love.*

Chrissy had taken her place on Rhona's other side and she'd felt a hand slip into hers as the predominantly male voices had risen in unison to sing 'Be Thou my Vision'.

\*       \*       \*

She was in the kitchen making coffee when the phone rang, just after midnight. She'd already spoken to Chrissy at eleven thirty; her assistant had taken to phoning during her nighttime breastfeeding sessions. According to Chrissy, her partner, Sam, managed to sleep through everything, only waking if she shook him. 'He's not got the right equipment anyway.'

These nighttime chats, Rhona knew, were more about her state of mind than Chrissy's, although looking down at her baby son was bound to bring back thoughts of McNab. The calls didn't last long, but she was always glad to hear Chrissy's voice in what had become her solitary darkness. Chrissy had tried on one occasion to get her to seek counselling for post-traumatic stress, but to her shame Rhona had greeted the suggestion with frigid silence. After that, Chrissy had taken it upon herself to be her nocturnal companion.

When the phone rang again, she'd thought

13

Chrissy had forgotten to impart some vital piece of news about baby Michael's progress, like an imagined smile, but it was an unfamiliar voice she heard. The operative couldn't tell her the full details, just that her presence was required at a suspicious death in Kelvingrove Park.

*       *       *

The street outside the flat was deserted, patched by darkness where a street lamp had failed. She unlocked the car remotely, shivering in the frosty air. In the distance rose the majestic edifice that housed Glasgow's famous Kelvingrove Museum and Art Gallery, and on the hill behind was the towering outline of Glasgow University. Surrounding all this lay the park, a place of Victorian splendour, its landscaped curves following the River Kelvin from which it took its name. Criss-crossed by numerous leafy walkways and cycle paths, it was a favourite haunt for all age groups in daylight but, like most inner city parks, it was not for the faint of heart after dark.

As she turned in at the park gates she saw the pulsating blue lights of three squad cars. There had been general disquiet among residents about the siting of the funfair, but their objections had been overruled by the city authorities—something they would probably regret now.

The entrance to the funfair was cordoned off, and a constable had taken charge. McNab had been the Crime Scene Manager on numerous incidents she'd been involved with, and Rhona was used to seeing his familiar figure, hearing his jocular welcome, and watching him eye up any

14

female personnel he hadn't yet persuaded into bed. The young constable who handed her the log book didn't even know who she was and insisted on checking her ID before letting her pass.

Walking onto a scene knowing the team she'd worked with for so long—her family—no longer existed was the most difficult part of each new case. She'd thought her new role as an independent expert under the auspices of the university would help. She liked working alongside Roy Hunter, the former DCI who had developed a digitised crime scene management system that made *CSI Miami* look like a bunch of amateurs. Spherical High Definition recording of major crime scenes, software that incorporated every item of information gathered—maps of the area, post-mortem findings, her own forensic notes, including DNA and fingerprint results. All of this was regularly updated and available twenty-four hours a day via laptop, phone or PDA. A far cry from notebook drawings, and definitely the future of policing.

Despite her new status, the absence of McNab, Chrissy and DI Wilson, who was currently awaiting a court appearance for assaulting a prisoner, had only served to accentuate her feeling of isolation. So she was relieved when she spotted one friendly face in the guise of DS Janice Clark, who had been promoted recently and taken over McNab's role as Crime Scene Manager.

'Michael would be proud of you,' Rhona told her.

'He taught me everything I know.'

Rhona left a moment of silence before she spoke. 'What's going on?'

15

'The body of a teenage girl was found in the Hall of Mirrors.' Janice grimaced, and Rhona noticed she looked pale.

'That bad?'

She gave a swift nod. 'The pathologist is in with her now.'

Rhona didn't ask for details. She would see for herself soon enough. She made her way over to a black tent fronted by a ticket booth, where a curtain had been pulled back to allow entry. The place smelt of diesel from the generators and damp, trodden grass. A narrow corridor lit by an orange light led to a second curtain, also tied back.

The first image that greeted her inside was herself, kitted out in a boiler suit, resembling a white balloon. The ludicrous reflection was more disquieting than amusing.

Blazing arc lights and metal treads set out on the wooden flooring led her towards the rear of the tented structure. The route was indirect and she had to pass various distorted images of herself before eventually being confronted by a likeness of Dr Sissons, his height diminished, his lower half so squat that his torso was only inches from the floor.

'Disturbing, isn't it?'

She wasn't sure whether he was referring to the crime scene or his counterpart in the mirror. He stepped aside to give her a full view.

The victim was lying on her back, a loose dress drawn above her waist to expose her stomach, or what was left of it. Beside the body lay the whitish coil of an umbilical cord still attached to the plump reddish mass of a placenta. Rhona was still processing the implications of this when Sissons confirmed it.

16

'Her assailant cut out a foetus.'

Rhona was shocked. She was used to scenes of violent death, but that didn't mean she was immune to them. Most Glasgow killings were the result either of drunken violence or turf wars. Rogue males attacking other rogue males with results that filled accident and emergency departments with hideous regularity, giving surgeons plenty of practice in sewing together the victims of Glasgow's knife culture.

But she had never seen a knife wielded in such a way before.

She scanned the floor of the tent, but Sissons shook his head. 'Whoever did this took it with them.'

'Was it mature enough to be viable?'

'Judging by the size of the placenta, I'd say yes.'

Rhona breathed deeply and tried to distance herself from the horror of the scene. There was nothing she could do for the victim now apart from carry out her job properly.

'Did the removal of the baby kill her?'

'I don't see any other wounds. She probably bled out.' He indicated a small white mask that lay next to the head. 'Looks like she was knocked out with something first. Smells like stain remover.'

'Chloroform?'

'Probably.'

'I don't recall any foetal thefts being recorded in the UK, only in the USA.'

'Given time, what happens there happens here.'

Sissons's job was to certify death, so he was ready to leave. 'The PF's been, so you've got the place to yourself.'

Under Scots law, the Procurator Fiscal

determined whether the death was suspicious. Here, his presence would have been a formality. You couldn't die accidentally from a forced Caesarean section.

Sissons said goodbye and left her to her own devices. His clipped voice and hankering after a gong often irritated Rhona, but she had to admit he was a consummate professional.

She would attend the post-mortem, as would the DI in charge of the case, together with a second pathologist for corroboration—a requirement where a death was deemed suspicious.

Scots law was big on corroboration. The boys on the beat were always moaning about it. There had to be two of you before lifting and charging a suspect, so—unlike in England—you had no chance of pulling someone in, however guilty, if you were on your own.

She wondered who the officer in charge on the ground might be. Most likely it would be Bill's replacement, DI Geoffrey Slater; McNab's nemesis, he was still hanging around like a bad smell.

Still, that was not her main consideration at the moment. She wasn't planning to disturb anything but it would be better if the loci had been fully recorded before she set to work. As if on cue she heard footsteps and Roy Hunter's multiple reflections appeared in advance of the man himself. He answered her unspoken question.

'We've taken photos and a spherical recording already, so no worries there.'

'That was fast.'

'We aim to please, especially when the investigating officer is DI Slater.'

18

They exchanged a meaningful look.

'Is he planning to open up the back of the tent?'

Once she had taken samples from the body and its immediate surroundings, it would be useful to have clear access from the back for the other SOCOs.

'When you're finished.'

'Who discovered her?'

'The boyfriend, apparently. He says she went to buy candyfloss and never reappeared, so he went looking for her. When he discovered she'd bought a ticket for the mirrors he came in to check if she was still in here. He found her shoe first.'

'Where?'

'In the next aisle.'

Rhona imagined the boy's concern when he found the shoe, turning to horror when he came across the remains of his girlfriend. Assuming he wasn't the one to kill her in the first place.

'I don't like places like this.' Roy gave the nearest mirror a wary glance.

'You didn't enjoy the fairground when you were a kid?'

'The rides were OK, but I didn't fancy the ghost train or the mirrors. Too creepy.'

'*Something Wicked This Way Comes,*' said Rhona.

He frowned quizzically. 'Wasn't that the name of a show at the Tramway recently?'

'Ray Bradbury wrote the book. A carnival comes to town, bringing evil with it.'

'Art imitating life.'

'You couldn't make up what we have to deal with every day,' she said.

'Too right,' he replied. 'Well, I'll leave you to it.'

19

He left the tent and she set to work. Her job was to retrieve what forensic evidence she could from the body *in situ*. Before she began, she took time to study the scene. First impressions were important. She'd caught the faint sweet scent of the chloroform mask on approach. Now she took time to absorb the details of the victim; its exact position, the injuries and the resultant pattern of blood spattering. Roy had captured all of this, both as static photographs and in a moving 360-degree image, but there was no real substitute for actually being here.

The general public often misunderstood the role of forensic science in solving a crime, thinking it was to provide observations based on the results of tests. Unfortunately some DIs, like Slater, thought the same. The truth was, forensic science was about solving a problem, which depended on asking the right question. That's why she and Bill had worked so well together; he had listened to the questions she'd asked.

The majority of the blood lay pooled beneath the body, but luminol indicated low spattering on the canvas wall and evidence of spraying on the nearby convex mirror, which increased the likelihood that the perpetrator had traces of blood on them, however microscopic.

Chloroform would have rendered the victim unconscious, but if she'd been aware of her attacker before he applied the mask, she would probably have called for help or tried to fight him off.

The funfair was quiet now, but earlier Rhona had been able to hear it from the flat. Pulsating music, throbbing generators and plenty of screaming from the nearby rides would have drowned out any cries for help. Even so, the operation would have had to be swift, in case anyone else entered the tent.

As far as she was aware, a normal Caesarean section took around five to ten minutes for someone who knew what they were doing and who was interested in the welfare of the mother. Here, it looked as though the only concern had been the swift removal of the foetus.

The girl's pants and tights had been pulled down to her knees. In normal circumstances that would indicate a sexual motive for the attack, but in this case, it could simply have been done to bare the abdomen.

Rhona directed an ultraviolet light on the lower torso and its surrounds. The fluorescent glow indicated either semen or urine. She applied dampened blotting paper to the girl's inner thigh, then sprayed it with a solution of reactants. There was no colour change, so no seminal fluid was present.

She tried to recall what she'd read about foetal theft. A rare occurrence, it was also unusual for a violent crime in that it was generally carried out by women. The idea of a woman doing this to a young girl was extraordinary.

She took a blood sample from the umbilical cord before moving on to the victim, where she dealt with the head first, carefully swabbing the mouth and ears, registering no marks or bruising on the face or neck area. When she'd finished, she bagged the head and moved on to the hands. If the girl had tried to fight off her attacker, her hands would hold evidence of that.

21

She used the magnifier and was rewarded by two strands of coloured hair or fibre caught under the nail of the middle digit on the right hand. She bagged the fibres, then carefully scraped under each nail, before turning the hand over. She was surprised to find marks on the palm written in what looked like black crayon.

ṕżıoḃ

She took a series of images of the scribble, then used a swab to sample the material used to write it.

She repeated the same procedure with the left hand, cleaning under the nails before turning it over. There was writing on the left palm too, but it wasn't the same:

CḣɑıՐ

She held the left hand up to the full glare of the arc light and caught a glimpse of its reflected image in a nearby mirror. Although distorted by the glass, it now looked like a word.

Rhona took a small mirror from her forensic case and held it up to the palm. The scrawl was a word and the word looked like 'chain'. Whoever had written it had done it in mirror writing.

Excited by the discovery, she checked the right hand. This time she thought the backwards writing said 'daisy'. Someone had written 'daisy chain' backwards on the girl's hands. The writing wasn't smudged, which suggested it had been done either post-mortem—by the killer—or not long before she died.

Rhona bagged both hands, then began to tape the exposed skin on the remainder of the body, using numbered transparent plastic adhesive-coated strips, adhering them to a clear acetate surface, then sealing them in a clean polythene bag. When she'd finished, she moved on to the clothes.

Over her loose-fitting dress the girl wore a soft suede jacket, fringed and festooned with zips. Rhona checked the label. Gucci. So it hadn't come cheap. She examined the other items of clothing. All high quality. The dead girl had come from a family with money if she could afford designer wear.

Rhona set about removing the clothing. If the body was moved from the site with the clothing intact, the bloodstaining evidence on it might be compromised in transit. When she'd finished doing this, she double-checked the area for a handbag. Roy hadn't mentioned one, but maybe he'd videoed its position, then handed it over as evidence. None of the jacket pockets held a mobile. If there had been one, it had already been removed.

She now concentrated on examining the wound. The perpetrator had had to cut through various layers—the outer skin, then muscle, then the uterine layer. A midline longitudinal incision had been made using a sharp blade, judging by its edges, giving plenty of space to extract the contents of the womb.

Babies born by Caesarean usually had to have

amniotic fluid sucked from their nose and mouth before they could breathe. If the attacker wanted the child to live, then there was a chance they'd done that and spat the fluid out in the vicinity, along with some incriminating saliva.

Once she was finished with the immediate surrounds, she focused on the closest mirror. Convex in shape, it reflected light outwards, rendering everything smaller and covering a wider field of view than a normal plane mirror. Rhona was suddenly aware of her own reflection repeated around the room, a score of versions, all deformed in some way or another.

The sound of footsteps on the treads brought her head round. Now it was DI Slater who was multiplied twenty-fold. Not a pretty sight. He was short and heavily built, with the face of a boxer who'd taken a lot of hits. What he didn't have in looks, he made up for in cunning. When he'd been brought in to cover Bill's suspension period, Slater and McNab had been instantly at odds. The pair went back a long way; when they were partnered as rookie cops, McNab had found Slater self-serving, more intent on making himself look good than on getting the right result. And it had worked. Slater had reached DI level, while McNab stayed a DS and got killed saving someone's life.

'Dr MacLeod.'

Slater's voice always sounded like it had a sneer in it.

'Detective Inspector Slater.'

'Got your samples?'

'I'll be a while yet.'

He grunted as though humouring her. 'The incident tent's up. I'll await your orders as to when we open the back canvas,' he said sarcastically.

Rhona bit off a similarly toned reply. She didn't need to prove anything to Geoffrey Slater. Her only concern here was the victim, not Slater's inability to relate to anyone unless they provided a leg up the ladder.

'Do we know who she is?' she asked.

'The boyfriend says her name's Kira Reese-Brandon. A pupil at Morvern School for Girls, no less.'

Morvern was an independent school on the north side of the city, not that far from where they stood. Teenage pregnancies were fairly common in the impoverished areas of Glasgow, but not among the pupils of a school famous for producing scientists, advocates and doctors.

'Not our usual murder victim,' continued Slater.

'Not our usual murder,' Rhona agreed. 'Do the parents know?'

'The mother contacted the station an hour ago, worried when her daughter hadn't come home from the funfair. They thought she might have gone into labour. Apparently she was due in a couple of weeks. They checked the hospital, then called the station.'

Which meant Sissons was right, the pregnancy was almost full term.

'Any sign of the foetus?'

Slater shook his head. 'The dogs haven't found it.'

Rhona looked up, hearing the beat of rain on the overhead canvas. It was February and close to freezing. Add rain into the equation and it didn't bode well for a newborn abandoned in the open. Hopefully the care that had been taken to remove

25

the foetus meant that someone wanted it alive.

*     *     *

Rhona watched as the mortuary van pulled away, creating muddy tyre tracks in the sodden grass. The temperature had risen a little with the rain and her breath no longer condensed like a speech balloon in front of her.

She had sat with the body when she'd finished her forensic examination, recording everything she'd found. It was a habit Chrissy thought morbid and often chided her for. Sitting with the dead. Rhona thought it was the least she could do. It was also the quietest spot at any crime scene.

A team of SOCOs had arrived to scour the tent and surrounding area. Rhona bundled all the evidence she'd collected into the boot of the car. She would drop the bags at the lab, then try to grab a couple of hours' sleep.

She drove through the park gates to see sunrise touching the university spires. Morning lectures would begin in an hour. Students would sit in those towers, as she had done in years gone by, listening to the cooing of the resident pigeons while being lectured on Moral Philosophy. A world away from what had happened below.

When she eventually reached the flat she was staggering from exhaustion. She didn't bother undressing, just grabbed the duvet from the bed and settled down on the couch, sinking into a troubled sleep in which she was a child again, lost in a mirror maze, calling for her father.

# CHAPTER FOUR

Some would describe the location for Scotland's maximum security institution as bleak. Professor Magnus Pirie, a native of the windswept and treeless Orkney islands, saw beauty in the surroundings rather than desolation.

He rolled down the car window and breathed in the upland air. His sense of smell was legendary among family, friends and colleagues. He now regarded this ability as a gift, but its intensity could be overpowering at times. Not today, though. A fresh breeze brought the scent of juniper, frosted heather and peat bog.

To his eye, only the Victorian monstrosity he was approaching looked bleak, fashioned by man to incarcerate his fellow human beings.

Magnus had visited prisoners before in his capacity as a criminal psychologist, but this visit promised to be very different. The inmate he was about to meet was unlikely ever to be released, despite his exemplary behaviour over the last two years, or the hobby that had made him something of a celebrity.

Magnus had sat far into the previous night reading and rereading Coulter's diary, written during his first year of confinement. The note that had accompanied it had reiterated that the inmate had given up writing the diary since transforming his life. *I view the world differently now*, it had said.

Jeff Coulter had been ruled criminally insane after killing his six-week-old daughter. According to the pathology reports, he had simply snapped

27

the baby's spine.

It had taken a month to get the authorities to agree to this initial meeting, which Magnus hoped would be the first of many. The apparent psychological transformation of such a man fascinated him. A study of Coulter would provide ample material for an academic paper and provide a good discussion topic for his advanced psychology students.

There had been a great deal of controversy when Coulter had come to trial. Naturally the public were horrified by the crime of which he had been accused. This, coupled with the ongoing controversy over whether vulnerable children should be taken into care (Coulter's child had been on the protection register), meant that social workers in charge of the case had taken a pounding. Once the prosecution had proved Coulter killed the child, a decision had to be made. Was he suffering from a mental illness at the time, or was he psychopathic? In any book on psychopaths, the chapter on treatment for the condition was pretty well non-existent, because there wasn't one. If he was deemed mentally ill, however, he could be treated.

Coulter and his defence counsel had opted to plead mental illness. After many interviews with professionals specialising in psychiatric and psychological conditions, the results were inconclusive. Despite this, Coulter was incarcerated in the building on the horizon, and prescribed medication. It had apparently worked. According to Coulter, at least, he was a new man.

The State Hospital was due to move to a new purpose-built facility within the next two years.

From what Magnus knew of the older building, it was not before time. The treatment of the mentally ill—criminal or otherwise—had improved considerably over the past decade, but still had some way to go. In previous eras cancer had been the dirty word. Mental illness, although experienced by a quarter of the population at some time in their lives, had replaced it as the Cinderella of the medical establishment. The fact that the general public tended to look to the criminally insane for their understanding of mental illness only served to reinforce its stigma, in spite of a string of high profile celebrities who'd recently admitted to conditions such as depression and bipolar disorder. Fear drove this attitude, and when you saw a hospital like this, you could understand why.

Magnus followed the signs to the car park, which was half empty. He parked as near as he could to the modern glassed entrance, a welcome extension to the starker older building. The open plan interior, brightly painted walls and potted plants did succeed in softening the clinical atmosphere. Only the posters on the notice board indicated the true nature of the place he had just entered.

'Can I help you?'

Magnus slipped an identity card across the counter.

'Professor Magnus Pirie. I have an appointment with Jeff Coulter at nine thirty.'

The young woman gave him a pleasant smile, then examined the photograph, ticked off his name on her list and pushed a visitors' book towards him.

29

'Great accent. Where are you from?'

Magnus was used to such questions when away from the islands, even though at home he was regularly accused of losing his accent.

'Orkney.'

'Like that guy Cameron on *Big Brother*?'

Magnus was surprised.

'That's right.'

She grinned. 'I voted for him.'

Magnus wasn't sure whether he was expected to thank her for supporting a fellow Orcadian. He covered his indecision by clipping the security badge she produced to his lapel.

'Have you read the visitor literature?'

He had.

'Then you know there's a security search?'

The information had been clear enough. His briefcase would be put through an X-ray machine and he would walk under a metal-detecting arch, similar to those used in airports. If he sounded an alarm, he would be physically searched.

There had also been a long list of items he was not allowed to take through. Among them were aerosols, badges, lighters, glue, alcohol, drugs and, intriguingly, fishing lines, string and coat hangers. Magnus could see how those last items might be used as weapons, but had reminded himself that Coulter had needed nothing but the strength of his hands.

'Someone will come to collect you.'

She was true to her word. Seconds after her short phone call announcing his presence, Magnus heard the click of the lock on a nearby door and a woman emerged. She was small and slim, her hair straight and glossy, her features oriental. As she

30

approached he caught the scent of roses. She held out her hand, which seemed tiny in comparison to his own.

'Dr Jacqueline Shan.'

'Professor Magnus Pirie.'

'If you would like to come through, Professor.'

'Magnus will do fine.'

She acknowledged his offer with a slight nod, but didn't volunteer an abbreviation of her own. A swipe of her security card released the door lock and she ushered him through.

Magnus was immediately assailed by the smell of strong disinfectant. He strove to ignore it, trying to concentrate instead on Dr Shan's rosy fragrance.

After he'd successfully negotiated the various security measures, she ushered him into a small interview room.

'They will bring Mr Coulter to you here.'

'Are you his doctor?'

'I am one of his clinical team, but not his consultant.'

'Do you know him well?'

She thought for a moment. 'I have spoken with Mr Coulter many times.' Her eyes rested on Magnus.

He produced the diary Coulter had sent him. 'I just wondered if you'd read this?'

She glanced at the notebook.

'His diary . . .' he explained.

'I am aware of what it is, although I haven't read it.'

Magnus wondered if that was the reason for the trace of annoyance he'd sensed in her manner.

'If you could wait here, please.'

She left the scent of roses behind. Magnus tried to analyse it, coming to the conclusion it wasn't eau de cologne but oil, such as might be used in massage. He wondered if Dr Shan was a proponent of Chinese alternative medicine as well as psychiatry.

When Coulter arrived, he was accompanied by two orderlies, both heavy-set men. In contrast, he was much slighter, although wiry, the sinews of his arms visible in a short-sleeved shirt. His hair was shaved close, he wore a day's stubble and smelt of aftershave. Had he been dressed in a snazzy suit, he could have passed for any Glasgow guy about town.

He offered Magnus his hand.

'Professor Pirie. It's good to meet you at last.' He indicated that Magnus should take a seat.

Behind him the two orderlies took up a stance, one either side of the door.

'For your protection.' Coulter's voice held a tinge of pride.

Although Coulter was obviously in good shape, Magnus was pretty sure he could have held his own, being six inches taller and considerably heavier. The inmate might be able to snap an infant's spine, but Magnus didn't imagine his own would break so easily.

'So what do you think of my diary?'

A complete analysis of the unpunctuated, yet fascinating scrawl would take a lot longer than he'd had up to now. He decided to be non-committal.

'Thank you for sending it and for agreeing to see me.'

Coulter met his steady gaze, his own direct and intense. Magnus had the sensation that he had never truly been looked in the eye until now.

'I don't remember what I wrote in that diary or why I wrote it. I'm not the man I was then.'

The gaze was unrelenting, with none of the quick glances away that most people indulge in to soften their stare. The air around Coulter seemed to buzz with energy.

Magnus wanted to ask why he had sent the diary. Why not simply destroy it?

He, along with many others, had not been convinced by Coulter's plea of insanity, which was partly why he was here. The diagnosis presented to the court had been conflicting. Proponents of psychopathy had pointed to Coulter's arrogance, his lack of empathy, shallow emotions, violent outbursts and, most important of all, his lack of remorse, shame or guilt. When asked what he felt about the death of his baby son, Coulter had responded, 'I can always father another one.'

Yet the covering letter that had arrived with the diary had painted a completely different picture. One of sadness and remorse, and a need to make amends for what he had done.

But then again, psychopaths were also known to be inveterate liars.

'Would you like to see what I do now?'

'Is that possible?'

Coulter turned to his minders. 'What do you say, guys? Can I show the professor my babies?'

\*       \*       \*

The tiny hand was curled shut, the central nail clasped against the palm.

'Newborn nails are blueish in tone. They change

33

to pink a few weeks after birth,' Coulter told him.

Magnus watched as he chose colours, mixing blue and pink pigment, adding clear liquid.

'Glazing gel. Helps it to set and gives a glossy finish.' Coulter stroked the brush gently downwards. When he had completed all ten nails, he moved to the feet, where a delicate thread of veins marked the ankle. 'I painted those in. Realistic, eh?'

He lifted a tiny foot and showed Magnus the pink-blushed soles.

'You have to be sparing with the paint, build it up over a few coats, but it's worth it to get to this warm look.'

He began coating the toenails to match the fingers.

Magnus could hardly bear to watch. The small body looked so real, every sign pointing to life— 'stork bites' on the back of the neck, milk bumps on the cheeks, a sucking blister on the lip.

Coulter ran his finger down the delicate groove from the doll's nose to its lip.

'This is called the angel's touch.' His voice was almost reverential. 'Its length and depth is a baby's most distinctive feature before the eyes open.'

He laid the newborn gently inside a satin-lined box and handed Magnus a photograph.

'What do you think?'

The likeness made Magnus's skin crawl.

'Cot death at five weeks. Still, this one won't cry or shit its nappy.'

He snapped a lid on the box. Magnus wanted to remonstrate, as though the baby might not be able to breathe. He knew it was just a doll, yet his brain told him otherwise.

34

As Coulter cleaned his brushes and tidied up, Magnus pondered why a parent would crave a replica baby. Yet there they all were. Photographs on the wall of smiling parents, nursing dolls that looked like their dead children.

He tried to understand his own feelings of abhorrence. He would have been unable to hold that doll, had it been offered to him. Maybe it was the scent of paint and plastic instead of flesh and blood that had made him recoil. Something that looked human, yet wasn't.

Coulter was observing him, sizing up his reaction.

'It gets some people like that.'

Magnus strove to make his feelings less obvious.

'How did you start?'

'I saw a programme on TV about someone who did it for a living. I made it my Art Project. It takes a lot of skill and patience, you know.'

Coulter's enthusiasm was obvious. Psychopaths were known for grandiose schemes which rarely came to fruition. If he was a psychopath, he seemed to be bucking the trend.

'Jimmy Boyle took up sculpture in Peterhead. Now he's a millionaire.' He laughed at his little joke. 'I'm doing not too badly in the celebrity stakes myself.'

That much was true. The newspapers loved the story of the child killer turned fashioner of 'Reborns'. There was even talk of a movie.

But you couldn't get away from the fact that he was a murderer. Like similar killers Magnus had interviewed, on first acquaintance Coulter appeared friendly, solicitous, even charismatic, especially during his work on the doll. None of that meant he related in any way to Magnus's understanding of the world.

When Coulter had finished tidying his workbench, they returned to the interview room and sat down again, this time with a cup of coffee each. Coulter seemed to have something in particular he wanted to say, and while Magnus waited for him to get to the point, he observed the other man's body language. The intensity of his stare had lessened, but the buzz was still there, together with an underlying eagerness which was currently being suppressed. It could be that it was nothing more than self-importance. There had certainly been an air of showing off in the workroom and Magnus suspected Coulter had rather enjoyed his reaction to the doll. But that was natural enough. People who didn't mind spiders often took delight in the discomfort of those who were frightened by them. Magnus didn't care if he shared a room with a spider but he didn't think he would like to share it with a baby doll. Not one as realistic as Coulter's. A sudden memory of that lifelike face brought another wave of revulsion.

There was a greasy shine now to Coulter's skin. The room was warm, but Magnus didn't think that was the reason. It was excitement that was making the man sweat.

Coulter spoke quietly, as though he didn't want his minders to hear. 'Women write to me in here. Lots of them.' He shifted slightly in the seat. 'More now since I started making the dolls.'

This phenomenon was well documented, particularly among inmates on America's Death Row. Psychopaths were known to have an uncanny

36

ability to recognise and use the kind of woman who had a powerful need to help or mother others. Such 'nurturing' women tended to look for the goodness in people while minimising their faults. Magnus wondered how those who corresponded with Coulter managed to reason away a child murder.

Coulter resumed his intent stare. 'One of them, Caroline, suggested I get in touch with you about my diary.'

'Why me?' Magnus knew his response had been too swift.

Coulter suppressed a smile. 'She read about you in the papers.'

Coulter was waiting for him to ask for more information, relishing his interest. Magnus decided not to indulge him. If he was going to work with this man, then he must be the one in charge. Instead, he decided to indicate the interview was at an end.

'Maybe we can talk about this the next time we meet.'

He was rewarded by a flicker of annoyance crossing Coulter's face, then he was all smiles and enthusiasm again.

'I'll look forward to that.'

Touché.

'You understand that our next interview will last much longer?'

'Once I finish Jacob, the one I showed you, then I have to start on Melanie, but I should be able to fit you in.'

Magnus kept his face expressionless. It wouldn't do to remind Coulter that it was he who had requested this meeting, not Magnus.

'Good.'

They shook hands, then the minders escorted Coulter from the room.

Magnus waited, assuming someone would come to collect him. The smell of Coulter's spicy cologne still hung in the air. It mingled with other scents that the man had carried on his clothes. Paint, varnish, a faint odour of plastic. Magnus longed for Dr Shan and her flowery fragrance to arrive and dispel the memory of Coulter and his doll.

In truth, he was perplexed by the interview and his response to it. His mind was already analysing this, putting it down to an abhorrence of Coulter's work on the Reborn.

But it wasn't that, not entirely. It was more about the true nature of the man. Psychopaths were routinely branded as 'evil' by the policemen who pursued them and the victims that survived an encounter with one. Magnus thought 'evil' was less about something present, more about the *absence* of something. The absence, in essence, of a common humanity.

Had he been out-manoeuvred, giving Coulter what he had wanted? The inmate had succeeded in generating a meeting with him. He had displayed his new skills to great advantage and shown that it wasn't a short term commitment. He had even orchestrated what they would discuss the next time they met. Magnus was pondering this when the door opened and Dr Shan appeared, her face a little flushed.

He rose to greet her as she murmured her apologies at leaving him waiting.

'Please don't concern yourself. I am aware I'm probably disrupting your schedule.'

She ushered him out and they were back in the corridor. The earlier scent was still discernible, pleasant and soothing. It prompted Magnus to ask, 'I wondered if you would be able to spare ten minutes to talk about Mr Coulter?'

She continued walking alongside him, but Magnus had detected a start as he'd made his request. He also suspected the glance at her watch was just for show. She wasn't contemplating whether she had the time, but whether she had the inclination.

'If you would like to come to my office, we can talk there.'

She opened the door on a small but elegantly furnished space. On the wall behind the desk was a print of what looked like a Buddhist woodcut. Dr Shan saw him glance in that direction but said nothing, merely waving him to a seat across the desk from her. The flush had left her cheeks. She looked calm and contained.

'How did the interview go?'

Magnus decided to be honest. 'Outwardly well, although I have the feeling I did what he wanted.'

A smile played at the corners of her lips. 'Mr Coulter can be very persuasive. On my first interview with him, I realised he knew more about me by the end than I knew about him.'

Magnus admired her frankness. Exchanging weaknesses had broken the ice.

'He says he corresponds with someone called Caroline.'

'He receives a lot of letters, mostly I believe from women.'

'So you don't know this Caroline?'

She shook her head.

'You were aware Coulter was keeping a diary?'

'He wrote a lot when he first came in, but showed it to no one.'

'You weren't curious?'

'Many inmates write their thoughts down. Most of what they write is nonsense linked to their illness.'

'Is Coulter mentally ill?'

'His mental state has responded to medication.'

'He's got better?'

'He functions well, works hard at his dolls and is no trouble.'

'But?'

'There are no buts.'

Magnus didn't believe her.

'Would you like to see the diary after I've studied it?'

'We would have to ask Mr Coulter's permission for that.'

The barrier was back in place and Magnus wasn't sure why. Dr Shan rose, clearly intending to terminate the interview. Magnus took his cue from her.

'Thank you again for your help.'

She gave a little nod, then led him to the door.

\*        \*        \*

As he drove away, the brooding presence of the building stayed with him until it eventually disappeared from his rear view mirror. Once it was out of sight, he pulled into a lay-by and got out of the car. The wind buffeted him, snatching at his hair and clothes. Magnus breathed in the moorland air, replacing the memory of Coulter's smell. The sky grew darker and more threatening as he climbed back in the car. Had he had started on a journey he would live to regret?

## CHAPTER FIVE

The footprint had been a long shot, so long that Rhona had never divulged her attempts at retrieving it to McNab. The chances of lifting anything at all from the trousers worn by the prisoner Bill was accused of attacking had been very slim. If she did succeed, there was no guarantee there would be sufficient in the pattern or deposit for a match. And what if the match *had* been Bill's footwear, not McNab's? Would she have submitted it to the investigating officer, thereby supplying even more evidence against Bill?

She had tried to work on the principle that either man could be lying, Bill to cover up for McNab or McNab to protect his superior officer. The victim of the assault, known as the Gravedigger, had a vested interest in implicating Bill, which is what he had done.

The Gravedigger's clothes had been removed and bagged after the alleged assault. There had been no blood, only bruising, the result of a well aimed kick to the testicles. Despite the awkwardness of the situation, the duty officer had quietly insisted that both policemen give up their shoes. And thank God he had.

At first glance the trousers had shown no evidence of the kick, but an electrostatic image using an aluminium sheet had lifted dust marks

41

invisible to the human eye. The pattern route had been singularly unsuccessful, the partial print an inconclusive match to either man's shoes. It was her analysis of the dust particles that had pointed to the truth.

McNab had been in the back of the Gravedigger's van. Bill had not. McNab had kicked aside rubbish to get at what lay beneath, and he had deposited some of that rubbish on the Gravedigger's crotch. Microscopic, but without doubt a match. DI Wilson had not kicked the Gravedigger, however much he might have wanted to. McNab had told the truth all along.

A rush of emotion swept over her. McNab had been desperate to prove that his boss wasn't guilty of assault. So desperate that many believed he had lied to keep the DI out of trouble, even to the point of ruining his own career.

There were no shadows in the pristine glare of the laboratory, but that didn't mean she couldn't sense McNab's presence. She glanced up at the door, remembering the way he would always knock before entering her domain; his studied look, the way his mouth would turn up at the corner as he observed her at work. She remembered the last time he'd been here. It was the morning after she'd used him to fill the frightened loneliness of her night. He had replaced bad dreams and memories with something gentle and loving. The next day when he'd turned up here, she had been curt, extinguishing the thinly disguised glimmer of hope. She had told him as far as she was concerned it had never happened. 'Whatever you want,' had been his reply, but she had felt his hurt.

She shook her head to dispel such thoughts and

42

slipped the results back in the folder. She couldn't bring McNab back to life, but she had done her best to prove his story true. She glanced at the clock. There would be no word back from the court for another hour at least, and she had a post-mortem to attend.

*     *     *

The victim's body was regarded as a scene which must be as thoroughly investigated as the locus of the crime. The attending team in Scotland consisted of two pathologists, the investigating officer, on occasion the Procurator Fiscal, and herself.

When Rhona arrived, DI Slater was already kitted up and waiting to go in. His eyes above the mask regarded her coolly. Slater was used to post-mortems and she had no doubt he would be unfazed by the gruesome nature of this death. For some reason that irritated her. You had to have a certain amount of detachment in this job, if only to survive, but Slater's attitude smacked of cold disinterest. She had seen it in the last case they'd worked on together. His preoccupation with nailing a high profile Russian gangster with kudos attached had seriously endangered the life of a child. McNab had been the real detective then. Like a terrier he had dug away at the decade-old evidence, never giving up, even when Slater had ordered him to. For Slater, McNab had been a nuisance, despite the eventual proof that the DS's intuition had been right all along.

All of which illustrated Slater's real problem. He didn't listen, regardless of the quality of the team he had around him.

Slater appeared to be contemplating a remark, no doubt about the imminent court case, then apparently thought better of it. Rhona busied herself donning the suit and mask. As far as she was concerned, they had nothing to say to one another until the strategy meeting. She certainly wasn't planning on mentioning the submission of her forensic evidence in support of Bill.

Dr Sissons acknowledged their entry with a nod. His corroborator today was Dr Sylvia Barnes. Rhona had met her before and they exchanged smiles through the masks. Sylvia was in her thirties, married to an engineer, with young children. Rhona and Sean had had dinner at their family home in Newton Mearns. It had been a pleasant evening, if a little domestic for her taste. It was around the time Sean had fancied himself as a father, particularly when fuelled by whisky. Rhona had feared that freshly bathed and sweet-smelling youngsters coming to say their goodnights to the assembled dinner party would only serve to encourage him. He hadn't brought the subject up in the taxi on the way back to the flat, but she'd known it was on his mind.

The other two men were the PF and a SOCO to record the post-mortem via photographs and video. The purpose of the exercise was to establish how the victim had died. A decision on suicide, accident, murder or natural causes was the normal outcome. In many cases, this one included, it seemed a foregone conclusion, but that didn't matter, the procedure was the same.

Sissons began sampling the body. Blood, hair (body and head) and swabs from all orifices. Then it was time for the hands. The marks on the palms had not gone unnoticed. Now they were up for discussion. The SOCO took further photographs, while the pathologist verbally recorded their existence. Rhona waited to see if anyone realised what the marks might be, before she asked for a mirror and held it up in front of the right hand.

'It says "daisy",' exclaimed Slater.

Rhona moved the mirror to the left hand. 'This one says "chain". The words are in mirror writing. I haven't processed the material used to write them but I'd hazard a guess and say it was probably a make-up pencil such as kohl.'

'You think this was done by her assailant?' Slater said.

'It's not smudged, so she couldn't have used her hands after the words were written.'

'Daisy chain. Is anyone else thinking what I'm thinking?' Slater said.

'What exactly *are* you thinking?' Sissons's voice was clipped.

'Daisy chaining. You know. Group sex?'

Just hearing Slater say 'sex' made Rhona shudder. She tried to dispel the image of him indulging in group sex, or any kind of sex for that matter.

'I checked out the term on the internet. It's quite common. Used often for florists and organisations that involve children. Although DI Slater's right, it does have strong sexual connotations in some contexts. The mirror writing aspect is even more interesting. Research suggests it's an inherited ability which very few people have. Leonardo Da Vinci wrote many of his notes that way and it got him into trouble with the Church,

45

because of its satanic associations. And pacts with the devil were traditionally written backwards.'

'You're suggesting the death has satanic overtones?' Slater said.

'I'm just telling you what I found.'

While the scientific officer took finger and handprints, Rhona revealed she'd retrieved coloured fibres or hairs from under a fingernail.

'So which were they, fibres or hairs?' asked Slater.

'When I've had time to examine them, I'll tell you.'

She turned her attention to the scientific officer, who was now taking a footprint since Kira had been found with one shoe missing. Rhona was struck by how small the girl's feet were. Sissons had recorded her height as a little over five feet, but her feet were tiny even for someone that size. She had measured the shoe picked up in the maze as 22 centimetres, which meant Kira wore a 2.5 in British sizing.

'We already know the baby was only a week shy of full term,' said Rhona.

Sissons nodded and spoke into the microphone. 'No bruising on the front of the body, apart from a small pressure mark round the mouth consistent with a mask. Blood tests should reveal whether chloroform was ingested.'

'Would you say her attacker knew what they were doing?' asked Slater.

'It's a classical incision. Not the preferred method now, but effective. Yes, I'd say they knew, or made a very good guess.'

Sissons lifted the dark mass of the placenta and weighed it. '502 grammes, 21 centimetres long,

2.23 centimetres thick.' He moved on to the umbilical cord. '57 centimetres in length. The end neatly cut.'

'And was the baby likely to be alive when it was born?' Rhona asked.

'A full term baby would have a strong chance of survival, even under these circumstances.'

Sissons rolled the body over.

'Is that a tattoo?' Rhona pointed to a mark at the base of the spine.

Sissons pulled the overhead light closer. 'It's a flower.'

It *was* a flower, around two centimetres in diameter, yellow-centred with a cluster of white ray florets, some tipped with red.

'*Bellis perennis*. An eye of day,' Rhona said.

'What?' Slater said.

'A day's eye, or daisy. So called because it heralds the day.'

'So we have a daisy tattoo and the words "daisy chain" in mirror writing on the hands,' Slater said.

The external findings having been recorded, Sissons began to open up the body. The stomach contents, removed and weighed, would end up with Rhona at the lab. At first glance, the meal resembled burger and chips, favourite food of the masses.

'Her boyfriend said she went to buy candyfloss,' Slater said.

'I don't see any evidence of that, but Dr MacLeod will confirm.'

'If he's lying about it, he could be lying about other things.'

'Did he admit to being the father of the child?' Rhona asked.

Slater shook his head. 'He said it wasn't his, but he didn't care. Can we confirm this without a baby?'

'I took blood from the umbilical cord,' replied Rhona. 'We can use it in a paternity test.'

'So we can tell?' Slater repeated.

'Yes.'

The time spent on a post-mortem depended on the pathologist. Each had their own way of working and their own speed. Sissons was neither too fast nor too slow. Despite this, Rhona could sense Slater's desperation to get away. She had caught a strong smell of cigarette smoke in the changing room. Chances were he just needed a fag. At one point she wondered if Sissons had picked up on this and was deliberately slowing down the proceedings.

Slater's nicotine craving eventually won. He muttered something about needing the toilet and absented himself. They were at the final stages anyway and knew little more than they had surmised in the incident tent, the fibres Rhona had lifted from the body being the only possible material link with Kira's assailant.

*       *       *

Slater's boiler suit lay discarded in the changing room, his overcoat gone from the peg. Rhona stripped hers off and checked her phone. There were no messages. She did a quick mental calculation. Court proceedings could be delayed for any number of reasons. Janice had promised to call as soon as she had any word.

Outside, the air was sharp with frost. She

48

remembered leaving the High Court with McNab after the Mary Healey case on a day like this. They'd celebrated the outcome with coffee at the Central Café, one of the few surviving old-fashioned Italian cafés that had served Glasgow well. She turned in that direction.

*     *     *

She was relieved to find no sign of Rocco, the proprietor. She didn't know if she could cope if he mentioned McNab. She slid alongside a red formica table that held the usual accompaniments for Rocco's famous fish suppers: salt, vinegar and sauce. Spurning the menu card, she ordered a large mug of black coffee, while questioning her sanity in coming here. She had a sense of starting to live her life backwards, a sure sign of growing old, or going mad. McNab would have made fun of her for it.

They had sat at this table the last time, McNab looking half dead through lack of sleep and worry. She'd smelt whisky on his breath and known that as soon as she left, he would supplement his coffee with more.

If he were sitting opposite her now, they would be discussing the latest case. She tried to imagine what his take on it would be, what questions he would ask. McNab had a habit of getting right to the point.

'Why was she in the Hall of Mirrors on her own?' The voice in her head was as clear as if he were there. 'Kids would go in there together for a laugh, but not by themselves.'

It was such an obvious question. Rhona hoped

Slater had thought to ask it.

## CHAPTER SIX

The strategy meeting had been called for mid-afternoon, leaving time for the post-mortem to establish the cause of death. That gave her a couple of hours in the lab before she had to show her face again. Her repeated checks on her mobile had been futile. Rhona resisted attempting to call Janice. If she was in court, her phone would be switched off anyway.

She settled down to some work, relishing the silence. Kira's case wasn't the only one in the running at the moment, but it was the most serious and therefore the one occupying her mind. Knife crime was fairly common in Glasgow. The analysis of stab wounds, and the knives used to inflict them, was well documented. But Kira's death was unique. Rhona could find no record of anything similar happening in the UK in her computer searches.

Her examination of the body had produced three interesting pieces of evidence. The hair or fibre from under the fingernail, the scrawled mirror writing done with what she suspected was a make-up pencil, and a deposit of something she believed might have come from the handle of the knife the perpetrator had wielded.

Professional knives such as those used in slaughterhouses and in hunting required handles that weren't slippery even when covered in blood. Shark skin provided the perfect material for this.

Sharply pointed placoid scales, also known as dermal teeth or dentricles, gave the shark's skin the feeling of sandpaper.

Magnified under an electron microscope, the unique shape of the scales she'd found was clearly visible. The perpetrator had deposited microscopic dentricles on the body as they performed the Caesarean. The police hadn't recovered the weapon but at least they knew a bit more about it. She took a micrograph of the enhanced image to show at the meeting, then examined the fibre.

The detailed analysis and comparison of fibre evidence fell into three or four sequential phases. First came microscopy to compare samples and establish type, followed by microspectro-photometry (MSP) to record a colour graph. Thin layer chromotography (TLC) could then be used to strip out the dye using an appropriate mixture of solvents, and for man-made fibres, the use of infrared spectroscopy to confirm the chemical identity already established from the fibre's appearance under the microscope.

Most work on hairs was to do with comparison. Hairs turned up everywhere, inside balaclavas and stocking masks, on clothing, in bedding and often on blunt weapons. Matching of hairs could place an accused at the scene of crime, just as a victim's hairs found on an accused provided a link between them.

Human and animal hairs were essentially the same. Both consisted of an inner core, known as the medulla. This was surrounded by a cortex enclosed in a thin outer layer called the cuticle. The easiest way to imagine the form was to use the image of a pencil, where the lead was the medulla,

51

the wood the cortex and the paint the cuticle.

The item under the microscope was not man-made fibre, despite its bright red colour, as she had first thought. It was a hair dyed bright red. When present in human hairs, the medulla was amorphous in appearance, the width generally less than one-third the overall diameter of the hair shaft. Very fine human hair and naturally blonde hair contained no medulla at all. The hair she was viewing under the microscope had a distinctive medulla and had come from an animal. Which animal, Rhona had no idea.

She didn't hear the door open, so engrossed was she in her study. The suited figure was behind her before she registered its presence.

'Chrissy!' Rhona stood up and threw her arms around her visitor. 'What are you doing here?'

'Sam's at the university showing Michael off to anyone in the Faculty of Medicine who might be remotely interested, so I thought I'd pop in and see you.'

Above the mask, Chrissy's eyes searched hers.

'I heard about the girl in the park. What have you got?'

Rhona waved her to the microscope.

Chrissy settled herself on the stool and took a long look. 'A hair, but not human.'

'I agree.'

'Even though it's bright red.'

Rhona was about to remind Chrissy when her own hair had been a similar colour.

Chrissy got in first. 'I liked my hair that colour. I'd do it again but I might scare wee Michael.'

Rhona laughed. 'I miss you.'

'Not for much longer.'

'What do you mean?'

'I'm coming back.'

'But it's too soon.'

'My mum's desperate to look after her first grandchild, even if he is black.' She grinned. 'Hey, now the USA has a black President, it's cool to be black.'

'And your dad?'

'Mum put up with a lot over the years, but when the old bastard tried to stop her seeing the baby, she threw him out.'

Chrissy was the only girl in a family of wayward boys ruled by a domineering father. One son had broken the trend, Patrick, Chrissy's favourite. He'd left, hiding his homosexuality from his parents. Chrissy had covered for him, desperate that her father and brothers shouldn't find out and deny her mother access to her oldest son.

'Well, it would be great to have you back,' said Rhona.

'So tell me about the funfair.'

When Rhona had finished, Chrissy shook her head in disbelief. 'It sounds like an episode of *Buffy the Vampire Slayer*.'

'What?'

'I got hooked on the box set of *Buffy* when I was breastfeeding. My God, can that girl kick ass. And the boyfriend, Angel, is hot.'

'Didn't you get enough witchcraft on the torso case?'

Chrissy had met Sam while on that case. It was his Nigerian mother who'd alerted them to the practices of a witchdoctor in Kano, helping them solve it.

Chrissy was deep in thought, and not about

53

witchcraft. 'The hair's quite long, could it have come from a wig?'

Wig manufacturers often threaded animal and human hair, then dyed it to the required colour. It was a possibility.

'I could do a bit of research,' she suggested. 'Let you get on with something else.'

'Oh my God!' Rhona glanced at the clock. 'I'm due at the strategy meeting in ten minutes. Slater will drip sarcasm if I'm late.'

'Bill's not back?'

'His court case was scheduled for today. I haven't heard the outcome yet.'

\*　　　\*　　　\*

The meeting had already begun. Rhona slipped in at the back. Roy's footage of the locus was on the big screen, Kira's mutilated body reflected in the surrounding mirrors of the maze. Slater was in full flow, giving a rundown of their call to the scene via a 999 by the victim's boyfriend, David Murdoch, who said he'd found her.

The way Slater said this suggested he was of the 'first witness, first suspect' school of thought.

'The victim was last seen by David and two other friends, Alexandra Stewart-Smith and Owen Hegarty, sometime after eleven o'clock.' Slater's loaded pronunciation of the names suggested his interpretation of the difference in their social class. 'According to all three of them, Kira said she was going for candyfloss and never returned. The ticket seller on the mirror maze confirms she did enter alone, he thought about half past eleven, and seemed anxious to get inside. He also said the

54

tented structure could be accessed other than by the entrance and exit by slipping under the canvas. David's clothes have been sent to forensics for analysis. As yet there is no sign of the baby.'

When it was Rhona's turn, she showed them the enhanced image of the dentricles.

'I lifted these from the wound site. They're dentricles, microscopic but easily recognisable as traces from shark skin. Butchers' knives and hunting knives often have shark skin handles, to stop hands slipping when covered in blood.'

They absorbed that information and she moved on to the hair.

'It was lodged under the victim's fingernail which might indicate a struggle with her attacker. Because of the colour and length and the fact it's not human, we think it might have come from a wig.'

'You're suggesting the killer wore a bright red wig?' drawled Slater.

'I'm not suggesting anything, merely relating what we have at this moment.'

Detective Superintendent Sutherland intervened. 'Our main focus must be the missing baby. What's happening about that?'

'We're still searching the park and the Kelvin waterway, but no luck so far.'

'The baby's father?'

'David Murdoch maintains he isn't the father and Dr MacLeod says she can prove if that's true. So far, the parents either aren't saying or don't know.'

'Foetal abduction is unusual, to say the least. We need to know more about the psychology behind this. See if Professor Pirie is available.'

Slater's face turned puce. If he thought he had all but obliterated the old team with McNab's death, it looked as though he was wrong. Rhona masked a smile. If she couldn't have McNab or Bill, she would settle for Magnus.

Slater appeared about to argue when a cheer from the incident room stopped him in his tracks. When Rhona had passed through earlier, the atmosphere had been subdued. A major incident involved a lot of organisation, many man hours, especially where the death also involved a missing child.

The roar and excited babble might mean the baby had been found. Slater, for all his girth, was quick on his feet. He threw open the door, ready to admonish the crowd.

Rhona caught a glimpse of Janice's jubilant face and knew immediately the cause for celebration. Slater barked his order for silence, then demanded to know *what the hell was going on*.

It was Janice who answered. 'Detective Inspector Wilson has been cleared of the assault charge, sir.'

Slater's expression never changed. 'I'm delighted to hear it. Now, can we get back to work? We have a missing baby, in case you've forgotten.'

The return to desks was accompanied by subdued but delighted murmurs. Nothing Slater said or did could diminish the importance of the news to the men and women in that room.

# CHAPTER SEVEN

Rhona was shocked by how much Bill had aged in the weeks since she'd last seen him. She had never really considered his age before, even when she'd attended his fiftieth birthday party at the Jazz Club.

The last twelve months had hit him hard. Firstly there had been Margaret's cancer diagnosis, then the assault on his daughter, Lisa, McNab's murder and finally the court case. You didn't have to be fifty to look old after a string of bad luck like that.

She had gone in search of him after the meeting, suspecting he was somewhere in the building, avoiding jubilant colleagues and awaiting Sutherland's interview call.

She had finally persuaded Angus, the Duty Sergeant, to tell her where he was.

'He doesn't want to talk to anyone before he sees the Super.'

'I'll pretend I found him all on my own.'

Angus gave her a reluctant nod. 'He's in number six.'

The corridor was silent and empty. Bill had chosen the most far-flung interview room. No chance of anyone spotting him unless they walked the full length of the corridor. She wondered if he had heard the whoop of joy that had gone up on the announcement of his acquittal. Such an outburst of approbation would have embarrassed him. He would also believe it to be undeserved; Rhona knew him well enough to know that. Bill had been raised with the belief that whatever you

57

were asked to do, you did it properly. That went for everything, from the mundane to the important. And in respect of McNab and the Gravedigger case, he believed he had not fulfilled that obligation, nor his duty.

When she opened the door, he was seated at the table, a full mug of congealing coffee in front of him. She wanted to go over and hug him, but didn't.

The last time they'd met was shortly after McNab's funeral. They'd sat in Bill's local, and Rhona had tried unashamedly to stop Bill leaving the police force. Back then, they'd had no idea what the outcome of the assault charge would be. It was their individual guilt and despair over Michael's death that had dominated the interchange.

He looked up as she entered.

'Sergeant Willis refused to tell me where you were, so I came looking.'

'You're the first one to make it through his cordon.' He gave her the ghost of a smile. 'Thank you.'

'For what?'

'Your forensic evidence.'

'You should never have said you did it.'

'McNab reacted the way he did because of me. An assault charge would have finished his career.'

Everything he said was true. McNab was known for his ill-controlled temper. An assault conviction would have probably resulted in the end of his CID career.

'McNab would never have let it go.' She didn't add, *if he were still alive*.

Bill acknowledged that with a brief nod.

Both of them knew that it wasn't over yet. The disciplinary procedure would kick in now the court case had ended. Bill had disobeyed a direct order from a superior, which had resulted in an assault. There were mitigating circumstances and he was a respected officer, but whatever decision Sutherland made, would Bill accept it and carry on?

Before she could ask, the door opened and Angus stuck his head round.

'The Super will see you now, Sir.'

Bill rose, his expression stony. If persuasion couldn't make him stay, maybe the possibility of revenge would.

She put her hand on his arm.

'Word is that Nikolai Kalinin is back in the UK.'

He gave her a half smile, acknowledging her last-ditch attempt, then he was gone.

Since Bill's suspension, Slater had done little to pursue McNab's killers. The investigation into Russian mob activities in Glasgow had been his baby. He'd put all the team's effort into trying to nail Kalinin, and failed. Slater didn't like to be associated with failure, so he'd mothballed the case, using the excuse that McNab's killers had left the country. Intelligence suggested Kalinin had returned to Russia or was lying low on the Mediterranean, managing gambling interests there. With the best will in the world, the long arm of Scots law didn't stretch that far.

But the death of McNab was like a canker at the heart of Bill's team. The DI's acquittal would ease some of the sense of injustice, but it wasn't enough.

She chose to return to the lab via the park. The frenetic police activity of the past forty-eight hours had dwindled to a team of SOCOs still scouring the interior of the mirror maze, and a couple of uniforms conducting door to door enquiries with the inhabitants of the motor homes.

The funfair was back in business, or would be in the evening, apart from the Hall of Mirrors. According to the news, the murder had brought in the crowds, keen to look at the scene of such a unique and ghoulish crime. The fact that the baby had not yet been found, dead or alive, only serving to feed the frenzy of interest.

Past the site of the funfair, the park achieved normality. Open spaces, wooded river banks, cycle tracks and a rollerblading structure. Close by was an enclosed children's playground. It housed a climbing frame and slide and a small roundabout, as well as two sets of swings, one with toddler-type seats. The play area was deserted. No chatting mums, no children. Maybe it was the time of day or maybe it was because of Kira and the missing baby.

As Rhona approached, a girl appeared, opened the gate and went inside. She took a seat on one of the swings and began to pull herself upwards.

Drawing nearer, she realised the girl was pregnant. And she *was* just a girl, not much older, at a guess, than Kira. As Rhona passed, a young male vaulted the low railing and called to the girl; the name sounded like 'Mel'. The girl slowed the swing down and jumped to the ground before walking to meet him. They embraced.

Without getting closer Rhona couldn't be sure, but the young man, his arms now about the girl, looked very like the photo she'd seen in the strategy meeting of David Murdoch, the dead girl's boyfriend. If it was him, it suggested David was

60

friendly with more than one pregnant teenager.

Rhona came to a halt, but the couple weren't interested in her, only in each other. The girl was talking rapidly, the boy trying to calm her. Rhona could hear nothing of the interchange. She brought out her phone as though answering a call and surreptitiously photographed the pair.

Her first instinct was to send the image to McNab, tell him what she'd spotted. She even brought up his number before she realised what she'd done. She stared at the screen, angry with herself for not deleting the contact already, yet unable to do so even now. She thrust the mobile back in her bag. She would email a copy to DS Clark when she reached the lab, check if it was David she'd seen.

By the time she exited the park the pair had disappeared; the distant view was of a deserted playground, an empty swing swaying back and forth.

\*       \*       \*

'OK. Listen to this. Yak hair is considered to be the best material to use for wigs.'

'Yak hair?'

'Bear with me on this. The victim had hair under her fingernail. It isn't human. So she picked it up from an animal. An animal that was dyed red? I don't think so. More likely she was in contact with a dyed fur jacket, or a wig. I started with wigs. Basically, the most expensive ones are made with virgin hair which has never been chemically treated. Remy hair, human hair that has been treated, comes next in quality. Next best is a weave

61

of human and animal hair. Further down the price scale it's synthetic. Apparently yak hair is pretty good in a weave because it can be curled, permed, relaxed and coloured just like human hair.'

Chrissy had launched into full flow as soon as Rhona appeared. Now she'd paused for breath, Rhona told her the news about Bill.

'Ya *beauty*!' Chrissy punched the air. 'All down to us of course.'

Chrissy took any forensic success to be a personal achievement.

'It's not over yet.'

'What do you mean?'

'Bill was in with Sutherland when I left.'

Chrissy put her hands on her hips. 'He won't demote him. Sutherland's not that stupid.' She took in Rhona's doubtful expression before going on vehemently. 'Everyone hates Slater. They want Bill back. Sutherland'll pretend to be the big noise . . .'

'Which he is.'

'But he'll try to make Bill stay.'

'I don't think it'll work.'

For the first time during the conversation Chrissy looked unsure.

'I hope you tried . . .'

'I tried,' Rhona said more sharply than she intended.

Chrissy's face fell. 'Things will never be the same again, will they?'

'Things change. Besides, you have Sam and Michael now.'

'And who do you have?'

'You know me. I like my own company.'

Rhona hoped her tone made it clear the

discussion was at an end. Just to make sure, she changed tack.

'Sutherland has asked for Magnus to be consulted on the fairground case. Slater wasn't too keen, but he has no choice.'

Chrissy had a soft spot for the Orcadian professor of psychology and liked the idea of a discomfited DI Slater. The small consolation seemed to perk her up.

'I'd better be going. I'd said I'd meet Sam about now.'

'So when will you be back?'

'I'll come in for a couple of hours every day. See how Mum gets on. If it works out, I'll do more.'

'Great.'

Just the thought of having Chrissy back was like a shot in the arm.

# CHAPTER EIGHT

Despite the coldness of the late afternoon, Magnus stepped out onto the balcony, where the wind coming up the river whipped at his body. The tide was in, surging from the western seaboard, up the 600 square miles of waterway that lay west of the Clyde. Below him, grey water seethed, white-tops like snapping teeth.

He thought of his home in Orkney, overlooking Scapa Flow. How the Flow would change minute by minute, second by second. Once, coming back from a camping trip on the nearby island of Hoy, he had been caught midway as the tide turned and the wind rose, heralding a storm. Everything had changed in an instant and life had become something to be fought for, his wits and sailing skills the only thing between him and oblivion.

He'd reached the safety of his small harbour and the exhilaration he'd felt as he'd fought the waves stayed with him the entire evening. As a result, he'd been unable to settle to anything and had walked the beach, despite the deteriorating weather, before he could finally go to bed.

Magnus felt something akin to that feeling now.

When the cold began to seep into his bones and his teeth to chatter, he turned and went back inside. The scent of water and city wind was replaced by the comforting smell of his home. Warm wood and polished leather. The musty smell of the books that lined the shelves mingled with the aroma of fresh coffee.

The box file lay closed on his desk. He knew when he opened it the comforting smells would be replaced by something else. Something that conjured up very different images and thoughts, fascinating and disturbing.

He decided to enjoy one more pleasant scent before he began. He fetched the decanter and poured some whisky into a brandy glass. The peaty aroma immediately met his nose. He added a little water, then swirled the liquid slowly round, before taking a mouthful. The powerful combination of kick and scent would go some way to anaesthetising what was to follow.

He settled in the swivel chair and turned to face the desk, and the box file. Setting the glass down, he unfastened the catch and opened it.

The effect was extraordinary. It was as though Coulter was now in the room with him. The pages he had pored over had absorbed his scent, sweat from his hands, the distinctive sweetness of his aftershave. Even the faint, lingering disinfectant odour of the hospital was discernible.

Who knew how long Coulter had laboured over each handwritten page, handling each sheet of paper countless times? Magnus wasn't distressed by the barrage of smells which brought Coulter into the room, but he would have preferred to read the diary objectively without the feeling that Coulter stood over him. He could ask one of his students to type up the notes for him. He would need to do that eventually anyway, if he was planning to use them in his classes.

But for now he would have to manage.

He clipped back the restraint and studied the opening paragraph of the first page. He had read it before but he did so again now, absorbing the flow of words as they were written.

*When Geri came back with the Baby I was surprisd it was so pretty like a doll I said I wood change the nappy Geri didnt want me to but I said Id be Gentel I pinched the leg for fun and she cryed and kicked me I wanted to pinch her all over becos she wos mine*

The passage was similar in tone to the other hundred odd pages written in the mawkish, rambling and semi-literate hand on lined prison notepaper. The spelling confusions, missing words and intermittent use of capital letters confirmed Coulter as poorly educated.

Yet, if you ignored the lack of normal punctuation, the writing had an elegant form

65

similar to a stream of consciousness. He was reminded of a comment attributed to James Joyce on the subject of his novel, *Ulysses*.

'I've put in so many enigmas and puzzles that it will keep the professors busy for centuries arguing over what I meant, and that's the only way of ensuring one's immortality.'

Is that what this was all about, Coulter's desire for immortality? His memoir to be picked apart interminably by psychology professors like himself and their students. To have books written about him, like other 'notorious' killers? Coulter's work on Reborns had redeemed him, at least in the eyes of those he'd helped. Why expose his 'other' self through the diary, if not for notoriety?

Psychopaths were known to take advantage of prison facilities, taking any courses on offer, attempting to shape a positive image of themselves with which to impress a parole board. Coulter was regarded by the hospital authorities as a model inmate, someone who had apparently turned a chaotic and violent life around. Someone who had found 'his calling'. Coulter no longer lived by the narrative that had informed the diary. He had said so himself. *I am no longer that person.* Was that really true?

Even in this short extract, Coulter's storytelling skills were evident. His ability to portray himself as a young father, delighting in the delicate wonder of his newborn baby daughter. Yet beneath the playful tone, Magnus sensed something else.

Coulter had insisted on changing the nappy, even though his partner wasn't keen. He'd told her he would be gentle. Once in charge, he began to refer to the baby as *she*, where before, he'd used *it*.

He pinched the little leg hard enough for the baby to cry out, which made him want to pinch it all over because, he said, he was her dad.

The memoir wasn't easy to read. It would take time and patience to deal with the flow of consciousness and to make sense of the poor spelling and punctuation, but the real challenge would be to determine what psychological sense it made.

Coulter, faced with a sentence that would keep him behind bars for the remainder of his life, had taken a route with a well established history. Criminal memoirs weren't new. From the days of the gibbet, murderers' life stories had been sold, usually on their demise, both for profit and as treatises on morality.

In Coulter's case, however, there was no evidence of remorse or guilt. In fact, the murder of his baby daughter was never mentioned at all. An initial trawl of the manuscript had shown it to be peopled solely by his numerous partners and their offspring (in it, he admitted to fathering nine children, the first at the age of fourteen). He talked about these babies fondly, yet some he'd never even seen, having left the mother before they were born. He often seemed to forget or never knew the babies' names or sometimes even their genders. Mothers' names, too, were misspelt and muddled up.

In the past, fathering numerous children had been common, usually in the hope that some would survive to pass on your genes. Nowadays one or two were the norm, their survival down to their parents' care and protection. But there were still plenty of instances where women had numerous children, often by different fathers. Fathers who took no part in their children's support or upbringing.

Magnus had picked up a sense of egotistical pride in Coulter's reminiscences of his progeny, as though his masculinity was evidenced by his virility. Even now, he went on creating children. *My babies*, he'd called them, only now they weren't real.

Magnus lifted his glass and took another sip of the golden liquid. He tried to imagine what he might write in a memoir of his own life. Unlike Coulter, he would have very few partners to declare and no offspring that he was aware of.

Would the narrative he wrote be honest or would he choose his words carefully, hiding the real Magnus beneath a revisionist tale? Would his students be able to glean anything of the man he was, or thought he was? Would he, knowing how it was done, be able to fool them?

It was an intriguing thought. Maybe even an exercise that might prove useful, for his students at least.

He wondered if his profession had destroyed his capacity to take people, even himself, at face value. To enjoy life as it happened, rather than constantly analysing it. Then he recalled an early meeting with Rhona, where his silent study of her thoughts had proved just as erotic as her scent and physical appearance.

In his profession, you had to be aware of what people were thinking, as opposed to what they were saying. He ran over his dialogue with Coulter in his mind. Both of them had been intent on establishing who was in charge. After that, Coulter had sought to intrigue Magnus. And he had succeeded. Showing him the Reborns had been a master stroke; seeing Coulter at work was much more powerful than simply being told about it.

His mobile vibrated against the surface of the desk, and he closed the lid on Coulter's musings and picked up the phone. The caller ID surprised him—it was as though by thinking about her, he had conjured Rhona up.

'Rhona!' he said, keeping his tone light.

'Hi, Magnus, how are you?'

Did she want the truth or the accepted reply?

'Fine, and you?'

'Busy. I thought you might like to know that Bill has been cleared of the assault charge.'

'I'm very pleased to hear it.'

She ran the details past him. 'Internal discipline kicks in now.'

He could sense her disquiet.

'You suspect he'll step down?'

'Yes.'

He found himself profoundly saddened by such a thought.

'But that's not why I'm calling. Sutherland wants you involved in the fairground case. I wondered if DI Slater had got in touch.'

'Not yet.'

She made a small annoyed sound in her throat.

'I have been following it on the news.'

'The abridged version,' she said.

'Do you want to meet up and you can tell me the rest?'

There was a moment's silence before she responded. 'Can you drop by the lab?'

'When?'

'Tomorrow, about eleven?'

69

'OK.'

He rang off, happy that he would see her again, whatever the circumstances.

# CHAPTER NINE

Bill stood at his front door and imagined life inside. Margaret would be in the kitchen by now, making the evening meal. Lisa was probably upstairs in her room studying. She was working for her Advanced Highers, her sights set on becoming a doctor. If she failed to get the qualifications she needed, it would be that bastard's fault. Bill cursed the Gravedigger under his breath for the umpteenth time.

'You have to let it go,' Margaret had told him. 'He wants what he did to Lisa to eat at you. If you let it, he's won.'

When she said it, it made sense. Standing here alone, hate filling him, such a notion seemed impossible. He took out his key and slipped it in the lock as quietly as he could. He needed more time before facing Margaret.

There was something comforting in the familiar sight and smells of the hall. Robbie's wet sneakers had been abandoned at the bottom of the stairs. A damp jacket hung steaming on the radiator. The left hand door lay ajar, television playing to an empty sitting room.

He went upstairs.

As he turned on the shower, he realised Margaret would hear the water running and know he was back. The thought made him feel guilty. He

70

should have gone through to her right away. It wasn't as though she would castigate him for his choice. She'd stood by him in all his major decisions, knowing that none of them were made without a lot of soul-searching.

Two brightly coloured scarves hung on the dressing table mirror. They'd been Margaret's favourites when she'd lost her hair through the chemotherapy. He wondered why she didn't put them in the drawer or throw them out now they were no longer necessary. Then the thought struck him that she kept them out to remind her that she'd survived.

Survival. Margaret knew better than most people what staring death in the face meant. The thought chastened him, and he dressed quickly and went downstairs.

She was standing at the open oven, her back to him, stirring a casserole dish she'd lifted out. On the kitchen table stood a bottle of Jura and two tumblers.

She spoke without turning. 'Why don't you pour us both a drink?'

He did as requested, adding water from the cold tap. The casserole back in the oven, she turned, her face flushed by the heat.

'Well?'

He handed her a whisky. He'd already texted her the court result so that wasn't the news she was waiting for, glass in hand.

'I got a ticking off from the Super.'

'That's it?'

He nodded. Sutherland had been brusque but kind. More than he deserved. She was waiting for him to continue. When he didn't, she said the

71

words for him.

'You didn't resign.'

He met her eye. 'I didn't resign.'

She toasted him with her glass and he saluted her back. Even now, as the whisky warmed his chest, he wondered why she didn't demand he leave the Force, point out that the job had endangered his family.

She took a seat at the table. Bill was struck, looking down at the new-grown hair, how much younger it made her look, the cap of curls resembling an infant's.

He joined her.

'What's happening about finding Michael's killer?'

'Nothing.'

'It's time you did something about that.'

He agreed. It was time.

*      *      *

Bill had developed a way of observing his daughter that wasn't direct. It had begun on her return from hospital and had continued since then. The mental checklist he went through each time he viewed Lisa exhausted him. It had worsened in the idle hours spent sitting at home awaiting the trial. Lisa was his first thought when he opened his eyes in the morning and the last when he closed them at night.

That was the reason he'd decided to go back to work, even if it meant being demoted. Surely if he had a case to work on, it would stop him thinking about what had happened to his daughter. If he was at the station, he would stop watching her.

It was Robbie who brought up the fairground case while they were at their meal, breaking the rule that what happened on the job wasn't discussed at home. Margaret had already told them he'd been reinstated.

'Does that mean you'll be in charge of the fairground murder?' Robbie's tone was casual.

'Why do you ask?'

'I just wondered. David Murdoch's in my year at school.'

'Who's David Murdoch?' Lisa chimed in.

'The boyfriend of the girl who died.'

A flash of fear crossed Lisa's face. Bill cursed his son silently for his thoughtlessness.

'Is David a friend of yours?'

'He's in my maths class.' A fairly non-committal answer.

Margaret threw Bill a warning look.

'I'm glad you're going back, Dad.' Lisa gave him a wan smile.

'So am I,' he said and meant it.

The rest of the meal passed off without incident.

Once the kids went back upstairs, Margaret asked him outright if he would be handling the investigation.

'DI Slater was there to cover for me. If the court case had gone the other way . . .'

'He might have been permanent?'

'They would probably have brought in someone new, or promoted someone.'

'DS McNab would have made a good DI.'

'Yes.' Better than Slater, he thought. The team would have worked for McNab, not the badge.

'It says in the paper that the dead girl went to Morvern.'

They had contemplated sending Lisa to the all girls' school at one time, because of its reputation for producing doctors. Bill was glad now they hadn't.

'She's OK, you know,' said Margaret.

'I'm not so sure.'

She rose and started stacking the dishes. 'We've got to put it behind us,' she said sharply.

His mobile rang before he could respond. He checked the screen. 'I'll take it in the hall.'

\* \* \*

When he left the kitchen, she replenished her glass. Margaret, the daughter of a Presbyterian minister, wasn't a drinker. Not normally.

Her hand shook a little as she raised it to her mouth. That had gone well, she congratulated herself silently. She had been surprised. He'd given every indication that he planned to resign, or ask for early retirement. Part of her wanted him to do that, but one thing she knew: Bill would not survive without the job. The kids would be gone soon, university, then a life of their own away from the family home. That was to have been their time together after thirty-odd years of marriage. Just the two of them.

Except there might only be one.

## CHAPTER TEN

Petersson recognised Rhona immediately, although he'd only seen her once before. It had been at Bill

74

Wilson's fiftieth birthday party at the Ultimate Jazz Club. By the time he'd spotted her, she was already being chatted up by Sean Maguire, Irish saxophonist and part owner of the club. He'd asked Bill to introduce him anyway. He remembered the quizzical look she'd given him at the mention of his name. *I've heard of you.*

It had pleased him that she'd known who he was. Then she'd left with the Irishman, dashing his hopes and squashing his ego.

But here she was again. And this time, alone.

He lifted two glasses of red wine from a passing tray and joined her in front of a modern painting that consisted of stripes in black, grey and white that rolled like waves across the canvas. He offered her a glass.

'Makes me sea-sick.'

'The painting or the wine?'

He took a sip and grimaced. 'Both, I fear.'

She smiled.

'You may not remember me . . .'

'I do. Einar Petersson, the journalist.'

'We met at . . .'

'Bill's party.'

'You have a good memory.'

'Yes, I do.'

'What brings you here?' He gestured at the groups of Glasgow art lovers who were scrutinising the offerings on show.

'I bought a painting from this gallery. "Sunlight over the Cuillins on Skye" by Sharon Mitchell. I love it. It hangs above my fireplace to remind me of home. How about you—are you an art collector?'

'I fancied a free drink before dinner. Plus my

75

flat's nearby,' he lied.

'I thought you were London based?'

'I am. Most of the time.'

'Then what brings you north?'

'A visit to Iceland to see my parents, then a bit of nosing around in Glasgow.'

'Something important?'

'Might be.'

He could tell by her expression that his vagueness wasn't holding her interest.

'I was sorry to hear about DS McNab.'

Her face drained of colour and she almost dropped her glass. He reached out to steady her arm.

'Hey, are you OK?'

'I didn't know you knew him.'

'I didn't, but I heard he got on the wrong side of the Russian contingent.'

She looked more angry than shocked now.

'Nikolai Kalinin.'

'You think Kalinin killed him?'

'Him or someone ordered by him.'

'Kalinin's a hard man to track down.'

She looked up swiftly. 'You've tried?'

'I'm thinking about it.' That too was a lie, but a necessary one. He wanted to find out what she knew, without giving anything away himself.

He could tell she was tempted, but cautious. After all, he was a newspaper man. It all depended on how keen she was to catch McNab's killer.

'Fancy going somewhere else? Preferably a place that provides better wine?' They both knew there was nothing really wrong with the wine.

She gave him an inscrutable look.

'Where did you have in mind, exactly?'

76

He mentioned a members only club not far from where they were. 'They serve good champagne. The food's excellent too, if you haven't eaten.'

She took a moment to reply. 'OK.'

He was relieved she hadn't turned him down and hoped it didn't show. He knew a fair bit about Dr Rhona MacLeod, and a pushover she wasn't.

## CHAPTER ELEVEN

Rhona stared into the early morning darkness. Properly awake now, she reached out and checked the place beside her in the bed. It was warm but empty. She thought Petersson might have already left, then she heard the shower and realised he was in the bathroom. It looked as though he was planning to leave without telling her, but felt the need to shower first. Was he going home to someone who would smell her on his skin? Or was he naturally fastidious?

She decided she didn't care either way.

She rose and went to the bathroom, pausing for a moment to survey his tall, muscular body through the shower glass. She couldn't make out the long purple scar on the left hand side of his torso, though she remembered tracing the line of it beneath her fingers.

*An argument with a knife,* he'd said.

The tattoos on his upper arms and chest were dark smudges, their intricate pattern blurred by watery streams. Last night she had simply registered their presence. She hadn't been interested in why he chose to decorate his body or what designs he had chosen.

She opened the cubicle door and stepped inside. He'd turned the shower to massage and the sudden drum of the needles on her head made her gasp. He circled her body with his.

'I didn't want to wake you. I have to be somewhere.'

She didn't ask where.

'Something to do with what we discussed last night. Before we moved on to other things.'

He made to kiss her but she avoided him by stepping out and grabbing a towel. She had to play this carefully.

As she dried herself, she went over last night's conversation. He'd drunk most of the second bottle of champagne, while she'd had very little. She'd wanted to be in control of what she said and did.

She felt a small twinge of guilt at her behaviour, then reminded herself it was no big deal. They had met socially and she'd brought him home for sex; something that had happened before with other men, and would no doubt happen again. But Einar Petersson's attraction wasn't his body or what he could offer her sexually. His attraction came from who and what he was, an investigative journalist who had successfully exposed a number of nefarious activities in high places.

Slater wasn't up to the challenge of finding Nikolai Kalinin, let alone building a case against him. Bill, she suspected, was out of the picture. On her part, she was willing to do whatever was necessary to progress the case. In her own time and at her own expense. Professionally there was an element of risk involved in such a decision, but she was willing to take that chance.

Petersson was beside her, rubbing himself dry.

'Perhaps we could meet up later?' he suggested.

'Why?'

He met her gaze. 'Because we both want the same thing.'

\*       \*       \*

When he left, she dressed, made herself coffee and settled at the kitchen table. At five a.m. the city still slept. The only sound in the room was the intermittent soft snore of the cat, who refused to be awake at such an hour. Rhona switched on her laptop. She had three hours before she left for the lab and planned to use the time to study more of Petersson's investigative career.

Her thoughts had been focused on revenge ever since McNab's death. Her dreams had taken on the same hue, one dream in particular returning time and time again. In it, she relived her meeting with Kalinin, sharing the meal with him as before, drinking his wine. This time when he made his move she went along with it, because that way she could get him in the bedroom alone, away from Solenik's watchful eye. In there she had the chance to pay Kalinin back for what he had done to McNab.

For a while, reliving the dream had helped her focus her anger but her vengeful dreams were now no longer enough.

McNab's murder was her 'soul crime'. Unresolved, it would continue to haunt her, perhaps forever. It was a common enough occurrence among policemen. Some went to their graves still trying to get to the truth of such cases. Soul crimes hung about their owners like a bad smell. They forgot all the murders they'd solved, focusing only on those they hadn't.

After the killing, feeling among McNab's colleagues had run high. No one cared that the investigation into the Russian mafia that Slater had pursued so relentlessly had gone belly up. What they cared about was that it had taken McNab with it. Some even blamed DI Slater for his demise, which was unfair but understandable.

Her response had been to blame herself. She should have gone with McNab and Chrissy that night when he'd asked her to. If she had been there, she would have held him back in some way, just as she had done on numerous other occasions. She would have prevented his death. She'd replayed her alternative scenario a million times, often so vividly that for a few seconds it felt like the truth.

She and Chrissy had been the ones to process the crime scene. She'd had to fight for the privilege. Slater argued that she was in shock; she couldn't be dispassionate; she might miss something. She'd listened in silence, then gone ahead anyway, knowing he wanted her out of there because her raw anger embarrassed him.

When the SOCO van had appeared that night, she'd donned a suit over her blood-splattered clothes and set to work. Chrissy had joined her. Wordlessly they'd searched, eventually finding what they were looking for. Ejected from the car window, the bullet casing had rolled down a nearby gutter. They'd sucked that gutter clean, bringing its contents to the lab, where they'd spent hours sifting through the mass of putrid gunge. Eventually they'd found it.

Retrieving a print from a casing had been well-nigh impossible until recently, when Dr John Bond, a scientific officer with Northampton Police, had developed a new forensic technique which relied on the subtle corrosion of metal surfaces by the chloride ions in human sweat. You could clean the metal surface, heat it to 600 degrees or paint over it. It made no difference. The corrosion remained. Dust the casing with fine conducting powder, pass 2500 volts through it and the pattern was visible. Not the print residue of the person who loaded the gun, but evidence of the physical changes their sweat had made to the metal itself.

Rhona had sent the casing south. It had taken time, but they'd eventually come back to her with a partial print, which found no match on any police database. That told her one thing. Since Kalinin had been lifted and printed, he hadn't been the one to load the gun. But she was in no doubt he was the one to order the shooting.

Chrissy, the only eye witness, had seen the gun emerge from the window but had not had a clear view of the man who fired it. She was also sketchy on details of the car, a black limo with smoked windows. They'd caught it briefly on camera later in the city, then lost it completely. Since they hadn't recorded it heading south, it might still be in Glasgow, hidden in a lock-up or garage. Every possible sighting had been followed up, but the probability was it had already been stripped down and given a revamp, plates and all.

Paddy Brogan, McNab's contact and manager of the gambling club, had seemed genuinely shocked

81

by his murder. After all, he'd invited McNab to play that night, to thank him for getting Kalinin off his back. According to his staff, Brogan had never left the building, so he was off the hook, for now.

All in all, the perfect crime.

Rhona hadn't attended the post-mortem. No one close to McNab had; Superintendent Sutherland had made certain of that. Slater had been the only one to see McNab's body on the slab, to see the effects of the bullet on his internal organs. Even that hadn't spurred him on to find McNab's killer. With Bill suspended, they had no one, it seemed, willing or able to progress the case.

Until Einar Petersson had appeared on the scene. Outside the law, with an axe of his own to grind where Kalinin was concerned, he could turn out to be exactly what she needed.

# CHAPTER TWELVE

On arrival, Bill had been summoned into Sutherland's office, where Slater was already waiting. They'd briefly acknowledged each other's existence, then Sutherland had asked DI Slater to fill them in on what had happened so far. Slater had done so with an ill grace, but beneath it Bill suspected he wasn't unhappy about his return. Working here after McNab's murder couldn't have been easy, especially since he'd brought the Kalinin case with him.

The official handover took half the morning. Afterwards Bill reclaimed his office and sat down in his favourite chair. If he was honest, he'd been afraid that Slater would have thrown the chair out. Now *that* would have upset him.

He settled against the old leather and swivelled to face the window, enjoying the familiar creak as it turned.

'Coffee, Sir.'

DS Clark placed a mug on the desk.

'That's not your job any more, *Detective Sergeant*,' he smiled.

'It never was, Sir.'

He accepted the mild rebuke.

'We're ready when you are, Sir.'

*    *    *

'All leave is cancelled until we find the baby.'

A babble of voices erupted at his announcement. It was what should have happened in the first place. They had all known that, except Slater.

'According to the pathologist, there's a good chance it's alive, despite the circumstances of the birth. Finding that baby is our top priority.' Bill looked round the assembled team. DS Clark couldn't keep the grin off her face. At least someone was pleased he was back.

And he *was* back. With a rush of emotion, he realised how pleased he was about that. The same intent faces, the sharp sense of excitement. He was addressing a hunting party, desperate to find its prey. This is where they caught the scent. Nosing their way through the mess of a crime scene.

But they had already lost precious time.

He'd listened to Slater's version of events, but it wasn't enough. He wanted to know what these people thought, the questions they felt compelled to ask. He wanted facts, but also feelings and intuition. That was what distinguished the men and women of CID from the uniform brigade.

'Let's start with motive,' he said.

Janice spoke first. 'All recorded cases of foetal theft have been carried out by a female assailant.'

'Why?'

The others began to join in.

'Jealousy. They want a baby themselves and can't have one.'

'Mental illness.'

'A fake pregnancy that needed a result.'

'And how many of those babies died?' he continued.

'None.'

'So this one is statistically alive, if indeed that was the motive. Other possible motives?'

Silence.

'A girl was mutilated and killed here,' he urged.

'A jealous boyfriend?'

'Revenge for something she did?'

'Someone who hates women.'

'A lust kill?'

'Was she sexually assaulted?' asked Bill.

A chorus of nos.

'Then why a lust kill?'

'He gets off on torture.'

'And why take the baby?'

'To kill it later?'

'She was rendered unconscious,' he reminded them.

'He wanted it to be easy?'

'He?'

'He, she, they.'

84

'You think there might be more than one?'

They hadn't thought of that. The hubbub broke out again, and Bill gave them time to talk the possibility through.

'So there wasn't necessarily only one assailant?'

They nodded their heads in agreement. Bill moved on to witnesses.

'The guy who sold her the ticket.'

'Last witness, first suspect. Who interviewed him?'

DC Campbell raised his hand.

'He says no one followed her in until the boyfriend, about twenty minutes later. He was getting ready to shut the place down.'

'His alibi?'

'The guy on the candy floss van opposite says he never left the booth.'

'You believe him?'

'He seemed pretty sure.'

'Any other witnesses?'

'The pals backed up David's version of events.'

'Who else saw Kira go into the tent?'

Janice answered, 'No one we've interviewed so far.'

Bill now asked the question that had been bugging him.

'Why the mirror maze? And why alone?'

'Curiosity?'

'It started to rain?'

'Maybe she fancied the guy in the booth.'

'Or she was avoiding someone.'

'The boyfriend, maybe?'

'He was on the Waltzers.'

'Someone else?'

'An old boyfriend? The baby's father?'

'Let's have R2S's 3-D recording up on the screen. I want to know who had a direct line of sight to the mirror maze entrance, what Kira could see from the entrance and why she went in there.'

There was a whirring sound, then the wall screen was washed with white light.

Bill continued. 'Did we take a note of names before we let people leave?'

'We recorded the names of those who were there, but some would have left before we arrived,' said Janice.

'Put out a request for anyone in the vicinity to come forward, even if they think they didn't see anything. Imply that we have CCTV footage.'

'We haven't.'

'They don't know that. Guilt might urge some to come forward in case we turn up on their doorstep. The place was crowded with teenagers, and teenagers take mobile phone pictures on nights out. Let's put out a call for any images of that night to be emailed to the police website. We might get lucky. Kira's mobile wasn't found with the body. I take it she had one?'

'Top of the range, according to her parents.'

'So where is it?'

'Perhaps the killer took it.'

'Why?'

'Maybe there was something on it.'

'Has it been used since it went missing?'

'No record of usage since that night, Sir.'

'What about a handbag?'

'We didn't find one with her. There was a purse in her pocket containing approximately twenty pounds, a couple of receipts, a bus pass and a credit card.'

'A credit card?'

'The family's well-off, Sir.'

Of course. Morvern School for Girls was anything but cheap.

He now offered up the evidence of the mirror writing and asked them what they thought. The responses sounded like a rehash of Wikipedia: pacts with the devil, secret codes, Leonardo Da Vinci. He was interested in the small number of people who had the ability, and also wanted to know everything there was to know about the term 'daisy chain'.

'DC Campbell. Find out which hookers offer daisy chaining to their clientele here in the city. Also anything about it you can find online. Look in places where young people hang out. Facebook, Bebo, sites like that.'

A cheer went up as Campbell blushed furiously. Bill ignored it.

'Carmichael, find out where she got the tattoo, and get the name of anyone else they tattooed with a daisy.'

A voice called, 'We're ready, Sir.'

Bill turned to face the screen.

## CHAPTER THIRTEEN

After the briefing, Bill decided to visit the school. Independent schools insisted they knew their pupils on an individual basis, so it would be interesting to see how well Morvern School for Girls had known Kira Reese-Brandon.

He and Margaret had visited the school a couple

of years back, and he had to admit he'd been seduced by it. Even Margaret, a staunch advocate of state education, had been swayed. If he'd said he wanted Lisa to go to Morvern, she would have gone along with it. It wasn't hard to see why.

The façade itself was impressive. Where most secondary schools, particularly those built in the Seventies, looked in danger of falling to bits, Morvern was housed in a beautiful, century-old building, carefully maintained.

He climbed the four wide steps to the pillared entrance, the school flag fluttering above him, and pushed open one of the double doors. The scent of wood polish met him as he entered the panelled reception area. Ahead, a second set of doors led to a spacious marble-floored entrance hall. There was a kind of hush, an air of quiet application, that he'd noticed before in other places of learning.

This school had a history, all of it good. It sold itself on a reputation for intellectual and professional excellence, and it had plenty of evidence to back up its claims; a cursory glance through the top names in the Scottish medical and law professions would find a high proportion of Morvern old girls. That was why they had considered sending Lisa here for her senior years. Bill felt a momentary twinge of regret.

He gave his name to the receptionist, who lifted a receiver and relayed his message to someone. A few minutes later a woman appeared from the direction of the entrance hall.

'Detective Inspector Wilson.' She held out her hand. 'I'm Diane Porter, Principal of Morvern.'

Her voice had a rich timbre, but it was difficult to place the accent. It wasn't received pronunciation, more a cultivated Scots, he decided. She was tall and well-proportioned, her hair a springy black sprinkled with grey. Unlike many women in the professions, she wasn't wearing the customary dark power suit, but a smart skirt and sweater, casual yet chic.

'If you would like to come through to my office?'

She led him into the entrance hall. Two senior girls appeared from a nearby corridor and she exchanged pleasantries with them, using their first names. The girls eyed him curiously, but Ms Porter did not introduce him.

To the right was a substantial wooden door with a brass plate that read 'Principal's Secretary'. She opened this and led him inside where a woman sat behind a desk.

'Joan, this is Detective Inspector Wilson.' The secretary seemed unfazed by the arrival of a policeman and merely smiled a welcome.

'Can you order us some tea please?'

'Of course, Ms Porter.'

He was finally ushered through a further door marked 'Principal' and into a large, high-ceilinged room filled with winter sunlight and the scent of hyacinths.

Near the window stood a leather-topped walnut desk with intricately carved legs. On it sat a laptop, a phone and a tray of papers. On the neighbouring wall hung a row of portraits of what he took to be former Principals. All of them wore black gowns and looked down on him with piercingly intelligent eyes. Before the desk was spread a rectangular rug which featured the school crest and the words of its Latin motto.

She followed his gaze. '*Sapere aude*. Dare to be wise.'

He remembered the motto from the school prospectus. He'd thought it appropriate for a school that had promoted women's education in the sciences when it hadn't been popular or advisable to do so.

'I understand you've come about Kira. Such a terrible business.'

There was a quiet knock at the door.

'That will be the tea.'

Joan entered, carrying a silver tray with a china teapot, two delicate cups and saucers and a plate of chocolate biscuits. Obviously the fees of nine grand a year could stretch to such niceties. She set the tray on a glass surfaced coffee table that sat between two leather armchairs and a couch near an ornate fireplace.

He took a seat as requested while she poured the tea. The civilised setting seemed at odds with the reason for his visit.

She handed him a cup and saucer. He took a sip of the tea. Earl Grey. One of Margaret's favourites, but not one normally served up at the police station. His team preferred builders' brew. He relinquished the fragile china, setting it safely on the table.

'What kind of student was Kira?' he began.

'Very able. Gifted, I would say. Her strength was mathematics, although she was good at everything, including music. An all-rounder. She planned to do maths at Cambridge.'

'Before she became pregnant.'

A pained expression crossed Ms Porter's face.

'I believe, after the birth, she intended to

continue with her studies.'

'How would that work?'

'The baby was to be put up for adoption.'

'How did Kira feel about that?'

'Initially, I believe she wanted to keep it, but eventually she came round to the idea.'

'She was persuaded?'

'Not by the school.'

'Have you any idea who the father of the child was?'

'No.'

'You didn't ask?'

'I felt that was a matter for the parents.'

'There was no question of an abortion?'

She shook her head. 'Kira's family are practising Christians.'

'Who don't approve of abortion?'

'Kira agreed with them. She didn't want the child aborted.'

He changed tack. 'Does the expression "daisy chain" mean anything to you?'

She seemed taken aback by his question, but when she answered, her voice bore no trace of nervousness.

'There's a support group for parents of autistic children which uses that name. We have some very able pupils here who exhibit some of the features within the autism spectrum, so I'm aware of the group.'

'Savants?'

'Some have areas of brilliance which are not necessarily reflected in other aspects of their life.'

'Was Kira one of those pupils?'

'Kira was a mature, well-adjusted girl with a very good brain.'

'Who should not have got pregnant?'

'We were surprised, yes.'

'You don't have many teenage pregnancies at Morvern?'

'Not normally, no.'

He decided to press further. 'How many of your pupils have become pregnant in the last decade?'

She hesitated. 'Five.'

It hadn't mentioned that in the prospectus.

'So one every couple of years?' It was still higher than he'd anticipated.

She shook her head, her cheeks flushing a little. 'No. Five this year, in fact.'

Bill was stunned.

'You've had five pregnancies within the last year?'

'Yes.'

'That's extraordinary. Have you any idea why?'

'Teachers are often confronted by copycat behaviour. Fads, for the most part, which usually confine themselves to fashion. Jewellery, hair styles, body piercings. Dieting is the one we tend to look out for. Self-harm is another.' She paused. 'The atmosphere between sensitive, emotional, bright adolescent girls is often highly charged.'

'You're suggesting getting pregnant was the fashion fad this year?'

'I assume we are speaking in confidence?' She looked to him for confirmation, and he nodded. 'I suspect it was more of a pact.'

'A group of girls got pregnant as a pact?'

'Our experience during the last six months or so suggests this may have been the case. The girls here are all high achievers, expected to succeed. There is a lot of pressure on them from parents, from their peers.'

'And from the school?'

'Morvern supports its pupils in every way we can, but we do expect them to make the most of the gifts they've been given. However, it is not always easy being clever.'

'And getting pregnant is one way out of the clever club.'

'It may appear to be.'

'Did you ask Kira to leave the school when you discovered she was pregnant?'

'No. We supported her when she wanted to stay.'

This surprised him. An obviously pregnant girl wearing the Morvern uniform was not a great advert for the school.

As if interpreting his thoughts, she said, 'Kira came in in normal dress.'

It was one way to save face, both for Kira and the school.

'And what about the others?'

'It wasn't apparent at the time that there were others. That came later.'

'So there have been four reported pregnancies since Kira?'

'Yes.'

'And what happened to those girls?'

'In view of the circumstances and after discussions with their parents, they all left, including Kira.'

'I take it these girls were friends?'

'Yes. A small clique of very high achievers.'

'You suspect Kira's pregnancy started a trend?'

'We became aware of two more pregnancies six weeks after Kira's was revealed.'

'And the remaining two?'

'A month after that.'

'Did you bring the girls together as a group and try and work out why this had happened?'

'The parents decided that wasn't appropriate.'

'And they removed their daughters from the school?'

'Yes. If they hadn't, the governors would have asked them to.'

One pregnancy could be attributed to a wayward pupil. Five pregnancies in so short a time would look like the school's fault.

He thought about the mirror writing on Kira's hands and the daisy tattoo on the small of her back. He didn't want to reveal either fact but he was interested in finding out if they could have had anything to do with this supposed pact.

'Did any of these girls have a tattoo?'

'Parents are advised that tattoos and piercings other than in the earlobe are not permitted.'

In his experience, forbidding a teenager to do something often achieved the opposite result. You needed evidence of being eighteen to get a tattoo in a licensed parlour but fake ID wasn't uncommon.

'I'd like the names of the other pregnant girls.'

'You plan to interview them?' She looked concerned.

'You said these girls were close friends, maybe even close enough to form a pregnancy pact. I need to speak to them about Kira. I also need to see their school records.'

'Our student records are normally confidential . . .'

'But not to the police,' he said firmly.

She rose. 'Everything's on computer now. We don't store hard copies. I'll organise Joan to help you access them.'

'Thank you. Also, did Kira have a guidance teacher, someone responsible for her pastoral care?'

'We have a tutee system in our sixth form. Dr Frank Delaney was Kira's tutor.'

'May I see him before I look at her records?'

'Of course.'

She walked over to the desk and buzzed through to her secretary, summoning Dr Delaney to her office.

'This may take a few minutes. If he is with a class, his Head of Department will have to organise cover.'

She returned to the coffee table and asked if he wanted more tea. Her calm demeanour had returned, her hand steady as she poured.

'Do you have any idea why Kira was killed?' she asked.

'No, we don't.'

'And what about the baby?'

'We're still looking for it.'

Dr Delaney arrived a few minutes later. He was very tall, easily six foot four, and stick thin. His face was all angles, the nose prominent and sharp, the look penetrating. Bill imagined him flapping the black gown as he strode around the classroom like a giant raven.

The Principal introduced them, then said, 'I'll have Joan retrieve Kira's records for you. If you just come through when you're finished here.'

'Thank you.'

Bill thought he glimpsed concern in Delaney's

95

eyes at the thought of being abandoned, but it didn't last long. When Ms Porter had closed the door behind her, Delaney folded his long frame into the seat.

'This is a terrible business. I still can't believe it. Kira was so alive. Her parents must be devastated. Is there anything I can do to help?'

'Tell me about her.'

'That's easy. Multi-talented. Fun. A powerful intellect, particularly in Maths. She was one of my best pupils.'

'Is that why you became her tutor?'

'The girls are allowed to choose a tutor. Provided not too many choose the same one, they are usually matched with their first choice.'

'So you had a special bond?'

Delaney gave him an inscrutable look. 'It's not unusual for a pupil to choose a tutor who is an expert in her area. It's a sensible career move.'

'That's why she chose you?'

'I assumed so.'

'Do you have any other tutees?'

He looked a little uneasy. 'I had three originally, including Kira. Only one remains.'

'What happened to the other one?'

'Samantha left for the same reason as Kira.'

'Because she was pregnant?'

'Yes.'

'Do you think the group of girls who got pregnant had formed a pact?'

He didn't look surprised by the question.

'"Pact" is probably too strong a word. Despite being brainy, Kira was also regarded as cool. That's one of the advantages of single sex education for girls. They don't need to pretend

96

they're not good at something to be cool. No boys in the classroom to play down to.'

'You think Kira had influence over the other girls?'

He shrugged. 'I don't mean she told them what to do. She was like a celebrity to them. Someone to emulate. If Kira did something unusual, then it was an OK thing to do.'

'Why do you think the girls got pregnant?'

'You mean was it accident or design? I have no idea, I've been asking myself the same question ever since Kira sprung her news.'

'She told you first?'

'I suspect I knew before her parents, but not before her friends.'

'Was she upset?'

'Not in the least. She was pleased. I was the one who was upset. I knew she could go far in Maths.'

'And a baby would stop her doing that?'

'Mathematicians do their best work early in their career. She knew that. In fact, she told me she was thinking of switching to Medicine instead.'

'That must have disappointed you.'

He gave a rueful smile. 'All teachers live through their protégés in some way. Yes, I admit I was disappointed.'

'You said you had three tutees?'

'Sandie's the only one still here.'

'Did she know Kira?'

'Yes. In fact, she was with her the night she died.'

An Alexandra Stewart-Smith had been on the list of friends with Kira that night. Sandie, David Murdoch and another boy, Owen Hegarty. He'd glanced over their statements but hadn't yet met

97

any of them. David he would speak to later today, but if Sandie was here, he could chat to her now.

'I'd like to meet with Sandie if she's in school today.'

'She was in Maths first thing.' Dr Delaney rose.

Bill was struck again by his height. His presence dominated even a room as large as this. An ideal requirement for a teacher, although Bill's own maths teacher had been a tiny, bird-like woman they'd christened the Hen because of her rotund shape and stick-thin legs. The Hen may not have been tall, but she had scared the living daylights out of him and everyone else in the class.

Dr Delaney asked him to wait while he relayed his request to the Principal, and Bill was happy to do so. He spent the time at the magnificent windows observing west end Glasgow going about its business. If they could have afforded to live near the centre, this was the area he would have chosen. The home of Glasgow University, the Botanic Gardens, close to a variety of independent shops, and a short underground trip to the city centre.

Most people thought of Glasgow as the murder capital of Scotland, all street gangs, knives and booze. But there was another side to the city and this area typified it for him. It was vibrant, peopled by a mix of families, students, the average earner and the well-to-do. Morvern wasn't the only independent school in the neighbourhood, although it was the only single sex establishment.

An anachronism really, a single sex school, particularly in this day and age. After all, life was made up of two sexes and kids had to live in the real world. Yet a lot of what had been said about

98

Morvern was true. A higher proportion of girls from here entered the more male-dominated professions. On paper it looked as though single sex education worked—for girls, at least.

When Diane Porter returned, she was accompanied by a nervous-looking girl dressed in a school uniform of kilted skirt and dark green sweater over an open necked white shirt. Gone were the days of the school tie, apparently, even in the independent establishments.

'Sandie, this is Detective Inspector Wilson.'

'Hi, Sandie.' He gave her an encouraging smile. 'I know you talked to my colleague, DI Slater, and I read your statement. Thank you for that. I'm taking over from DI Slater on Kira's case. When I realised you were in school today, I just wanted to introduce myself and have a little chat.' He hoped that sounded friendly enough.

It seemed to work. She sat down opposite him, the wary look gone from her face.

'Would you like me to stay with you, Sandie?'

Sandie looked to the Principal and then to Bill. Her reply surprised him.

'No, I'm OK on my own.'

Ms Porter's expression suggested she would have preferred to stay, and he couldn't blame her. As well as her school being linked to a murder, there was a possibility that the press would get hold of the pregnancy pact story. If they did, the school's reputation would take a further battering. He was surprised the multiple pregnancies had remained a secret until now—it only went to show that affluent Glaswegians were very good at keeping their problems out of the public domain.

He waited until Ms Porter had left before

joining Sandie at the coffee table.

'I'm very sorry about what happened to your friend.'

She gave a little sniff. 'She just went for candyfloss. No one else likes it, so we went on to the dodgems.' She gave him a pitiful look. 'I should have gone with her.'

'Did she ask you to?'

She looked uncomfortable. 'Not exactly.'

'What happened wasn't your fault.'

'I know.'

'Tell me about Kira.'

She seemed unsure how to answer. 'We were friends,' she said finally.

'Best friends?'

She shook her head. 'Kira had lots of friends. No one special, except maybe David.' Her tone changed when she mentioned his name.

'They were close?'

She sounded peeved. 'They had this thing. Always whispering to one another like you weren't there.'

'How long had they been going out?'

She gave him a sharp look. 'A while. He wasn't the father, if that's what you think. He said he didn't care it was someone else's. How weird is that?'

A little weird—if it were true.

'Was Kira seeing someone else?'

'Well, she must have been if it wasn't David's.'

'But you didn't know who?'

She shook her head.

'Why do you think Kira went into the Hall of Mirrors on her own?'

She looked irritated. 'She was like that

sometimes. Just did things on her own. She even went to the cinema alone.' She looked to him for confirmation of how odd that was.

Bill didn't find it strange at all. He'd done the same thing himself during his suspension and was surprised by the variety of people who'd shared the daytime showings with him.

'She never thought it was sad to do things on her own.'

'And you do?'

She struggled for a moment, then shook her head. 'Nothing Kira did was sad.'

'Even getting pregnant?'

'She was happy about it.'

'What about the other girls?'

Sandie gave a brief look round as though someone might be listening at the door.

'We're not supposed to talk about that.'

'I've spoken to Ms Porter already.'

'My father threatened to take me out of the school if word got out.'

'And you don't want that?'

'I need to pass my exams. I want to study Medicine at Edinburgh.' She said this as though it was a passport to prestige and riches.

It probably was.

He was silent for a moment. It hadn't been obvious in her statement, but Bill was gaining the impression that Sandie hadn't liked Kira very much. He wondered how many of the gang had. People tended to become leaders because others were in awe of them or simply feared them. Leaders who were loved were thinner on the ground.

'Did you see yourself as one of Kira's gang?'

'I didn't get myself pregnant just to please her if that's what you mean.'

'Did Kira *ask* the others to get pregnant?'

'No! I don't know. She didn't talk to me about it, anyway.' She sounded relieved and annoyed at the same time.

From what Bill had read, Slater hadn't known about the daisy chain reference on Kira's palms when he'd initially interviewed those with her at the funfair. Bill didn't want to make it common knowledge, but if it was linked to this pact he needed to know.

'Have you heard the phrase "daisy chain"?'

Her face coloured a deep red, then went white. She looked as though she might throw up.

'Are you OK?'

Her hands gripped the sides of the leather chair.

'Is this to do with Kira's death?' she said fearfully.

'It might be.'

The words came out in a rush. 'That's what we called ourselves. The Daisy Chain. Kira chose the name. We had to have tattoos done. A daisy somewhere on your body where it wasn't obvious. The school doesn't allow tattoos, even if you can't see them. How stupid is that?' She regained a momentary calm as annoyance set in, then fear returned. 'Kira made us swear we wouldn't tell anyone about that.' A suspicious look crossed her face. 'Who told you? Was it David?'

'No.'

'Then how do you know?'

'I can't tell you that, I'm afraid.'

She leaned towards him. 'If Ms Porter finds out about the tattoo, she'll ask my dad to remove me from the school. He'll go mad.' She slumped suddenly in the chair, a beaten teenager with too much on her shoulders.

'I won't be the one to tell her.'

She gave him a grateful look.

'Can you think of anyone who would want to harm Kira? Who might want to take her baby?'

Her face creased. She was close to tears. 'No. Everyone liked Kira. She was special.' Her voice was tinged with envy.

He thought it was time to change the subject. 'Why do you want to study Medicine?'

She looked surprised by the question. 'Dad's a doctor. It runs in the family.'

It sounded as though Dad had made the decision for her. He took out his card.

'Will you promise to call me if you think of anything that might help?'

She nodded.

'Can I speak to you again some time soon?'

'Dad won't like it.'

'I'm afraid the law takes precedence over your dad's likes and dislikes.'

She looked pleased at the thought.

He watched her leave. In the kilt, green tights and flat shoes, she looked nearer twelve than seventeen.

He spent the next half hour going through Kira's school records. They made interesting reading. The description of her as an all-rounder was an understatement. She was an excellent swimmer, played the flute and the violin, was captain of the hockey team and a champion school debater. She'd regularly taken part in the UK Mathematics Trust annual Challenges and had won a gold certificate every year. She'd sat six subjects at Higher Level, Scotland's gold standard examinations, and passed all six at Band 1 level. In Maths and Physics she hadn't dropped a single mark and had been singled out by the Exam Board. She'd been destined to sit four Advanced Highers this June, three science papers and one in Pure Maths, but she was also taking Greek and Mandarin taster courses.

Her results at Higher Level alone would have guaranteed her a place studying Medicine at any Scottish university where breadth of knowledge was seen as the guarantor of success. The Advanced Highers were there to appease the English universities, more used to the English A level qualifications. With this girl's ability, any self-respecting university should have sent a taxi to collect her.

He thought of Lisa, who had a similar workload. She'd already been offered a place at Edinburgh on the strength of her Higher results. If all went well, she would move through in October to begin her studies. He should be pleased for her, but in truth he dreaded the day she would no longer be under his roof and under his care.

He finished by reading Kira's personal statement for her university application. He'd read through Lisa's statement before she'd submitted her UCAS form. He was struck again by how articulate both these young women were, by their ability to identify their strengths and outline their ambitions. When he'd been that age, he'd had no idea what he wanted to be or do. Even if he had known, he doubted whether he would have had the skill to put his thoughts into words.

According to the Principal's secretary, Oxbridge applications had to be in by November. Kira had met that deadline, applying to read Maths at Cambridge. It seemed she had subsequently changed her mind—or hedged her bets—and applied to do Medicine at three Scottish universities through her UCAS application. Ms Porter had told him that Kira's baby was to be put up for adoption, and that she fully intended to take up her place at Cambridge. Dr Delaney hadn't seemed so sure. Bill suspected only Kira had known what she really intended doing, and he could no longer ask her.

He turned his attention to the other names on the pregnancy list. Louisa Sommerville, Melanie Jones, Jocelyn Calderfield and Samantha Wells.

The similarity with Kira was striking. All had been on their way to university. Louisa to study Chemistry, Melanie had chosen Law, Jocelyn, Medicine. Only Samantha had broken the mould and chosen Archaeology. The dates the girls left Morvern were on their files. The reason given was simply 'withdrawn'.

He glanced at his watch. He was due to see Kira's parents shortly. He decided to call the station first and ask DS Clark to contact the other girls' parents and arrange a time to meet them. His first concern was whether these girls were still pregnant. It seemed more than likely that Kira's death was linked to her participation in the Daisy Chain, which meant the other members of the gang might also be in danger.

# CHAPTER FOURTEEN

The Reese-Brandons lived on a quiet road high above the River Kelvin. Below, the walkway ran between Partick and Kelvinbridge, crossing and recrossing the river via numerous bridges. It was a popular route for walkers, cyclists and joggers as well as providing a green shortcut through this area of the city.

It wasn't unlike the Water of Leith in Edinburgh in that respect, although Bill suspected the Water of Leith was less rubbish-strewn than the place he now looked down on. It made him angry, this aspect of Glasgow and Glaswegians. In February, with the undergrowth dead and the trees laid bare, it was easy to spot the garbage they'd left behind. Even the river wasn't safe from their wanton waste. A little further up river, under a magnificent ironwork bridge sporting the Glasgow coat of arms, was the bizarre spectacle of an upside-down ironing board, its flat surface on the river bed, water swirling round its erect legs.

Up here, in the heights of Hamilton Drive, he could forget the litter and just admire the gracious row of two-storey houses that sat back from the road, each with a long, sloping stretch of front garden. Walking along this road with the rush of water nearby, it was hard to believe you were in the heart of Glasgow. Yet a five minute walk downhill from here would find you on busy Byres Road or in the cobbled alley of Ashton Lane with its famous bars and restaurants.

He stood for a moment outside the garden gate

106

before walking up the path through a carpet of yellow crocuses and white clusters of snowdrops and past a yellow Volkswagen parked in the driveway. The brass doorbell rang out and a few moments later a figure appeared behind the stained glass of the door panel.

Mrs Reese-Brandon was not what he expected. Kira had been slightly built, blonde and blue-eyed. Her mother was tall and dark-haired, her skin olive, her eyes brown. He wondered for a moment whether he had made a mistake and this was not Kira's mother after all.

'Mrs Reese-Brandon?'

She gave a brief nod. When she spoke, her lightly accented voice was anxious. 'You're not from the newspapers?'

'I'm Detective Inspector Wilson. I called earlier.' He showed her his warrant card.

She gave a quick glance behind him as though he was part of an advance party.

'You'd better come in. My husband hasn't come back from work yet.'

She ushered him into a splendid hall. In the middle stood a round polished table with a large vase of heavily scented lilies.

'My husband wanted to be here.' She looked perturbed.

'We could wait for him if you prefer.'

'I'm not sure.' She glanced at her watch, then seemed to make a decision and led him through to a sitting room overlooking the front garden.

She checked through the window. 'I'm sure Ronald will be here soon.'

'I'm happy to wait.'

She relaxed a little. 'Won't you sit down?'

He chose the sofa, and she sat in the closest chair.

'I'm very sorry about your daughter.'

Her face crumpled a little, then she brought herself under control.

'If only we could find the baby. Kira's gone, but if the baby is still alive . . .'

'Then you would have something of her?'

'Yes.'

'But I understood that the baby was to be offered up for adoption?'

'That was before this happened,' she said firmly.

He wondered if her husband agreed.

She leaned forward anxiously. 'They said the baby could be alive?'

'Foetal theft is very rare. In fact, this is the first reported case in the UK. But in cases in the USA, the babies have been found alive.'

'I hope so. I do hope so.'

What he'd said was the truth, but he didn't want her to hold out too much hope.

She settled back in the chair. 'Kira was such a bright girl. She was good at everything she turned her hand to. She was taking Mandarin, did you know that? She wanted to go to China.'

He nodded sympathetically. 'Her pregnancy came as a shock to you?'

She clasped her hands nervously in her lap. 'We couldn't believe it. It ruined everything.' She looked at him uncomprehendingly, and her right hand rose to the small crucifix that hung round her neck.

'Do you know who the father was?'

'Kira refused to tell us. She said we didn't need to know. No one needed to know.' The idea obviously shocked her.

'I've talked to Ms Porter and Dr Delaney,' said Bill. 'They told me about the other pregnancies.'

Her face darkened with anger. 'Those girls copied everything she did, what she wore. If she'd jumped in the river, they would have followed her. How stupid is that?'

'Did Kira ever mention a pregnancy pact?'

'A *pact*? What do you mean?'

'The girls all got pregnant about the same time.'

'That had nothing to do with Kira. You can't blame her for that.' They heard footsteps outside, and she rose and went to the window. 'That's Ronald now. I'll fetch the coffee.'

She left the room, and Bill heard a brief exchange of words in the hall before Kira's father entered the room. Ronald Reese-Brandon was a little taller than his wife, in his fifties, with iron-grey hair and very blue eyes. His immaculate suit looked like bespoke tailoring. Bill knew he was a banker at Barclays, having moved there during the Royal Bank of Scotland's recent troubles.

Bill introduced himself, and while they were shaking hands, the other man began to question him.

'You've caught Kira's killer?'

'Not yet.'

'Then why are you here?'

Bill's reply was cut off as Kira's mother reappeared with a tray. Her husband watched impatiently as she went about the business of setting out the china on the coffee table. She offered Bill a plate of fancy biscuits.

'Just leave it, Maria, will you?' snapped Reese-Brandon.

She abandoned the plate and shrunk back into her chair.

Bill tried to explain about the handover, but the other man cut him off.

'It's unacceptable to move police personnel around in the middle of a murder enquiry.'

He had a point.

'DI Slater was a temporary appointment, while I was . . . on leave,' Bill lied.

'You were on holiday when my daughter was murdered, and as a result of that we have to relive the nightmare?'

His wife put a hand on his arm. 'Please, Ronald.'

He shook himself free. 'We told DI Slater all we know. I suggest you read his notes.'

'There are some things I need to ask you myself.'

Reese-Brandon's mouth was a thin, determined line.

'We have nothing more to say to you.'

Bill decided to abandon the softly softly approach.

'I believe your daughter made a pregnancy pact with four other students. They called themselves the Daisy Chain. Kira chose the name and encouraged the others to have a daisy tattoo done, as she had.'

Reese-Brandon glowered. 'My daughter did not have a tattoo. I would not allow it.'

'The tattoo was at the base of her spine. It was recorded at the post-mortem.'

The man looked stunned. Bill understood what he was feeling; you can bring them up and love them, but you still don't know your own children.

'Even if this were true, what has it got to do with

her death?'

'We found the words "daisy chain" written on her hands in mirror writing. We believe her assailant wrote them.'

'Oh my God!' Maria Reese-Brandon covered her face.

'This would suggest that whoever killed your daughter knew about this club. Which is why I need to know too.'

Reese-Brandon's face sagged. Bill was suddenly aware of the grey half-circles under the man's eyes.

'We know nothing about a club. Kira had a group of friends who copied what she did. She was a remarkable girl, a leader. But I cannot believe she urged these girls to get pregnant.'

'Only one of the group didn't get pregnant,' replied Bill. 'Alexandra Stewart-Smith.'

Mrs Reese-Brandon looked up in surprise. 'Sandie wasn't really one of the group. Kira stopped bringing her round. She said Sandie flung herself at boys.'

Bill wondered if that accounted for Sandie's thinly disguised resentment of Kira.

'The other girls, did they meet here often?'

Kira's mother looked concerned at the suggestion that her hospitality had made matters worse. When she answered, her tone was defensive. 'Kira often brought friends home. They would chat in her room, play music. There's nothing sinister about that.'

'Did she ever bring David Murdoch here?'

Her husband answered. 'We knew nothing about this boy until DI Slater told us.'

'You didn't know Kira was seeing him?'

'If I had, I would have stopped it.'

111

'May I ask why?'

'He wasn't the sort of boy Kira should be seeing,' he said sharply.

Bill forbore asking if David wasn't suitable because he attended a state school. Instead, he said, 'What if David is the father of Kira's baby?'

There was an intake of breath from Mrs Reese-Brandon, who looked pleadingly at Bill. 'If David is the father, would he have rights over the baby?'

'For God's sake, Maria. The baby's clearly dead. How often do I have to tell you that?'

*   *   *

Maria watched the Detective Inspector leave, pausing for a few moments near the crocuses as though admiring them. In the past she would have done the same, because they meant that spring was on its way. How she loved spring in these northern climes. It wasn't the same in the Mediterranean where she'd grown up. Until she'd experienced a Scottish winter, she'd never truly understood how your heart lifted when you realised it was almost over.

She went upstairs and slowly opened Kira's door, breathing in her lingering presence. How long would that scent last? She hadn't opened a window in this room since they'd told her. She couldn't even bring herself to change the bed. She went there now and crept under the duvet, breathing in her daughter from its folds. Would she be doing this years from now, her sanity gone with her daughter's last breath?

Not if she had the baby. If she had her grandchild to look after, she could survive. How could she ever have agreed to Ronald's demands that it should be adopted? To give your own flesh and blood away, whatever the circumstances of its conception, was wrong. Ronald was so adamant that the baby was dead, but the detective wasn't sure, and neither was she.

She closed her eyes, imagining what Kira would say if she came home now and found her here. She laughed at the idea. How her daughter would rant at her. Complain that she had no privacy. She clasped the crucifix in her hand and intoned a prayer that the baby would be found alive. She imagined holding the tiny body in her arms, nursing it, changing it, watching it sleep. All the things she had never had the chance to do with Kira.

*       *       *

Bill was annoyed with himself for letting the interview get personal. If Robbie hadn't told him that David Murdoch was in his class, it wouldn't have happened. Ronald Reese-Brandon's casual dismissal of anyone outside his social sphere had annoyed him. He'd also got the strong impression the man wasn't as keen on finding the baby as his wife was, and that keeping the baby, rather than going ahead with adoption, seemed to be her idea.

He'd asked to see Kira's room before he left. Her father had initially refused, then conceded, but it was Maria who'd accompanied Bill upstairs.

The bedroom, overlooking the front garden, was bright and warmed by winter sunlight. He had been relieved when Mrs Reese-Brandon had shown him inside, then left him alone; going

113

through a dead teenager's room with her distraught mother looking on wasn't an idea he relished.

The room was large, and he'd immediately thought how Lisa would love to have so much space. It was also incredibly tidy, especially for a teenager. He wondered if her mother had done this recently, or whether it had been the norm when Kira was alive. He'd surveyed the kingsize bed, the brightly coloured duvet, the wall-to-wall wardrobes. Opening one of the mirrored doors had revealed a well-stocked rail, a selection of shoes racked neatly beneath. He'd checked her desk next, under the window. There was a selection of textbooks, mostly Maths and Physics, and an old-style blue school jotter which Bill picked up and flicked through. The complex combination of x's and y's suggested algebra or calculus.

One of the things he would normally look for when a teenager went missing was a diary. According to her mother, Kira hadn't kept one, but then she hadn't known her daughter had a tattoo. It occurred to him that if a clever girl like Kira had chosen to keep a diary, it might not be in the usual manner. He decided to take the jotter with him.

Mrs Reese-Brandon was waiting for him at the bottom of the stairs.

'I'd like to take a look at this in more detail, if I may.'

'But that's just her school-work.'

'I know.' He didn't elaborate.

She made him promise to let her know as soon as they found the baby. Her desperation to have something left of her daughter distressed him, but he knew he would be exactly the same in her shoes.

Once outside the house, he checked the time. He wasn't far from the university, and he was keen to see Rhona at the lab before his interview with David Murdoch. He felt he owed her an explanation for his change of heart. And maybe a thank you too.

He was passing the Reading Room when his mobile rang. It was DS Clark.

'Sir, can you come to the ivy steps on the Kelvin Way. We've found something.'

## CHAPTER FIFTEEN

Roy was in the process of building the body map, a digital representation of the victim on which the wounds photographed at the post-mortem would be shown. The digital body was Kira's exact shape and build, but the facial features were standardised, like a doll. This body map would be used to indicate to the investigative team the exact details of her injuries. It would also be used in court for the benefit of the jury, provided they caught her killer.

Rhona had seen many of these body maps, but was still impressed by them. Only recently she had watched as a child's injuries had been mapped onto a three-dimensional representation of its small body. She had observed as the programme peeled back the skin to expose the skeleton, just as would have been done at the post-mortem. The action had revealed a replica ribcage, showing just how many times each rib had been broken and subsequently rehealed. Behind the ribcage, further

115

injuries to the internal organs had been recorded visually. The jury viewing that body map on the big screen would have had no difficulty in appreciating the catalogue of abuse the two-year-old victim had suffered since birth.

Her own contribution to Kira's body map was already prepared. A series of drawings of the clothing Kira had worn, the areas for forensic investigation identified by shading. These drawings would sit alongside an actual photograph of the item of clothing on the big screen. The jury would then view these as she went through her evidence. Provided, of course, the case ever came to court.

The results of her tests, including DNA sampling, were already on the body map, the DNA samples currently in red because they weren't yet identified. They would turn green if or when they had a match. Selecting these markers with a pointer opened up details of the sample and its results. Wounds on the body map could also be selected, opening up the larger photographic version.

In Kira's case, there was only one wound.

There were two ways to perform a Caesarean operation. The most common method involved a horizontal incision in the abdomen, usually just above the pubic hairline, where the wall of the uterus was thinnest, thus involving less blood loss. Had this method been used, Kira might have lived.

Instead, her assailant had used the classical incision, a vertical cut from the navel. Such an incision provided a larger opening than the low transverse version and was normally used in emergency situations, when the baby's life was deemed to be in danger. It also caused a lot more bleeding, as had happened in Kira's case.

Rhona was struck again by the terrible waste of a young life and how easily it might have been avoided. If David had only gone looking for Kira earlier, or someone else had decided to enter the maze before it closed for the night, she might have been saved.

'What do you think?'

Roy's question brought her back to the present.

He'd selected Kira's right hand, magnifying it four times to display the indecipherable lettering. He double-clicked on the message which slowly turned to reveal its mirror image. *Daisy.* He repeated the same action on the left hand to expose the word *chain.*

'I've fed in the traces you found. The fibres under the fingernail and the substance on the fingertip.'

He demonstrated by selecting the middle digit of the right hand. Immediately a window opened up to show a magnified image of the two red fibres. They were currently marked as 'animal, type unknown'. The trace evidence found on the fingertip wasn't fully analysed either, but the record of its existence was there.

'I'm still working on the general crime scene view and the map of the surrounding area.'

'It's great,' she said, stifling a yawn.

He gave her a searching look. 'Are you OK? You don't look as though you got much sleep.'

Rhona felt a flush creep up her neck.

He grinned. 'Sorry. Didn't mean to pry, but I'm glad it's not work that's exhausted you.'

Rhona, who had no intention of mentioning Petersson, changed the subject.

117

'We should have something on the fibres soon. Chrissy's working on them.'

'Chrissy's back? I thought she had months left of maternity leave?'

'She's decided to come in part-time. Her mum's looking after Michael.' Rhona faltered a little on McNab's namesake.

'That's great news. I'll send the latest version of this through to DI Wilson.'

Her first thought was that he'd simply spoken too quickly and Bill's name had been the first one in his head. After all, he'd worked with him often enough.

He caught her look of confusion. 'What?'

'You said DI Wilson.'

'I know, and it sounded good.'

Her heart took off. She could feel its quickened beat in her throat.

'You don't know?' he said.

'I know the case was dismissed.'

'Bill's back at work as from today.'

'He didn't resign?'

Roy shook his head, smiling. 'And he kept his rank.'

'What about Slater?'

'Sent back from whence he came.'

Relief and elation flowed through her. 'Thank God. Is he taking over from Slater on the funfair case?'

'Yes.' Roy was enjoying being the harbinger of such good tidings. 'I expect he'll be in touch to tell you all this himself.'

'Just as long as I know it's true.'

'He's called a forensic meeting for tomorrow. That's why I wanted this up and running.' Roy

118

scooped up his laptop. 'You can access the current version from your machine. Send me anything else you come up with before the meeting and I'll do my best to add it in.'

She made a mug of coffee when Roy left and sat with it at the window, wishing Chrissy was here to share the news about Bill. Looking down on the park in the winter sunshine, she experienced a sense of *déjà vu*. They were back at the beginning; Bill, Chrissy and herself, before McNab had come on the scene. Back then, the case they were working on had also featured Kelvingrove Park, and the investigation had put her back in touch with Liam, the son she'd given up for adoption as a baby. She felt a pang of remorse—was she just as swiftly wiping McNab from the canvas of her life?

\*　　\*　　\*

Magnus chained his bike to the stand, then stood for a moment to admire the view across the park to the Art Gallery. He hadn't been here since the Gravedigger case, when he'd visited the lab with Rhona. He remembered how irritated she had been to be saddled with him at Superintendent Sutherland's request. He winced again at the memory of his first appearance at a strategy meeting, his arrogant questioning of the investigative team, as though a psychologist could know more about the mind of a serial killer than someone with thirty years' experience of criminals.

Rhona and Bill had put up with him, at times even given credence to his opinion, which in retrospect hadn't been a wise move on their part. DS McNab, on the other hand, had thought him a

119

fool, and hadn't been afraid to show it. And he'd been right.

After checking in at reception, Magnus took the stairs to the second floor, where Rhona was waiting for him on the landing. He thought she looked tired and not at all well; her eyes were dark and haunted. He tried to hide his shock behind a breezy greeting.

'Hey.'

'Hey, yourself.' She examined him. 'You look well.'

'So do you.'

She acknowledged his lie with a raised eyebrow. He thought about asking what was wrong, then decided against it. If he'd learned anything in his time with Rhona, it was how closely she guarded her personal life. Feelings were not up for discussion, least of all with a psychologist. He followed her into her office.

'Bill's back.' Her face lit up in a momentary smile.

'I'm delighted to hear it. What about DI Slater?'

'Gone,' she said, wrinkling her nose.

He remembered Slater. Bill had asked Magnus back to help on a second case, but then Slater had taken over and things had got complicated. Magnus had sensed how unhappy the investigating team had been under his leadership, and how much his bullying tactics and arrogance had pissed people off. He hadn't respected his colleagues or listened to their opinions, and as a result things had gone badly wrong. Magnus suspected Rhona and the others also partly blamed Slater for McNab's death.

Despite her obvious pleasure at Bill's return,

120

there was clearly some underlying tension in Rhona. He wondered if Sean was back on the scene, or whether she was still coming to terms with McNab's death. Magnus hadn't attended the funeral—not because he didn't want to, but because he hadn't thought it appropriate. McNab had distrusted and disliked him, and Magnus couldn't blame him for that. He was only sorry he hadn't had the opportunity to make things right between them.

'I was very sorry to hear about Michael,' he said inadequately.

She gave him a swift look that spoke volumes. Now he knew the reason for the pain in her eyes.

'Have they had any success in tracking down Kalinin?'

'Slater didn't even try,' she said sharply.

'Maybe now Bill's back . . .'

She cut him short. 'Maybe.'

She offered him a coffee and then began to bring him up to date on the fairground case. Magnus was immediately intrigued.

'There's never been a foetal theft recorded in the UK before.'

'That's where you come in.'

'They want a possible profile for the perpetrator?'

She nodded.

'They could probably get that by studying similar reports from the States.'

'There's something else.' Rhona told him about the mirror writing.

If he was intrigued before, Magnus was doubly so now.

'You're assuming her assailant wrote the

121

message on her hands?'

'It was fresh and unsmudged, in soft crayon, possibly make-up.'

'Mirror writing as a skill is pretty rare.'

'I know. Plus we found a daisy tattooed on the small of her back.'

'A daisy.' He paused, thinking. 'You need more than one daisy to make a chain.'

'That's what I thought.'

She fired the overhead projector via a laptop and brought up an image of the crime scene on a screen.

'Roy's still working on this but there's enough to give you a sense of what we have.'

Magnus watched as she went through the 360-degree shots of the mirror maze. Roy had done a great job recording the scene while avoiding the multiple reflections in the mirrors, but it still had all the hallmarks of a teen horror movie. An enclosed space, a girl on her own, a narrative that juxtaposed sex and death.

'Why was she in there?'

'We don't know. Her friends said she went to buy candyfloss and never came back.'

'Who found her?'

'The boyfriend.'

'The baby's father?'

'He says not, but when I DNA-test the blood from the umbilical cord, we'll know for sure.' She brought up the body map.

He watched, fascinated, as she magnified the palms of the hands, clicking to spin the writing and reveal what it said.

'That's an impressive piece of software,' he said.

'You haven't seen the half of it yet,' she replied.

'So this move to independent expert status is working out OK?'

'I end up with a lot of the cases I'd have been on anyway, but the difference is I get to choose. It suits me much better.'

Magnus wondered how true that was. He knew how much working in the team had meant to her, both professionally and personally. Bill Wilson had been like a father figure as well as a colleague. Chrissy was always willing to state the truth, no matter how uncomfortable it might be. And McNab. Awkward, determined, impetuous to the point of danger . . . and great at his job. And he had seen the way the Detective Sergeant had looked at Rhona, felt the energy that flowed between them. McNab had loved her, and now he was gone.

The random nature of sudden death could stop people in their tracks. Those left behind lapsed into a feeling of futility, often resulting in depression. Others set about constructing an alternative life, one they thought they could control better. He suspected that was what Rhona was doing.

She opened a screen window to display two red fibres.

'These are the other traces I found. Two hairs. Definitely not human. Dyed. Possibly yak hair.'

'Yak?'

'Apparently it's used in the manufacture of high quality wigs.'

'So her assailant might have been wearing a wig?'

'Either that or she picked up the fibres elsewhere before the attack. Yak hair is also used for hair extensions, although bright red is a bit extreme for normal day use. I also found traces of make-up on her finger. We're trying to identify the origin.'

He let her talk on, absorbing what she was saying with no further interruptions. When she'd finished, he sat in silence for a few moments.

'There's a forensic meeting tomorrow,' she said. 'You'll come along?'

'Of course.'

They lapsed back into what was now a slightly awkward silence. Magnus, suspecting Rhona wanted him to leave, stood up. He had planned to ask her to have a drink with him some time, but now he wasn't sure if such a suggestion would be welcome.

She led him to the door.

'You'll let me know what time tomorrow?'

'I'll text you.'

He found himself absurdly grateful that she still had his number in her phone.


# CHAPTER SIXTEEN

The narrow wooden steps climbed through a steep ivy-coated bank from the Kelvin Walkway to a mesh fence at the rear of the independent Glasgow Academy.

In the days when schools operated an open-door policy the path would have provided a back entrance, allowing pupils access from the walkway and the park. Now the area was overgrown and the gate padlocked, although some enterprising person had cut a hole in the wire big enough to squeeze through.

The surrounding ground cover of ivy was littered with empty cider bottles and crushed lager cans, suggesting the location provided an occasional drinking den, reasonably secluded, but with a clear view of the walkway below.

From the gate the path proceeded downwards in a zig-zag fashion, with steps at the steepest inclines. It was muddy, partially covered with long tendrils of ivy and blocked in part by the fallen branches of overhanging trees, one of which required clambering over.

It was at this spot the two thirteen-year-olds had made their discovery. Lunchtime had brought them here with their sandwiches and cans of Coke to sit on the log. Half-eaten slices of bread and cheese lay discarded beside a fallen yoghurt carton, suggesting lunch had come to an abrupt halt once they'd spotted the bag.

Bill crouched on a metal tread and took a closer look at its contents, the hair on the back of his neck rising. No wonder the boys had been so freaked. Who wouldn't be?

Soft fronds of dark hair curled damply on the brow. The eyes were closed, the lids a fragile cobweb of blue veins. Tiny white milk bumps freckled the nose above a cupid's bow mouth, opened to expose the tip of a pink tongue. A newborn, absolutely devoid of life.

How could a doll look so real?

It was so achingly realistic that he felt the need to check for a pulse in the soft folds of the neck, to touch the cheek and hope for warmth. He imagined the eyes opening and the startled mew of

125

a newborn's cry.

'Even the paramedics were fooled at first,' DS Clark told him. 'It's a Reborn, a doll modelled to look like a real baby.'

There had been a TV documentary on the subject of Reborns a few months back. He'd watched it with Margaret and had been shocked at the image of grown women cradling the dolls like real babies, and bewildered at the fact that some of them had asked for the dolls to be fashioned to look like their dead children. Margaret had been more circumspect: *I suppose it's no different from surrounding yourself with photographs, except that this way you can hold the dead child.*

'Take a look at what it's wearing,' Janice urged him.

The doll was encased in a pink sleep suit, fastened up the front. Bill remembered them from Lisa and Robbie's own baby days. The shape of the body was the same as a normal infant, fat-bellied, the bottom thickened as though by a nappy. On the right front of the suit was an embroidered flower motif, yellow-centred with white petals.

It was undeniably a daisy.

It could be a coincidence, but he was wary of coincidences, especially in a murder hunt.

He retreated via the metal treads DS Clark had laid and dipped under the ribbon. They weren't that far from where the murder had occurred. Walk a few hundred yards in an easterly direction and you would be at the funfair. In fact he had practically looked down on this area from Hamilton Drive.

The doll, although in a plastic bag, had not been hidden. Someone wanted it to be found. It looked in perfect condition, and—according to the TV programme he'd watched—they were not cheap to buy. All this, along with its proximity to both the locus of crime and Kira's home and the presence of a daisy motif on the sleep suit, meant they had to take its appearance seriously.

'Parcel up the doll and I'll take it to forensic myself. And get a couple of SOCOs to go over this area,' he said.

'They're on their way, Sir.'

Bill nodded his approbation. Janice was proving an able and astute replacement for McNab.

'The other girls in the gang. What's happened about them?'

'All four of them have had terminations. I went to interview them and their parents—it was a little creepy, actually. The girls all had the same haircut as Kira, all dyed to the same shade of blonde, and I kept forgetting which one I was interviewing.'

Bill wondered if the fact that they were no longer pregnant would be enough to keep them safe, assuming they had had nothing to do with Kira's death.

As though reading his mind, Janice said, 'I checked out their alibis for the night Kira was killed. None of them were anywhere near the funfair. In fact, they've been on lockdown since the pregnancies. Private tutors and heavy parental supervision until their exams.'

Bill liked the sound of that. If the parents were on the case, he didn't have to be. 'Alert the families to our concerns, but make it sound like our normal procedures.'

\*　　　\*　　　\*

He headed back to his car and drove to the university, the doll on the back seat. He thought of ringing ahead to warn Rhona of his imminent arrival, but decided against it. He had no idea what he planned to say or how he would explain his change of heart. He was also ashamed of giving her such a hard time when she'd tried to persuade him to stay.

He recalled their meeting in the Beechwood Bar after McNab's death. The DS had arranged that get-together, no doubt hoping that the presence of both himself and Rhona would change Bill's mind about taking responsibility for the assault on the Gravedigger.

He remembered how Rhona had sat there, constantly looking across when the door opened, as though expecting McNab to enter. Despite her pleas, he'd left her that night intending to chuck it in, whatever happened with the court case. At the time he'd believed it himself.

What had changed his mind?

If he were honest, it was Rhona's accusation that he was betraying McNab; that it was up to him, to both of them, to bring his killer to justice. And he couldn't do that if he was out of the Force.

He signed in and made his way up the stairs to the lab. Through the glass panel he could see that Rhona was on her own. Of course, Chrissy would still be on maternity leave. He stood outside the door, remembering an earlier visit here when he'd realised something was personally amiss with Rhona. At the time they'd been investigating the death of a male university student. Her involvement in that case had made her face up to issues in her own past and had also led her into danger.

She was a consummate professional with one weakness—she took some cases personally. He had the same failing himself. You were constantly warned against it, but you would have to be made of stone not to. It took its toll on you, he could vouch for that.

She glanced up, sensing someone watching her. Above the mask, he saw her eyes light up.

## CHAPTER SEVENTEEN

'I'm so glad you're back.'

'Thank you for reminding me why I should be.'

'I was a bit harsh.'

'You only said what I needed to hear.'

'And Margaret's OK with your decision?'

'I think she's relieved to get me out from under her feet.'

They savoured each other's pleasure for a moment.

'I've asked for a further meeting with Superintendent Sutherland to discuss how we progress the Kalinin case,' Bill said.

'How did he react?' Rhona tried to keep her tone neutral.

'I got the impression he wasn't keen.'

'Why?'

Bill shrugged. 'I don't know, but I plan to find out.'

Rhona was so heartened by that she almost blurted out about Petersson, but something stopped her. Luckily, at that moment, Chrissy arrived. No subdued reaction to Bill's reinstatement from her. She flung her arms about him and practically whooped for joy.

While Rhona made coffee, Chrissy regaled Bill with tales of baby Michael and brought him up to date on Sam.

'You haven't been to hear him play in ages,' she said accusingly.

'When is he next on?'

'At the weekend.'

'I'll be there, if work allows.'

Chrissy turned pointedly to Rhona. 'Will you come too?' she challenged.

'I'll think about it.'

There was a moment when she thought Chrissy might raise the subject of Petersson, her supposed boyfriend. Rhona didn't want that, so quickly changed topic.

'A Reborn's been found in the park near the funfair. Bill brought it for us to take a look.'

'You found one of those creepy dolls?' Chrissy said excitedly. 'Where is it?'

'In the lab.'

'Great!' Chrissy, all else forgotten, immediately began the process of kitting up.

\*     \*     \*

The doll lay exposed on the table. Even now, in the bright glare of the laboratory lights, small limbs loose, eyes closed, it looked for all the world like a real baby.

'It's remarkable.' Rhona touched the tiny hand, fully expecting it to open and grab tightly onto her

130

finger.

'It's so realistic I feel like picking it up and nursing it myself.' Chrissy looked as bewildered as Rhona felt.

She realised they were talking in hushed tones as though trying not to wake a sleeping infant. Was this why people kept these dolls? So that they could behave as though there was a real baby in the house?

She carefully removed the sleep suit with her gloved hands and laid it to one side. Underneath was a pretty pink vest and what looked like a proper disposable nappy.

'OK, that's really weird. Why would anyone put a real nappy on a doll?' Chrissy said.

'Little girls put nappies on dolls. It's all about pretending.'

'This doesn't feel like pretending. It feels creepy.'

Rhona undid the fasteners between the legs and pulled the vest gently over the head, then took off the nappy. The vinyl arms and legs had been inserted into a cotton body and fastened with plastic cable ties. Undressed, the doll looked less real.

Rhona remembered being afraid of a ventriloquist's dummy when she was a child, imagining it coming alive when its master was asleep. The idea used to give her nightmares. And yet she had never seen a ventriloqist's dummy that looked remotely real. Not like this baby had done when fully clothed.

They worked separately, Chrissy taking the clothing and the bag while Rhona concentrated on the doll itself. She would examine its tiny body as

131

thoroughly as she had Kira's. If, as Bill suggested, there might be a link between them, then trace evidence would reveal this.

She began to gently take apart the doll, removing the head before snapping the cable ties that held the limbs in position. She laid these to one side before cutting through the cotton body shape to remove the stuffing. She'd already examined the fine hair that had been rooted in the head: cashmere, commonly used for dolls' hair. She now checked inside the head cavity, spotting what looked like writing close to the folds of the neck joint. She fetched a magnifier and took a closer look.

*Daisy JC*

Could Daisy be the model name of the doll? She'd done enough research online to realise that for commercial purposes the various models were given male or female names. If this was a *Daisy* doll, maybe *J* and *C* were the initials of the artist who'd brought it to life.

She went back online and searched for a model called *Daisy*. There wasn't one, although she did find an advertisement for embroidered daisies to sew onto your doll's clothing. She then tried various combinations of *JC* and *Daisy,* with no luck. If *JC* was indeed the artist, she needed more than just their initials to identify them.

She abandoned that line of enquiry and returned to the doll itself. A closer study of the head revealed that it was vinyl, overlaid with a type of polymer clay which had been sculpted to give it its facial characteristics. The ears were entirely polymer, sculpted again to a unique shape, just like human ears. She took time to admire the workmanship—whoever had made this doll was indeed an artist.

She went back to her photographs of the doll, taken before she had dissected it. The more she examined them, the more she wondered if the reason the doll was so realistic was because it had been modelled on a specific baby, with all its distinctive features. If so, who was that child? If it did exist, maybe someone would recognise it.

She emailed Bill her findings so far. Checking on possible DNA from the doll would take longer, but if he decided to reveal its existence to the press, then a photograph might help locate the owner, or the mother of the baby it was modelled on.

Petersson called her in the early afternoon.

'Have you had lunch?'

She hadn't, caught up as she'd been with the doll. 'Not yet.'

'Can we meet?'

'Now?'

'It's important.'

She waited for him to explain why, but he didn't.

'What about the café at Kelvingrove? The one in the basement.'

It would involve a short walk through the park, but she appreciated his attempt to stay clear of the lab.

'OK. Fifteen minutes?'

'I'll be there.'

She told Chrissy she was going out for some fresh air. Chrissy gave her an inscrutable look and for a moment Rhona thought she might suggest coming with her.

'How long for?' Chrissy asked.

'An hour at most.'

'I might be gone by the time you come back.'

Chrissy was sticking to part-time, although the hours were longer than she'd first suggested.

'I'll see you tomorrow then.'

Chrissy was clearly suspicious of Rhona's sudden desire for fresh air, so Rhona made a quick getaway.

Spring had brought a riot of colour to the park in the form of pink and purple crocuses and banks of yellow daffodils, although a brisk wind still made her eyes water.

Despite it being mid-week, the museum was busy because of the *Doctor Who* exhibition which had finally reached Glasgow as part of its UK tour. The enthusiasts looked to be predominantly students, although there were a few folk in their sixties and what looked like an enthusiastic primary class.

Rhona skirted the crowds and headed downstairs.

## CHAPTER EIGHTEEN

Petersson took out the rabbit's foot and turned it over in his hand. Although it was discoloured and bald in places, he still felt its luck. It had been instrumental in saving his life before, and he suspected he would need it again before long.

The rabbit's foot had been a present from his grandfather on his ninth birthday. Perhaps *afi* had had a premonition of what was to come, because it turned out that the luck arrived just in time. After the party, he'd gone skating on an ice-covered lake and strayed too far from shore. The ice had cracked under him and he'd fallen in. His father and grandfather had managed to haul him out and found the rabbit's foot frozen to his right hand. Petersson had been clinically dead for four minutes before they made his heart beat again.

Then there had been the night when, as a teenager, he'd 'borrowed' his father's car to transport two friends to a party in Reykjavik. Too much alcohol had rendered him fearless, resulting in a somersault on a slippery road. All three of them had escaped serious injury, suggesting that his little amulet's protective influence might extend wider than himself.

Although now a grown man of thirty-seven, Petersson was still superstitious. He might kid himself that his continued existence was because he was smarter than those he pursued, but deep down he knew that wasn't true.

Many of the criminals he'd investigated had turned out to be just as superstitious as himself, particularly those from Eastern Europe. Did Kalinin have a lucky charm, shielding him from the law? Even as he mulled this over, Petersson knew he was looking at the real reason on the screen in front of him.

He'd spent the hours since leaving Rhona's bed in front of his computer. He didn't normally find it difficult to separate pleasure and work. In her case he had revelled in the combination of the two, although he was well aware that had she not deemed him useful, he probably wouldn't have reached her bed. But he was glad he had, and hoped to be there again soon.

He reread the intercepted message. It had taken

a long time to hack into the system and find something, longer still to decode what he'd found. Those years at university honing his programming skills, his ambition to write the next generation of computer games, had served him well. Creating a complex digital world of adventure through online gaming had been fun, but not half as much fun as poking around in other people's digital lives. In truth, his career might have gone either way; he could have made a very good living from hacking, or chosen to use his skills another way and bring down those who operated on the wrong side of the law. The trouble was that those who operated outside the law weren't always bad, at least not in his eyes. So he'd revised his moral code. He went after those *he* decided were bad. People like Kalinin, but also those in the establishment who saw themselves as above the law. All of which made him a lot of enemies. Now, reading this message had produced the same icy chill as that plunge through the ice when he was nine.

He wondered whether Rhona MacLeod had any idea what she was dealing with. He knew about her visit to the Russian's penthouse flat in search of a missing woman, Claire Watson. He'd been impressed by that, although he'd deemed it foolhardy. He also questioned why the policeman, McNab, had allowed such a thing to happen. He could only assume that neither of them had known the true nature of the man they'd decided to challenge. The Russian had a well-documented propensity for torture. Torturing men he saw as part of the job; women, Kalinin tortured for pleasure.

Petersson rose and went to the small kitchen

area. He opened an overhead cupboard, brought out a half-full vodka bottle and poured a double shot. He took the clear liquid into his mouth and swirled it around before swallowing. The blast of warmth that hit his chest did nothing to remove the creeping chill. The message changed everything, and he would have to adjust his plans accordingly. He felt the familiar throb of his purple scar. Even now, two years later, he could still relive the moment when the knife had entered, could taste again the blood that had spurted into his mouth.

He dragged his mind back to the present. He hadn't died then and he had no intention of dying this time, but it was risky getting involved with Rhona MacLeod, especially now. The existence of the message he'd intercepted had made him uneasy about the Russian mafia investigation after the death of DS Michael McNab, and DI Slater's role in it. It had also raised questions about Dr MacLeod herself.

He put the vodka back in the cupboard and rinsed the glass before calling her. She answered almost immediately. When she agreed to meet in the museum café, he had no idea what he would say to her. He would have to decide on the way.

*        *        *

Rhona spotted Petersson sitting by the window in the conservatory area and composed her expression before going to join him. He sensed her approach and looked up. She expected a smile of welcome at least, but he looked too preoccupied for that. She pulled out a chair and sat down opposite.

137

'I haven't ordered yet.' He pushed the menu card towards her as the waitress came over.

She gave it a cursory glance, her hunger evaporating.

'Coffee will do. A pot.'

He gave their order, waiting until they were alone again before he spoke.

'Something's happened.'

'To do with Kalinin?'

'Almost certainly.'

His expression was unnerving her. 'What?' she asked sharply.

'Tell me what you know of Fergus Morrison.'

Rhona hesitated. Whatever she said now was common knowledge, so she wasn't giving anything away.

'Private Fergus Morrison went AWOL after seeing a friend blown apart in Afghanistan. When he was living rough in Glasgow, he witnessed the murder of a man named Alexsai Petrov by Kalinin. Morrison used Petrov's body to fake his own death by hanging his dog tag round the neck and setting fire to the skip he was in. We found the body and I forensically identified it as Petrov.' She paused. 'But you know all that.'

He was waiting for her to continue.

'Morrison agreed to give evidence against Kalinin. He was put in the witness protection scheme.'

'Fergus Morrison is dead,' said Petersson.

'What? But how?'

'He was shot.'

'When did this happen?' If it had been in Glasgow, surely she would have heard about it?

'London, a week ago.'

138

She looked at him, surprised. 'What was he doing in London?'

'Slater had him transferred to a safe house there after they got McNab.'

Why had Slater not told her he'd sent Morrison south? Then again, why would he? He was aware of her antagonism towards him and, unlike Bill, he wouldn't deem it necessary to include her in any decisions that might be made in the Kalinin case. After all, she was only an expert witness, not a police officer. Even if she was the one who'd held McNab in her arms and watched him die.

The coffee arrived. Rhona watched as Petersson poured two cups and pushed one towards her. When she attempted to lift it, she realised her hand was trembling. She replaced the cup without drinking.

'Morrison was the only witness alive who could place Kalinin at the scene of crime,' she said.

'Which is why he was assassinated.'

Assassinated. It sounded so melodramatic.

'Kalinin's clearing the decks of anyone who has anything on him.'

A terrible thought occurred to her. 'Anya. What about Anya?'

Anya Grigorovitch, the young Russian woman whose lover, Alexsai, had been Kalinin's victim.

'I went to the Russian café. Anya and her brother Misha are no longer there.'

'Then where are they?'

'I hoped you might know.'

He was staring at her intently.

'I don't.' If she had known, would she have told him? 'I need to speak to Bill about this.'

'I thought Slater was handling the case?'

'Not any more,' she said with relish.

Petersson looked put out. It was obvious he was used to being the first one in the know. Rhona felt at an advantage for the first time since she'd walked into the café.

'Fergus Morrison's death isn't common knowledge, for the moment,' he said.

'Why not?'

'I presume they want Kalinin to think he's still alive.'

Rhona studied this man she knew nothing about, apart from his reputation for exposing those who thought they were above the law. Did she believe him?

'How do you know all this?'

His voice dropped even lower. 'I have a CHIS contact.'

CHIS—Covert Human Intelligence Sources. In layman's terms, a dedicated police unit for handling snouts and grasses. She shouldn't be surprised that Petersson had such contacts in his line of work.

'If this is true and they're worried about Kalinin taking out contacts up here, shouldn't Bill be told about it?'

'If you mention it, he'll want to know how you found out.'

Rhona wondered what she was getting into. If Bill was back on the job and progressing the Kalinin case, maybe she should back off and leave it to him?

Petersson appeared to be reading her mind. 'Believe me, your DI's got no hope of nailing Kalinin.'

'Slater might have given up, but Bill won't,' she

said firmly.

'Like McNab didn't?'

The warning in Petersson's words left her cold. 'He was in the wrong place at the wrong time,' she said.

'No. McNab was in the right place at the right time. Kalinin made sure of that.'

## CHAPTER NINETEEN

David Murdoch was waiting in an interview room, and Bill took a moment to study him through the one-way glass before going in. He was tall and rangy, long legs in tight jeans stretched out under the table. His hair was carefully arranged, a poker-straight fringe combed sideways, no doubt held in place with gel or spray. The hairstyle seemed to be constantly on his mind. He periodically smoothed the fringe as though in the interim it might have had the audacity to curl.

Bill had read David's statement. He'd studied all the statements, and they matched; David, Owen and Sandie all agreed that Kira had wanted candyfloss. They hadn't been willing to wait in the queue, so they'd gone to the dodgems without her. When the ride was over and Kira still hadn't reappeared, they'd crossed to the Waltzers. After that ride, David had gone looking for her.

Bill checked the boy's personal details. David Murdoch was seventeen years old. His mother was dead and he lived with his stepfather. He had no brothers or sisters. He was in the fifth form at school, doing a mix of subjects, including Maths at

Intermediate level—so not a match for Kira's mathematical ability. Bill wondered what they'd had in common.

David stood up as he entered, looking worried.

'Hi, David. I'm Detective Inspector Wilson.' Bill held out a hand. 'Thanks for coming in to see me.' The hand in his was soft, and he caught a trace of scent—or was it hair gel? They sat down.

'Why do you want to see me again?' asked David.

'I've taken over from DI Slater, so I thought we should talk.' Bill paused. 'I'm very sorry about Kira, David. I know you were good friends.'

David nodded wordlessly.

'Can you tell me how you met?'

A glimmer of light appeared in David's eyes.

'It was in the park. She was sitting on a bench, reading a book. She spoke to me first,' he added defensively.

'You had things in common?'

'Music, books. We both read a lot. And we liked the same films.'

He bowed his head so that the fringe obscured his eyes. Bill suspected they had filled with tears.

'Do you feel up to telling me what happened the night she died?'

There was a snuffle from behind the curtain of hair. 'I told them everything in my statement.'

'I know. It's just that it's much better for me to hear it from you personally.'

David took a deep breath and began, echoing his previous statement. Was this just a well-rehearsed story, or were the events carved in his memory? This was the problem with recalling incidents; people began to repeat them like a

142

mantra, and it could become hard to tell what was a true memory and what had become familiar through repetition. Nevertheless, there was no mistaking David's horror and revulsion when he reached the point in the story where he'd discovered Kira's body.

He stuttered to a halt. 'I'm sorry.'

'It's OK.' Bill gave him a chance to recover, then said, 'I keep wondering why Kira didn't come back to you. Why she went into the Hall of Mirrors on her own.'

David looked up, similarly puzzled. 'I wondered about that too. I asked her to go in there with me earlier, for a laugh. She wouldn't.'

'You didn't mention that in your statement.'

'I didn't think it mattered,' he said, perturbed.

'Everything matters,' Bill told him firmly. 'Every second you were together that night matters.'

David looked worried. 'No one asked me about it before.'

'Is there any reason you can think of why she might have gone in there?'

David shook his head.

Bill changed tack. 'Did Kira have a boyfriend before you?'

A flush crept up his neck. 'Kira wasn't exactly my girlfriend. I mean, we didn't, we weren't . . .'

'Having sex?'

He nodded. 'We cared about each other, but not in that way.'

A thought crossed Bill's mind. He decided to voice it outright. 'Forgive me asking such a personal question, David, but I promise it is relevant. Is that because you prefer boys?'

David blushed a little, then looked as though he

143

might deny it. Finally, he said, 'I haven't made up my mind yet.'

Which helped explain why David seemed happy to accept Kira's pregnancy, Bill thought.

'Did Kira tell you who the baby's father was?'

David shook his head.

'Did you ask?'

'We didn't question one another about anything. If she'd wanted to tell me, she would have.'

They must have made a strange couple, but it seemed to have been working.

'Was Kira still planning to go to Cambridge to study Maths?'

'She'd decided to do Medicine here in Scotland so she could keep the baby.'

'I thought an adoption had been arranged?'

'She talked about that at first, but then she changed her mind. You can't take a baby from its mother if she doesn't agree,' David added fiercely, sounding as though he was quoting Kira.

If Kira's father had had his heart set on having the baby adopted and for his daughter to take up her place at Cambridge University, it seemed he would have had a fight on his hands.

'Why did Kira change her mind about the baby?'

'She found out she was adopted.' David subconsciously put his hand up to his mouth, as though he'd said something he shouldn't.

'She told you she was adopted?'

'I wasn't supposed to say anything, but it doesn't matter now.' A flash of anger crossed his face. 'Her parents didn't tell her. She found out by accident. Can you believe that?'

'How did she find out?'

'She heard them talking about her, and the

144

baby.'

'Did her parents realise Kira knew?'

David shook his head emphatically. 'No. She kept waiting for them to tell her, all through the pregnancy, but they never did.'

So the Reese-Brandons hadn't been completely straight with him. Maybe they'd simply thought the fact that their daughter was adopted could have nothing to do with her death. They were probably right, but it did throw some light on why Kira was so determined to keep her child.

'When you found Kira, did you look at her hands?'

A spasm of pain crossed the boy's soft features. 'I just saw the blood and what they'd done to her stomach.'

'There was a message in mirror writing on the palms of her hands.'

'What?' David's mouth fell open.

'You know what I mean by mirror writing?'

'You can only read it in a mirror.'

'Can you write like that?'

He looked frightened. 'No!'

'Can anyone you know do it?'

'Kira . . .'

'Kira could do it?'

'She tried to. She said Leonardo Da Vinci was a mirror writer. She was a big fan of his.'

Bill thought about Kira's school records. She had been good at everything. Science and Maths, but also languages and music. It wasn't surprising she was a fan of a polymath like Leonardo.

'Do you think the person who killed her wrote on her hands?' David whispered.

Bill didn't answer.

145

A film of sweat had blossomed on the boy's brow, making his heavy fringe stick to his skin. It was warm in the interview room, but not overly so.

'Don't you want to know what was written on Kira's hands?'

'I . . .'

'Or perhaps you already do?'

'I never saw any writing, I swear it.'

Bill waited a moment before continuing. 'I understand Kira was in a girl gang?'

David looked startled. 'It wasn't a *gang*. Kira and her mates just got together sometimes.'

'To do what?'

'Play music, talk.'

'Anything else?'

The dark flush was back, creeping up the boy's neck to blossom in his cheeks. 'I don't know what you mean.'

'What did this gang call themselves?'

'They didn't have a name.'

'That's not what I heard.'

David darted Bill a look as though trying to read his mind.

'I don't know who you've been talking to, but the gang was just a bit of fun. Kira was popular. Other girls liked to be associated with her.'

'They liked copying her, you mean?'

'Yes.'

'How?'

'Her clothes, hair, that sort of thing. Sometimes even the expressions she used.'

'What about the daisy tattoo they all had done?'

David's head, which had been sinking towards his chest, shot up. His face was completely scarlet now. 'I never saw her tattoo.'

146

'But you knew about its existence?'

'Kira did it for a laugh. The others copied her.'

'She didn't tell them to have it done?'

'Kira didn't tell people to do things, they just did it to be like her.'

'So the Daisy Chain gang all got pregnant, to be like Kira?'

There was a stunned silence.

'She didn't ask them to.'

'So it wasn't a pact?'

David shook his head again, vehemently. 'Kira thought they were stupid. She said so.'

It was the first time in their conversation that Bill believed him.


## CHAPTER TWENTY


The video footage was high quality, as you'd expect from Kira's BlackBerry—or, to give it its full name, the BlackBerry Bold Snakeskin 24k Yellow Gold Luxury Mobile Phone. According to DS Clark, it had cost a grand. Bill couldn't conceive of spending that amount on a phone.

'It's not the dearest.'

He looked at her in amazement.

'The most expensive one I found online was half a million pounds.'

Bill forbore thinking about such extravagance. Bad enough that parents doled out a grand on a seventeen-year-old.

The mobile had been discovered near the spot they'd found the Reborn. Janice had supervised a forensic search of the area, which wasn't easy given the thick covering of ground ivy. They had to be grateful that it wasn't mid-summer when the ivy would have been supplemented by even more undergrowth.

The video clip had been downloaded from the camera and was now ready to play. Bill gave the IT guy a nod and he set it running. The baby—or doll?—was dressed in a pink sleep suit embroidered with a daisy motif, and appeared to be asleep. The camera hadn't been positioned close enough for a clear view of the features. The clip only lasted a few seconds.

'Just at the end there. I thought I saw it move,' Janice said.

'Play the clip again,' Bill ordered.

Like Janice, he found himself imagining that the left eyelid flickered just before the end.

'Can we find out if it really did move?'

'We could slow down the clip, divide it into frames and compare them.'

'Do that.'

A BlackBerry like Kira's could have been sold easily and profitably on the black market. Whoever had attacked her hadn't been interested in stealing her mobile or her wallet, even though it had had money and a credit card inside. The phone and the video clip had been left near the Reborn for them to find. But for what reason? To try and convince them that the baby was still alive?

Bill decided he would be interested to hear Magnus's take on all of this. He checked his watch. 'OK, I want the clip available in the forensic meeting in half an hour.'

Before that, he had his session with Superintendent Sutherland.

'That is not your concern.' The Superintendent's expression was closed.

Bill replied nevertheless. 'The team are still very angry about McNab. That won't go away if they believe we're not pursuing his killer.'

Sutherland looked irritated.

'SCDEA are dealing with it in Scotland, and SOCA at the London end.'

Kalinin was known to mastermind a large international operation, dealing mainly in drugs and human trafficking. The Scottish Crime Enforcement Agency had the remit to tackle organised crime in Scotland. If SCDEA and SOCA, their equivalent south of the border, were involved, it suggested the decision had been made to go after Kalinin on organised crime rather than for his involvement in McNab's murder. If the serious crime agencies believed they had a better chance of nailing the Russian on his London record than simply on McNab's murder, that made sense. It still rankled though.

'So let's leave them to get on with it, shall we?'

Sutherland began to shuffle papers, a clear sign that the interview was over. Bill took his leave.

He went through to his office and sat down in his chair, swivelling it around to face the window. McNab had often joked about this chair, saying that every time they heard it squeak, it meant the boss's brain was working. This memory only served to feed Bill's anger and guilt. He had failed his DS just when McNab needed him most.

He thought to himself that this would be the

point in one of Margaret's beloved crime novels where he would go to the filing cabinet and bring out the booze. Often fiction wasn't that far from the truth. There *was* a bottle of whisky in the filing cabinet, but he was planning to leave it there for now. Good whisky shouldn't be drunk to block out the frustrations and disappointments of life, but to savour its triumphs. He'd save it for when Kalinin went down.

The Super was right, in part. SCDEA was better equipped to pursue Kalinin, although it still stuck in Bill's craw that he couldn't handle it personally. But that didn't mean he was about to give up. He knew one or two people at SCDEA who owed him a favour. Maybe it was time to call those favours in?

That decided, he switched his attention to the forensic meeting. Forensic evidence had become an intrinsic part of most enquiries, but it took an expert to recognise just what type of forensic evidence was pertinent to solving each crime. He was reminded of a rookie detective's desire to DNA-sample all condoms found in the vicinity of an assault on a prostitute, until it was pointed out to him that that would involve a minimum of two hundred tests—not the best use of forensic or police resources.

Too much information in a case could prove as counterproductive as too little. The brain could only handle or process so much at any given time, which was where Roy's software came in. Using it, the collected evidence could be viewed as an interconnected whole, from a body map to a full-scale plan of the crime scene and its surrounding area.

He logged on to his computer and brought up Kira's body map, where the forensic work Rhona and Chrissy had completed had already been entered. Bill read the details from the screen, then magnified the tattoo, noting the position of the daisy; on its side, as though ready to be linked in a chain. He recalled how, as a child, he'd watched the careful construction of such chains, the daisy stem split by a fingernail, the head of the next one inserted. A tricky and frustrating business, given that the daisies often wilted before a decent length chain could be produced.

He moved on to the mirror writing, clicking on it so that it revealed its true meaning. David Murdoch had been shocked by the fact that someone had written on Kira's hands, but then the entire investigating team felt the same way, mistrusting mirror writing because of its association with satanism. Police officers were conservative that way—they could cope with psychopaths and serial murderers, but they didn't like the occult. They didn't relish chasing the devil, and neither did he.

## CHAPTER TWENTY-ONE

Magnus looked around the assembled faces. Just like the old days, he thought. Well, not quite. He glanced over at Rhona, who caught his eye and held it. So he wasn't the only one thinking about McNab, whose place was now occupied by the newly promoted Detective Sergeant Clark.

Bill began by leading them through the evidence

entered on the crime scene software, allowing the rest of his team to offer comments and suggestions along the way. Magnus was struck by the difference between Bill's approach and Slater's, which Rhona had described to him. Slater had apparently dominated the proceedings, displaying a need to be centre stage and in total control. According to Rhona, he'd also been renowned for his distrust of forensic evidence, particularly if it suggested something that didn't match his preferred version of events.

Bill operated in an entirely different manner. No one here was afraid to offer a suggestion, however odd it might sound, and Magnus agreed that they might need to think out of the box on this one. He had already spent half the previous night reading up on foetal theft and the psychological reasons behind it, and there was something about this crime that didn't fit. He wasn't yet willing to say why he thought this, neither did he have any evidence to support the belief, but it was there all the same.

Magnus listened intently to everything that was said, offering no input of his own until Bill revealed that they'd found a lifelike doll in the park not far from the funfair. A picture of the doll lying below a rotting tree trunk appeared on the screen. Magnus was suddenly assailed by the smells of Coulter's workroom: warm plastic and sharp varnish, the cloying scent of moulded clay.

'You found a Reborn near the scene of crime?' he said sharply.

All eyes had turned to him.

'You know something about these dolls?' Bill asked.

Magnus hesitated, realising that what he was about to say might cause uproar in the room. 'I visited an inmate at the maximum security prison who makes Reborns. His name's Jeff Coulter.'

'The man convicted of killing his baby?' The question came from Rhona.

'Yes.'

Expressions of revulsion reverberated around the room. Magnus couldn't blame them. The thought of a baby killer making replica babies had elicited much the same response from him.

'Coulter got in touch with me and asked if I was interested in studying the diary he'd kept at the beginning of his incarceration,' he explained. 'I visited him and he showed me some of his work on the dolls.'

Rhona interrupted him, agitated. 'When I took the Reborn apart, the words *Daisy JC* were inscribed inside the head cavity. I thought that *Daisy* was the model type, but the head had been sculpted, probably to match a real baby. The initials JC I assumed to be those of the artist.'

'Could *JC* be Jeff Coulter's signature?' Bill asked.

'It would be a hell of a coincidence, but I suppose it's possible,' Magnus said. 'There can't be that many people making Reborns in the UK, and Coulter had a display of photographs on his workshop walls of a lot of satisfied parents with their replica children.'

'Would you remember if this doll was on one of them?'

Magnus frowned. 'I have to admit I found the photographs quite disturbing, so I didn't examine them in detail. Also, I'm not sure I can really tell

153

one *real* baby from another, let alone a doll.'

'Roy, can you bring up the close-ups Dr MacLeod took of the doll?'

The photos appeared as a collage on the screen, starting from the doll intact, to the separated pieces, and finally the interior of the head.

'Let's take a look at it as a whole.'

Roy selected the first image and enlarged it.

The little body lay on a lab table, eyes closed, limbs relaxed as if in sleep. Magnus's first reaction was one of fear that it might suddenly wake, roll off the surface and fall to the floor. He tried to concentrate on the facial features. Were they in any way familiar?

Although the smells in the room had remained sharp in his memory, the visual images of the dolls had not.

'I don't recognise it. I just glanced at the photos on his wall. He was working on a little boy, he called it Jacob. The next order, he said, was for a girl doll called Melanie.'

'Melanie? You're sure of that?'

'That's the name he gave her . . . it.'

Bill thought for a moment before asking, 'People send Coulter photographs and he copies them?'

'Yes. Pretty accurately, judging by the letters of thanks.'

'OK, let's take a look at the mobile clip.'

Roy brought it up next to the Reborn image.

'How many of you think they're the same baby?' Bill asked.

There was a chorus of murmurs, then a little more than half the hands went up.

'What about you?' Bill asked Magnus.

154

Magnus was taken aback. He had known nothing about a video clip.

'Where did you get this?'

Bill explained about Kira's mobile.

'And the mobile was left near the doll?'

'Yes.'

A shiver of anticipation went through him. In psychological terms, the presence of the mobile and its recording changed everything. Magnus wondered if Bill realised that. He studied the juxtapositioned images. The video clip had been taken just far enough away to make identification difficult.

'There is a similarity, but that may be down to the clothes.' As the short video neared completion, Magnus thought he saw an eyelid flicker.

'Is that a real baby?'

The muttering broke out again. Bill called for silence.

'We're not sure yet.'

'If it is, could it be Kira's child?'

'The clip was on her phone.'

'When was the clip recorded?' Magnus asked.

'Approximately twelve hours after we found her body.'

\*     \*     \*

Bill asked Rhona and Magnus to wait behind. Gradually the noise outside the room diminished as the team went back to the more mundane aspects of the investigation.

'Now, tell me what you really think is going on here,' said Bill.

Magnus took his time before answering.

155

'Stealing an unborn is usually an act of desperation carried out by a vulnerable woman, who craves a baby in her arms.' He paused. 'Someone in that position would be unlikely to carry out these . . . other actions.'

'You're referring to leaving the Reborn and the phone?'

Magnus was, but not just to those aspects. He nodded anyway, letting Bill carry on in his thought process.

'What if the perpetrator left the doll because they didn't need it any more, and the video was there to reassure us that the baby is still alive?'

'It wasn't obvious from the clip that the baby is, or even was, alive. But if we assume that what you say is true, then what was the purpose of the mirror writing and the reference to the Daisy Chain gang?'

'Maybe the person who took the baby wasn't the person who wrote on Kira's hands,' Rhona said. 'Although whoever it was had to have been there pretty swiftly after the event.'

'Or be present at it,' Magnus said.

All three digested this possibility.

'I think I'll bring David back in and have you sit in this time.'

Magnus nodded. 'If he was as close to Kira as he maintains, there may be more he hasn't told us.'

'I think there is,' said Rhona. 'I saw David in the swing park near the funfair yesterday. He was with another pregnant girl.'

Magnus glanced at Bill, but he didn't look that surprised by this.

'I visited Kira's school,' he said. 'Four of her friends fell pregnant at around the same time as

156

Kira. The Principal thinks there may have been a pregnancy pact. I also learned that the same group of girls called themselves the Daisy Chain, and all had apparently had a tattoo done like Kira. One of those girls is called Melanie.'

'You think that's significant?' Magnus asked.

'We have one dead girl and a missing baby. The perpetrator knew about the Daisy Chain gang, so more than likely they knew the rest of the gang were also pregnant. We can't rule out the fact that the others might be at risk.'

'The girl in the park with David,' Rhona said. 'I heard him call her Mel.' She pulled out her mobile. 'I took a photograph of them.' She located the photo, then handed the phone to Magnus.

The girl's dark hair was held back by a red hairband, her face thin but pretty. It might have been a photograph of young love, had it not been for the worried expressions on both their faces.

'That's David, all right,' Bill said. 'I think it's time I spoke to Melanie Jones.'

\*       \*       \*

Magnus slipped the jotter into his backpack. Bill had shown him the mathematical scribblings and asked him to take a closer look.

Perhaps it had been his mention of Coulter's diary that had prompted the request? Bill seemed to know that Magnus had combined Maths and Psychology at university. He wondered how Bill had found that out, then decided that DI Wilson was the kind of officer who would make a point of knowing everything about his team that might prove useful.

A sharp wind caught at his jacket as he unpadlocked the bike and swung his leg over the crossbar. On the way back to the flat, his mind ran through all that had been said. Bill wanted any possible link with Coulter to be followed up, so Magnus had suggested he contact Dr Shan initially and ask her to check whether Coulter initialised his dolls. He would also send her an image of the doll they'd found and ask her to find out if it had been made by the inmate.

If there was anything forthcoming, DI Wilson would arrange an interview at which he wanted Magnus present. Recalling his own meeting with Coulter, at which he had felt outmanoeuvred and possibly outmatched, Magnus wondered how the senior detective would handle Coulter. It was something he looked forward to observing.

After discussion, Bill had decided he wouldn't release the image of the Reborn or news of the recording to the press until they were sure whether the baby in the video was alive. He promised to let Magnus know the result as soon as the tech boys finished their analysis.

When he reached the flat, Magnus poured a whisky and went out onto the balcony. Below him, the river churned as it fought the incoming tide. There were no rivers like this in Orkney, but he had often watched this tidal struggle in Scapa Flow. He recalled the feeling he'd had as he left the prison after his conversation with Coulter, the sense that he'd started on a path he would live to regret. Magnus took a mouthful of whisky. He had one thing to be thankful for in all of this—he had been given another chance on Bill's team. A chance he didn't want to mess up.

He went back inside and set about making himself something to eat. He was anxious to look at Kira's notebook and after that to go back to his study of Coulter's ramblings, but he would do both better with food inside him. He switched on the radio as he sautéed garlic, then added prawns and spinach to the frying pan. The evening bulletin had nothing new on the search for Kira's killer or the missing newborn, so Bill had been true to his word. Magnus knew that the DI couldn't keep a lid on the latest developments for long, but the last thing they wanted was Coulter to find out before they had a chance to check if the doll was one of his.

He whisked up a couple of eggs and poured them into the pan, stirring the mixture lightly. While he waited for the omelette to set, he considered having another whisky but settled instead for opening a bottle of red wine.

Rather than taking his meal to the desk with him, he forced himself to sit at the dining table. Eating alone wasn't much fun and he was doing it a lot these days, but better to do it properly than shovel in the food while reading Kira's notebook.

Half an hour later he had cleared the plate, drunk two glasses of wine and made himself a pot of coffee. Now he was ready. He carried his cup to the desk, retrieved the notebook from his bag and opened it.

## CHAPTER TWENTY-TWO

David's jacket was nowhere near the quality of Kira's—a supermarket copy of a brand she might have worn. It resembled leather but wasn't, although it was a reasonable imitation, complete with fashion zip details. The jeans were from the same supermarket, as was the shirt. Rhona suspected the whole lot would have cost less than one item of Kira's outfit.

In freefall, a drop of blood was spherical, the form of least energy; it would not break up unless it was acted upon by another force. The size and shape of the stains produced depended on three variables: the volume, the height and the surface on which the drop fell. The greater the volume and height, the larger the stain. However, if the surface was absorbent—like the rough wooden floorboards of the mirror maze—this generally resulted in smaller stains.

Images of the blood patterning at the crime scene suggested that Kira was already prostrate when the knife entered her body, and that she had not put up a fight, probably having already been rendered unconscious by the chloroform. That meant her attacker would have had to crouch or kneel next to her to perform the Caesarean.

If David had knelt close to the body, the knees of his jeans would have been bloodied and blood from the soles of his trainers would probably have imprinted on the back of his jeans. She'd found blood, but not in a pattern which matched either of these scenarios. In David's statement, he'd said that he'd slipped and fallen close to the body, which could account for the smears on the back of his jeans. But blood hadn't been the only trace evidence she'd found.

Rhona checked the image in the comparison microscope. There was no doubt that the two

160

scales she'd retrieved from the right leg of David's jeans came from the same knife handle as those found on Kira's body. Could David have picked these up when he'd knelt by her body, or had he been in contact with the knife used to cut Kira open?

Rhona began to consider an alternative scenario to the one given by David. What if he had arranged to meet Kira in the mirror maze with the intention of removing the baby? The main stumbling-block in this version of events appeared to be timing. Had there been enough time between David leaving the others and raising the alarm for him to perform the operation and dispose of the baby?

The guy in the booth had reported that David entered shortly before midnight, at which point Kira had been in the tent for roughly twenty minutes. The lights had been flashed five minutes after David entered to warn him that the maze would close shortly, and the 999 call had been logged at twelve minutes past twelve. David had had between ten and fifteen minutes to immobilise Kira and extract the baby, which was long enough to perform the Caesarean section, but not to hide the baby. Unless someone else had done that for him?

David had been adamant that he wasn't the baby's father, admitting to Bill that he might be gay. He'd said he didn't care that Kira was pregnant with someone else's baby, and that their relationship was special. What if the opposite were true? What if David was insanely jealous that Kira had slept with someone else and had killed her because of that?

But if that was the case, why take the baby?

Another interpretation of events suddenly occurred to her. Maybe Kira wasn't supposed to die. Maybe the baby was removed to prevent its paternity being established. But if you knew how to perform a Caesarean, would you also know that the umbilical cord could be used to establish paternity? One thing she was certain of, foetal theft was only one possible motive for the attack.

Rhona updated the software with her latest findings and texted Bill to let him know what she'd discovered. It seemed even more important now to find out if David was the baby's father.

She decided to take a break and make herself a coffee. It would have been nice if Chrissy had been around to talk things through with, but this wasn't one of her days.

As Rhona added milk to her mug she heard the ping of an incoming text. She was about to ignore it, but then it occurred to her that it might be from Bill or Petersson. The message said, *Dead man walking*.

Rhona checked for the caller ID, but the number had been withheld. She immediately thought of Petersson. Codes were right up his street. Maybe the cryptic text was his way of telling her that the dead soldier wasn't dead after all. She brought up his number. It took six rings before he answered.

'Rhona? I was just about to call you.'

'Did you just send me a text?'

'No.'

'That's weird.'

'Why? What did it say?'

' "Dead man walking". I thought there had been a mistake and you were telling me Fergus

Morrison was alive.'

'Morrison isn't alive, and I didn't send you a text.'

'Then who did?'

'Did you check the number?'

'It was withheld.'

Unnerved by the pregnant silence on the other end, Rhona decided to change the subject.

'What were you going to call me about?'

'I have some news. Can I come round later?'

'News about what?'

'I'll tell you when I get there.' He paused. 'Shall I pick up some food on the way?'

She was about to refuse, then thought better of it. It would save her a trip to the shops on her way home.

'OK.'

'What do you fancy?'

'Anything but chicken and vegetables,' she said.

*       *       *

Petersson took charge of the meal. She'd expected something ready cooked, but that apparently wasn't his style. As he unpacked the bag at the kitchen table, she spotted salmon, salad, wine, bread and a bottle of balsamic vinegar.

He handed her the bottle of wine.

'It's chilled already. Can you open it while I get started?'

It was obvious from his preparations that Petersson expected her to wait until the meal was served before she started on her questions. Rhona opened the bottle and poured two glasses.

She sipped at the white wine as Petersson tossed

163

cubes of salmon in balsamic and began to gently fry them over a low heat. The sour-sweet scent made her mouth water.

Ten minutes later they were sitting down to the meal and their second glass of wine.

'Eat first, then we'll talk,' he ordered.

They were at the coffee and whisky stage before he decided it was time. There was a quiet satisfaction in his voice as he told her.

'I have reason to believe that DI Slater was closer to Kalinin than a detective should be.'

Rhona waited, her heart thumping.

'Kalinin's continued freedom from prosecution has worried me for some time. Either he's the luckiest bastard on the planet or he has a guardian angel.'

'And that guardian angel is Slater?' she said, her stomach churning. Maybe eating first hadn't been such a good idea after all.

He nodded, watching her reaction.

'That's a big accusation. I hope you can prove it.'

'My source is reliable, although I can't prove it, yet. That's where you come in.'

'Me?'

Petersson reached for the whisky bottle and poured himself another. Rhona waved away his offer of a refill and waited.

'Tell me exactly what happened the night McNab was shot,' he said.

A chill crept through her. She had no desire to relive those moments.

'Is that really necessary?'

'I believe so.'

Rhona moved her hands below the table in case

164

Petersson should see them tremble, and began.

'Michael took Chrissy, my forensic assistant, to The Poker Club to celebrate. He asked me to go with them. I refused.' Her voice broke a little, and she cleared her throat before continuing. 'Kalinin appeared there with Anya Grigorovitch in tow. Michael thought Kalinin was still in custody. DI Slater had released him, but hadn't warned Michael of that fact.' She could hear the ice-cold anger in her voice. 'Michael and Chrissy left the building immediately. He was trying to flag down a taxi when the car appeared and he was shot.'

'When did you arrive?'

'Anya called me from the Ladies' room after she realised Michael was there. She thought Kalinin was planning something. I came straightaway, but . . . I was too late.'

'McNab was already dead?'

'No.' She stumbled over her words, remembering the look in McNab's eyes when he'd said her name. 'I tried to stem the bleeding but he died shortly after I got there.'

'Did you go with the body in the ambulance?'

She shook her head, trying to read Petersson's expression. Where was all this leading?

'Tell me about the autopsy.'

'Post-mortem,' she mechanically corrected him. 'I didn't attend.'

He looked puzzled. 'Can I ask why?'

'DI Slater thought the death was too personal.'

'But he was there?'

'I assume so.'

'Who performed it?'

'Under Scots law, two pathologists must be present for collaboration purposes. I assume

165

Dr Sissons would have been one of them.'

'But you don't know that for certain?'

'No.'

'Can you find out exactly who attended the post-mortem for me? I'd also like to see the report.'

She had never wanted to see the report before now, having no desire to read the details of how the bullet had shattered McNab's internal organs.

'Why is this important?'

'I'm not sure yet. But if we want to identify Slater's role in all of this, we have to know the details of that post-mortem.' He gave her a half smile. 'We'll get the people responsible for McNab's death.'

'Is that a promise?'

'That's a promise.'

\*     \*     \*

If she kept her eyes closed, there was a similarity: in the long, lean line of his body under her hands, in the stubbled roughness of his cheek, the movements, the sounds. No two men made love in the same way, but Petersson performed with the same raw passion as McNab. If she kept her eyes shut, she could pretend for a moment that it was Michael she held inside her.

She felt his lips lightly touch her left lid, then her right. Rhona opened her eyes and looked into his.

The first time had been calculated. She'd wanted him on her side and sex had seemed the right card to play. This time was different. This time she had used him as a means of remembering. It had worked, up to a point. His blue eyes were examining her. Free now of lust, they sought something more from her, something she was unwilling to give.

She moved to extract herself, his body suddenly heavy. Reading the signs, he lifted himself clear and rolled beside her. She should rise now, go and shower, a sure sign of disconnection. Sex was one thing, relating was another. And as far as she was concerned, Petersson was a tool in her fight against Kalinin.

As she went back into the bedroom after her shower, Rhona heard the click of a key turning in the front lock. She glanced at Petersson, who was still in bed, his eyes closed. Rhona pulled on a dressing gown and opened the bedroom door.

She knew it was Sean before he appeared round the corner in the hallway. It was he who looked startled.

'I'm sorry. I didn't see any lights. I thought you were out.'

A mewing broke the silence that followed, as Tom came racing out of the kitchen and made straight for Sean's legs, weaving in and out and purring.

'I came for the fiddle and the rest of my things.'

'I put them in the spare room.'

'I'll get them and be out of your way.'

Too late, she heard the creak of the bed and the padding of feet, as the door she had half-closed behind her swung open. She knew Petersson was still naked. She could feel his proximity in the heat from his body and the smell of sex from his skin.

Sean's gaze rose from her face to the taller figure behind her, then he shifted his eyes back to hers and waited. The moments ticked past.

167

She was damned if she was going to introduce them. She was damned if she would even acknowledge the awkwardness of the situation. As Sean turned and headed for the spare room, Rhona felt Petersson's hand rest lightly on her shoulder. She turned quickly, shaking it off.

'You'd better go.'

She wasn't sure if she wanted him to leave before Sean or after. What if bad timing meant they left together? Petersson, perhaps sensing her disquiet, dressed quickly. In minutes he was ready to leave.

'Let me know what you find out,' he said at the front door.

She nodded, then closed the door swiftly behind him and retreated to the bedroom. From there she could hear Sean moving around, murmuring to the cat. Rhona remained motionless, thinking she should go out into the hall, at least. That she should not be rude.

She felt her heart lurch in her chest, then take off like a steeplechase. This was stupid. There was nothing between them now. She did not have to explain her actions to Sean. As if to spite herself, she opened the bedroom door and went into the hall. The spare room door stood ajar. Sean was standing by the window, the fiddle case in his hand. He turned to face her.

He was thinner than she remembered, his dark hair longer, but the eyes were the same deep, dark blue.

'You look great,' he smiled.

'Thanks.'

He lifted the holdall he'd brought with him, now full, and hoisted it over his shoulder.

168

'I'll be off then.'

She stood aside to let him pass. The cat was making a determined effort to restrict his exit, and Rhona swept it into her arms.

'He's grown.' Sean rubbed Tom's head affectionately.

She hadn't wanted another cat after what had happened to Chance. It had been Sean who had taken the initiative and got her one. She'd been annoyed with him at first, then grateful as her affection for the kitten had grown. Sean had been good at interpreting her needs even when she wasn't aware of them herself.

She heard herself say, 'Where are you staying?'

'I was at the club for a while, but . . .' He hesitated. 'Now I'm seeing Angie.' He left the rest unsaid.

Her heart slowed and settled like a hard lump in her chest. She had no right to be surprised or upset.

'I was really sorry to hear about McNab.'

She nodded stiffly.

'Chrissy told me.'

She imagined Chrissy in the jazz club, chatting to Sean, and felt excluded, despite the fact that she had been urged to accompany her there on numerous occasions.

'Rhona . . .'

'I'll get the door for you.'

He stood for a moment as though he would speak, then thought better of it. As he slipped past, she caught the scent of him. The memory was stronger than his smile or the colour of his eyes. She felt violated by the surge of feeling that assailed her.

Then he was through and standing on the landing.

'Sam's back playing at the club. I thought you might come and hear him with Chrissy and Bill some time.'

The gang, she thought, all there bar her. And whose fault was that?

'Soon,' she said.

'See you then.'

'Yes, see you.'

She closed the door and stood against it for a moment, then walked quickly to the front room and glanced down into the street. Sean was loading the holdall and fiddle case into a smart little red sports car. A blonde head was visible in the driver's seat. Angie, no doubt.

Rhona forced herself to vacate the window in case Sean looked up. Too late, she remembered she had not asked Sean to return his key.

## CHAPTER TWENTY-THREE

'Why do you ask?' Sissons was regarding her quizzically.

'I just wondered.' Rhona tried to keep her tone light.

'I didn't perform the post-mortem myself.'

'What about Sylvia?'

He shook his head. 'Dr Barnes wasn't present either.'

'Then who did do it?'

'As far as I am aware, it was performed by a pathologist sent up by SOCA.'

'But McNab was killed on our patch. His murder is under our jurisdiction.' She realised her tone had changed, but it was difficult to hide her astonishment and irritation.

'I am well aware of that. However, I assume the Met were putting a case together on the Russian connection and . . .'

'McNab's death was part of that,' she finished for him. 'I assume there was a report filed on the results of the post-mortem?'

'One presumes so.'

'Do you have a copy here?'

Something in Sissons's body language suggested she was about to be dismissed.

'Dr MacLeod, as I understand it, you were with DS McNab when he died. You found the bullet casing. What more is there to know?'

He was right. She was sounding weird, obsessed.

'In normal circumstances I would have been present at the post-mortem. I would like to read the report.'

He sighed, rose from his desk and went to a filing cabinet. She watched as he rifled through various drawers, making no attempt to disguise his irritation. Eventually he turned.

'I can find no written record at the moment.'

In normal circumstances three hard copies would have been produced for dissemination and sent to the police. One to be given to the Fiscal, one for the senior investigating officer and one for the case file.

'What about an ecopy?'

He regarded her with a stoical annoyance.

'I suggest you talk to the office staff about that.'

This time she *was* dismissed, and she took it in

171

good grace. She'd known Sissons long enough to realise that he'd already gone out of his way to help her.

Had Sissons or Sylvia performed the post-mortem, an ecopy of the report would have been in the system in case the Strathclyde police wanted it in pdf format. But if responsibility for investigating McNab's death had moved elsewhere?

She would check with the office staff first.

If there was nothing on the system, she would try and locate the whereabouts of any hard copies, assuming they hadn't gone south.

She decided she didn't fancy approaching Detective Superintendent Sutherland to ask if he had a copy. Bill might have access to one but she wasn't keen on alerting him to her interest. He had a knack of reading her motives. The only other alternative was the Fiscal, who might just humour her.

*       *       *

Rhona was pleased to find Dorothy Jenkins on duty in the admin office. Dorothy had been working in the job for as long as Rhona had. They exchanged a few pleasantries about the weather, then Rhona presented the secretary with her request. Dorothy accepted it with equanimity and immediately set about checking the system for a copy of the post-mortem results.

'I don't recall seeing them though. I vaguely remember someone else came to perform the post-mortem on the policeman.' She paused. 'They're not in the usual place.' She scrolled down the list. 'We had three around that time. See the date.'

Rhona didn't want to register the date.

'I believe a pathologist from the Met did the post-mortem, so would that have been stored differently?' she said.

'Really? That's unusual.' Dorothy thought for a moment, then began a different search. 'Maybe they wrote it up on their own system,' she offered when nothing was forthcoming. 'But I expect there must be hard copies around somewhere. You could try the senior investigating officer, or the Fiscal.'

'I will.' Rhona tried to keep her voice light. 'Thanks for your help.'

Dorothy gave her a sympathetic look. 'It was a terrible thing. A young man like that, with everything to live for.'

Rhona simply nodded.

She left the Forensic Pathology department and made her way onto University Avenue. The biting wind that fought her progress reminded her of the night of the snowstorm when she and Chrissy had been stranded in Fern Cottage, Chrissy only days away from giving birth. It was hard to comprehend that in such a short space of time so much had happened. A death and a birth. She allowed herself to contemplate for a moment what McNab's reaction to the birth of young Michael might have been, then shook herself free and concentrated on reality.

She would find out which Procurator Fiscal had been involved and contact them. If they didn't have a copy of the report, surely they would have been able to name the pathologist involved. She would then contact them direct.

She pondered what significance this had for Petersson's pursuit of Kalinin. How did it affect the possibility that Slater was on the wrong side?

Rhona recalled Petersson's reply when she'd suggested that McNab had simply been in the wrong place at the wrong time. His take on it had been quite different. He believed Kalinin had known exactly where McNab would be. In fact, the Russian had arranged it. If Petersson was right and Slater was on Kalinin's payroll, then his freeing of Kalinin from custody that night had made McNab's death inevitable.

The thought only served to make her even more determined to find out what Petersson wanted to know.

Back at the lab, a glimpse of Chrissy's suited figure through the glass raised her spirits. It would have been even better if she could have confided in her about her enquiries. She wondered if her assistant was aware that McNab's post-mortem had been performed by someone from outside the department—she couldn't imagine Chrissy keeping that to herself.

Chrissy looked up at Rhona's entry, her eyes inquisitive.

'Where were you?'

'Forensic Pathology.'

*Don't ask why*, Rhona prayed. Chrissy had a radar for lies. Luckily she seemed intent on asking questions on a different subject, one that made Rhona equally uncomfortable.

'So who's this new man in your life?'

Rhona was struck dumb.

Chrissy looked delighted at the result of her enquiry. She probed further. 'Tall, Nordic looking?'

How the hell did she know about Petersson?

'His name's Einar Petersson. And he's not my new man.'

'That's not what I heard.' Chrissy was toying with her now.

'I don't care what you heard.'

Chrissy raised an eyebrow and waited. Rhona hung on, knowing Chrissy would be forced to reveal more. She had been in Petersson's company in public three times. At the art show, the club they'd gone to afterwards and in the gallery café. If she hadn't been spotted at any of these places, then Sean had to be the source.

Chrissy was looking fit to burst. She eventually did.

'Sam told me.'

Had Sam seen them in the gallery café, or had Sean told Sam about his visit? She soon found out.

'Sean's not really serious about that woman, you know,' Chrissy said.

Rhona couldn't help herself. 'How long?'

Chrissy pulled a face. 'A couple of weeks, maybe. It won't last anyway.'

'A fortnight and he's moved in?' Rhona couldn't hide her dismay.

'Did Sean say that?'

'He implied it.'

'As far as I know, he's still sleeping at the club. Anyway, you've got Petersson or whatever his name is.'

'He hasn't moved in.'

'Sounded quite cosy to me though.'

'Sean told Sam that?' Now Rhona was annoyed.

'Sean . . .' Chrissy chose her next words carefully. 'Sam got the impression he was upset.'

Rhona found herself pleased by that thought.

175

After all, no one liked to be replaced too quickly, no matter what the circumstances.

## CHAPTER TWENTY-FOUR

It had been difficult to get to speak to Dr Shan at all. Now that he finally had her on the line, the task hadn't become any easier.

'We need to establish whether the doll we have is one of Coulter's.'

'I understand that.'

'So, if I send you a photograph . . . ?'

'It would be easier to show Mr Coulter and ask him.'

Magnus had imagined Dr Shan visiting the photo gallery without Coulter and checking an image of their find against those on display. He didn't want Coulter alerted to this. He didn't want the man to fancy himself as the centre of police attention.

'Psychopaths tell lies as a matter of course,' he said.

'I am well aware of that, Professor Pirie. However, Mr Coulter has not been *officially* diagnosed as having a psychopathic personality.'

Magnus knew the word *officially* was a direct dig at him. Coulter was being treated in the State Hospital as though he had a mental illness, not a personality disorder. He was apparently responding to drugs, if that could be believed.

Magnus tried a different tack. 'Could you check if and how he signs his dolls without alerting him to why we want to know?'

'That might be possible,' she said grudgingly.

'The Reborn we found has the initials *JC* signed in the head cavity.'

The silence that followed was heavy.

Eventually Dr Shan responded tersely. 'I can't take a doll apart. It's a patient's private property.'

'He likes talking about his work. Perhaps just a general enquiry?'

There was a loaded pause, then she said, 'I'll be in touch.'

Magnus wanted to ask how soon, but decided that would be pushing his luck.

'Thank you very much, Dr Shan.'

He heard the phone go down.

A complex woman, he decided. He reexamined his actions during the prison visit and the recent phone call, trying to work out how exactly he had annoyed her, then decided that he simply didn't know and probably never would. He could ask her outright, of course, but people rarely liked being asked about these things and also rarely gave an honest answer. He came to the conclusion that he had to accept that he simply pissed Dr Shan off.

He put on some coffee, then took out Kira's diary and laid it on the desk, with pen, paper and laptop nearby. It had been a good few years since mathematics had been an essential part of his life. He could only hope that it was like riding a bicycle and the thought processes would return once he stimulated that part of his brain again. He fetched a mug of coffee and settled to his task.

Bill had not specified his interest in the notebook, only that he wanted Magnus to take a look. A wise move on the DI's part. Suggest one particular focus and that's what the reader fastens

177

on. Better to keep an open mind. Magnus was aware that Kira had been an exemplary student, good enough to study Mathematics at Cambridge. He began to leaf through the jotter. The contents were predominantly algebraic in content, and he recognised partial fractions and some calculations using the binomial theorem. After that came at least ten pages of matrix algebra. Magnus felt a surge of pleasure at the carefully laid-out matrix calculations.

Kira's construction of the matrix form was beautifully scribed, the numbers and symbols written in a clear, small and precise hand. This was someone who loved maths as a poet must love the form and meaning of poetry.

The notes went through the various algebraic rules for addition, subtraction and multiplication, then how to find a determinant, obtain an inverse and transpose a matrix. All topics in the Advanced Higher syllabus which he'd checked online. Nothing special up to now, other than a promising mathematician at work.

Magnus turned to the next page.

There were some calculations using complex numbers followed by their polar form, $z=r(\cos\theta + i\sin\theta)$, then a space followed by a group of symbols

$$\iota\tau\beta\varepsilon\gamma\iota\nu\varsigma$$

which seemed unrelated to the topic she'd been working on.

Two blank lines followed, then Kira reverted to her previous calculations. Magnus began leafing through the jotter, looking for anything similar and found quite a few. Some were written within the text, some along the margins or the spine. Most were written in a tiny hand that would require a magnifying glass to make out the shapes.

He considered whether the collections of symbols might simply be doodles Kira had carried out while problem solving or whether they were in fact significant. Most of the symbols he recognised as Greek, others he wasn't so sure about.

Magnus was aware that every letter in the Greek alphabet except one was used in the language of mathematics, *omicron* or 'o' being too close to the Roman letter 'o'. He recalled, as a first year pupil in secondary school, being sent to sit at the back of a senior maths class. He had seen the strange symbols being written on the blackboard and hoped that one day he too would understand their meaning. Then, such symbols were like a foreign language the older students in the room understood, while he could only admire its strange forms.

Maybe Kira loved those symbols too, the ones less commonly used, and simply enjoyed drawing them on the page.

Magnus returned to their first appearance during Kira's work on complex numbers. He wrote a copy on paper of what he thought each symbol was, then went online and checked on the Greek alphabet.

'$\iota$' or the Greek *iota* he decided might be the English 'i'. '$\tau$' he believed could be translated as 't'. He studied the next letter for a moment or two and decided it was *beta*. The fourth was *epsilon*. The next he didn't have a clue about. In its slightly smudged state it could be anything.

He studied the alphabet again, then sought to

enlarge the typeface in order to compare the symbols with the unrecognisable one, before giving up and moving on to the sixth, which, if he had been right first time, was 'i' again.

Symbol seven he decided was *sigma* used to denote 's'. He was now left with:

'itbeγins' which looked very like 'itbegins'.

But what begins?

The phone rang as he sat back, satisfied by his translation but puzzled by its significance, if any.

He picked up the receiver.

'Professor Pirie?'

He immediately recognised Dr Shan's voice. 'Yes?'

'I tried raising the subject of his signing the dolls in general conversation as you suggested.'

'And?'

'It didn't work.'

*I bet it didn't*, Magnus thought.

'He has asked that you visit him again.'

Any request or interest from Dr Shan that Coulter deemed unusual would have either enhanced his ego or stirred his suspicions, or both. Magnus had given Dr Shan the job. He couldn't now complain if he felt she had not carried it out to his satisfaction.

He decided to take a different approach.

'Do you know if Coulter has sent the doll he was working on when I was last there?'

'No. But I can check with the mail department for you.' Dr Shan's tone was conciliatory.

'Thank you.'

'When do you envisage coming back to see Mr Coulter?'

'As soon as possible.'

This time he wouldn't have to go through the original channels, not if he had DI Wilson with him.

## CHAPTER TWENTY-FIVE

Slater had known nothing of a possible pregnancy pact or the existence of the Daisy Chain gang, so there had been no interviews conducted with its members.

Bill had set DS Clark the task of contacting the girls' parents. She'd reported back that the families involved had been angry at having their names given out by the school. No doubt Morvern's principal would be taking the flak over that. As to the reported pregnancies, DS Clark had established that only Melanie remained pregnant, the others having chosen terminations.

Bill and Magnus drew up outside a two-storey sandstone villa. Minutes from Byres Road, the house was in a highly desirable location within walking distance of Melanie's school.

They had already discussed how Bill planned to conduct the interview; Magnus was there to observe Melanie's reactions to the questions Bill posed.

He pulled the old-fashioned brass door bell and listened as a clanging resounded in the spacious hallway. The young woman who opened the door was dressed in dark clothes and spoke with an accent he took to be Polish.

Bill showed her his ID and introduced himself. 'We're here to speak to Melanie.'

She looked wary, but stood back to let them enter, then indicated a door on the left. 'In here, please.'

The room they entered was spacious and filled with a soft wintry light. Near the bay window a tall fern plant stood in a waist-high blue ceramic pot, its fronds reaching almost as high as the ceiling. They were urged to take a seat on one of the three thickly cushioned sofas which framed the ornate mahogany fireplace.

'I'll tell Melanie you're here.'

When the girl arrived a few minutes later, she was alone. In black leggings and a patterned top, she was small and slight, apart from the bump of her pregnancy.

Before Bill could ask, she said, 'Mother is at a medical conference in London. My father's out of the country on business. I don't need them here to speak to you anyway.'

Bill began his introductions. Melanie's reaction to Magnus's title was a guarded glance in his direction. They took their seats. Magnus next to Melanie on the sofa, Bill opposite.

'You know why we're here?'

'I assume it's about Kira,' she said, her manner composed.

'She was a friend of yours?'

'We were in the same year at school.'

'That's all?'

'We weren't close, if that's what you mean.'

Bill didn't argue. Instead he said, 'May I ask when your baby's due?'

The change in topic took her by surprise, but she quickly covered it. 'In three weeks.'

'You must be excited.'

'I'm having it adopted. I have a place at Edinburgh University.'

'To study Law, I believe.'

'How did you know that?' she said, suspiciously.

'I visited your school and spoke to your principal, Ms Porter.' Bill watched her wariness change to anger. 'I also know that Kira was a good friend of yours. As were Louisa Sommerville, Jocelyn Calderfield and Samantha Wells. In fact, you called yourselves the Daisy Chain.'

Melanie's face flushed.

'And that you all got pregnant around the same time.'

'The school had no business telling you that. My father will be—' she said angrily.

Bill interrupted her. 'Kira was found with the words "daisy chain" written on the palms of her hands in mirror writing. Which suggests that whoever killed her and took her baby knew about your little group.'

'That's impossible—apart from us, only David knew.'

'What about Sandie?'

Melanie curled her lip. 'She wasn't part of the gang.'

'Why was that?'

'Sandie acted like an idiot around boys. It was embarrassing.'

'Yet she didn't get pregnant.'

Intense irritation crossed her face, but she didn't respond.

'This pregnancy pact?'

'What do you mean, "pact"?'

'You were in a gang. You all got pregnant around the same time. That sounds like a pact to

183

me.'

'The pregnancies weren't intentional.'

'So Kira didn't persuade you all to get pregnant?'

'Of course not!'

Bill changed the subject. 'May I ask who the father is?'

She lifted her chin. 'That's none of your business.'

'If it helps bring Kira's killer to justice, it is my business.'

'My pregnancy is nothing to do with Kira.'

'Then it won't matter if you tell me the father's name.'

She thought for a moment. 'I don't know his name. I was at a party. I got drunk and had sex with someone.'

'Why didn't you have a termination?'

'I'd missed periods before because I was underweight. By the time I realised I was pregnant, it was too late.' She glanced down at the bump. 'Now I'm stuck with this.'

'Kira chose not to have an abortion.'

She shrugged. 'Kira always had to be different.'

'Can you think of any reason why someone would hurt Kira and take her baby?'

'No!' She looked frightened at the thought.

Bill waited a moment before asking, 'Why did you meet David Murdoch in the park the day after Kira died?'

'I didn't.'

'I have a photo that shows you two together in the children's playground.'

The question had unnerved her, but she rallied. 'David was very upset about Kira. I was sorry for him.'

'Is David the father of your baby?'

She laughed sarcastically. 'David's gay.'

'Gay men can father children.'

'Not mine.'

'Do you know who the father of Kira's baby is?'

'No.'

'Could you take a guess?'

'She was having sex with someone. Not David. Kira liked to be the first to do things.'

'So the gang decided to give it a try?'

She didn't respond.

'Was Kira frightened of anyone? The person she was having sex with?'

'Kira wasn't frightened of anyone, or anything.' Her tone was admiring, almost wistful. Then she appeared to remember something. 'Except clowns.'

'Clowns?'

'Kira was scared of clowns. We tried to watch a horror film with a clown in it one night and she totally freaked. She tried to pretend she wasn't frightened, told us she'd seen it before, but she was lying. She made us watch something else instead.'

They left her in the sitting room, the Polish girl showing them out.

'Well?' Bill said to Magnus as soon as they were in the car.

'I think there probably was a pact, or at least a decision to have sex, maybe even daring each other to see who could get pregnant first. It may be Kira was already pregnant and encouraged the others.'

'So that another pregnancy would dilute the impact of her own?' mused Bill.

'These girls were all expected to be something more than just mothers. Maybe they were

185

challenging that assumption.'

Bill recalled Ms Porter saying that it wasn't always easy being clever.

'The principal said Kira's family were practising Christians, that's why she didn't abort the baby.'

'Kira was old enough to have an abortion without their consent,' Magnus reminded him.

'Then maybe what David said was true. Kira discovered she was adopted and decided to keep her baby.'

'Or as Melanie said, Kira always had to be different.'

'I got the impression that Melanie was hiding something more than a pregnancy pact,' Bill said.

'I agree.' Magnus looked thoughtful. 'When she turned towards me, her breath smelt unpleasantly sweet, a symptom of the presence of excess ketones. Which suggests she isn't eating enough during pregnancy, or she's highly stressed.'

Bill recalled the girl's unnaturally thin frame. 'Or both.'

'I think Melanie's very frightened and not just about having a baby.'

'Maybe she's scared she'll be next,' said Bill grimly.

\*　　　\*　　　\*

Melanie rose awkwardly from the sofa and went to watch the policeman's car draw away from the kerb, putting her hands on the bulge of her belly. It felt taut, the skin stretched. She wanted her stomach to be concave again, to be able to trace her hip bones, to be empty.

Her heart had been racing during the interview.

She'd felt sure they must have heard it. She wondered why the psychology professor had been there. She'd wanted to ask but had been afraid to. She'd thought if she told them Kira wasn't a friend, they would just go away. It had never occurred to her that they would know anything about the Daisy Chain.

She fetched her mobile and brought up David's number, then remembered the steel in his voice when he told her not to phone him, that they must stay away from one another. It had been at her insistence they'd met in the park. She left the window and sat down heavily on the sofa, pushing the mobile away from her, knowing David would be angry if she called. It was all Kira's fault. The stupid gang, the tattoo. This thing inside her. And now Kira didn't have to face any of it.

Poor Kira. Her baby cut out, removed, never to be seen again. There were times she wanted the same thing to happen to her. To wake up and find it gone. But she didn't want to die like Kira. Who might have killed Kira? Her secret lover? But why would he kill Kira and take the baby she said was his? And why would he write 'daisy chain' on her hands unless he knew about the gang? Melanie looked down with loathing at the rippling bump that had taken over her body. What if she and the thing inside her were next on the killer's list? She closed her eyes and forced herself to take deep, heart-slowing breaths.

How had it all gone so wrong? At the beginning it had been a bit of fun. They'd downloaded erotic novels and read them together, voting on their favourite scenes. Then Kira had told them she was having sex with someone, acting out what she'd

187

read. She'd regaled them with every intimate detail of her encounters, then dared them to try it. And they'd played along. It had been impossible not to.

Taking chances had been her idea too. Testing fate, Kira had called it. Leaving it up to the gods. Then she said she wanted to see if she could get pregnant. She became obsessed with it. She wanted to get back at her parents, her father in particular. If she got pregnant, that would show him. Anyway, she'd assured them, if it happened, it would be easy to get a termination.

So Melanie had gone along with it, never thinking it could happen to her. She hadn't had a period for months, not since she'd begun dieting. Besides, when you were high and drunk, you didn't care. And now she was the one left to face the consequences. How unfair was that? She hadn't even seen the guy, because of the mask and the darkness. It was an erotic fantasy that had turned into a nightmare. When she'd told the policeman she had no idea who the father of her child was, it was the truth. None of them had known except Kira, and Kira was dead.

Melanie drew herself up from the couch and went into the hall. Blanka had said her goodbyes until tomorrow, leaving a settled silence in the house that Melanie normally liked but which now made her uneasy. She passed the hall table with her mother's list of emergency numbers beside the phone and slowly began to climb the stairs.

Once in her room, she closed the door and pulled down the blinds before lying down on the bed. This was the one thing she liked about being pregnant. She found herself able to doze off whenever she chose. Would she be able to do so now despite her unease?

She decided to give it a try.

The mask of Dionysos stared down at her from the opposite wall, the mouth partly open in the hint of a smile. Kira had proclaimed that Dionysos would unleash the primordial exultation which was dormant in them all. It had sounded great at the time. Little had she known.

Melanie switched on her iPod, put in her earphones and closed her eyes.

## CHAPTER TWENTY-SIX

'Clown wigs?' said Rhona.

'Apparently the best ones use only yak hair. You can do anything with it,' replied Chrissy.

Rhona thought about that for a minute. 'The writing on Kira's hands was done with a soft black make-up pencil.'

'So what? A clown killed her and stole her baby? Sounds like the pitch for a slasher movie.'

'You're the one who brought up the subject of clowns,' Rhona reminded her.

Chrissy nodded thoughtfully. 'A clown outfit isn't a bad disguise. With make-up or a mask you often can't tell if the person wearing it is male or female.'

'You don't normally have clowns at funfairs, do you?'

'No, but I don't think people would be surprised at seeing one.'

'Some people don't like clowns.'

'I'm one of them,' said Chrissy forcefully.

189

'I didn't think you were scared of anything.'

'Well, you're wrong. Ugly white faces with their huge, grinning, red mouths.' Chrissy shuddered.

'Isn't that a recognised condition?'

'Being shit-scared, you mean?'

'Fear of clowns.'

'It's called coulrophobia,' replied Chrissy.

'So you're coulrophobic?'

'Among other things.'

'Good job McNab didn't know about that.'

'I made sure he didn't.'

There was a small, awkward silence, then Chrissy said, 'This is what we have to do, you know.'

'What?'

'Mention his name more often. Remember him without feeling guilty about it.'

'I don't feel guilty. I feel angry.'

'I feel guilty.'

'Why?' Rhona said, surprised.

'He died saving me, remember?'

'McNab was the one they were after.'

'He still made sure I was all right.'

They lapsed into silence again.

'I'm going to the club to listen to Sam tonight. Why don't you come?'

'Not tonight.'

Chrissy gave her one of her particular looks, which indicated advice was about to follow. 'Better to know your enemy.'

Rhona couldn't resist asking, 'You've seen her?'

'She comes in.'

Rhona wanted to ask what she was like. She was blonde, she knew that much. And she had a smart little sports car.

'She's not like you,' Chrissy offered, reading her mind.

What the hell did that mean? Rhona decided not to ask. 'I'm busy tonight.'

'Ah,' Chrissy said, her eyes wide and knowing.

'Not with Petersson.'

Being 'busy' would mean sitting by the fire, the shadows of McNab haunting the corners of the room.

'If you change your mind, phone me.'

She said she would just to please Chrissy, although she had no desire to watch Sean on stage or scan the audience looking for Angie. She'd rather be alone with the ghost of McNab.

Chrissy's lecture over, Rhona retreated to her office. Thinking about McNab prompted her to pick up the phone and call the Fiscal's office, where she asked to be put through to Doug Cameron. They'd been on a number of jobs together, many of them also involving McNab, including the Gravedigger case. Her only concern was that Cameron might mention her request to Bill, but she would have to take that chance.

'Dr MacLeod,' Cameron said cheerfully.

'Hi, Doug. Hope I'm not interrupting anything?'

'Nothing that can't wait. What can I do for you?'

Rhona decided not to beat about the bush. 'I wanted a look at the post-mortem report on Michael McNab. As you probably know, I did the work on the bullet casing. I would be interested to read the pathologist's report on the injuries the bullet produced.' A valid-sounding question.

'You weren't at the post-mortem?' Cameron sounded puzzled.

'DI Slater didn't want anyone there who was too

191

closely involved. We were all still in shock.'

'I can understand that,' he said sympathetically. 'Did you try the SIO? He should have a copy of the report. Or Dr Sissons?'

'Forensic Pathology couldn't find one on the system. Apparently a pathologist from down south was used. Something to do with SOCA building a comprehensive case against Kalinin.'

'I see.' There was a pause. 'Can I call you back on this?'

'Sure. No rush.'

Rhona swore under her breath as she put the phone down. Was it her imagination or had there been a sudden note of caution in Cameron's voice? Maybe she shouldn't have mentioned SOCA? The delineation between Scots and English law could be a sore point at times.

Why was she beginning to feel that something wasn't right about all of this? She realised it had started when Petersson asked her about the post-mortem results on McNab. She had never needed to know what was in them before. The bullet hadn't left McNab's body, it had disintegrated inside him. She'd never wanted to know the full extent of the damage it had done.

*       *       *

Rhona moved the plastic bag containing the carry-out meal to her left hand and fished in her pocket for the key. When she opened the front door, she was surprised not to hear scampering paws as Tom came to greet her. Then she heard a plaintive miaow from beyond the kitchen door.

She normally let the cat have the run of the

house. She must have inadvertently shut the kitchen door when she'd left that morning. Rhona deposited the bag on the work surface and doled out sufficient affection to satisfy Tom before opening the wine she'd bought on her way home. She poured a large glass and slipped the plastic container of chow mein into the microwave.

While it was cooking, she carried her glass through to the sitting room, lit the gas fire and turned on the lamps. She didn't want any shadows dancing in the room tonight. When she heard the ping from the kitchen, she suddenly realised how hungry she was. She heaped a plate high and carried it back through.

When she finished eating, she poured another glass, then fetched the duvet and got undressed in front of the fire. Tom came and nestled beside her, his purr comforting. She turned on the television, keeping the sound low, and when sleep didn't come, she watched the silent figures move about the screen. It was a crime drama whose characters she didn't recognise, although they appeared to be having as much difficulty in their fictional world as she was having in reality.

Eventually she must have dozed off because the entry buzzer startled her into wakefulness. She rose and walked through to the hall, still in her underwear, and pressed the intercom button.

'It's me. Can I come up?'

She didn't answer immediately.

'It's important,' Petersson insisted.

She pressed the release button and went to put on some clothes. When she opened the door, Petersson was standing impatiently on the mat. He strode in, bringing a draught of cold air with him.

193

'Do you have any alcohol? Vodka?' he said sharply.

'No vodka, but there's whisky and a little wine in the kitchen.'

He followed her through. The white wine bottle stood on the table, more than half empty.

'Make it a whisky,' he said.

She fetched the bottle from the cupboard. 'Water, ice?'

'Straight.'

She poured a double and handed it over. He drank it down and held out the glass for another. She refilled it and handed it back. This time he took only a sip.

'That's better. Can we go through?'

She led him into the sitting room where the evidence of her previous occupation was obvious to see.

He suddenly looked contrite. 'I woke you up? I'm sorry.'

'I was watching TV,' she lied. She indicated a seat near the fire, folding the duvet up and laying it on the back of the sofa before sitting down herself.

'The autopsy report, did you get a copy?' he asked.

'No.'

'There is a problem?'

'More an oddity. Apparently the post-mortem wasn't done by any of the usual team.'

'Really?'

'Someone came up from the south to perform it. Something to do with SOCA's case against Kalinin. Maybe they had to conduct an autopsy under English law. That happens sometimes.'

Petersson didn't look convinced.

'What is it?' He was annoying her now.

He took a moment before answering. 'What if there is no report?'

'There has to be.'

'Not necessarily.'

Now he was really irritating her.

'What are you trying to say?'

'If McNab didn't die, there would have been no post-mortem.'

The shock of the statement floored her for a second. 'That's utter nonsense.'

'Why?'

'Because I was with him when he died.'

'What if he was revived in the ambulance?'

'He wasn't.'

'You weren't with him, so how do you know?'

'I was at his damn funeral, that's why, as were all his fellow officers.'

'Was it an open coffin?'

'Of course not.'

'So you never saw the body?'

'I was there when his heart stopped, remember?'

'When I was a boy, I fell under ice. When they pulled me out, I'd been dead for four minutes.'

'It's not the same. This is ludicrous. The kind of cover-up you're suggesting . . . people just don't do that.'

Petersson shrugged. 'Who saw the body after it left in the ambulance?'

'I don't know. Hospital staff. Mortuary staff. DI Slater attended the post-mortem, for God's sake.'

'Yet there is no record of it.'

'There must be. I just haven't located it yet.'

Petersson's questions were unnerving her,

195

springing hope in what had been a desert of despair. She couldn't, wouldn't allow that to happen.

'McNab is dead,' she said firmly.

Petersson observed her for a moment.

'*If* McNab *were* alive, he would be a key witness in the case against Kalinin.'

She raised her voice. 'But he's *not* alive.'

'Maybe we're meant to think that.'

Rhona was growing angrier by the second. Her eyes filled with tears.

'What you're suggesting is arrant nonsense. More than that, it is cruel.'

His look softened. 'I'm sorry if I'm distressing you, but I wouldn't say such a thing without a reason.'

'This had better be good,' she warned him.

'I've been investigating Kalinin for almost four years. For most of that time, all my leads have resulted in a dead end. Recently, I managed to hack into some files that led me to believe Kalinin had a supporter on the inside of the justice system.'

'That's when you told me about Slater?'

'It looked like DI Slater was slowing things down, making things easier for Kalinin.'

'In not pursuing the investigation into McNab's death?'

Petersson nodded. 'I began to dig further. That's when I discovered that Fergus Morrison had been murdered and that the news of his death had been kept secret. I also discovered that Anya and her brother had disappeared, supposedly having returned to Russia, although I can find no evidence to support that.'

Rhona thought of the gentle Anya losing her

lover to Kalinin. She had been so afraid she might lose her brother the same way, yet still she had helped McNab.

'All this leads me to believe Kalinin is set on removing anyone who might give evidence against him. Morrison. Probably Anya and her brother.' He paused. 'I also think he's looking for McNab.'

'Kalinin thinks McNab's alive?'

'He has reason to.'

'What reason?' she said sharply.

'Morrison was tortured before he was shot. The torture had all the hallmarks of Solonik.'

Rhona shuddered. The sadistic Solonik had once tortured McNab, almost gouging his eyes out with his thick, blunt fingers.

'Someone had been sharing the safe house with Morrison. Kalinin suspected it was McNab, and Solonik's job was to find out if that was true.'

'And was it?' She couldn't believe what she was saying.

'That's what I'm trying to find out.'

Rhona leaned back, feeling queasy. Petersson moved to sit beside her.

'Are you OK?'

She shut her eyes, willing her stomach to stop churning. 'So what do we do?'

'You locate the post-mortem report, if there is one. Speak to the hospital staff. Use any excuse. Check with the mortuary. Find out who was on duty that night, who drove the ambulance. Use your position, tell them it's about forensic evidence in a case against McNab's killers. Say whatever is necessary to get to the truth.'

'But why would Slater be a part of this?'

'If he's crooked, he's covering his own tracks in

197

some way. He released Kalinin that night, remember? Or maybe the opposite is true and he hid the fact McNab was alive so they could bring him out later to testify. If Kalinin believed him dead, he would give up pursuing him. It's not the first time SOCA have hidden a witness that way, and for that reason.'

'SOCA couldn't hide McNab without help from Scotland. Superintendent Sutherland was in overall charge, he had to have known.'

'That's what we're going to find out.'

She looked at his strong, determined jaw, the ice-blue eyes.

'Why are you doing this?'

'I told you already. We want the same thing.'

When Petersson left, she crawled back under the duvet, but the chill generated by his words would not dissipate.

That was the problem. Petersson's argument made a kind of sense, although she couldn't let herself begin to believe it.

But what if it was true and McNab was alive?

One thing was certain. Now that Petersson had planted a doubt, she would have to find out.

*     *     *

Petersson strode away from Rhona's apartment building. He was convinced that she hadn't known or even suspected that the policeman's death might have been a cover-up. Her shock had seemed entirely genuine. Now that the possibility had been presented, she would pursue it, probably without regard to the consequences. If, as he suspected, McNab was in hiding, she was his best

198

chance of finding him.

It was, he thought with satisfaction, the outcome he had hoped for.

## CHAPTER TWENTY-SEVEN

Magnus thought he had isolated all the Greek phrases from Kira's notebook, although he couldn't be entirely sure. Some had been hidden in calculations and others had been written backwards, which had confused him until he'd fetched a hand mirror.

He had eleven separate words or phrases. Now he set about deciphering them, using the method that had provided him with 'It begins'.

There were twenty-four letters of the Greek alphabet, corresponding for the most part to a single letter of the Roman alphabet. He studied the table he'd printed out.

| | | | | | |
|---|---|---|---|---|---|
| Αα | Alpha | a | Νν | Nu | n |
| Ββ | Beta | b | Ξζ | Xi | x(ks) |
| Γγ | Gamma | g | Οο | Omicron | o |
| Δδ | Delta | d | Ππ | Pi | p |
| Εε | Epsilon | e | Ρρ | Rho | r |
| Ζζ | Zeta | z | Σσς | Sigma | s |
| Ηη | Eta | e(I) | Ττ | Tau | t |
| Θθ | Theta | th | Υυ | Upsilon | u (y,v,f) |
| Ιι | Iota | i | Φφ | Phi | f |
| Κκ | Kappa | k | Χχ | Chi | ch |
| Λλ | Lambda | l | Ψψ | Psi | ps |
| Μμ | Mu | m | Ωω | Omega | o |

199

His method of transcription was simplistic and didn't take into account all the Romanised forms. It also involved making guesses at the letter 'h', which apparently could be represented by a tiny, apostrophe-shaped mark. Despite this, his method did seem to be giving him a result.

The second entry on the diary had appeared one page further on. It was embedded inside a set of parentheses, split in four by plus signs as though representing a calculation.

$$(\Delta\iota + \acute{\omega}\nu + \upsilon\sigma + o\varsigma)$$

Ignoring the plus signs, he wrote down the string of symbols and consulted his table.

$$\Delta \; \acute{\omega} \; \nu \; \upsilon \; \sigma \; o \; s$$

He muttered to himself as he wrote down their Roman equivalents, leaving a space for the letter he wasn't sure of. 'Delta, iota . . . not sure, nu, upsilon, sigma, omicron, and another version of sigma.' It spelt . . .

**Di nusos**

He said it aloud, in case it rang a bell, then realised what the third symbol might be.

'Omega! So another letter "o" . . . and upsilon can be a 'y'. Dionysos.'

Magnus went online and looked the name up. Dionysos was easy enough to find. As the son of the Greek god Zeus, he was the god of wine— among other things—and had inspired a religion. His female worshippers, known as the Maenads, were said to be inspired by him into a state of ecstatic frenzy, through a combination of dancing and drunken intoxication. Apparently they lost all self-control during this state and engaged in uncontrolled sexual behaviour.

He thought of Melanie and her pregnancy, apparently the result of just such a drunken party. There were eleven other phrases to translate. What else would they tell him about Kira and the life she had led in the run-up to her death?

He closed the notebook and set it to one side. Kira's scribblings would have to wait. It was late and he wanted to look over some material before his next meeting with Coulter. He'd been correct in his assumption that an interview would be easier to arrange if DI Wilson requested it. They were due to meet Coulter at nine thirty the following morning.

He retrieved the box file from the shelf and opened it. Immediately he caught Coulter's scent again and wondered if the smell of cologne and sweat would ever leave the well-thumbed pages.

He leafed through until he found the paragraph he sought. In the context of the current investigation, it had a certain resonance.

*I can make them do what I wont becos they worship me and I can make them pregnant*

Coulter's grandiose assessment of his power over women was at least partly accurate, if the story of his nine offspring was true. His current prison correspondence also suggested certain women were drawn to him, possibly increasingly so since his work on the dolls had become public.

Magnus had found Coulter manipulative, powerfully so. But he had to admit that he had played the role of reformed character well, particularly during their time together in the workshop. He could imagine the man making a strong impression on women using that act.

He recalled Dr Shan's guardedness when discussing her patient. Had Coulter managed to manipulate Dr Shan's thought processes the way he'd done with other women? If he had, it might account for the doctor's displeasure at Magnus's appearance on the scene. Maybe she wanted to keep the study of Coulter to herself.

Those sent by the courts to a State Hospital were rarely released, and medication was used to keep symptoms of their mental illness at bay. Patients who had turned their lives around and now contributed in some way to society were few and far between.

If Coulter had proved to be such an exception, then there was cause for celebration. A visible success for Dr Shan.

*If* Coulter had reformed.

It all came down to your understanding of the concept of evil. From what Magnus had read and seen, he was inclined towards the view that true psychopathy was innate and could never be reversed. If Coulter had been mentally ill at the time of the murder and had been treated for it, then he was a success. If, on the other hand, he was a psychopath, then he was reflecting back what he knew Dr Shan wanted to see, and taking pleasure from his manipulation of her. Magnus believed the latter to be the case.

A flurry of rain splattered the windscreen, and Bill flipped on the wipers.

'The tech boys are of the opinion the video is of a doll, not a live baby,' he said. 'They say the flicker we saw was caused by the camera moving. Also, DS Clark has spoken to the other members of the Daisy Chain. Their stories are all the same. Too much to drink at a party, had sex, got pregnant.'

'Pretty high hit rate.'

'I suspect we're talking about more than one try. Despite what they all say, I think there was a pact, probably instigated by Kira.'

They lapsed into silence. Ten minutes later, the bulk of the State Hospital came into view. Their admittance was swift, and this time they didn't need to wait for Dr Shan to escort them; the receptionist took one look at Bill's ID and let them through immediately.

Dr Shan was waiting for them on the other side of security, looking, Magnus thought, as composed as ever. He had picked up the scent of roses before they spotted her. She acknowledged his smile before greeting Bill.

'Detective Inspector Wilson, I presume.'

'Dr Shan. Thank you for arranging the meeting so quickly. I assume you haven't told Coulter what it's about?'

She shook her head. 'I only mentioned Professor Pirie's visit. Mr Coulter knows nothing about you accompanying him.'

'Good.'

'If you'll come this way please.'

They went back down the corridor—the smell of disinfectant overwhelming—to the interview room Magnus had used on his previous visit. A few minutes later Coulter arrived, accompanied as before by a pair of male orderlies. He paused at the door, registering Bill's presence. Magnus thought he saw pleasure cross Coulter's face, but it resumed a neutral expression as he took a seat opposite them at the table and waited for an introduction.

'Mr Coulter, I'm Detective Inspector Wilson. I'd like to ask you a few questions.'

As before, the air about Coulter seemed to buzz with energy. Magnus wondered if Bill was picking up on it too.

'What about?'

'Your dolls.'

Coulter gave a sly smile. 'You want to buy one, Detective Inspector?'

Bill ignored the question. 'I understand you make them to order?'

Coulter nodded.

'Would you recognise a doll you'd made?'

'They're my babies. Of course I would recognise them.'

Bill took a photograph from the envelope he carried and slid it across the desk. Magnus was surprised to note it didn't feature the doll from the park.

Coulter swiftly glanced at the picture.

'I never made that.'

'What about this one?' Bill pushed another photograph forward.

Coulter made an exasperated noise. 'These are crap, production line stuff. Mine are special.'

A third photo was pushed across the table.

This time Coulter's face lit up. 'Now you're talking. That's my Daisy. Beautiful, isn't she?' He picked up the picture and examined it closely.

'That one is definitely yours?'

'I'd know Daisy anywhere. See that angel's touch. It took me forever to get that right.' He met Bill's eyes. 'Anyway, I always sign my dolls so no one else can claim my work.'

'Where do you sign them?'

'Inside the head. The doll's name and my initials, JC.'

Magnus was surprised that Coulter had given out the information they sought so easily. Either he knew nothing about the case or he was a very good actor.

Bill abruptly rose to his feet.

'Thank you very much for your help, Mr Coulter.'

The man's jaw dropped. 'That's it?'

'Yes.'

Coulter's eyes darted between Bill and Magnus. 'Where did you find Daisy?'

'What makes you think we found it?'

A flash of fury sparked in Coulter's eyes, but his tone was nonchalant when he answered.

'Daisy's mother would have told you who made her, so you didn't get Daisy from her.'

Coulter was no fool.

'What was her name?' said Bill.

'Who?'

'The woman who ordered the doll.'

Coulter looked like a man who was back in charge. 'I only remember the dolls' names.'

'I can check with prison records to find out

205

where it was sent.'

'You do that, Officer.'

Magnus wondered if it was all over. Each man was silent, waiting for the other to speak. Magnus watched Coulter closely. He could sense the adrenalin surging through the man, the air around him sizzled with it.

'Aren't you going to ask me who I'm working on at the moment?'

'What are you working on at the moment?'

'Her name's Melanie. The professor knows that. Don't you, Professor?'

Coulter had been on the edge of his seat, desperate to say the doll's name.

Bill indicated to the orderlies that they were ready to leave, but Magnus could see Coulter wasn't finished. There was something else he wanted to say. If Bill knew that too, he didn't show it, and they were at the door before Coulter succumbed.

'I remember the woman's name now. The one that ordered Daisy.'

They stood waiting.

Coulter looked triumphant. 'Reese-Brandon, that was it. Mrs Reese-Brandon ordered Daisy.'


## CHAPTER TWENTY-EIGHT

'I think he has a contact on the outside,' Magnus said.

'I agree. And I think that contact is aware of information not known by the general public.'

'Which means it's someone closely connected to

the case.'

They had adjourned to Dr Shan's office after the interview. Bill had insisted on speaking to her before he left the premises. Someone had shown them there and gone in search of the doctor.

'You interviewed him two days ago. Did he give any indication then of knowing about Kira's death?'

Magnus thought back. 'I didn't know myself then. We sparred a bit verbally, then he asked if I wanted to see his workroom. He did some work on Jacob. I got the impression he was showing off. Then he mentioned that his next order was called Melanie.'

'Did he make a point of telling you the doll's name?'

'Perhaps, but at the time the fact of his naming the dolls seemed abhorrent to me, so I remember it more because of that. I think he liked making me feel uncomfortable.'

'I think Coulter knew we were here today because we'd found the doll,' said Bill.

It was almost impossible to keep developments secret; news travelled even if it wasn't made public, and the two boys who had found Daisy wouldn't have been able to keep quiet about it. But Coulter was locked up. Bill had a gut feeling that Coulter had a source directly linked to the case.

'Possibly,' replied Magnus. 'But remember that Coulter's a skilled liar. He's just as likely to have made that story up about Kira's mother ordering the doll, particularly if he's been following the story on the news.'

The door opened and Dr Shan came in, looking concerned.

'The orderly said you wanted to talk to me before you left.'

'Something Coulter said suggested he has a contact on the outside directly linked to the case we're investigating.'

She considered that for a moment. 'One of his former partners visits him,' she said. 'And as I mentioned to Professor Pirie, Mr Coulter receives a lot of mail, mainly from women. He also makes phone calls, which are allowed of course.'

'Can you supply me with details of any visits he's had in the last month, plus letters he's sent and received, and any calls he's made?'

She looked perplexed. 'I can tell you how many letters arrive and are sent, but we don't read our patients' private mail. We do operate a PIN system for calls.'

'So you know when he made them and the numbers he contacted?'

'In theory.' She hesitated. 'As you're probably aware, Detective Inspector, mobiles make their way in here, despite our best efforts.'

'Then I'd like Coulter's room and workshop searched for one.'

Dr Shan was growing more perplexed by the second. 'Are you sure that's necessary? Mr Coulter has been an exemplary patient up to now. It seems . . .'

Bill interrupted her praise. 'Is there a record of who buys his dolls?'

'Probably.'

'I want to know who bought a doll called Daisy and when it was delivered. I also need to know who ordered the one he's currently working on.'

'But you could have asked Jeff that yourself.'

'I would rather see the official records.'

Bill didn't add that he was disinclined to believe anything Jeff Coulter told him.

*     *     *

On the way out, Bill said, 'You're happy to go past the Reese-Brandon house on our way back?'

'If Kira's mother did order the doll, we need to know,' answered Magnus.

Forty-five minutes later they were back in the city and drawing up outside the house. The same pale yellow Volkswagen was parked in the small driveway to the right of the garden path. Bill hoped that meant Mrs Reese-Brandon was at home, preferably alone.

He rang the bell and saw her approach through the glass again. She hesitated long enough for Bill to think she might not open the door. When she eventually did, he realised from her expression that she thought he'd brought bad news.

'Is it the baby?' Her face was drained of colour.

'No, we haven't found it, I'm sorry. I came to speak to you about another matter.'

She led them into the same room as before, where Bill introduced Magnus and explained about his involvement in the case.

She listened, but Bill wasn't sure she was taking much in. She just wanted to know why they were there.

'We've found your daughter's mobile phone.'

'You have? Where?'

'In the park, a few hundred metres from the funfair.'

She looked as though she might cry.

209

'Ronald bought her that for her birthday. Kira loved that phone. He was very good to her, you know?' She said this as though they might think otherwise.

'Mrs Reese-Brandon, was Kira adopted?'

She looked stunned by the question. 'How do you know that?'

'David told us Kira overheard you and your husband discussing it.

'Kira *knew*?' she cried.

'For most of her pregnancy, I believe.'

Light dawned in her eyes. 'That's why she refused to give up the baby. Why she fought Ronald so hard. Before that happened, they were close.' She gestured to the sideboard where an array of framed photographs depicted Kira at various ages, mostly with her father. 'He used to call her his princess. After she told us she was pregnant, everything changed. It was terrible.' She put her hands to her face. 'I should have told her. I wanted to, but Ronald said it wasn't necessary because I was the only mother she'd ever known.'

Bill gave her a few moments to regain her composure.

'There's something else.'

She looked at him, stricken.

'Did you ever commission a lifelike baby doll? They're known as Reborns.'

She looked at him in amazement. 'How could you possibly know that?'

'You did?'

'Yes.'

'From a man named Coulter?'

'Yes, but . . .'

'Where is this doll now?'

210

'I ordered it for Kira. I thought it would help if she had to give her own baby up for adoption. I sent the dollmaker a baby photograph of Kira. We didn't get her until she was two, but there was a picture of her when she was newly born. The adoption agency gave it to me.'

'Where is the doll?' he repeated.

She grew distressed. 'I tried to give it to Kira. She hated it. She demanded I get rid of it.'

'And did you?'

She shook her head. 'I couldn't. It looked so like her.'

'Where is it?'

'At the back of my wardrobe, in a box.'

'Can you fetch it for me?'

She rose and left the room. She was back minutes later, as they knew she would be.

'It's gone.' She looked wildly at Bill. 'I don't understand.'

He brought out the photograph.

'Is this the doll you ordered?'

She took the photograph and stared at it in amazement. 'Yes. But where did you find it?'

'With Kira's phone, in the park.'

Her legs seemed to give way beneath her. Magnus, moving swiftly, caught her before she hit the ground.


# CHAPTER TWENTY-NINE

David tried Melanie's number again, but it rang three times, then went to voicemail. He slipped the phone out of sight as a teacher came round the

211

corner and busied himself at his locker, pulling out a book he didn't need and stuffing it in his bag. The corridor was busy with students as classes changed rooms for the next period. He was due at Maths, but had no intention of going. He really needed to talk to Melanie. He'd told her not to get in contact, but that was before he discovered the police knew about the Daisy Chain. The feeling of dread that had come over him when he'd discovered those words had been written on Kira's hands threatened to overwhelm him again.

He thought about the possibility that Kira had written the words herself. She had been good at mirror writing and was almost ambidextrous—she could write maths calculations with either hand. But could she have written on both her own hands in mirror writing? And why would she? He wondered again why she had gone into the mirror maze. Had her story of going for candyfloss been the truth? Or had she been planning to meet someone and not told him?

Kira had never told him who the father of her baby was and he hadn't asked. She didn't like being questioned. He knew in his heart that if he hassled her, she wouldn't spend time with him any more. So he'd stayed quiet about everything, listened to her tales of the Daisy Chain gang, done what she asked so he could just be near her. He'd even agreed to take part in one of their sessions, wearing that weird mask. He'd been drunk and high and it had felt great. A kind of release. He'd suddenly realised he didn't have to worry about his sexuality any more. He could accept that he liked to go either way. He wasn't a freak. He could have the best of both worlds. Kira had told him that the

Greek god Dionysos would release him, and she'd been right.

David joined a group walking along the corridor before taking a detour into a nearby toilet. He would wait until everyone got to class and the corridor went quiet, then leave. If a member of staff challenged him, he would make an excuse about going to the dentist, or say he wasn't feeling well. He would go and see Melanie, tell her the police knew about the Daisy Chain, suggest they come clean and tell the Detective Inspector everything that had happened. But before that, he would have to explain to her about the mask.

He left the building unchallenged and headed for the bus stop. While he waited for the bus, he went over the events of that night for the umpteenth time. When Kira had left them at the dodgems, she'd seemed perfectly normal. He'd gone on two rides, both lasting around five minutes, then looked for her for at least half an hour before he got to the mirror maze. Both Sandie and Owen said they'd headed home after the Waltzers. David remembered seeing Sandie messing with her mobile, probably putting in the Waltzer guy's number.

If Kira *had* set out to meet someone, that person had to be the one she saw last and possibly the one who killed her. David forced himself to stop thinking about it, reminding himself that it was the police who solved these things, not him. He was in enough trouble already.

He reached Melanie's house twenty minutes later. There were no cars in the drive, suggesting neither parent was at home. Relieved, he went straight to the front door. Melanie had told him that the cleaner would let anyone in who came to see her. Her parents were another matter.

He rang the doorbell and waited for the sound of footsteps. When there were none, he peered through the glass panel, trying to get a view of something more than the hall, then pulled out his phone and rang Melanie's mobile. When there was no response, he tried the door and it swung open.

David stood in the silent hall. There had to be someone here, otherwise the door wouldn't have been left unlocked. He decided to take a chance and call Melanie's name, his voice echoing in the hallway.

'Mel! Are you here?'

He'd only been in the house once before. Melanie's parents had been away and the Daisy Chain had decided to have one of their sessions here.

He stood outside the bedroom door for a moment, listening, then knocked and called her name again. When there was no response, he opened the door and glanced inside. At first he thought the room was empty, then he realised Melanie was asleep on the bed.

He entered quietly, not wanting to wake her and give her a fright. She was lying on her back with one arm outstretched. He was surprised how thin her arm was, then remembered the sharpness of her hip bones beneath him. That's how he'd realised it was Mel he'd been with at Kira's party, before the mix of alcohol and dope had taken over. Once that had happened, he'd no longer been David Murdoch, mediocre maths student and sad bastard who didn't know which way to swing. Wearing the mask, he'd felt like Dionysos himself.

The blind was pulled down, leaving the room in a half-light. He whispered her name, then had the sudden thought that she might wake up and scream, so he put his hand gently over her mouth, just in case. It only took a second to register that something was wrong.

'Mel?'

He grabbed her arm and shook it. When there was no response, he felt for a pulse at her neck and couldn't find one. Horrified, he sprang to his feet, his mind racing. Melanie was dead, but she was still pregnant. There was none of the gore that he'd seen with Kira. Should he call an ambulance? The police? He dismissed the idea almost immediately. Young women like Melanie didn't just die, even if they were pregnant. The police were already suspicious of him. He couldn't report another dead body. He felt his stomach heave into his throat and made a run for the bathroom. There was no way he could reach the toilet, so he turned and vomited in the bath instead.

When he'd emptied his stomach, he dragged himself up and turned the cold tap on full. Grabbing a back scrubber, he used the wooden handle to clear the plug-hole until the water ran away freely. Then he went to the sink, splashed his face and dried his hands and face on a towel.

He tried to compose himself.

He would leave immediately. Chances were no one had seen him come in. He glanced around, suddenly worried that he had left some trace of himself in the room. Scenes from *CSI* came flooding back to haunt him. Forensic torches flashing round darkened rooms. Gloved hands. Tiny quantities of blood and skin displayed under microscopes.

He recalled with horror everything he'd done since entering the house. The door handles he'd touched. Oh God, he'd touched Melanie, and been sick in the bathroom. His DNA could be on the towel.

He stood frozen.

They would forensically examine the room and the body and find his DNA. They would blame him for Melanie's death.

He forced himself to calm down. All that stuff was fiction. Most of it anyway. He would wipe the door handles with the towel, and Melanie's arm and mouth. He would rinse the bath again and take the towel with him.

He used the towel to turn on the water full blast. Once he was convinced the bath was clean, he wiped the tap. Then he wiped every surface he thought he might have touched, including door handles.

Melanie was proving more difficult. He would have to approach the body again, which he really didn't want to do. He wondered if he should use the damp towel or get a dry one? He knew you should rub fingerprints off with a dry cloth, but what about skin? Could they find his fingerprints on her? Or maybe flakes of his own skin?

His brain couldn't cope with the question.

In the end he decided to use the towel as it was. He forced himself forward and knelt down by the body. Was it his imagination, or had she grown cold and stiff since he'd run into the bathroom?

Her arm felt very thin, the wrist as narrow as a child's. He turned the hand palm up and saw there was something drawn on it. It was a daisy.

Someone had drawn a fucking daisy on her hand. There was no blood, no signs of a struggle, but Melanie hadn't just died because something went wrong with the pregnancy. Someone had murdered Melanie and drawn a daisy on her hand.

Before Kira, he had never seen a dead body. Now he had seen two in the space of a week. The dead Kira haunted his dreams, and now Melanie would join her. He smothered a small sob as he reached out and scrubbed the towel backwards and forwards over the girl's partially open mouth.

Rising swiftly, he stuffed the towel inside his jacket. He had to get out of here before someone came home. He slipped out of the door, avoiding the handle, and stood for a moment on the landing. When he heard nothing, he headed down the stairs.

# CHAPTER THIRTY

Rhona had vowed to concentrate wholly on the outstanding lab work for the duration of the morning. Over lunchtime she would attempt to find out what had happened to McNab's body after she had last seen it. She was still using the past tense in her thoughts about him, and was determined to keep it that way.

In the cold light of dawn, Petersson's suggestion that McNab might have survived seemed hardly credible. That wasn't enough for her; she would have to prove it wasn't true. But that would come later. At the moment she was intent on finding out whether David had fathered Kira's child.

217

In paternity suits, a blood sample was normally taken from the umbilical cord immediately after the birth. A test was performed under controlled circumstances, the results of which could be used to determine paternity. In this instance, she'd taken a sample soon after arriving at the scene.

She studied the pattern of alleles produced from DNA profiles of Kira, the baby and David.

| Locus | Genotype of | | |
| --- | --- | --- | --- |
| | Kira | Child | David |
| D3S1358 | 15, 16 | 16, 17 | 14, 15 |
| VWA | 18, 19 | 18, 18 | 14, 16 |
| D16S539 | 10,11 | 9,10 | 9,10 |
| D2S1338 | 19,23 | 23,24 | 20,23 |
| D8S1179 | 13,13 | 13,14 | 12,13 |
| D21S11 | 28,29 | 28,30 | 28,31 |
| D18S51 | 13,16 | 13,14 | 12,15 |
| D19S433 | 12,15.2 | 15.2,16 | 15,16 |
| TH01 | 9.3,9.3 | 7,9,3 | 7,9,3 |
| FGA | 19,22 | 22,22 | 24,26 |
| Amelogenin | XX | XX | X, Y |

Locus D3S1358 gave the child's genotype as 16,17. Allele 16 must have come from Kira, but 17 certainly didn't come from David. This effectively excluded David from being the father. The pattern was repeated throughout the table. She had the genotype of the father of the missing foetus, but it wasn't David. The result also indicated that Kira had given birth to a baby girl.

Rhona thought back to the video of the Reborn, dressed in a pink sleep suit with a daisy motif. It

218

was common now to be asked if you wanted to know the sex of your baby, and Bill had told her that Kira's mother had ordered the Daisy doll. Maybe Maria had known Kira was going to have a girl.

She would feed the DNA results on the baby's father into the national database where they would be compared to known sex offenders, although the facts up to this point suggested that Kira had deliberately got pregnant.

David definitely wasn't the father, but his actions that night were still under scrutiny, not least because of the shark skin dentricles found on his jeans. She hadn't identified traces of saliva in the environs, so whoever delivered the baby hadn't cleared its airways in the tent. Her hope of obtaining a DNA profile of the assailant that way had met a dead end.

Despite all their efforts, she and Chrissy still had nothing that could be linked to an assailant apart from the yak hair, the dentricles and the likelihood they were capable of mirror writing.

\*　　　\*　　　\*

Rhona tried the city mortuary first because she was known there and her seemingly casual request wouldn't appear odd. Her luck was in. The mortuary assistant on duty was Sandra Boyce, someone she knew personally. She fed her the usual story about studying the bullet casing and wanting to see the results of the internal injury.

'They didn't bring him here. Last I heard, the body went south. Something about it being part of a SOCA case.'

219

That seemed hardly credible. The post-mortem for a death on Scottish soil should have taken place here. Trying not to sound too aghast, Rhona thanked Sandra for her help.

'To be truthful, I was relieved not to be involved. It was too close to home.'

Rhona agreed with her. She rang off. If the mortuary wasn't able to supply her with what she wanted, the next step was the hospital. She realised she had no idea which hospital McNab had been taken to, although she'd assumed it had been the A&E department at the Royal Infirmary. Getting information from the hospital wouldn't be as straightforward as phoning the city mortuary. They weren't going to tell her anything over the phone, no matter who she was. She would have to make a visit.

The drive across town gave her time to wonder what the hell she was doing. It would be easiest to meet up with Bill in private and tell him the whole story, taking a chance on him thinking she had lost her marbles through grief, guilt or a mixture of both. The alternative would be to confide in Chrissy, who would no doubt track the required information down in half the time it would take her. But something stopped her. A much-used phrase of her mother's came to mind: *Least said, soonest mended.* Dragging others into this meant admitting she gave credence to Petersson's arguments. When she had hooked up with the journalist, it was in the hope that he would discover enough to nail Kalinin. Now she was faced with something else entirely, and she had no one to blame but herself.

What if she dragged Bill and Chrissy into this,

and it all went pear-shaped? She didn't want that to happen, particularly after the disciplinary proceedings Bill had had to endure. No. She would make her enquiries alone, or just with Petersson. No one would be exposed, except herself. After all, she wasn't the first bereaved person to wish someone alive again.

\*     \*     \*

Her route to the Royal Infirmary took her into the area where it had all begun. Duke Street, the derelict Great Eastern Hotel, the Molendinar burn, the Necropolis. All haunts of the Gravedigger, whose vengeful actions against those who had caught him had poisoned all their lives. *Every contact leaves a trace.* It seemed Locard's exchange principle applied to more than just physical evidence.

She went straight to Accident and Emergency and was relieved to find it wasn't busy. Her enquiry at reception took her into an office where, once her identity was properly established, she was put in the charge of a woman called Eileen, who would check back on the records of that night for her.

After around ten minutes' searching, Eileen discovered three gunshot admissions that night. Two men and one woman. All three had been taken to surgery.

'Can you give me their names?'

'Who are you looking for?'

'Michael Joseph McNab.'

'That's one of them.' Eileen flipped through a few screens. 'I'm sorry. He died during surgery.'

Surgery? Rhona felt her heart lurch. 'You mean

221

he was alive when they brought him in?'

Eileen studied the screen. 'It says he was revived in the ambulance and taken to the operating theatre.' She regarded Rhona sympathetically.

'How long did he live?'

'The time of death is given as 12.27.'

Rhona thanked her and left. As she exited the building, an ambulance drew up, lights flashing. Immediately a paramedic threw open the back door. He was joined by the driver and they quickly lifted out a figure on a stretcher. It looked serious. She watched in morbid fascination, rewriting what she'd believed until now to be the story of that night. In this version, McNab was the live body on that stretcher, his heart shocked into beating in the ambulance, only to have it stop again on the operating table. So Petersson had been right about one thing. The rest of his story—McNab's recovery and retreat into hiding, SOCA's involvement, Slater's cover-up—were all figments of Petersson's imagination.

As the doors sucked shut behind the paramedics, Rhona roused herself and began to walk briskly away, not caring where she was heading, only knowing that she couldn't get behind the wheel of a car in her present state of mind.

She gave the cathedral a wide berth and went up the road that led across the Bridge of Sighs and into the Necropolis. When she reached the top, she leaned back against the nearest stone edifice and fought to collect her breath and her thoughts.

Suddenly she realised what had been niggling at her since she left the hospital. At first she'd only registered that McNab had been revived in the ambulance and then died on the operating table.

Now the memory of one small detail displayed on that computer screen flashed into her mind.

McNab couldn't have died on an operating table in the Royal Infirmary at twenty-seven minutes past midnight, because at that precise moment she had been holding him in her arms.

## CHAPTER THIRTY-ONE

Bill was eating dinner with Margaret and the kids when the call came through. He vacated his place at the table and went through to the hall. As he closed the door behind him, he caught a glimpse of Margaret's concerned face.

'Detective Sergeant?' He kept his voice low.

'Sorry, Sir.' Janice always started with an apology. She knew the moments with his family were precious, so if she had had to call him at home it must be serious.

'We've received a call from Mrs Jones, Melanie's mother. She found Melanie when she got back from her trip.'

'Dead?' said Bill.

'Yes, Sir.'

'Like Kira?'

'No. The foetus hasn't been removed. But there's a mark on her hands that looks like a daisy.'

'I'll be there shortly.'

\*       \*       \*

Bill observed the girl he'd questioned only the day before. She lay on top of the bed, fully clothed, as

223

though she had simply dozed off. There was no evidence of a struggle, no obvious injuries, no blood. In his time on the Force he'd rarely visited death scenes that looked as peaceful as this one.

Sylvia Barnes, the pathologist, was there already. She rose from her position next to the bed.

'What happened?' Bill asked her.

She indicated the girl's eyelids, where tiny haemorrhages spider-marked the pale skin. 'There are also pressure marks on her chest. Nothing on the neck, so she probably wasn't strangled.' She pointed to the large, square pillow that lay alongside. 'I think she was probably held down and suffocated with the pillow while she slept, but we'll find out for sure at the post-mortem.'

'There was no attempt to remove the baby?'

'No,' she said. 'There is this, however.' She turned Melanie's right palm outwards, exposing a crude attempt to draw a daisy. 'Looks like the deaths are linked.'

'Or someone wants us to think they are,' he said. 'What about the timing?'

'I gather the mother spoke to her late morning, but didn't get a reply at two p.m. She found the body at six thirty p.m. when she got home, and thought Melanie was sleeping until she touched her hand. The time frame corresponds to the body state. Melanie probably died in the last four to six hours.'

Bill stood for a moment, understanding how Melanie's mother might have convinced herself that her daughter was asleep. He would have done the same. Yet something happened to a body when life left it. The stillness of death was unique. Mrs

Jones may have prayed that her daughter was only sleeping, but Bill suspected she'd realised the truth even before she'd touched her.

*       *       *

Mrs Jones looked like an older version of Melanie. She was slim, pretty and impeccably dressed. Shock had drained her face of colour so that her discreetly applied make-up seemed overdone. She was sitting on the sofa her daughter had used when Bill had interviewed her. A female constable sat alongside, a comforting hand on the woman's arm. When Bill asked what had happened, Mrs Jones confirmed the story he'd already heard.

'When I tried to call her the second time, I assumed she was resting. She's been sleeping a lot lately. I thought she was asleep when I went into the room,' she faltered. 'Then I realised there was something odd. She was so still. I touched her hand and it was cold. I called 999. The paramedics were here in minutes, but they said Melanie had been dead for some time.' Her voice broke.

Bill gave her time to collect herself before asking, 'Did Melanie tell you I came to see her yesterday?'

She looked surprised. 'Why did you want to see Melanie?'

'To ask about her friendship with Kira Reese-Brandon.'

'Melanie stopped seeing Kira months ago,' she said sharply.

'Why?'

'Kira was a bad influence on Melanie. First the dieting, then the parties.'

'Tell me about the parties.'

'They were using houses where someone's parents were away. It was all Kira's idea.'

'Was it Kira's idea for them all to get pregnant?'

'It doesn't matter now, does it? Nothing matters. Melanie's dead.'

'Does the name David Murdoch mean anything to you?'

'No.'

'Is there anyone you can think of who might have wanted to harm Melanie?'

'She was never in any trouble until she started going around with Kira.'

## CHAPTER THIRTY-TWO

The house was easy to find. Many of the houses in the area had been converted into expensive flats, but this was one of the few that hadn't. It had retained the graciousness of a well-built Victorian townhouse. And now it had police tape blocking the entrance.

Chrissy had been in the lab when Rhona had returned from her visit to the mortuary and the Royal Infirmary. It had taken all Rhona's powers of deception to weave a convincing alibi, but she suspected she'd been saved from an interrogation by Chrissy's distracted air. Rhona wasn't sure what was worrying her—some concern over baby Michael, problems with Sam, or maybe even something about Sean that she didn't want to tell Rhona.

They seemed to have silently agreed on a trade-off: Chrissy would withhold the Spanish Inquisition if Rhona didn't pry into what was bothering her. In truth, Rhona found this disconcerting. A worried and reticent Chrissy was more distressing than an eager, enquiring one.

When the call came through about Melanie Jones, they decided to both attend the scene. The silence in the car was unusual and uncomfortable. Rhona tried to concentrate on the short drive from the lab and not think about what horror Chrissy was failing to discuss with her. She'd already decided that it did not involve Sam or the baby, since nothing would keep Chrissy from talking about them. Which only left Sean. She suspected something had happened, something Chrissy did not want to reveal.

Rhona set her mind against such musings, reminding herself that she and Sean were over and what he did now was none of her concern. Nothing Chrissy knew would change the situation between them.

She pulled up outside the villa and fetched her forensic bag from the boot. The house was already cordoned off and she'd spotted Bill's car parked nearby. All she knew was that the body of Melanie Jones had been found by her mother at six thirty p.m. under suspicious circumstances. The girl had been almost full term with a baby, and had almost certainly been a member of the Daisy Chain gang. Rhona hoped she was not about to view something similar to what she'd found in the mirror maze.

Bill met them in the spacious hall. 'It's not like before,' he reassured them.

'I'm glad about that,' Chrissy replied fervently.

As Bill led them to the stairs, Rhona caught a

glimpse of a middle-aged woman as she passed a sitting room, a female PC in attendance.

Rhona was struck by the quiet order of the bedroom they entered. She'd imagined a room much like her own as a teenager, messy and lived-in, but Melanie's space was nothing like that. It was pretty and boring, as though an interior decorator had just finished work on it. There was nothing to tell you what kind of teenager Melanie had been. No posters, none of the usual paraphernalia that gave an indication of the character of the room's inhabitant. Only one item seemed incongruous. On one wall was a dark green mask of a man's face with an open mouth, framed by bunches of purple grapes.

Melanie lay opposite on a double bed. If you ignored the faint, sweet scent of a body starting the process of decay, you could imagine her asleep. Rhona was immediately struck by how thin the girl's arms and legs were, only the pregnancy giving a roundness to her form.

'Roy's completed the camera work. I'll leave you to do the rest,' Bill said.

'How long have we got?' Chrissy asked.

'As long as it takes.'

Rhona concentrated on the body and bed area, Chrissy on the remainder of the room. As they'd climbed the stairs, Bill had told them that in Sylvia's opinion Melanie had been suffocated. It was clear why. Petechiae, tiny purple and red spots caused by small areas of bleeding under the skin, were obvious on the face, neck and eyes. Nearby lay a continental-style pillow in a white embroidered case—a convenient murder weapon.

Rhona began the usual routine. Head first, then

228

hands. The body was losing its flaccidity as rigor mortis set in; brought about by complex post-mortem biochemical changes, it invariably began in the face, jaw and neck before spreading downwards to affect the arms, trunk and legs. Within twelve to eighteen hours, the entire body would become rigid, before the rigor mortis disappeared in the same order as it had appeared, twenty-four to thirty-six hours after death.

The eyes that stared up at her were cloudy. In life, the crystalline structure of the cornea was dependent on hydration, but after death the water of crystallisation was lost and the desiccated eye became opaque.

When she'd swabbed and bagged the head, Rhona began to sample the hands. Under different circumstances, the roughly-drawn daisy might not have been recognisable as such; if Melanie and Kira had been killed by the same person, then their skill at mirror writing didn't extend to drawing. Either that, or they had been in a hurry.

After swabbing and securing the hands, Rhona set about taping the exposed skin. The patterned top had been raised—she presumed by Sylvia—to expose the hard mound of the foetus and the girl's pressure-bruised chest. Rhona imagined someone placing a pillow over the face of the sleeping girl, leaning on it to prevent her escaping. Melanie's sudden awakening. Her realisation that she could no longer draw breath. It wouldn't have taken much strength to hold her down long enough to smother her.

She left the clothes in place since there were no bloodstains that could be compromised by the body's removal to the mortuary. Once she'd finished processing Melanie, she bagged the offending pillow. The rest of the bedclothes would have to wait until the body was removed and taken to the mortuary. She took a seat beside the bed and was beginning to write up her notes when Chrissy called her from the bathroom.

'Come take a look at this.'

The en suite was as neat as the bedroom, decorated all in turquoise with a matching bath towel.

'Stand at the door,' Chrissy ordered. 'Take a look round and tell me what's missing.'

Rhona did as requested, scanning the room. When she didn't answer immediately, Chrissy said, 'Beside the sink.'

Rhona followed her pointing finger to a hook, but Chrissy could wait no longer.

'The hand towel. Where's the matching hand towel?'

'OK . . .' said Rhona hesitantly.

'And someone's recently been sick in the bath.' Chrissy indicated something she'd pulled from the plug hole that looked like a cube of carrot. 'I smelt it when I knelt down.'

'Maybe Melanie suffered from morning sickness.'

'In my experience, most people, pregnant or not, usually vomit into the toilet, not the bath. Also, whoever it was tried to use this to clear the plughole.' She waved a wooden back brush at Rhona. 'Another thing, there are no fingerprints. Not on the taps or the door handles. Melanie might have been a bit obsessive about neatness, but I can't see her wiping the handles after she used them.'

Rhona had to agree with that. 'So your theory is?'

'Someone wiped them with the missing hand towel and took it with them.'

It sounded plausible.

'I'll check the toilet seat, then I'm done. Let's hope he had a piss before he left.'

Eventually Chrissy signalled that she was finished and they headed downstairs together. Mrs Jones had disappeared from the sitting room, probably gone to stay with friends or neighbours while the team took over the house. Cold air met them at the open front door, and Rhona pulled down her mask and breathed it in.

'Tidiest bedroom I've ever been in.' Chrissy might be neat at work, but she certainly wasn't at home. 'I don't think the girl had anything to do with the décor. The whole place looks like something out of *Homes and Gardens*.'

'Like you read *Homes and Gardens*,' Rhona laughed.

'You know what I mean,' Chrissy said in distaste. 'Everything matched. Curtains, lampshades, headboard. Even the bloody thingy above the window.'

'The pelmet,' Rhona offered.

'Jesus.' Chrissy shook her head. 'The only thing different was green boy.'

'You mean the mask?'

'Very sexual. Bunches of grapes, an open mouth. I'm surprised her mother allowed it in the house. Definitely worth a closer look. What about you? Anything interesting?'

'No yak hair, if that's what you mean.'

'And the daisy?'

231

'If it was a daisy.'

'An attempt by someone to make us think it was the same perpetrator when it wasn't?'

'Maybe. But the fact that the girls were both pregnant and part of the Daisy Chain gang does suggest a link.'

'We're not in the business of suggestion,' Chrissy said firmly.

'No, but we *are* in the business of asking the right questions.'

Chrissy glanced at her watch, a worried look on her face. 'I'll have to go. Sam's on at the club tonight.'

'Give little Michael a hug from me.'

'You could always come back and see him,' Chrissy offered. 'Sam's cooking dinner before he goes.'

'Tempting, but I'd better hang on here until the mortuary van arrives.'

'See you tomorrow then.' Chrissy looked a little put out. Either there was something she wanted to discuss, or she had sensed Rhona was hiding something from her.

Rhona spent another hour working on her notes before the mortuary van arrived. Once the body was removed, she began stripping the bed and bagging the items, and when she lifted the pillow below Melanie's head, she discovered a mobile. It seemed Melanie had taken her phone to bed with her. Rhona flipped it open and checked for any outstanding messages. No texts, but there were two missed calls. One was her mum, probably calling from the train, and the other was from someone called David. Bill had already left the scene, so she phoned him.

'What time was this call?'

'Two thirty-five.'

'After the mum?'

'Yes.'

'Give me the number.'

She read it out to him.

'Thanks. Are you finished over there?'

'Yes, I'm headed home now.'

'Anything apart from the mobile?'

'Chrissy thinks someone vomited in the bath and it looks like the surfaces and door handles have been wiped, possibly with a hand towel that's been removed.'

'I'll check with her mother about the towel.'

Rhona waited until she was in her car and ready to go before contacting Petersson, who picked up on the first ring. Rhona realised she hadn't rehearsed what to say, although it turned out not to matter.

'Come round to my place,' he said.

'I've just finished work. I need to shower and eat.'

'You can do that here.'

'What's up?'

'You know what's up,' he replied. 'You didn't find the post-mortem report, did you?'

'I—' she began.

'McNab was alive when he entered the hospital.'

She heard herself say, 'He died in the operating theatre.'

Petersson snorted in exasperation, then said, 'I'll see you shortly.' He reminded her of the address. 'I'll have food ready.'

She ended the call, her hand trembling, then sat in silence. She shouldn't be thinking about this,

233

torturing herself with some wild fantasy about people coming back from the dead. She wasn't in a Shakespearean play; in her world, dead people stayed dead. Like the girl she had just processed in that bedroom. She should be thinking about that. She'd told Chrissy their job was to ask the right questions, but her mind wasn't fully on that job. It was elsewhere, in futile pursuit of the impossible.

Her mobile pinged—an incoming text. As if rebuking her for her wandering thoughts, the message from Bill told her she was needed at the post-mortem, scheduled for nine thirty the following morning.

Petersson's flat was in a tall, stately Victorian block near the Botanic Gardens. She took her time getting out of the car and locking it, making a point of not looking up to the second floor window. She knew she was kidding herself, pretending that she could climb back in the car and drive away from Petersson and his wild theories. She had a sudden flash of McNab's ironic grin. How he would have mocked her, called her *Dr* MacLeod in a sardonic tone, with a twinkle in his eye.

What if the shoe had been on the other foot? McNab, she knew, would have gone into the jaws of hell for her, just as he had done for Chrissy.

She walked up the short path to the front door and pressed the buzzer.

'Come on up.'

The door clicked open. The stairwell was lined with maroon and blue tiles in perfect condition, the upper half looking as though it had been newly painted cream. Only the stone stairs betrayed the age of the building, worn down by the countless footsteps of the inhabitants of the century-old building.

Petersson was waiting at the open door. He stood aside to let her enter.

'First on the right,' he instructed.

She hesitated. The hallway was a room in itself, and held a dining table that sat eight people.

'I thought you'd prefer to eat in the kitchen,' he explained.

She went through into a large room that appeared to serve as both kitchen and study. An alcove in one corner, which would have historically contained a bed for a kitchen servant, was now lined with shelves of books and housed various items of computer equipment including three monitor screens. Two places had been set on a circular table next to the window, and Rhona caught the aroma of something cooking in the oven.

'You've time for a shower before we eat,' said Petersson. 'All rooms lead off the hall. I've left the door to the bathroom open for you.'

Rhona wanted a shower desperately, if only to wash off the scent of death. She made her way back through the hall, suddenly awkward in someone else's home and resisting the desire to open the numerous other doors that led from the hall. The bathroom turned out to be more of a wet-room, with blue corner tiles enclosing a many-spouted shower unit and a drain in the tiled floor. The lack of a cubicle made her feel exposed, and she locked the door before stripping off. She ignored the various wall spouts in favour of the rose fitting overhead, and was surprised by the power of the water that cascaded down on her. She found a tube of something that professed to be both shampoo and shower gel. It had a strong astringent smell, obviously male, but she didn't care. It was better than the lingering aroma of the chemicals associated with forensic work. She applied it liberally all over.

There was a knock on the door as she turned off the water.

'There's a robe behind the door,' called Petersson. 'Might be a bit big though.'

She ignored the offer and put her own clothes back on.

Petersson was dishing up when she entered the kitchen. He'd switched off the fluorescent strip lights above the work surfaces, and softer wall lights now lit the room.

'Take a seat.'

'It smells good.' She realised just how hungry she was.

'Venison casserole and a decent red.'

He poured a good measure of wine into each of the balloon glasses.

'I'm driving,' she reminded him.

'The meat and veg will soak it up.'

They ate in silence, for which Rhona was grateful, as it allowed her time to work out what she planned to say. She wondered if Petersson was thinking the same thing.

When they'd finished the silent meal, he lifted away the empty plates and offered her more wine, which she declined.

'Coffee would be good,' she said.

He set up the coffee machine, then stacked the dishes in the dishwasher.

'That was delicious. Thanks.'

'No problem. Are you happy to talk in here?'

'I assume you're not bugged?' she joked weakly.

'I know *I'm* not,' he said in all seriousness.

She set her coffee mug back down. 'You're suggesting I might be?'

'I have no idea. Do you?'

The thought had never occurred to her.

He smiled to put her at ease. 'I was only joking.'

She suspected he hadn't been. 'All this suspicion must come with the territory,' she said.

'Journalists in Russia are routinely murdered. Especially when they're intent on unmasking the *mafiya*.'

'This is Scotland,' she reminded him.

'Now merely an outpost of the Kalinin empire.'

She was unnerved by the intensity of his blue eyes. There was something about Petersson that reminded her of the Russian.

'I wouldn't have survived this long if I hadn't taken precautions,' he said.

There was a pause. Each of them was waiting for the other to open the real conversation. Rhona decided it might as well be her.

'The mortuary had no post-mortem report. They suggested it went south.'

'And the hospital?'

'As I said, they told me McNab was revived in the ambulance, but later died in surgery.'

'Mmmm.' He regarded her steadily. 'And?'

'And what?'

'I've seen the hospital records.'

'Why? How?'

'It's not that difficult. NHS Scotland has made a recent habit of leaving patient records lying around . . . I did a piece about it for a well-known local paper.'

'Then why ask me to do it?'

'If there was something wrong with their record of events, I thought you would spot it.'

She nodded. 'The time of death was wrong.'

He raised an eyebrow and waited.

'They registered his death at 12.27. He was with me then, not even in the ambulance. I was searching for a pulse, so I looked at my watch. But there's no reason for the hospital to falsify the time.'

'No. But from my experience, when people start amending data, idiosyncrasies occur.'

'If McNab was alive he would have contacted me by now,' she said sharply. It was what she had been thinking all along.

'And put you in danger?'

'He would have found a way.'

'Maybe he has, and you didn't pick up on it?'

'No.' She studied his expression. 'What else do you know?'

'SOCA moved a man to a new safe house recently, after a tip-off he was in danger of discovery. That man was described by my contact as "a dead man walking".'

'What?' She jumped as though someone had laid a red-hot poker against her bare skin. 'That's what the text said. The one I thought came from you.'

Horrible possibilities began to crowd her mind. McNab, alive and in danger. Perhaps the text was a call for help? He'd never trusted Slater, always thought he was on the make. But did Slater even have anything to do with this?

'What do we do?'

'You give me your phone, and I find out where

238

that text came from.'

'Have you got the software to do that?'

'Yes.'

She thought about Roy Hunter and his mobile tracker programme, which had recently located a hitman who'd killed an innocent couple to punish their gangster son. She should give Roy the mobile, ask *him* to find out where the message came from.

As if reading her mind, Petersson said, 'It's better if we keep this to ourselves.'

'Better for who?'

'When you contacted the Fiscal about McNab's post-mortem, what was the reaction?'

Rhona recalled the sudden silence on the phone, the guarded replies. Petersson smiled grimly.

'You and me. No one else. That way we keep him safe.'

'McNab is dead.'

'Say it often enough and you might convince yourself.'

Rhona rose abruptly from the table. 'I have to go.' She pulled on her jacket. 'How long do you need the mobile for?'

'I'll work overnight. You can have it in the morning.'

She reluctantly gave him her phone. 'Write down your number for me.'

He took a card from the desk drawer and handed it to her. 'It's on here. What time do you leave for work?'

'I have a post-mortem at nine thirty.'

'I'll drop the mobile off by eight.'

She didn't look back as she descended the stairs, but she knew he was at the door watching her.

Giving him her mobile felt too intimate, more so than having sex with him. By the time she'd reached her car, she was already regretting it.

## CHAPTER THIRTY-THREE

It was a double post-mortem. Sylvia had removed the foetus, which now lay alongside the mother. It had been a girl. This time they had no need to take blood from the umbilical cord, as they had the baby itself to check for paternity.

Sylvia's first thoughts on Melanie's death were proved correct as the telltale signs of suffocation were recorded. Melanie had been undernourished, especially considering her pregnancy; and the baby, although full term, was less than five pounds in weight.

They found a daisy tattoo, just like Kira's, etched on her upper thigh. Apart from the daisy scrawled on her hand, there was nothing else that suggested the same perpetrator for both killings. Yet the sense that the deaths were linked was strong in everyone's minds.

The manner of death recorded, Rhona and Bill left Sylvia to finish up and went together to change out of their gowns.

'What happened about the mobile number?' Rhona asked him.

'It goes to voicemail, a standard recording.'

'So we don't know if it was David Murdoch.'

'We're checking on it,' said Bill. 'I want you to swab everyone who was at those parties. DS Clark has a list of names from the other girls in the Daisy

240

Chain. This gang and their pregnancy pact caused the death of these two girls. Neither death was a random act.'

'Where do you want me to do this?'

'Make it at the station. Let's scare the shit out of them. That way we might get some answers.'

'When?'

'As soon as possible.'

'You know David isn't the father of Kira's baby?'

'I saw the result you posted up.' He paused. 'There's something else, which may be important. Melanie Jones told me that Kira was afraid of clowns. She had a phobia. And you said the hair you found under her fingernail was the kind used in clown wigs.'

\*      \*      \*

Rhona drove to Petersson's flat immediately after the post-mortem. She had waited as long as she could before leaving for the mortuary, calling Petersson constantly from her home phone but getting no answer. She had kept her irritation under control while in the mortuary and during her conversation with Bill, but now she was angry. Had Petersson taken her for a ride? What was he really up to? Why had she believed any of his stories, and given him her phone?

As she drove, she decided that if Petersson wasn't at his flat she'd go straight to Roy, tell him she'd lost her mobile and ask him to track it for her.

She found a metered parking place but didn't have the change to buy a ticket, which only added to her fury. When she eventually pressed the buzzer, she was seething. There was no reply. She pressed for another occupant and requested entry, and was relieved to hear the door catch click open.

As she climbed the stairs to the second level, her mind was whirling with conspiracy theories. Petersson had wanted her mobile, and had been very persuasive. Details of all her contacts, both professional and personal, were on that phone. So was the strange message. Perhaps Petersson wanted access to the message because he intended to find McNab himself. Her blood ran cold—what if Petersson had been working for Kalinin all the time?

She stood outside for a moment, trying to marshal her thoughts, then pressed the bell firmly, hearing it resound throughout the flat. She was surprised to hear shuffling footsteps on the parquet flooring of the hall. The door opened and a crumpled and bleary-eyed Petersson stood before her.

'What the hell do you think you're doing? You told me you'd have my mobile back by eight.'

'Rhona, come in.' He stood back to let her enter. 'I'm sorry. I must have fallen asleep.'

'I rang you a million times.'

'My mobile's set to silent.'

'You're lucky you've *got* a mobile.'

'I'm sorry. Yours is in here.'

She followed him into the kitchen. The table, which had been so neatly set for dinner the previous night, was now strewn with empty coffee cups and food wrappers. He walked to the desk and picked up her mobile.

'It took longer than I anticipated. I remember sitting down at the table with a coffee, then nothing until I heard the doorbell just now.'

Relief swept through her as she took the mobile from him.

'I hope it was worth it,' she said.

'It was. Come and see.'

He pulled up another chair and motioned her to join him at the computer, then brought up a city centre map with three red markers on it.

'Central London,' he said. 'That message came from a pay-as-you-go mobile in the Hammersmith area. It was connected to a network four times in twelve hours. Since then, nothing.'

'From where?'

'I only have the nearest cell site used, so I can't be exact.'

'And the number?'

'I've tried calling it. I get a dead tone.'

'How does that help us then?' She knew her voice was rising in pitch and annoyance, but couldn't prevent it.

He ignored her. 'Who do you know who might call you from Hammersmith?'

Had Sean and Sam not been back in Glasgow, she would have said one of them. Otherwise, she could think of no one.

'It could have been a mistake, a wrong number. I've sent a text to the wrong person before now.'

'It was the code name my contact gave me.'

'I only have your word on that.'

He said something sharply in Icelandic. It sounded like a curse.

'Look, if you don't believe or trust me, I suggest we call it quits.'

It wasn't the reaction she'd expected. 'I didn't say I didn't trust you.'

'But you obviously don't.'

'I'm a scientist. I believe in things I can see and measure.'

He laughed suddenly, an infectious sound. It transformed his face, his eyes crinkling in pleasure.

'What?' she said, annoyed that he might be laughing at her.

'OK, I'm having a thought, which of course you can't see or measure. Does that mean it doesn't exist?'

'I don't think that's relevant.'

'I do. The thought is this: DS Michael McNab is holed up somewhere in Hammersmith. He may or may not be under the protection of SOCA. In any case and for some reason or other, he is trying to get in touch with you. This is, I believe, endangering his continued existence.'

'Then what did we bury in a coffin in that cemetery plot?'

'It's usually a set of weights.'

'Usually?' she said in disbelief.

'I know of at least five burials of men who are walking about with new identities and lives. If McNab *is* alive, you will never know him by that name again, unless we get Kalinin.'

'You said three calls were made, as well as the text to me. What were the other numbers?'

'I'm still trying to trace the recipients.'

'Show me the other numbers.'

He didn't move for a moment, and the thought crossed her mind that the other numbers didn't exist, but then he pointed and clicked on the screen. A tag opened up at the other two red dots. Each speech balloon contained a number and a time.

244

Rhona didn't recognise either number, although that didn't necessarily mean anything. She had a poor memory for phone numbers and struggled to remember her own, resorting to programming it in her address book under 'Me'. She remembered how oddly Chrissy had behaved earlier, as if she'd had something to say. On a hunch, she retrieved Chrissy's number. It wasn't a match.

'I've done that already. Neither number matches any in your address book.'

She felt obscurely irritated at this breach of her privacy, although it had been the obvious thing for him to do.

'So where do we go from here?' she said.

'I think you should leave it to me now.'

'Why?'

'You found out what you could about the post-mortem and the hospital.'

'I haven't finished with that yet.'

'I think you've done enough.'

'That's not for you to say,' she responded angrily.

'I'll keep you informed.' He sounded equally determined.

'I think it's time we spoke to Bill.'

She was pleased to see the suggestion rattled him.

'I wouldn't advise that. Not unless you want McNab to die a second time.'

'Bill could never be a threat.'

'I agree, but if even a rumour of this gets out and Kalinin gets wind of it . . . I told you someone on the inside is helping him.'

'And what if it's you?' she snapped.

He stared at her in amazement. 'You actually

think I work for Kalinin?'

'Do you?'

He regarded her for a moment, then drew up his shirt, exposing the long purple scar.

'I got this while on an assignment in the wake of the murder of a Russian journalist, who was about to reveal some interesting international connections of Kalinin's. I followed her leads just short of the man himself. I had names, mobile data, dates, times.'

Rhona couldn't take her eyes off the scar.

'I regained consciousness in a hospital in Prague with a drain in my side. According to the doctor, the knife went up and under the ribcage, straight for the kidneys. I'm lucky to be alive, or so the doctor said.' He let the shirt fall. 'I told you. We both want the same thing.'

After Rhona had left, Petersson sat down abruptly at the table. His side ached as though it had never healed. It was always the same when he was tired. He rubbed at the scar absentmindedly.

Despite his exhaustion, his performance, he decided, had been adequate. Nevertheless, he wondered how much she had believed. He had been warned about Dr MacLeod. Only now did he acknowledge that he had not taken the warning seriously enough.

## CHAPTER THIRTY-FOUR

Magnus closed the notebook. Eleven phrases, not all sequential, yet all seeming to follow the same theme. Kira had been studying Greek as well as

Maths, he knew; what he'd found embedded in the differential calculus and complex number calculations could be her playing with her newly found knowledge, or something more significant.

He studied the list of transcribed words on the notepad.

| | |
|---|---|
| ιτβεγινς | it begins |
| Διωννσος | Dionysos |
| σετΣυςΦρεε | sets us free |
| διΔμΥρΡαΛυΣτ | did Myrrha lust |
| ΔαύγτεΡλουερ | daughter lover |
| ισΜεΛλιςδΗσιρε | I smell his desire |
| ΣεξιςΚοντροΛ | sex is control |
| ΘΗνφολλΩ | they follow |
| ΛικΕςέεΠ | like sheep |
| νοθινγιΣφοΡβιΔδεν | nothing is forbidden |
| εΥΗρυΘινΓιςπΛεασΥρε | everything is pleasure |

Myrrha, daughter of Theias of Assyria. Mother of Adonis. Was Kira likening herself or another to Myrrha? Ovid wrote of Myrrha in his *Metamorphoses Book X*. Myrrha, both daughter and lover to Theias. Her story was a disturbing one, as all Greek myths tended to be. But did it have any relevance to what had happened to Kira?

Magnus had no desire to expose himself to ridicule. He had interpreted something wrongly before, with grave consequences. One thing he was sure of—Kira may have been a model and gifted pupil, but she had another life. The theme of sexual awakening was strong, and the reference to Dionysos helped paint a picture of imagined or real excess. Bill had mentioned parties held by the Daisy Chain gang, where they indulged in alcohol,

247

drugs and unprotected sex.

Most—if not all—teenagers had lives their parents knew nothing about, just as parents had their own secrets, sexual or otherwise. Bill had told him that Kira's tutor had described her as having celebrity status, the rest of the gang fashioning themselves on her. This was not unusual in teenage peer groups; teenage behaviour was concerned predominantly with conforming to the norm, with not being singled out in any way as different. And Kira had decided what the norm should be in the Daisy Chain. Where she went, the rest would follow, so if she got pregnant, they must do the same. As a group they had taken hedonism to extremes, and in that sense they could be seen as acting out the role of the Maenads, Dionysos' female worshippers.

The reference to Myrrha, however, had different implications. Magnus decided to call Bill and talk to him directly about it.

The detective answered almost immediately and launched into a disturbing story concerning Melanie Jones. It was the first Magnus had heard of the second death. Even as he listened to Bill's account of Melanie's mother finding the body, and the post-mortem confirming suffocation, Magnus was questioning his interpretation of the diary.

'Is it possible,' Bill was asking, 'that Coulter was aware of some threat to Melanie and her baby?'

Magnus recalled Coulter's watchful eyes. Had he been looking for a reaction to his use of the name 'Melanie' for the new doll?

'I don't know,' he said honestly, no longer trusting his own judgement.

'What if we're right, and Coulter does have

248

someone on the outside who's feeding him information, or even acting on his behalf?'

'You think Coulter could be controlling this from inside the prison hospital?'

'It wouldn't be the first time murders have been masterminded by prisoners. The questions are: how could Coulter achieve that, and why would he want to?'

'I can tell you why, easily,' Magnus said. 'I don't believe Coulter has changed, merely adapted his behaviour to suit his circumstances, a common skill in psychopaths. Everything he does is concerned with increasing his position and influence. He could be playing all of us, including Dr Shan.'

'Well, not any longer.' Anger crackled in Bill's voice.

Magnus changed the subject. 'I called you because I may have found something in Kira's notebook.' He explained about the Dionysos reference and the cult of the Maenads, then waited for Bill's reaction, feeling a little foolish.

When Bill spoke, he sounded intrigued. 'This Greek god, Dionysos—if you were fashioning a mask of him, what would it look like?'

'A mask? Well, he's often associated with wine, so probably a vine or grapes would be incorporated.'

'We found one in Melanie's room. Green, smiling, with bunches of purple grapes around his face.'

'That sounds like it could be him.'

So his interpretation of the Greek references to Dionysos in the notebook might be correct. Magnus went on to describe the part that disturbed him the most—the story of Myrrha and her relationship with her father. He could sense the tension on the other end of the line as Bill listened without interruption.

When he finished, Bill said, 'Thanks, Magnus. That's one thing I hadn't thought of. More fool me.'

## CHAPTER THIRTY-FIVE

Bill called the meeting to order. The men and women in the incident room had been working flat out for seven days without finding the missing baby, and they now had another dead girl.

Most already assumed Kira's baby to be dead too. Bill hoped they were wrong.

He glanced round as silence descended, taking note of Magnus at the back next to Rhona. They were already aware that he would call on them as required.

The important thing was to try and present an overview of the situation, since so many of the team had been working on their own piece of the investigation. To keep up the momentum, everyone should be made aware of how important their own contributions were. Bill dealt with the most recent death first.

'There were no signs of a break-in, and when Melanie's mother arrived home, the front door was off the latch. Either Melanie had failed to lock it when she went for a nap, or she let her killer in because she knew and trusted them.'

They studied Roy's recording of Melanie's bedroom. Everything looked so normal, and in

250

death Melanie appeared simply to be asleep on the bed. It was nothing like the horrific scene in the mirror maze.

'Melanie was suffocated, probably with one of her pillows. There were no signs of a struggle. She was a slight girl, easily overpowered, especially if the perpetrator found her asleep. Hopefully forensics will tell us more when they've processed the material.' Bill then brought up a photo of the mask on the screen, and asked Magnus to come forward.

Magnus explained about the Maths notebook as the relevant pages replaced the mask overhead. There were a few groans and mutterings from the assembled team about having been crap at Maths at school, but Magnus's clear explanation and delivery soon had them all listening intently.

He showed them the opening message which he translated as 'It begins', then explained how he had pieced together the name Dionysos. He flicked the image back to the photograph of the mask and explained the cult of the Greek god and the young female Maenads who worshipped him.

Bill interrupted, seeing that the team were wondering what this had to do with Melanie's murder, and filled them in on the drunken teenage parties and the girls' apparent obsession with pregnancy. Then he ran through the details of their meeting with Coulter.

'We think someone may have been feeding Coulter inside information about the case. Ian, Sarah, you've been looking into this—what have you come up with?'

DC Ian Murphy looked embarrassed to be put on the spot and stumbled a bit as he stood, to catcalls from the floor.

Bill raised his hand to silence them.

'Let's hear it.'

Murphy cleared his throat, then read from his notebook. 'Geri Taylor, Coulter's former partner and the mother of the infant he killed, is still in contact with him. In fact, she has visited him twice in the last month.'

That pronouncement sent shocked whispers around the room. Murphy waited until they subsided.

'Apart from Ms Taylor, eleven women write to him regularly, one more frequently than the others.'

'Who is she?' Bill asked.

'Her name is Caroline Sweet.'

Someone hummed the opening bars of Neil Diamond's 'Sweet Caroline', causing some slightly sheepish laughter. Bill ignored it.

'Address?'

'A post office box, Sir.'

'Coulter said someone called Caroline suggested he send me his diary,' said Magnus.

'OK, we need to find this woman. What about phone calls?'

'He makes one every fortnight, to Geri Taylor.'

'That's it?'

'Yes, Sir.'

'No sign of a mobile?'

'Not yet, Sir.'

Bill didn't doubt that Coulter was using means other than the official PIN-controlled calls to keep in touch with the outside world.

'What about the workroom? He may have hidden the components of a mobile phone among the doll material,' Magnus suggested.

'Was the workroom searched?' Bill asked Murphy.

'Dr Shan says it was.'

'I want that room searched again, forensically this time.'

Bill turned back to address the room. 'The doll found in the park was modelled on Kira as a child and bought by Mrs Reese-Brandon, who says it went missing from her house. Kira knew about the doll, so she may have mentioned its existence to the other girls or to David. We need to know who was aware that doll existed. Also, Coulter says he's working on a Reborn he calls Melanie. He made a point of telling us the name.' He paused. 'If Coulter knew about these girls, I want to know how and why.'

Rhona was next up. She came forward, and Bill thought how pale and tense she looked; McNab's murder had hit her hard, and he wasn't convinced she'd dealt with it yet. He'd wanted to talk to her but had held off, hoping that his own discreet enquiries about Kalinin and SOCA might soon bear fruit. He made up his mind to have a quiet word with her on her own as soon as possible.

Rhona began, her voice clear and steady. 'We retrieved yak hair from under Kira's fingernail, which is often used in making high quality wigs for clowns. Kira was known to have had a phobia about clowns.'

Bill nodded. 'If there was anyone dressed as a clown in the vicinity that night, I want to know about it.'

Rhona went on. 'The blood from the umbilical cord proved that David Murdoch was not the

253

father of Kira's baby, although we recovered two dentricles from his jeans. Shark skin dentricles, probably from the knife used to section Kira after she was rendered unconscious using chloroform.'

Someone at the back raised a hand. 'How would the boy have known how to perform a Caesarean section? Do we know if he had any medical training?'

Rhona shook her head. 'We don't think so, but full details of the Caesarean method, particularly the older version, are available on the internet. Butchers' knives and hunting knives, both of which often have rough shark skin handles to prevent the hand slipping in blood, can also easily be bought online.'

Bill allowed a few moments for all that to sink in, then clapped his hands together decisively.

'OK, I want David Murdoch, Sandie Stewart-Smith and Owen Hegarty brought back in. I also want all the kids known to have attended these parties to be fingerprinted and swabbed.'

Bill dismissed the team, aware of Magnus's curious eyes on him. Bill had decided to ask the professor not to mention the Myrrha angle to the team yet. It was too explosive. Rhona and Magnus followed him into the office and he closed the door behind them before he spoke.

'We're going back to see Kira's parents. I want them both swabbed.'

'Are they suspects?' Rhona said.

Bill turned to Magnus. 'Tell Rhona what you told me.'

# CHAPTER THIRTY-SIX

'Is this really necessary?'

Ronald Reese-Brandon had aged ten years since their last meeting. The arrogant façade had dissolved, allowing a glimpse of the tortured soul beneath.

'It's useful for elimination purposes.'

Kira's mother sat on the sofa, clasping and unclasping her hands, occasionally looking up at her husband as though for guidance, which was never forthcoming. Mr Reese-Brandon finally gave in and slumped down beside her.

'OK, let's get it over with.'

Rhona produced the mouth swabs. Kira's mother looked as though she might burst into tears at any moment and her husband was grimly silent, but both of them submitted to swabbing.

When it was over, Reese-Brandon quickly rose.

'Now can I get back to work?'

'Can you spare a few more minutes? I wanted to ask you both a couple of questions about the doll your wife bought.'

His pale face flushed.

'What doll?'

'Your wife told us she purchased a Reborn doll, made to look like Kira as a baby.'

Reese-Brandon turned on his wife. 'I told you not to do that. I forbade it.'

She cringed.

'You were unaware she had bought the doll?' said Rhona.

'We discussed it. I told her it was a terrible idea.

255

The doll would only remind Kira of the baby. We wanted her to forget it and get on with her life.'

'Nevertheless, your wife did purchase the doll and showed it to Kira.'

'I never knew this.' He threw his wife a look of contempt.

'We found the doll in the park not far from the funfair. According to your wife, she thought it was still here, in a box in her wardrobe.'

Reese-Brandon had regained some of his strength.

'I had no idea the doll existed, here or anywhere else.'

'So you didn't remove it from the wardrobe?'

'How could I, when I didn't know it was there?' His tone was exasperated.

'You're sure about that?'

'Of course I'm sure.'

'I also need to take your fingerprints.'

'This is ridiculous!'

'Dr MacLeod will do it here, or you can come down to the station.'

'My daughter's been murdered and you spend your time hounding us instead of looking for the culprit?'

Bill didn't answer. Reese-Brandon couldn't refuse, no matter how much he blustered.

When Rhona had finished processing the prints, Kira's mother looked as though she could take no more, but Bill had to harden his heart and keep questioning her.

'Melanie told me that Kira was afraid of clowns. Is that true?'

Mrs Reese-Brandon raised her head wearily. 'Yes, she was terrified of them. I don't know why, but it started when she was very young. If she went to a birthday party and they had a clown, we would have to leave.'

'So if someone wanted to frighten Kira, that would be the way to do it?'

'She would have had a panic attack. It was the only thing that truly scared her.'

*     *     *

'What did you think?' Bill asked Rhona, once they were in the car.

'The father was dominant. The mother submissive, although not averse to going against his wishes in secret.'

'Did he know about the doll, do you think?'

'He looked pretty disgusted when the subject came up,' replied Rhona.

'If the doll was in the cupboard, then only a few people had access to it. Kira, possibly David, maybe the gang, and of course, her parents.'

'I didn't get any prints from the doll, but there was a partial on the mobile.'

'I'd like that checked against everyone who went to Kira's parties.'

'I'm not sure we have enough, but we can give it a try.' Rhona paused. 'Most people wouldn't willingly give their mobile away. Even to a friend. It's much too personal.' She bit her lip anxiously. 'Can you drop me at the lab?'

He nodded. 'There was something I wanted to talk to you about before you leave.' Bill watched her jaw tighten, but her voice was deliberately casual.

'Oh, what?'

'I've been making some discreet enquiries about the Kalinin case,' he said, avoiding McNab's name.

'And?'

'My contact at SOCA says that Fergus Morrison's dead.'

Rhona turned to him, her eyes wide. 'You . . . you know that for certain?'

'No, but I plan to ask the Super outright.'

'Oh, Bill.'

'I know,' he said. 'Morrison was the only remaining witness to the skip murder.'

She seemed to be struggling with herself, as though she wanted to say something.

'I'm sorry,' he said.

She turned abruptly away.

'I'll do my best to find out more.'

'No, don't,' she snapped.

'But, Rhona, we agreed we wouldn't give up on this.'

She was staring blindly out of the rain-splattered window.

'We can't bring McNab back, whatever we do,' she replied.

\*        \*        \*

Rhona was surprised to find the lab deserted, then realised that it was Sunday. Chrissy would be home with Sam and baby Michael. She briefly felt a pang of jealousy mixed with regret, then dismissed it. If she were at home now, even if she had someone to share the day with, she would do nothing but think. Not a pleasant prospect. She was better off here, and she had promised Bill a speedy return on the Reese-Brandons' DNA tests.

Hopefully the task would keep her mind off other matters. Bill's revelation that Fergus Morrison was dead had confirmed Petersson's story; she hated to admit it, but a high percentage of what he'd suggested so far had turned out to be true.

McNab had been revived in the ambulance, his post-mortem results were not available and Fergus Morrison was dead, presumably assassinated by Kalinin to prevent him from testifying. She'd wanted to ask Bill if he knew whether Misha and his sister were OK, but had stopped herself, realising that once she began, she would have been unlikely to stop.

Now, worry began to nip at her. Petersson hadn't wanted Bill involved, as he suspected someone on the inside. Bill was discreet, but if the informer—whoever it was—got to hear of Bill's continuing interest in the case, what would they read into that? Would it serve only to reinforce the idea that McNab was alive and they were hiding him to testify later?

No. Bill had openly mourned McNab. No one could believe his anger and determination to discover the truth stemmed from anything other than a desire for his killer to be brought to justice.

She imagined Bill's reaction if she had dared to suggest that McNab was still alive. He would have thought her deranged, or ill; unable to face up to death. He might have been right.

# CHAPTER THIRTY-SEVEN

Twenty frightened kids, plus at least the same number of angry or worried parents. Bill had asked that they all be sent to wait in the biggest space they had, the canteen, and provided with tea, coffee and whatever teenagers were drinking these days if alcopops and cheap cider weren't on the menu.

David Murdoch and Owen Hegarty were the only kids not attending a private school in the city. Kira had spread her net wider than Bill had thought, at least for the parties. He suspected, though, that the inner circle had been restricted to the Daisy Chain and David.

When he entered the room, all heads turned his way and a couple of the parents made an attempt to approach him. Bill held up his hand and asked for quiet; fortunately for him, they obeyed. He suddenly realised what it must be like for teachers in front of an unruly class, and had a moment of sympathy for his wife.

'Thank you for coming along today,' he began. 'I'm sure you're all anxious to help in our enquiries into the murders of Kira Reese-Brandon and Melanie Jones, and of course the abduction of Kira's baby.'

He looked around at the parents' faces. For the most part, these people were law-abiding. In fact, a few of them might be involved in upholding the law themselves. He was counting on the fact that they would go along with him on this.

'All of you children'—there was an indignant

rumble from the assembled teenagers, which Bill ignored—'were friends or acquaintances of Kira's. As such, you attended parties that Kira organised. It's important therefore that we eliminate you from our enquiries. You can do this by giving us your fingerprints and a sample of your DNA.'

More muttering, louder this time. One man, dressed in a smart grey suit, stepped forward.

'I assume the DNA samples and prints will be removed from your database afterwards?'

'If no charges are brought.'

'And my son's record will be clean?'

'Under those circumstances, yes.'

The answers seemed to satisfy most of the adults, although the kids didn't look impressed.

'You'll be called in one at a time and an officer will take a mouth swab and a set of prints. When that's done you may leave, unless DS Clark wants a chat with you. And thank you in advance for your co-operation.'

Bill withdrew before any more questions could be posed. He wanted to reinterview the three who had been present at the funfair that night, and since they'd already been processed for DNA and prints, he had asked DS Clark to send them straight in. Only David hadn't turned up.

He asked to see Sandie first. This time she wasn't in school uniform, which made her look at least five years older. He beckoned her over and she glanced curiously around the room before taking her seat.

'Is this a real interview?'

'What do you mean?'

'Will you turn on a tape?'

'Not unless you want me to.'

261

'Shouldn't I have my mum or dad with me?'

'Are they here?'

She shook her head. 'They're busy. I've nothing to hide anyway. They know that.'

She settled herself in the seat and looked directly at him.

'Let's start with Kira's mobile,' said Bill.

'What about it?'

'Did she have it with her at the funfair?'

'God, yes. She always had it with her.'

'Do you specifically remember seeing it that night?'

She thought for a moment. 'Yeah. She dropped it and I picked it up for her. Her belly had got so big it was hard for her to bend over.'

'You're sure?'

'Yes. Why?' she said, guilelessly.

He decided not to mention the partial print they'd retrieved from the mobile. If it was hers, she had accounted for it, assuming she was telling the truth.

'Kira wasn't a *good* friend of yours, was she?'

'No.'

'Then why were you at the funfair with her?'

'I wasn't with Kira. I was with Owen.'

'You went there with Owen Hegarty?'

'Yes. We saw David and Kira and joined them for a bit.'

'Kira's mother said her daughter didn't like you.'

Her face flushed. 'I didn't like her, either.'

'Why?'

'She thought she was better than everyone else. She told lies about people.'

'About you?'

'She said I was a slag, when she was the one that

262

got pregnant.'

Bill changed tack. 'Did Kira ever mention a life-like doll? One her mother had made for her?'

She was shaking her head briskly before he'd even finished the sentence.

Bill pushed the photo of the 'Daisy' Reborn across the table. Sandie avoided looking down initially, then gave it a swift glance.

'That's horrible.' She screwed up her face.

'You never saw this doll before?'

'Never.'

'You're sure of that?'

'I'm sure.'

He waited for a moment, then asked, 'What was Melanie Jones like?'

'She was a silly cow. She got herself pregnant to be like her precious Kira.'

'Anything else?'

'She was anorexic. Her arms and legs were like sticks.'

'You didn't like her?'

'She wasn't as nasty as Kira. She was just a sheep.'

'Can you think of anyone who might have wanted to harm Melanie?'

'No.'

There was no sorrow in her voice. Whatever the Daisy Chain had said or done to Sandie had hurt her deeply. Despite this, Bill suspected that if Kira had ever offered Sandie a place in her gang, she would have accepted with delight.

Bill told her she could go and asked that Owen Hegarty be sent in.

Owen was small and slightly built, not much taller than Sandie. He had black hair, blue eyes and an Irish look about him, as suggestd by his name. He smiled pleasantly at Bill and took a seat. They had nothing suspicious on Owen so far; his story checked out and there had been no trace of his DNA on Kira or at the crime scene. His only questionable behaviour had been his attendance at one of Kira's parties.

'Tell me about the parties, Owen.'

It looked like the question he had been waiting for. Bill wondered how often he had rehearsed his answer since he'd been contacted by DS Clark.

'It was like any party. I had a few beers, smoked a joint, met some girls.'

'Where?'

'Kira's place. Her parents were away.'

'And?'

'I didn't get any, if that's what you're asking.'

Bill pushed a picture of the mask towards him.

'Did you see this at the party?'

Owen took a look. 'No. What is it?'

'A mask of the Greek god, Dionysos.'

'Kira was into Greek stuff. She was always showing off, saying things in Greek that no one could understand.'

'So no one wore this mask at the party you went to?'

'Not that I saw.'

'Did you know Melanie Jones?'

'The skinny one who died? She was at the party, but she went off into a room with someone.'

'Who?'

'I never saw him. Kira said it was Melanie's turn.'

'Her turn?'

'Kira was high, giggling and stuff. That's what

264

she said. I thought she meant Melanie was going with a guy.'

'Have you spoken to David recently?'

'I haven't seen him since Friday morning. He was in class first thing, then he skived off.'

'He left school?'

'He didn't turn up at the other classes and he wasn't about after school.'

Bill let Owen go and immediately went in search of DS Clark. There were only a couple of teenagers left in the cafeteria. He headed for the incident room. Janice was at her desk, concentrating on something on her computer screen.

'Did you reach David Murdoch?'

'No. I've sent someone round to the house.'

'Owen Hegarty says David came into school on Friday but left early. I want him found.'

'Right, Sir.'


# CHAPTER THIRTY-EIGHT

The name 'chromosome' derived from the Greek: *chroma* for colour, and *soma* for body. Rhona wondered if Kira had discovered that fact while learning Greek, or whether she had only been interested in the glamour of the legends.

The word had originated because different chromosomes were receptive to certain dyes. They produced a pattern of colour that painted a genomic picture of each human being; twenty-four different chromosomes, of which twenty-two were autosomes and two sex chromosomes. Males had an X and Y chromosome, females two Xs. Once you added the twenty-two held in common, the magic number of forty-six chromosomes defined each of us as unique.

She had begun with Melanie's baby—a girl who, had she lived, might have inherited her mother's dark hair and her slight build. Alternatively, she might have grown tall like her father, whom Rhona now knew to be David Murdoch.

The pattern of paternity she had sought in the blood from Kira's baby's umbilical cord, she now recognised in the DNA of Melanie's unborn child.

According to Bill, Melanie had been utterly and convincingly dismissive of his suggestion that David might be the father. Was it possible she didn't know who had impregnated her? Was that what the mask was all about?

Rhona thought of the picture of Kira that was beginning to emerge. Extremely intelligent, but also manipulative and controlling. Her impressive intellect and charismatic personality were used to devastating effect on those she called her friends, and probably on David too. According to Bill, David had spoken of Kira as though she could do no wrong. He had declared their relationship to have been unique, that he'd loved her and her unborn child, even knowing it wasn't his and despite his sexual ambivalence.

Sandie had called his devotion 'weird'. Perhaps it was.

But that's what a cult did to its members, blinded them to any faults in their leader. It seemed Kira had indeed played at being God, with devastating consequences.

Rhona turned to the swab samples she had

taken from Kira's parents. Mrs Reese-Brandon had told Bill that Kira was adopted and the DNA confirmed this, with no pattern to suggest a familial connection between Kira and either of her parents.

Rhona now checked the DNA comparison that Bill had specifically requested—a paternity check on the umbilical cord using the DNA sample taken from Mr Reese-Brandon.

Magnus's research into Myrrha had revealed that, according to myth, the goddess Aphrodite had inspired Myrrha with lust to commit incest with her father.

But in Kira's case, it wasn't a myth. The DNA pattern did not lie; the child Kira had been carrying had been fathered by her own adoptive father.

If Reese-Brandon had been abusing his daughter and suspected the child might be his, had he killed Kira and removed the child to cover this up?

\* \* \*

Bill lowered the phone, his stomach churning. He had known there was something wrong in that household, and Rhona's call had just confirmed his worst fears. Instinct had told him that the atmosphere had been generated by something more than losing their child. Why hadn't he considered this as a possibility before Magnus worked on the diary? It wouldn't be the first time he'd brought charges against a father for raping his daughter.

Had he been misled by the big house and the

private school? He knew full well that sexual abuse happened in all social classes. Or was it simply because the research had shown that foetal theft was usually carried out by women?

He was annoyed and angry with himself. He should have paid more attention to Reese-Brandon's reactions, to his assertion that the baby was dead even when his wife had tried to hope otherwise. Why had he been so sure of that?

Bill checked himself. Even if Reese-Brandon had fathered the child, it did not automatically mean that he'd killed his daughter and removed the foetus.

He thought of Melanie, smothered in her own bed. Had she known something that might have led them to the killer? Was that why she'd died? There had been no sign of a forced entry, suggesting she had willingly let her attacker in. What if Reese-Brandon had gone round there that afternoon? What if something Melanie had said made him think she knew the truth about his relationship with his adopted daughter?

Most people wouldn't know that the umbilical cord contained only the baby's blood, so maybe he'd thought that by removing the baby he'd removed the evidence of paternity. According to his wife, Kira and her father had been very close. She had been his 'little princess', until she'd got pregnant. He had been initially set on an abortion, but Kira had defied him.

The situation must have become intolerable for him; if Kira had gone on to give birth, he would have had to watch the baby grow up, knowing it was his. She could have held this secret over him forever—constantly threatening imminent disgrace, if not prosecution. The pregnancy had put her in control.

Bill wondered if it had been engineered that way. Had Kira got pregnant on purpose? Or had the pregnancy afforded her a means of getting back at the man who was abusing her? The man who should have been her protector?

He thought of his own daughter, Lisa. He would never be capable of imagining her as a sexual object. She was as precious to him as the air he breathed.

An hour later, DS Clark delivered the news that Ronald Reese-Brandon was waiting for him in interview room one.

'Any luck with David Murdoch?' he asked her.

'No, Sir. His father's not seen him since Saturday, when he went out and didn't come back.'

'He has no idea where he is?'

'He says he's tried phoning him but gets no answer. We're doing the same.'

'Friends?'

'Seems he wasn't much of a socialite, apart from with Kira.'

'Keep trying the mobile and let's put out a missing person on him. We need to find that boy.'

Kira's father was sitting stiff-backed at the table and didn't look round as Bill entered and took his seat opposite.

'Thanks for coming in, Mr Brandon.'

'My name is Reese-Brandon.'

Bill ignored the reminder. The truth was he'd had enough of the double-barrelled label. One surname was enough for most people.

'We have the results of the DNA tests.' He took a moment to study the man's expression. Did he

269

already know what was coming? 'At my request, Dr MacLeod compared your DNA to that of Kira's baby.'

Ronald's arrogance had been replaced by suspicion and surprise.

'I don't understand.'

'We don't need a baby to test for paternity, Mr *Brandon*. The umbilical cord does the job just as well. Our results show you to be the father of your daughter's child.' Bill had trouble keeping the contempt out of his voice.

Reese-Brandon blinked twice, very fast, then seemed to regain his composure. He straightened himself in the chair and said, almost triumphantly, 'Kira wasn't my daughter.'

'Your *adopted* daughter,' Bill retorted.

'She wasn't my adopted daughter either.'

'Your wife told us . . .'

Reese-Brandon interrupted him. 'Maria and her former husband adopted Kira when she was two. By the time I met Maria, she was divorced and Kira was twelve. Kira was not related to me in any way.'

'You deny she was your daughter?'

'She was patently not my daughter in any natural or legal sense.'

'What about morally?'

He gave a deep sigh. 'I cared deeply for Kira, but not as a father.'

Bill tried to control his distaste and rising anger. 'When did your . . . sexual relationship begin?'

'Kira revealed her feelings towards me on her sixteenth birthday. I reciprocated.'

Bill frowned. 'Are you seriously trying to tell me this was a consensual affair, initiated by Kira?

What did your wife have to say about it?'

At last the man looked uncomfortable.

'We planned to tell her once Kira had left for university and we began living together.'

'But the pregnancy changed all that?'

Reese-Brandon said nothing.

'Were you aware the child was yours?' Bill persisted.

He swallowed hard before answering. 'Kira told me she wasn't sure.'

'She'd been sleeping with someone else?'

'She was a teenager. There were parties, as you know. She said she'd got drunk one night . . .'

Bill cut him off. 'Kira told you you weren't the father?'

'No. She simply said she wasn't sure. She was too young to have a child, and she had a brilliant future as a mathematician. I wanted her to have a termination.'

'But she said no.'

'She told me she couldn't in case the baby was ours. She wanted it. I accepted that.'

'I have an alternative version of events, Mr Brandon. You abused your daughter and got her pregnant. When she wouldn't abort the baby, you killed her and removed the foetus to hide this fact.'

'That's utter nonsense. I loved Kira. I would never have harmed her.'

'I don't believe you.'

'I want to speak to my lawyer.'

'We haven't charged you, Mr Brandon. Under Scots law you don't need a lawyer yet.'

'Then I have nothing more to say.'

\*      \*      \*

Bill felt an overwhelming need to get the man out of his sight. When he entered the observation room, Janice Clark was standing at the window. She turned to him, a shocked expression on her face. She'd seen and heard a lot in her time on the Force, but she was still young enough to be surprised by what people were capable of.

'What do you think, Detective Sergeant Clark?'

'I don't think their relationship was the way he described it.'

'Why?'

'She was twelve when they met, he was forty, at least.'

'You think he abused her?'

'I think he manipulated her.'

'Clearly,' said Bill. 'But by the end, from what we know of Kira, maybe she was the one manipulating him.'

'Perhaps he taught her well.'

'But did he kill her?'

'He has an alibi for that night.'

'I wonder if his wife will back him up once she knows the truth.'

'You're going to tell her?' Janice looked alarmed.

Bill shrugged. It wouldn't be pleasant, but it had to be done.

'What if Mrs Reese-Brandon had already found out about them?' said Janice. 'What would she have been capable of?'

'We can't rule that out,' replied Bill. 'We'll have to speak to her again.'

He would have to let the husband go, for now. They had nothing to place him at the scene of crime; no sightings, no mobile calls. But he had a motive, if he didn't want his sexual relationship with Kira to be revealed.

Reese-Brandon was an intelligent man, and it wouldn't take a great deal of searching on the internet to discover that umbilical cords were routinely used to establish paternity. Would he not have planned in advance, and removed it from the scene? And even if he did kill Kira, what had become of the baby?

Bill didn't like the man—or what he had done with the girl the world regarded as his daughter— but that didn't make him a murderer.

Magnus had been right when he said the psychological aspects of the killing had changed with the delivery of the doll and the video on Kira's mobile. Whoever had done that was trying to manipulate them. He just couldn't see Reese-Brandon playing that kind of psychological game.

Bill put a call through to Maria Reese-Brandon and asked if she could come down to the station.

'I should check with my husband first. He'll want to come with me.'

'He's here already.'

She gave a small gasp. 'Why? Have you found the baby?'

'No. Your husband is helping us with our enquiries.'

'I'll come down.'

Bill replaced the phone. He would tell her the truth, and if she had been covering for her husband, he suspected she wouldn't do so for much longer. Of course, if Janice was right, Ronald might be the one covering for Maria.

She wore a red coat. The splash of colour made the room seem even drabber. Bill had asked DS Clark to stay with them while he broke the news. Maybe he was a coward, but he didn't relish the idea of confronting Maria with the fact that her husband had been sleeping with her daughter. No one should have to tell a mother that.

'May I see my husband?' Her voice was low, and he detected a tremble.

'After we've had our chat.'

She clasped her hands together on her lap and waited for him to explain why she was there.

'We have some news on the paternity of Kira's baby.'

She looked surprised. 'I don't understand. How can you tell?'

'The umbilical cord was left behind. It can be used to test for paternity.'

'Oh.'

There was no easy way to say this, so he made it as plain as possible. 'I'm afraid your husband is the baby's father. The DNA test is conclusive, there can be no doubt.'

He observed her expression as she processed the information. Puzzlement gave way to shock, then disgust. The colour drained from her face, leaving it chalk-white. She swayed as though she would topple. Janice had wisely sat next to her and, realising what was about to happen, put her arm round the woman to steady her.

Bill waited as his DS helped Mrs Brandon to put her head between her knees to encourage the blood to flow back into her brain.

He felt bad, but her reaction to the news of what he thought of as incest was so immediate and so powerful that it told him what he wanted to know. Mrs Reese-Brandon had had no idea that her husband was sleeping with her daughter.

Eventually a small amount of colour found its way back into her cheeks. She raised her head and looked at him.

'I'm sorry, I . . .'

'*I'm* sorry to be the one to tell you.'

Shock had rendered her almost incoherent. Bill watched as she struggled to make sense of what he had just told her.

'How could he have hurt her? She was his little princess. He was so kind to her. When we married, she was only twelve. It's difficult for a man to take on a child that isn't his. But he did, without complaint.' She looked at Bill, struggling to comprehend. 'That's why Ronald's here, isn't it?'

'Yes.'

'What did he say?'

Bill told her the truth, knowing it would come as a further shock. 'That they loved one another. That they planned to live together when she went to university. That's when they planned to tell you.'

Her mouth sagged. She emitted a shrill little laugh.

Bill went on doggedly. 'The night Kira died, you said your husband and you were together at home?'

She gathered herself, as though making a decision. 'Ronald was there until I went to bed at ten thirty. I heard him go out after that. I thought he was seeing someone else and I didn't want to face up to that, so I said he was at home.'

275

'You're sure he left the house?'

'I heard the car reverse down the drive. He didn't turn on the engine, but I heard the wheels on the gravel.' She met Bill's gaze, her eyes full of tears. 'You don't think he killed Kira? He isn't capable of that.'

From Bill's experience, men were capable of anything and everything, but he decided to throw Maria one crumb of comfort.

'We have nothing to place your husband at the scene of crime.' He refrained from adding, 'yet'. 'I'd like you to give a statement to DS Clark. Just write down what you've told me about the night Kira died.'

'I loved my daughter,' she said quietly. 'I would have loved her child too, whatever its parentage.'

He believed her. Maria Reese-Brandon had a bigger heart than he had.

'The Reborn you ordered for Kira. How did you get in touch with Coulter?'

'There was an article about him in the paper. I wrote to the State Hospital.'

'And how did you pay for the doll?'

'I sent a cheque made payable to the hospital. They extract the cost of the materials and the rest goes to the NSPCC.'

'Did you continue your correspondence with Coulter after that?'

She looked confused by the suggestion. 'No. Why would I?'

'Did you tell Coulter anything about Kira in your letter?'

She shook her head.

'And remind me, when was the last time you saw the doll?'

'A couple of months ago. I was tidying the wardrobe and took a look inside the box. I knew I should get rid of it, but it looked too like a real baby. I couldn't simply throw it out.'

'Who among Kira's friends might have had access to the doll?'

She thought for a minute. 'All of the girls were at the house at some time or other, even Sandie. And I'm sure David would have been there too. Kira tended to go her own way, despite what Ronald wanted.'

Her hand flew to her face in distress and she began to sob in earnest. She was crying not for herself and what she now knew, but for her dead child, whatever she had done.

*     *     *

Ronald Reese-Brandon stood up as Bill reentered the room.

'Can I go now?'

'Not yet.'

'But I've answered all of your questions. There's nothing else to say.'

'Sit down, Mr Brandon.'

'*Reese*-Brandon.'

'I have just spoken to your wife.'

'What did you tell her?' he demanded.

'The truth. That you'd had sex with her daughter. That it was you who made Kira pregnant.'

'You had no right to do that.'

'*You're* telling *me* what's right and what isn't?' snapped Bill.

'I would have preferred to tell Maria myself.'

'I have no reason to believe you would have. You and Kira seemed to be taking a long time about doing that.'

'This is private business, between my wife and I.'

'Mrs Reese-Brandon has retracted her previous statement. She now says that you did leave the house the night Kira died.'

'That's nonsense. She's only saying that because of what you told her.'

'Your car left at eleven o'clock. You reversed down the drive without turning on the engine.'

Brandon was apoplectic.

'She's lying!'

'Where did you go?'

'Nowhere. I told you, Maria's just angry. She's lying.'

'Where did you go?'

He shrugged. 'All right, I did go out. But I drove round for a while, that's all.'

'Where exactly?'

'Byres Road, through Partick. In circles.'

'Why?'

'I needed away from the house. From Maria.'

'You went to look for Kira?'

'No!'

'She called you and asked you to meet her at the funfair.'

'What? That's nonsense.' But Reese-Brandon's eyes had flickered sideways.

'She sent you a text, didn't she?' It was a long shot, yet Bill watched as the arrow struck home.

The other man's lips thinned and he gave a sharp nod. 'She wanted me to collect her. She was always doing that, especially since the pregnancy. She would go somewhere, then text me and ask me to pick her up. Kira was very demanding.'

'Did she text you from the BlackBerry you bought her?'

Reese-Brandon looked surprised by the question. 'No. She had a pay-as-you-go she used . . .' He came to a halt.

'When contacting you in particular?'

He gave a curt nod.

'So you went to the funfair to meet her?'

'I waited in the car near the station. She didn't appear, and eventually I went home. She did that sometimes. Called me out, then never turned up.'

'Did you try calling her?'

'She didn't answer.'

'And what time was this?'

'Around eleven thirty.'

'You didn't enter the funfair?'

'No.'

'You realise we have mobile footage of that night, from multiple sources?'

'You won't find me on any of it.'

## CHAPTER THIRTY-NINE

Magnus answered his mobile on the second ring.

'Can we talk?' Rhona's voice sounded tense.

'Of course. Do you want to meet somewhere for a drink?'

'I'll come round, if that's OK?'

He tried to keep his tone light. 'There's always Highland Park here for emergencies.'

She gave a small, forced laugh. 'I'll be there in about twenty minutes.'

As soon as she rang off, Magnus went to check out the fridge. If Rhona was coming from work, chances were she would be hungry. There was probably enough curry left over from the previous night, if he kept his own portion small. He selected a bottle of white from the wine rack and put it in the fridge. He knew she preferred white.

His preparations done, he sat back down at his desk and wondered about the purpose of Rhona's visit. He doubted it would be personal; it was far more likely to be something about the case. Kira's notebook lay open on his desk, where he'd been studying the final pages when Rhona had called. The entries had ended on an unfinished calculation, as though Kira had been disturbed midway through.

The emerging picture of Kira's character had given him hours of thought. There were many similarities between her personality traits and Coulter's, predominantly the narcissistic need to be centre stage and the desire to bend others to their will.

Coulter's diary, he'd returned to its box file. His comprehensive reading had given no indication of any outside contacts the inmate might have had. Despite this, he agreed with Bill that Coulter had inside knowledge of this case. Another search of the workshop and Coulter's room at the hospital was scheduled for tomorrow, along with a further interview. Magnus knew how much pleasure Coulter would be deriving from all the attention he was receiving.

The buzzer interrupted his train of thought and he rose to release the entrance door. He went to open the flat door and saw Rhona climbing the stairs. She looked weary, and he remembered that this was Sunday night and Rhona had probably worked on the case the entire weekend. She threw him a brief smile as she reached the landing.

'What a wonderful smell.'

'Chicken Tikka Masala, a Glasgow speciality. Want some?'

'I'd love some.'

He ushered her inside. Above the aroma of curry that pervaded the flat, he caught her perfume as she passed him in the doorway. He liked the way she always wore the same one. He had no idea what it was called, but its scent had become one with her in his mind.

'I didn't realise how hungry I was until I started to climb those stairs.' She dropped her bag on the sofa and slipped off her coat, tossing it over the back of the seat.

'A dram?'

'Please.'

He set about pouring the whisky and adding a little water. She accepted the glass and they went through the ritual of swirling the liquid and breathing in the aroma, which had become a comfortable shared routine.

She took a sip and he watched as she reflected on the taste. 'Good.' She dropped onto the couch, kicked off her shoes and settled her legs beneath her.

He sat across from her. 'Five minutes, then we eat.'

'I might need ten for what I have to say.'

'OK,' he said, cautiously.

She took another sip before she spoke.

'Something's happened about McNab.'

'They've picked up Kalinin?'

'No. Before I start, I want you to promise to tell no one what I'm about to say.' She held his gaze, her eyes serious, and he nodded his agreement. 'I may sound as though I've lost my marbles, but since you're a psychologist you'll be the best judge of that.'

She had both intrigued and worried him.

'Let's hear it.'

\*     \*     \*

After her revelation over whisky, then food, she had asked to go out on the balcony for some fresh air. They stood there now, a chill wind ruffling the grey waters of the river below. She had borrowed a thick, cabled sweater before they stepped outside. It hung well below her waist and her hands were hidden in its long arms. She huddled inside it against the chill.

'So you don't think I'm mad?' she said, after a long silence.

'No.'

'Do you believe he could be alive?'

'There's only one way to find that out for certain.'

'And that is?'

'Dig up his grave.' He was only half joking.

'Which we can't do. And what do you think about Petersson? Can we trust him?'

'Well, most of what I know about his investigative work casts him in a good light. But I'm under no illusions that he would do anything to pursue a story. That kind of tenacity comes with the territory, and it will include telling lies to get

282

what he wants. Discovering that the only witness who could put Kalinin behind bars is actually alive would definitely be a scoop worth fighting for.'

Rhona sighed. 'So what should I do?'

She had never asked his advice before. He felt flattered and slightly at a loss.

'I thought Petersson told you to do nothing more for the moment.'

'That's not an option,' she stated firmly.

She wasn't seeking his advice at all, he realised. She knew what she intended doing, and wanted to gauge his reaction.

'What are you going to do?' he said warily.

'First, find out if that call came from where he said it did.'

'How?'

'I'll ask Roy to help me with that. Also, Petersson said that the number gave a dead tone when he tried calling it. I want to know if that's true.' She folded her arms protectively across her body. 'There are things about Michael that Petersson doesn't know. If he really is trying to contact me, there are other avenues he might try.'

'Such as?'

Her face shone pale in the shadows. 'I'd rather not say until I've checked them out.'

'But you'll keep me informed?' He suddenly felt worried for her. If Kalinin did believe that McNab was alive, he would stop at nothing to discover his whereabouts, and a search would inevitably lead him to Rhona. Magnus wanted to tell her to leave well enough alone, as Petersson had apparently done. She must have been reading his expression.

'I'll be careful,' she told him.

She moved inside, leaving him to follow. Settling

back on the couch as he closed the balcony doors, she said, 'Can we talk about the Reborn case now?'

'OK.'

'Ronald Reese-Brandon is confirmed as the father of Kira's baby. Bill may have him in custody by now.'

So the Myrrha reference had meant what he'd thought it had.

'He murdered his daughter?'

'We haven't any evidence yet that places him at the scene of crime, but the pregnancy would be a strong motive.'

'Does Bill think it's a case of abuse?'

'Given Kira's age, it would usually be assumed so.'

'Maybe, but I'm not sure Kira could have been coerced into anything. I get the impression she liked being the one calling the shots in every area of her life.'

Rhona quickly filled him in on the latest from the second murder case, including her discovery of Melanie's mobile and the fact that David Murdoch had been reported missing.

'Why would David hurt Melanie? You said the baby was his.'

'I don't think he knew that. And if he wore the mask, she would have had no idea who impregnated her.'

'Kira was controlling everything, even down to who the Daisy Chain girls had sex with,' he said.

'Which might be why she died.' She fell silent for a moment. 'I'm coming with you tomorrow. Bill wants me to take a look at Coulter's workroom.'

He was glad of the prospect of spending more time with her.

'So I'd better get home.' She rose stiffly from the couch.

The suggestion was out before he had time to think. 'You could stay, have another dram. There's a spare room,' he added hurriedly.

She seemed to find his impromptu offer amusing.

'Thanks, but I like to end the day in my own place. And there's Tom to think of.'

'Tom?'

'The cat,' she reminded him.

When she left, Magnus helped himself to another drink, then went and picked up the sweater she'd borrowed and buried his face in her scent.

\*　　　\*　　　\*

It was an outside chance and she didn't hold out much hope, but it was worth a try.

She waited until she was home, not trusting her mobile any more. What Petersson had said about being bugged had unnerved her. He had had her phone in his possession for twelve hours. What if he was the one doing the bugging?

She picked up the handset of the landline and rang the answering service for her father's cottage on Skye, her heart beating rapidly. There were three voicemails.

The first was from the Gaelic College, asking if she was willing to let out the cottage again to a visiting lecturer. The second was a cold call about house insurance. The third began in silence, then a man's voice simply said, 'Rhona'.

# CHAPTER FORTY

He had tried turning off his mobile, but it hadn't helped. He'd simply felt compelled to switch it on every five minutes to check for messages. He'd finally decided it was better to keep it on and not answer. Since he'd decided to make himself scarce, there had been three calls from the police station along with many from his stepfather's mobile.

After finding Melanie, he'd gone straight home and taken a very long shower, then put all the clothes he'd been wearing in the washing machine and turned it on. After that, he'd raided the drinks cabinet and poured himself a large vodka. By the second glass, he'd made up his mind to sit things out, convincing himself he'd removed any trace of Melanie from his person.

He'd stayed in his room when his stepfather arrived home from work, insisting he'd eaten already, and played computer games until ten o'clock, when he'd turned on the TV to find no mention of Melanie's death on the Scottish news. That had made him feel better, as though finding her body hadn't really happened at all.

The next morning he'd been woken by his stepdad leaving for work. Not long afterwards, Owen had destroyed his carefully constructed peace of mind by leaving a voicemail saying the police knew about the parties and that they were all to go down to the police station and be fingerprinted and swabbed. Owen had sounded quite excited about this, as though it was all just a game.

The thought of going back to that police station had scared the shit out of him. The police had already taken his fingerprints and a mouth swab 'to eliminate him from their enquiries'. Why the hell would they want him back there? He'd tried to stay calm, but when the call came he didn't pick up, just waited before listening to some woman on voicemail asking him to report immediately to the police station.

In the hours since finding Melanie, he'd come to the conclusion that the killer had smothered her. He'd seen it done numerous times on TV, a pillow placed gently over someone's sleeping face. And she was so little and skinny, it would have been easy. Then he thought about the way he'd covered her mouth tightly with his hand.

What if they found flakes of his skin on her mouth and thought it was him who'd smothered her? Once it had occurred to him, his brain had gone into overdrive, reliving everything he'd done in that room. Sitting on the bed, touching her arm, gripping her wrist. He'd shaken her arm up and down, for fuck's sake—his DNA must be all over her.

He'd tried to calm himself down by recalling how he'd wiped her mouth, her arm, her wrist and got rid of his fingerprints. It was then he realised he had no idea what he'd done with the towel.

After ten frantic minutes of searching he'd found it in the washing machine among his clothes. He'd gone on to hide the damp clothes in his wardrobe, thinking hanging them out on the line (which he never did) would have looked suspicious. He'd taken the towel with him and tossed it in a skip in the city centre.

Now he was standing in the line at McDonald's, trying not to look or act like a fugitive from the law—which, he had to keep reminding himself, he wasn't. Jesus, he'd never realised how many CCTV cameras were trained on the city centre. He'd counted at least eight on the way here. How the hell did the neds get away with anything? That must be why they all wore the same hoods and baseball caps, so you couldn't distinguish one from the other.

He took possession of his breakfast and headed for the darkest corner. No one even glanced up. He was back to being invisible, just like he'd been before Kira had taken him under her wing. He didn't know whether to be sad or glad about that.

As he ate, he worked on his plan. He could stay away for at least a couple of nights before Gary freaked. Since his mother had died, the two of them had pretty much kept out of one another's way; with her gone, they had nothing and no one in common. He was actually surprised Gary hadn't asked him to leave once he'd reached seventeen, and had always felt that's what would happen should he put a foot wrong.

Well, he'd certainly put a foot wrong now.

As he polished off the burger, he wondered if he might delay things by sending Gary a text saying he was staying with mates. But if the police went round to the house looking for him, that wouldn't wash for long.

He might be better to lose the mobile altogether. He was savvy enough to know that the police could trace him if he used it. He should throw it in a skip like the towel, say some ned had stolen it from him. He brought it out of his pocket and stared at it. The thing was, he couldn't bear to lose his phone. It would be like losing his right arm. He put it away again.

He was suddenly aware just how difficult it was to lie, properly and consistently. It seemed that one lie just tripped up another. He'd occasionally lied to Gary about where he was going, although Gary always looked as though he couldn't care less, but proper lying was much harder. Kira had been great at it. He'd been shocked at first by her ability to tell the Daisy Chain something that sounded true, but which he knew to be a lie. She was always so convincing. You just believed everything she said.

She'd assured him that he was the only one she would never lie to, and he'd believed her, although that night at the funfair he hadn't been so sure. She'd never mentioned liking candyfloss before, and when he'd offered to fetch some for her, she'd given him a look that had scared him.

He swallowed the last mouthful of Coke, then got rid of the tray. Where to now? He made a quick decision to head for Kelvingrove and put in some time at the *Doctor Who* exhibition. His plan was to stay warm and off the radar.

## CHAPTER FORTY-ONE

She'd spent ages listening to the message left on the Skye number. The voice had said her name, just once, then nothing more. When she'd eventually fallen asleep on the couch, she still had no idea who the voice belonged to.

McNab had known about her father's place on Skye. He'd even tried to persuade her to invite him there for a few days' walking, during their brief affair. All a ruse, of course. McNab hated the great outdoors. His plan had not been to see the Isle of Skye but to have a weekend of uninterrupted sex.

He'd called her there once, and she remembered how annoyed she'd been. She'd accused him of stalking her and told him to fuck off.

All that seemed a lifetime ago. McNab's lifetime.

She'd spent a restless night, the voice on the phone echoing through her dreams, and had been glad to finally glance at her watch and realise it was morning, albeit before sunrise.

Now, during a long, hot shower, she asked herself whether she should enlist Roy's help in trying to find out where the Skye call had come from. She would claim she had a potential stalker as an excuse for her request to check out the 'dead man walking' text, and it would be easy to add the Skye voicemail to that scenario.

Or maybe she should just tell Roy the truth?

If she did, she would have to admit to herself that she was giving credence to Petersson's story. She would also have to reveal that she'd supplied him with information about the post-mortem which, if not illegal, was unprofessional.

She stepped out of the shower, quickly dried her hair and got dressed. By the time the phone rang, she'd fed Tom and was pouring her second cup of coffee.

'I'll pick you up in ten minutes,' said Magnus.

'What about Bill?'

'He's not coming. Something about watching phone footage of the funfair that night. He wants you to sit in on the interview with Coulter before examining the workshop.'

\*       \*       \*

Rhona had never been to the State Hospital before, although she'd given evidence in court about a number of its inmates.

As they crested the hill, she caught her first glimpse of it. In the cold morning light of late February there was something Alcatraz-like about its position, but surrounded by mist-swathed moorland instead of water.

'Dr Shan has requested a meeting before we interview Coulter.'

'What's she like, this Dr Shan?'

'In her thirties, oriental, probably a Buddhist judging by the décor of her office. I think she resents my visits to her patient.' He paused. 'Coulter has . . . a *way* with women. He makes them feel special—chosen, even.'

'You think he has some influence over her?'

'Perhaps. What I do know is that Coulter can be very persuasive and very charming. Scarily so.'

'So I should be on my guard?'

'You can try.'

\*       \*       \*

The woman who approached them was exactly as Magnus had described. What he'd failed to mention was how beautiful she was.

It was Magnus who performed the

291

introductions.

'Dr Shan, this is Dr Rhona MacLeod. She will sit in on the interview.'

The woman appraised Rhona.

'You are a medical doctor?'

'A forensic scientist.'

Her finely plucked eyebrows rose in surprise. 'Really.' She looked to Magnus for an explanation.

'Dr MacLeod is here to examine Mr Coulter's workroom. DI Wilson wants her to meet Mr Coulter before she does that.'

A flash of something resembling anger crossed Dr Shan's face. 'We have already searched both Mr Coulter's living quarters and his work space, as you requested. We found nothing untoward.'

'You're probably right, but I'd like to take a look anyway,' Rhona said pleasantly.

Magnus wisely changed the subject. 'You wanted to speak with us before the interview?'

'I wanted to register my disquiet at your repeated visits to my patient. As he is confined here and under watch all the time, he cannot be involved in crimes committed outside these walls. Secondly, I believe your continued interest in him is affecting his progress.'

'How is that?' Magnus said, with genuine interest.

Dr Shan hesitated, perhaps sensing she should have phrased her complaint differently. 'He has become more agitated than usual, and continually asks when you will return. Visitors are few here, very few in Mr Coulter's case. It is unfair to give him hope that more visits will take place.'

'I get the impression that Mr Coulter likes being the centre of attention.'

292

'I don't believe that to be the case at all. I think he is unnerved by it.'

'He told you that?'

'Yes, he did.'

Rhona decided it was time to come clean. 'I apologise if that's the case, Dr Shan, but this is a necessary visit. It relates to a police investigation into the murder of two young girls.'

'Two?' Dr Shan looked shocked.

'Kira's pregnant friend, Melanie Jones, was found dead on Friday afternoon under suspicious circumstances.'

Dr Shan's hand fluttered to her mouth. 'I didn't know.'

'Jeff Coulter has fashioned two Reborns which may be linked to this case. One, called Daisy, he made for Kira's mother. It was found near the scene of crime. The other doll Mr Coulter said he had named Melanie, and he made a point of telling Professor Pirie that on an earlier visit. Since that visit, Melanie Jones and her unborn baby have both been killed.'

Dr Shan was speechless, her face a mask of surprise.

Rhona continued. 'We think at the very least Mr Coulter has been receiving information about these crimes that wasn't readily available from watching the news reports.'

Dr Shan recovered herself a little. 'All this may be just a coincidence.'

'That's why I'm here. To see if it is.'

Dr Shan indicated with a nod that she would delay them no more. 'I'll take you to the interview room and let the ward know you're here.' She picked up the phone.

*          *          *

Coulter was not the first killer Rhona had been in close proximity to. Some, like the Gravedigger, hadn't been from choice. Others had been in a court of law with at least a dock between. A smiling Coulter was a table's width away.

'Well, Professor, who do we have here?'

'Mr Coulter, I am Dr Rhona MacLeod.'

'*Dr* MacLeod? A psychiatrist?'

'No, a doctor of science.'

He took a moment to consider that.

'And what kind of science, exactly?' he said.

'I specialise in forensics.'

'Wow,' he laughed. 'Brains as well as beauty.'

His gaze was openly admiring but not overtly sexual. He was less intimidating than Rhona had expected; his eyes were friendly and his manner pleasant and unthreatening. He looked interested in her, but there was another quality about him. A sort of magnetism that drew and held her.

'So, Dr MacLeod, why are you here?'

Although he wasn't shifting in his seat, there was a sense of restless energy about him.

'To take a look at your workshop.'

'They already did that. They didn't find anything.'

'I know.'

He leaned back, folding his arms. 'Well, if you've got the time to spare, I'm happy for you to take another look.'

'I'd like to ask you a couple more questions first,' Magnus said.

Coulter switched his attention to him. Rhona

felt a strange surge of relief that he no longer held her in his gaze.

'Fire away,' he said with enthusiasm.

'Tell me about Geri.'

'You've been reading my diary!' He sounded pleased by this. 'Geri's my girlfriend.'

'She visits you here?' asked Magnus.

'When she can. She writes to me a lot and we talk on the phone.'

'Does she live alone?'

'What do you mean?'

'I just wondered, with you in here long term, whether she had another partner?'

'I told you, she's *my* girlfriend.'

The pleasant façade had cracked momentarily, but it was back up before they had time to see what lay beneath.

'What does Geri have to say about Caroline?' persisted Magnus.

'She knows other women write to me. If it helps, she doesn't mind.'

'I see. Tell me about Caroline.'

'What do you want to know?'

'Her age, what she does for a living, what she writes to you about.'

Coulter frowned. 'That would be breaking a confidence.'

'She writes to you in secret?'

'Some people might not approve.'

Magnus sat in silence for a moment.

'How's the Melanie doll coming along?'

Rhona watched as a small smile played on Coulter's lips. This was what he'd been waiting for. 'She's all ready. Do you want to take a look?'

The doll was tiny, with fuzzy, dark hair and rosebud lips. She was dressed in a pink suit with a daisy motif, just like the one they'd found in the park.

'Would you like to hold her?'

He held it out to Rhona, who was standing with Magnus in the doorway of the workroom. She wanted to refuse, but her arms seemed to move of their own accord as she accepted the doll from him. She had expected to feel revulsion, but found herself cradling it as though it were a real baby. And it did look and feel exactly like one, even down to its soft, floppy body.

'Don't you just love that wee face?' Coulter's eyes lit up as he gazed at the doll. 'Look, the eyelids even look slightly damp. Moist glaze medium does that.' He turned to smile at Rhona. 'Attention to detail is what makes these dolls special.'

She handed it back to him, and he took it gently, even cradling the head.

'Who's this one for?' she asked.

'Geri. A present.'

'Did she choose the name?'

'Yes.'

Rhona wondered if the Reborn had been made to replace Geri's own baby, the child he had killed.

Coulter laid the doll carefully in its box.

'When you examine the room, Doctor, you'll be careful with my tools?'

He indicated the neat row of instruments that resembled a surgeon's implements, and Rhona had a sudden unpleasant image of him carving the doll's face from clay, excavating the eye sockets with a scalpel.

When Coulter and Magnus left, accompanied by the orderlies, Rhona looked around the room. Coulter had been completely relaxed about the possibility of a search, with nothing in his manner to suggest he was worried. But then, if Magnus was correct in his assessment, the man was a practised liar.

The workroom was quite small, more like a large cupboard, a table filling one wall. Behind it were shelves stacked with materials, all labelled. A small jar of the glaze he'd talked about sat next to a selection of brushes. The numbers and different sizes made Rhona think of an artist's studio. A paint set named 'Peaches and Cream Complexion' was open. Perhaps it had been used on Melanie.

Magnus hadn't mentioned Melanie's death to Coulter, yet Rhona couldn't help but feel that he knew about it already. He had been relaxed, confident, almost triumphant about the newborn he'd given her name to.

Assuming Coulter was aware of Melanie's death, who could have told him? Not Dr Shan, whose reaction made it clear the news had come as a shock. It hadn't been made public yet, so Coulter would have to be in touch with someone close to the case. For that to be true, he had to have a means of communication.

He had to have access to a mobile.

Mobiles in prisons were either hidden whole, or were taken apart to hide, the SIM card being the most important part. Although it was a recent phenomenon, dogs were already being trained to sniff out mobile parts. It was the only option, short

297

of trying to block all mobile calls in and out of prison. Both methods were difficult to achieve, but were imperative if they were to prevent crime and drug empires being run from behind bars.

Rhona was sure she would unearth something to prove Coulter had found a way of communicating with the outside world. She set to work.


## CHAPTER FORTY-TWO

Bill could sense the energy when he entered the room, and wondered if it meant they had made a breakthrough. Multiple officers had been working on the mobile images gleaned from the calls they'd made to the public, and they wouldn't be so excited if they had found nothing.

Roy had placed mobiles at the scene via the calls they'd made and received. If their killer had made a call when at the funfair, he or she would be among those detected.

A hush descended as Bill walked to the front. Roy was seated next to a laptop, whose screen was duplicated on a whiteboard above him. On it was a map of the site, showing the location of every van and every funfair ride the night Kira was murdered.

Bill gave Roy a nod, and he began.

'Over sixty images were made available to us from that night; their locations are marked on the map. During the hour before Kira's disappearance we have a record of fifty calls bouncing off nearby masts, and all of these have been logged by the time the call was made. When we concentrated on the area around the dodgems, the Waltzers, the toilets and the mirror maze, the number narrows down to nearer twenty and the images to ten.' He paused. 'Just after Kira left the others at the dodgems, she showed up in the background of a short video.' He enlarged an image and set it to run.

The video showed a teenage boy kissing a girl before they both laughed towards the mobile in his outstretched hand. Behind them a pregnant female in a fringed jacket crossed the screen, face intent, walking quickly. It was Kira, looking very much alive.

'Five minutes later a photo taken near the line of female toilets finds this.'

He tapped the screen and a second image became enlarged. It was poorer quality than the video, but it was clear enough to see what the excitement in the room was about. Behind a kid with a candyfloss was a row of toilet cubicles. Emerging from one was a clown. There was an explosion of noise from those watching.

'We pick up the clown again a few minutes later.' Roy brought up another image. 'Next to the candyfloss van, in a direct line to the entrance to the mirror maze.'

'Anything that suggests the clown got in there with her?' Bill asked.

Roy shrugged. 'We can't tell. It would have to have happened via the exit or under the canvas at the rear, and no one was round there to take photos.'

'Let's see the shot near the candyfloss van again. Can we estimate the clown's height?'

Roy brought up a scale on the screen. The clown

was approximately two thirds the height of the van.

'We estimate it at 1.67 metres,' he said. 'Around five feet five.'

'Any sightings of the clown before that time?'

'None.'

Bill turned from the screen to address the group.

'OK, the clown emerged from a female cubicle, where we can assume they may have gone to put on the costume. So we have an average height female or a shorter male, in a red-haired clown wig, the colour of the fibres retrieved by forensic from under Kira's fingernail.' He turned back to Roy. 'Anyone else recorded in the vicinity of the maze around the time the victim went inside?'

Roy brought up three images. 'These were taken within a ten minute period.'

As Bill studied the photographs, his stomach flipped. 'Can you enlarge that one further?' He pointed at the third.

The image was slightly blurred, but unmistakeable. Tall and thin, dark-haired and hook-nosed. A raven, he'd thought when he first saw him at Morvern. Dr Frank Delaney, Kira's tutor, had been at the funfair the night she died.

\*  \*  \*

As soon as the commotion died down, Bill gave orders that Delaney be brought in for questioning. Then he headed for his office and closed the door. The coffee he'd fetched before the meeting sat cooling on his desk. He sat down on the swivel chair and took a swig. He didn't like hot coffee anyway. As he anticipated the caffeine hit, he

300

allowed a sense of satisfaction to flow through him.

He was reminded of the knitting his mother used to do when he was small. Fair Isle patterns, a weave of complex colour. But when things went wrong and she slid the knitting off the needles to rip it back, the pattern unravelled to reveal a set of single identifiable strands.

Kira—clever, manipulative, sexually promiscuous. A siren who influenced both men and women. In the video her expression had been intent. Was she heading somewhere in particular, to meet someone? Had Delaney also succumbed to her power and gone to meet her that night?

The last time her mobile had been used was to record the image of the doll for them to find, so it was logical to assume that whoever killed Kira took her phone and used it. The tech team had detailed all the calls and checked the numbers. The Daisy Chain gang had featured, David, home, a Twitter account she had set up. They were going through that account now. Bill had been shown some of the messages she'd posted online, direct messages received and sent, the people she'd been following and who had been following her. It had all looked like gobbledegook to him but it had to be studied, every last piece of empty-headed nonsense.

Bill glanced at his watch. They would have had to pull Delaney from school. Maybe even out of the classroom. No doubt the Principal of Morvern would comply with the police summons using her normal discretion, but he wouldn't like to be in her shoes if Delaney turned out to be a prime suspect in a murder case and the parents found out.

He fired up his laptop and logged on to the

crime scene software. He wanted another look at Delaney. This time he studied the expression on Delaney's face and decided the man was scanning the crowds. With his height it was easy. Was he looking for Kira? Had she been on her way to meet him when she went into the maze?

While he waited for news of Delaney's arrival, he picked up the phone and dialled Sutherland's office.

The DSI listened in silence while Bill outlined the developments in the case.

'Very well. Keep me informed.'

Bill caught him before he rang off. 'There's something else.'

'Can it wait?'

Bill decided to plough on regardless. 'It's about Fergus Morrison.'

'Who?' Sutherland knew full well who Bill was referring to.

'I heard he was dead, shot by an assassin. Is it true?'

'Where did you hear this?' Sutherland snapped.

'The rumour mill,' lied Bill.

'Canteen gossip.'

'It's not true then?'

'As I said, canteen gossip.'

The DSI was lying, and was aware that Bill knew it. He brought the discussion to an end. 'As I said, keep me informed about the *current* case.'

It was the signal to lay off, and Bill took it. He knew Fergus Morrison was dead, which meant the Kalinin case was dead in the water. If SOCA had something else up its sleeve, he wouldn't hear about it; the Super had made it clear that it was none of his business.

Bill knew he would have to tell Rhona that the rumour about Morrison's death was true, and regretted now that he had ever mentioned it to her. He feared he had only made matters worse.

He tried to refocus his thoughts on the fairground case and the man he was shortly to interview. Delaney had been plausible, pleasant even. Maybe he had been honest, for the most part. Good liars always stuck close to the truth; maybe Delaney had simply omitted the part where he was sleeping with his student.

There was a knock at the door and DS Clark stuck her head round.

'Delaney's here, Sir. Room five.'

Dr Delaney had exuded intelligence and confidence when seated in the Principal's study at Morvern. He looked considerably less confident now.

Police interview rooms tended to have an unpleasant smell. A lot of sweating went on in them, not to mention the actual bodily fluids left behind by some previous occupants. Bill was used to the odour, in the same way that the doctors and nurses who walked hospital corridors daily no longer smelt illness, disinfectant and death.

Frank Delaney looked deathly. When Bill entered, he rose from his seat and Bill noted again his spindly frame, shorn of its presence and authority without the black gown. He seemed to have shrunk in his twill trousers and tweed jacket.

Bill indicated that he should sit back down, then took his own place opposite. The eyes that met his drooped into dark shadows, and the hollows under Delaney's sharp cheekbones reminded Bill of a skull. Only the voice, when Delaney spoke,

303

retained strength and confidence.

'Why am I here?'

'Because you were at the funfair the night Kira Reese-Brandon died.'

There was a moment's silence during which Bill thought Dr Delaney would deny this, then he shrugged.

'I came out of the tube station and the lights attracted me. I went for a look.'

'You went to meet Kira.'

The man looked puzzled. 'What? Of course not. I had no idea Kira was there. How could I have known?'

'And you didn't see her?'

'No, I did not. I was only there a few minutes. As I said, I took a look out of curiosity, then left.'

'Why didn't you mention this before?'

He shrugged. 'It didn't seem important. As I said, I was there only briefly.'

'Is Kelvin Bridge your local tube station?'

There was a moment's hesitation. 'No, but there were a couple of yobs on the train making a nuisance of themselves. I decided to avoid trouble, get off and walk the rest.'

Bill sat back in his chair. A few beads of perspiration had appeared on Frank Delaney's broad brow.

'What was the nature of your relationship with Kira Reese-Brandon?'

'I was her tutor. You know that.'

'That's all?'

He bridled. 'Of course that's all.'

Bill shook his head.

'I think you were infatuated with your star pupil. I think you arranged to meet her that night at the funfair.'

'That is both ridiculous and offensive.' Delaney made to rise.

'Sit down,' Bill said brusquely.

He reluctantly retook his seat.

'Were you having a sexual relationship with Kira?'

The man's jaw clenched. '*No.*'

'Then why were you meeting her at the funfair?'

'I wasn't. I told you . . .'

'We have evidence that places you near the mirror maze close to the time of Kira's death.'

Now a rivulet of sweat trickled down the doctor's gaunt cheek, and he brought out an old-fashioned handkerchief and dabbed at it.

'I had no idea Kira was at the funfair. I told you, I got off the train because there was trouble.'

'And were drawn to the lights of the funfair?'

'Yes. I took a quick look and left.'

'The mirror maze was at the far side. It would have taken more than a few minutes to walk there.'

Dr Delaney shifted uncomfortably in his seat and said nothing.

Bill leaned forward. 'If you only wanted a quick look, why walk so far and in that particular direction?'

'I was looking for the toilets.'

Bill was sure he was lying.

'Did you find them?'

'There was a queue. I decided not to wait.' He seemed pleased with his quick answer.

'I'd like you to provide us with a swab for DNA purposes.'

'I don't think that's necessary,' said Delaney, affronted.

'You refuse?'

'I decline, because it's unnecessary.'

'If you had no contact with Kira that night, a swab will prove this.'

Delaney wanted out of there and a swab could provide him with an exit. But if he had had direct contact with Kira that night, it would put him in the frame for her murder. His decision would be very telling.

'I'll give you a few minutes to think this through,' said Bill.

The other man winced as Bill scraped back his chair and left the room. Bill closed the door behind him and took up a place at the observation window.

Dr Delaney sat very still, his eyes directed at the opposite wall. Bill wondered if he was aware he was being watched and didn't want to give his feelings away. Then something happened that shocked him; Delaney started to cry: deep, silent sobs that convulsed his body. Bill stood for a few minutes watching what appeared to be genuine grief. But were Delaney's tears for himself or the dead Kira?

Bill reentered the room and sat opposite again.

Eventually Delaney lifted his head and spoke. 'Kira wouldn't get rid of the baby in case it was mine. She said if it was, think what a mathematician it would be. I wanted her to have a termination, go to Cambridge, become what I knew she was capable of.' He met Bill's eye, his face anguished. 'I loved her. She was . . . extraordinary.'

'She'd been sleeping with someone else?'

He shook his head. 'Once. A drunken teenage

306

party. A mistake. She was adamant she wouldn't shirk her responsibilities. She wouldn't kill our baby.'

The same story she'd fed Ronald Reese-Brandon. Bill wondered how many more she'd spun that lie to.

'I think it's time you gave that DNA sample.'

'You'll be able to tell if I am the baby's father?'

'Yes.' Bill could have told him then that he wasn't, but he didn't.

'You went to the funfair to meet Kira that night?'

'She texted and asked me to.'

'Did the text come from her BlackBerry?'

He shook his head. 'She used pay-as-you-go phones for privacy. She was always changing them.'

'When did she text?'

'Half eleven.'

'Do you still have that text on your phone?'

'I planned to delete it, but after Kira died I couldn't bring myself to.'

Bill asked him for his mobile, and Delaney took it from his pocket and pushed it across the table.

'What did the message say?'

'To meet her near the mirror maze at eleven thirty.'

'Did she mention why she wanted to see you?'

'No. I don't understand. Why is the text so important?'

'Because I suspect Kira didn't send it.'

# CHAPTER FORTY-THREE

Even as she'd dismantled the latest Reborn, Rhona had to acknowledge how beautifully made it was. Coulter had been right when he'd told them his dolls were special.

Inside the head, Rhona had found the inscription *Melanie JC*. There was nothing else besides stuffing, tie tags, paint, varnish and glaze. Coulter hadn't objected strongly when Dr Shan told him that Dr MacLeod wanted to remove the doll for further examination. In Magnus's opinion, Coulter was revelling in the attention their visit had brought, even if it involved the removal of the doll. Rhona suspected he also knew she would find nothing in it.

Her systematic search of the workroom had identified few places available for concealment, and the doll had been the last possibility. If Coulter had access to a mobile, he wasn't keeping it in his room or where he worked. Nor, it appeared, was he keeping it inside this doll. So they had no physical link between Coulter and the case, apart from the fact he seemed to know all about it.

Rhona fetched a cup of coffee from the machine and sat down with it to think. Forensic work wasn't about testing, she reminded herself. It was about asking the right questions.

Coulter knew what was going on, which meant that someone close to the case was telling him— either someone involved in examining the case, or a witness.

She ran through possible contacts. Perhaps Maria Reese-Brandon? She was a vulnerable woman and they knew she had purchased a doll from him, and Coulter was good at manipulating women.

Was their contact sufficient for him to have influenced her? How had she first found out about Coulter and his Reborns? Could Kira's mother be 'Caroline'? Most importantly, if she knew about the baby's parentage, was she capable of killing her daughter? Rhona reminded herself that Kira's death may not have been intentional if removal of the baby had been the primary act. But would any mother leave her daughter to die?

The second possibility was Dr Shan. She continually defended Coulter. If she seriously believed he had been an ill man and through her care and medication had turned his life around, her defence of him was understandable. But what if Magnus were to prove that her diagnosis of Coulter had been wrong, and Coulter had been manipulating her? How damaging would that be for Dr Shan, both personally and professionally?

A startling yet totally plausible thought occurred.

Rhona left the lab, discarded her forensic suit and fetched her mobile.

Magnus answered on the third ring.

'Any luck?'

'Nothing in the doll,' she said.

'Oh.' Magnus sounded disappointed.

'But there is something.' She paused. 'Conan Doyle had Sherlock Holmes say: "When you have eliminated the impossible, whatever remains, no matter how improbable, must be the truth."'

There was a moment's silence. 'And what remains here?'

'Dr Shan must have allowed Coulter to use her mobile.'

*       *       *

When Rhona had hung up, Magnus sat down slowly, shaking his head in disbelief. If that was the answer, he was astonished by its simplicity. He began to recall each encounter he'd had with the doctor, placing each of her behaviours and responses within this new context: there was her irritation at his initial visit—perhaps she had been the real reason why it had taken so long for him to receive permission to visit Coulter; her annoyance when Coulter had given him permission to study his diary; the dismissive tone she had used when he'd raised the subject of the diary with her. Until he arrived on the scene, Dr Shan must have believed herself to be the sole recipient of Coulter's confidences.

Then there was her reaction to the revelation that Coulter might be in clandestine contact with the outside world. Dr Shan had had no fear of a hidden mobile being found, because she knew there wasn't one.

How would Coulter have persuaded her to allow such a breach of protocol? Perhaps Dr Shan so badly wanted to believe Coulter was better, that he was remorseful for what he had done, that she had been susceptible to his persuasive powers.

The first time Dr Shan's defences had slipped had been on their last visit. She had seemed truly shocked by the revelation that another girl had

310

died and that her name had matched that of Coulter's doll.

That would have been the moment to confess her involvement. Yet still she'd said nothing, and Magnus thought he knew why. Dr Shan may have had some idea about whom Coulter had been in touch with, and believed that contact had no connection to the case.

When he called the station, DS Clark told him the boss was in the interview room with Dr Delaney.

That surprised Magnus. 'Is Delaney a suspect?'

'The boss spotted him in one of the mobile shots taken near the Hall of Mirrors.'

'When he's free, could you tell him I'm on my way down and I need to talk to him?'

'Will do.'

A burst of adrenalin spurred him into action. Locking the front door, he took the stairs to the ground floor three at a time as he pulled his coat on. His bike stood chained against the railing that fronted the river, and as he fumbled with the padlock he realised he was buzzing with energy just like Coulter had been the first time they'd met. The memory of that meeting released a strong olfactory recollection of the man: his astringent aftershave, the light sweat brought on by adrenalin as Coulter had squared up to his opponent. Coulter had thought he would play with Magnus and ultimately fool him.

Magnus allowed himself a smile as he wove his way expertly through the downtown traffic towards the police station. Psychopaths commonly overestimated their own ability and underestimated that of others.

Bill left Delaney to sweat in the interview room a while longer. A SOCO had been requested to take prints and a DNA sample now that Delaney was officially a suspect, having been at the scene of crime and possessing a motive for killing his star pupil. But that wasn't enough to charge him. They would need physical evidence that he did meet with Kira that night, that he had been close enough to kill her.

Ronald Reese-Brandon, and now Frank Delaney. Similar stories, similar motives; love and hate, polar opposites that were never far apart.

But if it had been either of the men, what had they done with the baby? How had it been spirited away from the crime scene—hidden under a coat, or carried in a bag? Had it been crying, and if so, why had no one reported hearing it?

He called Roy Hunter and told him he had another mobile he wanted him to take a look at. If Kira's alleged text instructing Delaney to come to the funfair was still there, he wanted to know when it had arrived and where it had been sent from.

He retreated to his office and sat down, muttering his thoughts out loud.

Kira had been close to at least three men: the two he had recently confronted and David Murdoch, who had apparently disappeared off the face of the earth. The longer the teenager stayed off the radar, the more he became a suspect. First on scene, first suspect—it was a cliché because it was so often the case.

He wondered if David had known about Kira's

312

affair with her father, or her relationship with Delaney. If David had truly loved her, would he have put up with her behaviour? Maybe Kira had made a point of telling David everything, even the intimate details. That would be how she kept her power over him. And Kira had liked to have power over men.

Bill knew he'd have to also consider the women linked to the case. He used a pen to stir the remnants of his coffee, before taking a mouthful and starting to scribble notes on the pad on his desk.

\*　　\*　　\*

A while later, he called Janice Clark into his office. 'This woman who's writing to Coulter . . .?' he said.

'Caroline?'

'No, the partner. What do we know about her?'

Janice, a well-trained cop, rattled the details off from memory. 'Early twenties. Lives in Partick. No previous convictions. Wasn't implicated in the death of the infant.'

'Have we visited her since this case opened?'

DS Clark hesitated. 'I did see a report from social services.'

'They're still involved with her?'

'Her last baby died in suspicious circumstances, obviously, and now she's expecting another.'

'Geri Taylor is pregnant?' Bill couldn't hide his surprise.

DS Clark looked flustered. 'It appears so, Sir.'

Coulter had been adamant with Magnus that she wasn't seeing anyone else.

313

'Why wasn't I told this?'

DS Clark flushed in confusion.

'I'm sorry, Sir. I didn't realise . . .'

'Do we know yet if Caroline Sweet has been using the PO box to correspond with Coulter?'

'I'm not sure. I'll check.'

'Do that,' he snapped.

He regretted his tone almost immediately. Of course his detective sergeant didn't realise how important this snippet of information about Geri's pregnancy was; Magnus's meetings with Coulter had been kept between him and Bill. He should have checked all Coulter's connections with the outside himself, not blamed his subordinates for his own failings. He moderated his tone. 'Can you find out about the PO box for me? Also, I'd like to see the social services file on Geri Taylor.'

'Yes, Sir. Also, Professor Pirie called. He's on his way in and wants to speak to you.'

'Please show him in as soon as he gets here.'

A mortified DS Clark left his office. Bill watched as the door closed behind her. What the hell was going on here? Two young women dead, one infant dead in the womb, another missing, presumed dead. A psychopath behind bars still managing to manipulate people. Adultery, incest, teachers sleeping with their pupils, adolescent drug use and orgies.

No wonder DS Clark couldn't keep it all in her head. Even McNab would have struggled with this one, although his former DS's capacity to comprehend man's inhumanity to man had been legendary.

He'd thought earlier that he was beginning to see a pattern, but now he was less sure. Nothing fitted.

So Coulter's partner was pregnant, but not by him. Not unless conjugal visits had become a feature of life in the State Hospital. Bill wondered if Coulter knew about the pregnancy. Dr Shan had stated that Geri had visited Coulter twice in the last month, so had Geri disguised her condition? Maybe she wasn't that far along.

Bill remembered how short Coulter's temper was. Although the man had said Geri was fine with him writing to other women, he couldn't imagine Coulter being quite so easy with the idea of Geri having a relationship. He asked Magnus what he thought as soon as he arrived.

'I think Coulter would take that very badly indeed. He was extremely angry when I dared to suggest Geri might have taken another partner since he'd been incarcerated.' Magnus paused. 'There's something else.'

'What?'

'Rhona didn't find anything in the room or in the latest Reborn. She suggested Coulter might have been using Dr Shan's mobile to contact someone on the outside.'

'You think that's a possibility?'

'I do, although I wish I'd thought of it sooner.'

'I wish I had too.'

Bill called the incident room, and when DS Clark answered, she immediately told him that the social services report on Geri Taylor was on its way. Bill cut her short.

'I'd like Dr Shan, Coulter's psychiatrist, contacted and asked to come down to the station.' He'd already decided not to mention the mobile, in case she conveniently lost it before she got there.

315

'Make it sound like a standard request.'

He thanked her, hung up and turned to Magnus.

'I'd like you present at the interview, if that's OK?'

'Yes, of course.'

'Before Dr Shan arrives, I need to bring you up to date on Delaney and Kira's father.' He paused. 'Both men admit to having a sexual relationship with Kira. She apparently told both of them that the child was probably theirs.'

Magnus seemed unsurprised.

'Either man could be a suspect,' he said. 'Both have motives, particularly if they believed Kira was playing them off against one another,' he added thoughtfully. 'But why leave the doll and the mobile for us to find?'

'To convince us that Kira's killer was psychologically damaged?'

'And why kill Melanie?'

'The two deaths might not be connected.'

'Two pregnant girls, both members of the same gang . . .'

'Melanie's killer didn't remove the foetus.'

Magnus nodded thoughtfully. 'We're missing something.'

*That's why you're here*, thought Bill. Instead, he said, 'If it *is* either of those two men, that means Coulter isn't involved.'

'And yet he believes himself to be,' said Magnus.

'Is that not in the nature of a psychopath?'

'But Coulter still has information he shouldn't be privy to.'

'I'm hoping the arrival of Dr Shan might enlighten us on that score,' replied Bill.

Magnus regarded Dr Shan with interest as she took a seat in Bill's office. He wondered if Bill was as aware of her fragrance as he was. It was not particularly strong, but he found it very noticeable. DI Wilson had decided not to have her shown to an interview room, but had her brought here to his office. Magnus had accompanied her from reception, and on the way she had passed through the incident room. He believed from her reaction that this was her first time in a police station, and a quick glance behind as he opened the door to DI Wilson's office confirmed that it was certainly the first time the investigating team had seen anyone quite like her; the dropped jaws of the men and the envious looks from the women had been proof of that.

Now Bill opened the interview with a pleasant smile.

'Dr Shan, thank you for coming in. I'm sorry we couldn't come to see you at the hospital.' He indicated the window separating them from the incident room. 'In the middle of an enquiry it can be difficult to get away.'

Dr Shan nodded. 'I quite understand, Detective Inspector.'

'Dr MacLeod has confirmed that she did not find any evidence that your patient was concealing mobile parts either in his workroom or inside the recently completed Reborn he called Melanie. Nevertheless, Mr Coulter is in receipt of information on this case which is not available to the general public.'

Magnus thought Dr Shan might respond to this,

317

but she pursed her lips and said nothing.

'We believe therefore that you allowed Mr Coulter to use your mobile phone to make contact with someone outside the hospital.'

She frowned, her composure faltering. 'That isn't allowed under hospital rules.'

'Nevertheless, you did so, did you not?'

She seemed struck dumb.

Bill's voice hardened. 'I repeat, did you allow a patient detained in a State Hospital to make private calls using your personal mobile phone?'

Magnus was impressed at how little the doctor's shock showed in her bearing, but he could sense her distress. He watched her eyes flicker as she absorbed the accusation, then rapidly weighed up her response. She seemed to come to a decision.

'I did allow Mr Coulter to call his partner on just two occasions. He was distressed by a letter from her and wanted to speak to her privately.'

'He was alone with your mobile phone on two occasions only?'

Dr Shan looked uncomfortable. 'During our meetings, I was sometimes called away.'

'And on those occasions you left your mobile in the room with him?'

She looked even more uneasy. 'I may have done.'

'Isn't that against the rules?'

'Coulter has proved himself to be trustworthy.'

'Did you ever check to see if he made a call?'

'No.'

'But you suspect he might have.'

'It is possible.'

'In light of this, I must ask you to hand over your mobile for examination.'

318

'But it has all my personal numbers, not only my work.'

'We will respect your privacy, Dr Shan. We're only interested in calls made by Mr Coulter.'

Magnus caught a faint, acrid whiff of sweat under her floral scent. Dr Shan, for all her Zen training, was in a dark place at this moment. Having given her trust to someone, she was now faced with the spectre of betrayal. He wondered if she had ever harboured a suspicion that she was wrong about the extent of Coulter's rehabilitation. Or had Coulter simply fooled her as he had fooled others?

'Please give me your phone,' said Bill.

She hesitated, then reached into her bag and passed the mobile across the desk.

'When should I expect it to be returned?'

DI Wilson's expression was unreadable. 'When we're finished with it.'

## CHAPTER FORTY-FOUR

Chrissy had laid out her trophies and was studying them intently: the trap from under the plughole of the bath, the green Dionysos mask and a toothbrush.

Rhona was particularly intrigued by the last item. Toothbrushes were good sources of DNA, as good as the mouth swabs taken from potential suspects. However, there had only been one toothbrush in Melanie's bathroom—a pink electric one, which you would assume was hers and therefore contained only her DNA.

319

'We don't know that,' Chrissy said wisely. 'Someone in that room puked in the bath.' She indicated the trap, which had been unscrewed to reveal a matting of long, dark brown hair and a mess of gunge that resembled vomit. 'If I puke, for whatever reason, I always clean my teeth afterwards. I don't care whose toothbrush I use.'

Rhona made a mental note to hide her toothbrush whenever Chrissy came round.

'What about the toilet seat?' she asked.

'He, she or it did not piss before they left.' Chrissy sounded disappointed. 'No prints on the seat from being lifted by a man. Nothing on the handle from flushing, either.'

'And the mask?'

Chrissy grinned. 'As fertile and entertaining as the god himself. What was his name again?'

'Dionysos, or Bacchus if you prefer Roman lore to Greek.'

'Well, Dionysos has been busy. I found various traces of DNA on our god here, lots of skin flakes and also some semen. Looks like that inviting mouth was used for more than just kissing.' Chrissy wiggled her eyebrows. 'What about your body?'

'The taping picked up traces of DNA around Melanie's mouth and her right arm. I also found something else.'

'What?'

Rhona beckoned Chrissy over to the high-powered microscope, where she settled herself on the stool and peered through the lens.

The partial shark skin dentricle had been picked up by the tape from the top Melanie had been wearing. If they were unsure whether the two deaths were linked, this evidence alone was enough to convince them.

Chrissy turned from the microscope. 'You think whoever smothered Melanie was planning to cut out the foetus?'

'Why else would they have the knife with them?'

'So what went wrong?'

'They were disturbed before they could operate? That seems the most likely scenario,' said Rhona.

'No trace of chloroform?' Chrissy asked.

'None. She was simply smothered, although I'm not sure that the pillow was the murder weapon. From the evidence we have, I think someone may have put a hand over her mouth.'

'The same person who killed Kira?'

'It seems more than likely.'

'We're getting closer,' said Chrissy, unable to disguise her delight.

*But not close enough*, Rhona thought.

\*     \*     \*

She'd once worked on a case where skin flakes had been found on the deceased's hand. The evidence had placed a suspect at the scene, but it hadn't proved they had killed the victim. The truth turned out to be quite different; the suspect had arrived at the scene and had held the hand of the victim as they died. That small act of compassion had made them a prime suspect, at least for a while. No wonder the general public feared getting involved and so many people reported incidents anonymously.

Rhona studied the results of the DNA analysis of the traces of foreign skin found on Melanie's

321

body. Someone had covered her mouth and nose, probably with their hand. The same person had grasped her arm. She suspected, but had yet to confirm, that the vomit Chrissy had discovered in the bath would belong to the same person.

Forensically, she could place David Murdoch in Melanie's bedroom. She could prove through trace evidence that he had covered Melanie's mouth and nose and held her arm.

According to Owen Hegarty, David had left school early on Friday, which would have given him time to visit Melanie before she died. His stepfather had said David spent Friday evening in his room, then the stepdad had left for work early on Saturday and hadn't seen or heard from David after that. The teenager had simply disappeared.

From all accounts, his sexuality notwithstanding, David had been besotted with Kira. She had taken pity on him, scooped him into her bright sphere of existence. Without Kira, David was nothing, in his eyes at least. Why would he kill her, and why would he kill Melanie? Did he know Melanie was carrying his child?

When Rhona had seen them together in the park, he'd appeared to be comforting an obviously distraught Melanie. He hadn't looked capable of killing her, or anyone else.

But Melanie had let *someone* into the house, someone she'd known and trusted. Someone like David.

What had happened in that bedroom?

If David had been the one to vomit in the bath, had he been shocked by what he'd done, or by what he'd seen?

Rhona wrote up her report before logging into

322

the software and recording the DNA findings on the Melanie case profile. Then she called Bill.

Once she'd explained about the skin flakes on Melanie's mouth and arm, she told him about the shark skin dentricle.

'It came from the same knife?' he asked.

'Yes.'

'Melanie's death is in the evening paper. I issued a photo of David as a missing person, to go with the story.'

'You already suspected he was involved in her death?'

'He disappeared around the time she died. It was too much of a coincidence.'

'And now we can place the knife at both scenes,' she said.

'Good work,' said Bill. 'Also, I spoke to Maria Reese-Brandon. I told her that her husband had fathered Kira's baby and she went into shock. I don't think she had any idea what was going on between them. Anyway, he's lost his alibi for that night, as his wife now says he did go out.'

'You think he went to meet Kira?'

'He admits he did—says Kira texted him and asked him to pick her up, but then never appeared.'

'I found no evidence to place him in the Hall of Mirrors.'

'That doesn't mean he wasn't there.'

There was a moment's silence before Bill said, 'And what about David—would he have had enough time to remove the baby and hide it before he called 999?'

'Just about.'

'Maybe David did kill Kira. Maybe he found out

323

about Frank Delaney and Ronald Reese-Brandon and flipped out.' He paused. 'But why would he kill Melanie?'

'Because she had reason to suspect him?'

They would never know the answers to their questions until they found David Murdoch.

## CHAPTER FORTY-FIVE

David checked the path below before rising from his hiding place. With dusk approaching he felt more confident about venturing out. He'd now spent two nights on the street; the first, he'd slept in an alley behind Sauchiehall Street and found the experience terrifying, with drunks looking for a fight and the police looking for the drunks. He'd moved to Kelvingrove Park after that. It was colder and wetter, but he'd felt safer hidden among the undergrowth on the steep incline from the Kelvin walkway.

His legs felt unsteady as he ploughed his way through thick ivy towards the path. He needed food, but if he bought cheap alcohol it might both stave off the hunger and help calm his anxiety. He made his way swiftly by the river walk towards Kelvinbridge, hood up, head down.

When he reached the main road he headed for a corner shop. He'd checked the stands every day for anything on Melanie and there had been nothing so far. He was beginning to believe he'd dreamt it. Maybe she hadn't been dead after all? Maybe she'd just been unconscious and he'd panicked for no reason.

He walked in and picked up a bottle of strong cider. He had enough for that and a chocolate bar, which was better than nothing. He approached the counter.

The male assistant pointed at a sign that said, *ID required for all purchases of alcohol.*

David checked his wallet as though looking for ID. 'Sorry, mate, forgot to bring it.'

'No ID, no alcohol.'

'That's OK. I'll just take the chocolate.'

David handed over his basket. The guy removed the cider and stood it to one side, rang up the chocolate and handed him his change.

David thanked him and made a point of putting the chocolate bar in his backpack while the next customer took his place. He waited until the assistant was occupied with the next guy, then snatched the cider and bolted for the door. On the way to the door, his head whipped back as he spotted the headline on the topmost of a pile of newspapers.

### Friend of funfair victim found dead

Next to a photo of Melanie was one of himself. He registered all this in a split second, then scrambled out of the door as the shopkeeper was still coming around the counter.

Darting across Great Western Road, he made for the underground station. Entry was by escalator from street level, and he ran down the moving stairs. His quick glance back had showed no one following—chances were the man would do nothing. Why hassle the police for a bottle of cider?

He hung around inside for a while, his heart thumping against his ribs. When he was certain no one was following him, he reemerged and took the steps down to the park. Heading for the nearest bench, he opened the cider, gulping down as much as he could at one go.

When he was sure his stomach wasn't about to reject it, he swallowed some more. Already the gnawing hunger was retreating, and with it the numbness in his fingers and toes. He screwed the lid back on and tore the wrapping off the chocolate bar. He ate slowly, letting each square melt on his tongue before adding another.

While he savoured the chocolate, he worried whether the guy in the shop might have recognised him from the photo in the paper, then realised that he didn't look like that any more. In the picture, his hair had been styled, and one of the first things he'd done when he went on the run was wet it and brush it back. Without the gel to hold it in place, it had sprung back into its natural curls, and now he looked like the geek he'd been before Kira had taken him in hand. The memory of Kira brought a wave of self-pity; this was what life was like without her. He took another slug of cider, then anchored the bottle inside his jacket.

Where to now?

He gazed at the lights of the funfair. It had only been scheduled to stay for a week but notoriety had brought out the crowds, delaying its departure.

The alcohol had taken effect, lifting his mood. He was seized by the drunken idea that if he visited the funfair, he could pretend the last nine days had never happened. Maybe he could even convince himself for a while that Kira was alive and waiting for him there.

He rose unsteadily to his feet, slung the

326

backpack over his shoulder and headed for the lights. The path ran alongside the river, and he realised that if he walked far enough he would end up directly below Kira's house.

The night of the party had been only the second time he'd been allowed inside. On both occasions her parents had been away. The first time, they'd drunk vodka from the drinks cabinet, and he'd got pissed and revealed his sexual confusion and inexperience to Kira. She had vowed then to help him end his abstinence.

The second time had been for the party, when Kira had produced the green mask and insisted he wear it. High as a kite, he'd had sex with Melanie. She hadn't been the only one that night—drugs, drink and the mask had combined to make him lose all his inhibitions. He'd felt like he'd actually become Dionysos.

He laughed at the memory of another encounter on the stairs to the back cellar. Then, wearing the mask, he had been the focus for someone else's lust, someone he knew would never admit to such leanings. That had been the most liberating experience of his life, because he finally realised what Kira had said was true.

*Everyone can take what they want.*

There was a vibration in his pocket as his phone registered an incoming message. He stood, swaying slightly, undecided. Should he read it? What if it was the police? He glanced round surreptitiously. The crowds continued to walk past him as though he was invisible. If Kira had been with him, everyone would be staring at them. She always looked so cool. He smiled at the memory, then his face crumpled and tears oozed from his eyes. *I am*

327

*pathetic*, he thought, *and I don't care*. There was nothing to care about any more. He pulled out the phone, checked the sender's name and opened it.

*W R U? I need 2 spk 2U*

He texted back: *at funfair.*

The reply was almost instantaneous. *W8 thr am cmg I know who kild Kira*

He spotted the mirror maze in the near distance and staggered towards it, alcohol swirling through his brain. The lights and throbbing music of the funfair enveloped him, heightening the acuteness of his memories like a drug. Kira. He recalled the scent of her skin—milky and sweet, like a baby's. Her voice. He laughed at the memory. She always sounded so posh, even when she was swearing.

He stopped, realising he was at the mirror maze. The pain flooded back. He whimpered and slid to the ground, anchoring his arms round his chest. He felt the bulge of the cider bottle and pulled it out, opened it with shaking hands and began to drink in large, rapid gulps, desperate to blot out the image of Kira's bloodsoaked body. When the bottle was empty he threw it to one side. The world swam before him, ebbing and flowing, but the acute pain had lessened to a dull throb.

Some time later, he didn't know how long, he heard a voice and looked up. The words made no sense. He lowered his head again because it felt too heavy and settled his eyes on the boots that stood before him. They were red. He thought about stepping in Kira's blood, sliding in it. Falling. He felt the thump as his head hit the wood and winced. His eyes were closing and he forced them open again. That smell was back, jolting his memory. He slid further down, began curling himself into a ball. Now he was inches from the red boots. And he remembered. The flash of red under the mirror when he'd fallen.

'You were there,' he said in disbelief, his voice slurred.

## CHAPTER FORTY-SIX

Bill skimmed through the social services report, looking for confirmation that Geri Taylor was pregnant.

Magnus had seemed saddened by Dr Shan's confession, although Rhona had already suggested to him that the doctor might be involved. Before leaving, he had said, 'I want to take another look at Coulter's diary, to see if anything in there suggested who else he might have been in touch with. I can't help but feel that's why he wanted me to have it.'

'If I discover who Coulter called, or who Caroline is, I'll let you know,' Bill had promised.

Now Bill glanced at his watch and realised guiltily that he should have called Margaret and let her know he wouldn't be back to eat with the family. Time had simply run away from him.

He closed the file and slipped it in a folder to take with him. He wouldn't read it properly until Margaret was asleep, to give her at least a couple of hours of his time. He nodded to the night shift on his way out, but DS Clark was nowhere to be seen. He hoped she was at home relaxing—after the bollocking she'd got from him today, she deserved it.

When he reached home, Margaret was in the dining room, a pile of jotters on the table in front of her. She gave him a weary smile.

'It's curry,' she said. 'Just pop the plate in the microwave, and put the naan bread in the toaster.'

He busied himself in the kitchen, suddenly ravenous. When the microwave pinged, he extracted the steaming plate, flipped the naan from the toaster and carried it all through to join Margaret at the table.

'You look tired,' he said, concerned.

'I'm OK. But I'm heading for bed when I finish this.' She had two more books to mark.

'I could join you, bring us both up a whisky?'

She smiled. 'That would be nice.'

She bent back over her marking, and he studied her soft, new curls as he ate his dinner. They reminded him of Lisa's baby hair. He wanted to ask Margaret if she really was OK, if her return to work had been too soon after the chemotherapy. But instead he pondered how easy he found it to forget everything when he was working on a case, even his wife's cancer. Thankfully it was in remission, but he still felt ashamed that it wasn't in his mind every minute of the day. For a long time it had been, but you could grow used to anything in time.

'Are the kids home?'

'Lisa's next door with Diane, and Robbie's in his room. There.' She placed the last jotter on the pile. 'How long will you be?'

'Ten minutes?'

'Any longer and I'll be asleep.'

He watched her climb the stairs through the open door. Did she always look so tired at the end

330

of the day? He made a mental note to check that Lisa and Robbie were pulling their weight, although he was guiltily aware that, as usual, he wasn't.

The spicy curry had lost some of its flavour. He took a couple more forkfuls, then pushed the plate to one side. He would go upstairs and spend some time with Margaret, then when she fell asleep he would come back down and study the social services report on Geri Taylor.

He poured a couple of whiskies, went through to the kitchen to add water, then headed upstairs. Margaret was already in bed, a book open on her lap. She smiled at him as he entered.

'I was sure you'd get engrossed in that file you brought home and forget to come up.'

'You know me too well.' He handed her a glass, kicked off his shoes and stretched out on the bed beside her.

They sipped in companionable silence. This was what love was, he thought. Someone you could be quiet with.

He planted a kiss on the side of her head.

'What's that for?'

'Because I love you.'

'And I love you too.'

He switched the glass to his other hand and put his arm about her. She nestled close against him. He wanted to make love to her, but didn't want to impose himself.

'Get undressed,' she ordered.

\*         \*         \*

Later, Bill closed the file and pushed it to one side.

According to the report, Geri Taylor's baby was due any time. Bill couldn't imagine how she could have visited Coulter in recent days and hidden her pregnancy. Might his partner's pregnancy have anything to do with Coulter's behaviour in this case?

He was done thinking about Coulter tonight. He poured another small whisky, double-locked the door and began to climb wearily to bed. He was on the third stair when the silent mobile vibrated in his pocket.


## CHAPTER FORTY-SEVEN

David lay close to the back canvas wall of the mirror maze, a plastic cider bottle by his side. In the dark he would have looked like a drunk, passed out on the grass.

The paramedic team had pulled aside his heavy jacket to reveal a knife, its blade buried deep in his left side under the ribcage. David's cold hands still gripped the shaft as though he had made the thrust himself, like a Roman falling on his sword.

'He was dead when we got here.' The female paramedic looked not much older than Lisa, her hair pulled back in a ponytail, a stud glinting in her nose. 'We found this.' She handed Bill a scrap of paper. On it was scrawled, *I killed them.*

'Could he have done that to himself?'

'It's do-able, if you're determined and the knife's sharp enough.' She shrugged. 'He's all yours now.'

She picked up her bag and the two headed off

towards an inquisitive and growing group of bystanders.

'Get a tent up,' Bill called to the nearest uniformed officer. 'And get rid of the vultures.'

\* \* \*

The shadows were back, advancing and retreating. Sitting in the semi-darkness, bunched under the duvet with the cat on her lap, Rhona was comforted by their presence.

McNab would always be there, just out of sight in the corner of her eye. She had decided she preferred his ghost to the nagging hope that he might still be alive.

Further calls to the answerphone on Skye had yielded only silence. She'd enlisted Roy Hunter's help as planned. After anxiously listening to her concocted tale about a stalker, he'd agreed to check her mobile and also the phone number on Skye.

She'd been itching to ask him to compare the voice to McNab's, but sensibly had not. She would have to be content with discovering the origins of both calls.

Petersson hadn't been in touch since Saturday morning when she'd harangued him at his flat about her mobile. She found herself hoping she would never hear from the Icelander again, and suspected his silence meant he had been using her as much as she had him. But one thing kept nagging at her; she could not deny that everything he'd told her had turned out to be true. She wondered if Bill had challenged Sutherland on Fergus Morrison's death.

The phone rang, and she checked the caller ID. Not Petersson. Good. She answered it.

'David Murdoch's dead,' said Bill.

'What?'

'Found knifed near the mirror maze. He left a note saying he killed both girls. Are you OK to come down?'

*　　　*　　　*

It was all too familiar. The throbbing music, the lights, the morbidly curious crowds. And the forensic tent, propped against the wall of the larger mirror maze marquee and blazing in the hastily-erected arc lights.

She donned her suit and mask, slipped on latex gloves and picked up her forensic case. Despite the thinness of the layer that now separated her from the funfair, the sounds outside seemed to drop away as she entered the smaller tent. When she pulled back the mask a little and took a deep breath, the first scent she distinguished was the sweet, sickly odour of cheap alcohol. After that came blood, then the rank undertone of emptied bowels.

She stood for a moment and took in the scene.

The body was slumped close to the canvas. She estimated it was a couple of metres short of the exit, which placed David's body roughly level with the place they'd discovered Kira nine days before.

He lay curled in a foetal position, knees bent up, both hands on the knife that jutted at an angle from his chest. Through his fingers Rhona could make out the rough, grey, shark skin handle.

He was unshaven, the formerly straight fringe

now wavy and swept greasily back. His startled eyes were bloodshot, his fingernails grimy. The jeans were covered in mud, trainers soaked through. It looked as though he'd been living rough since he'd left home.

The placement of his hands round the knife handle puzzled her—the grip looked unnatural and she wasn't sure why. If she had been intent on thrusting a knife into her guts, how would she hold it? She mimicked gripping an invisible knife, and instinctively her right hand curled over the left. In David's case, the left hand was on top. Had he been left-handed?

She gently loosened his grip, which proved easy as David's fingertips had been scarcely engaged with the handle's surface. That wasn't surprising; as he'd lost control of his limbs, his hold would probably have loosened. Of course, there was a possibility his hands had never held the knife in the first place. She dusted the handle for prints.

Bill had said he'd left a note, admitting to killing both girls. Knives weren't uncommon in suicides, if you were desperate enough. And David looked like a desperate boy.

As she worked, the noise outside diminished further as the funfair shut down for the night. The police would be busy asking the same questions as before, trying to find someone in the crowds that had milled around the rides and stands who might have seen the last few minutes of David Murdoch's life.

When she finally emerged, Bill was waiting with coffee. A nearby snack van had stayed open at his request to feed and water the SOCOs and uniforms still present.

Rhona added two sugars before taking a grateful sip.

'What do you think?' Bill said.

'Well, the angle of entry could fit with a self-inflicted injury, so it may well have been suicide.'

'Anything else?'

'He's been sleeping rough. Probably drinking rather than eating. There was no obvious sign of an attacker. I loosened his grip, took some samples from the handle and left the knife *in situ*. It looked like shark skin. Was David left-handed?'

Bill thought about it. 'I don't know. Why?'

'It's OK. I'll check.'

'I just don't get it.' Bill shook his head. 'If David did kill Kira and remove the baby, what the hell did he do with it?'

Rhona sighed. 'It doesn't fit with the Coulter situation either.'

Bill swore softly. 'I forgot to tell you! Coulter's partner, Geri Taylor, is pregnant. Apparently it's due any day now.'

'What? Are you sure?'

'It was in her file from social services.'

'Coulter took it very badly when Magnus even suggested Geri might have a new partner. I can't imagine what he would do if he knew she was pregnant. Have you spoken to her?'

'I planned to go there tomorrow. But if David was the killer, I don't know where we're going with the Coulter investigation.'

'He still appeared to know what was happening,' she reminded him.

Exhaustion had set in for both of them. Even strong, sweet coffee was no longer keeping it at bay.

'Are you awake enough to drive home?' said Bill.

'It's not far.'

'I'll let you know when the post-mortem is scheduled. It won't be early, that's for sure.'

## CHAPTER FORTY-EIGHT

Magnus woke with a start to find the first pink light of dawn filtering into the room. He was still sitting on the settee in front of the fire, Coulter's diary on his knee. Beside him on a coffee table stood the remains of a bottle of Highland Park. He checked the level; he'd hit it hard, but not enough to give him a headache.

He glanced down at the open page of the diary, trying to remember where he had got to before he'd fallen asleep. Then he remembered.

Five times he'd spotted the same reference. He'd gone so far as to mark each with a slip of paper. He rose, excited. Was it too early to call Bill? He checked his watch. He would give it half an hour.

He switched on the coffee machine and headed for the shower. Under a burst of water, he almost felt like singing, but settled for some joyful humming instead.

Excitement had generated real hunger. He poured a mug of coffee, then set about frying himself bacon and eggs. Ten minutes later he sat down to a full plate with toast and more coffee and thought about what his discovery might mean.

Coulter had sent him the diary as a test. He'd

planned everything, then written it in there to challenge Magnus, his own self-belief unassailable. How Coulter must have loved those hospital visits. The sparring between Dr Shan, his defendant, and Magnus, his chosen adversary. He remembered the man's knowing smile when he'd said, 'You've been reading my diary.'

He flipped through the diary again, double-checking in case lack of sleep or too much whisky had addled his brain. But the phrase was there.

*I can get her anuther*

Twenty minutes later he succumbed and rang Bill's number. He thought it was about to go to voicemail, then a woman's voice answered.

'Yes?'

'Is DI Wilson there? It's Professor Pirie.'

'Is it urgent? He only got home three hours ago. He's still asleep.'

'I'm sorry, but I think it probably is urgent.'

He heard the phone go down, then some whispered words, before Bill's muffled voice came on the line.

'Bill, it's Magnus.'

'You found something?'

'I believe the baby's alive, and I think I know where it is.'

\*       \*       \*

The red sunrise had been replaced by a bright blue February sky. They were ahead of the rush hour traffic, and the city streets were just waking up to a new day.

Bill drove west along the Clydeside expressway past the Finnieston bridge, eventually cutting up into Dumbarton Road. Magnus sat in the passenger seat.

Earlier, Bill had listened intently to the professor's theory about the references in Coulter's diary, before breaking the news about David Murdoch.

Magnus had puzzled over that, and for the first time doubt had begun to creep in.

'How does that fit with your theory?' Bill said.

'I don't know,' Magnus admitted.

Bill wasn't convinced, Magnus could tell, but the DI was willing to go along with his request.

Exeter Drive was a steep street off Partick's main thoroughfare, rising through red sandstone apartment blocks on the left and post-war flats on the right. They drew up outside the number Bill had been given, parked and climbed the steps to the communal front entrance, which was doorless, then on up to the first landing. Bill chose the central door, whose glass panel showed a light was on inside. As they approached, they heard the high-pitched cry of a baby.

Bill rang the doorbell.

A young woman opened the door to them, wearing a quilted dressing gown and slippers. Her face was fuzzy from sleep and she carried a baby's bottle, full of milk.

'Geri Taylor?'

She nodded, her sleepy expression replaced by wakeful suspicion.

Bill showed her his warrant card. 'Could we come inside?'

Fear flooded her face and she made an attempt to shut the door, but when Bill's foot prevented her, she turned and fled, running down a narrow hall and through a doorway. Bill raced after her, reaching the inner door before she could shut it in his face.

When Magnus followed, Geri was standing as far away from Bill as was possible in the tiny sitting room, hugging a bundle to her chest. A pushchair stood near the window and baby clothes hung on a drying rack close to a gas fire. The room smelt of baby: regurgitated milk and watery urine. The bundle against her squirmed, emitting a hungry cry.

'Why don't you sit down and feed the baby,' Bill said quietly. 'We can talk when you've finished.'

Geri's eyes darted between them warily. A further piercing shriek decided things for her. She sat down on a nearby couch and offered the bottle to the baby's eager mouth. The screaming ceased immediately.

Her eyes were on the baby all the time it fed, and her face was placid and happy now. She looked every inch the besotted new mother.

Magnus wondered if he could be wrong, but knew in his heart he wasn't.

There were three babygros hanging on the drier. All were pink, with a daisy embroidered on the front.

Geri propped the baby upright on her knee and rubbed its back to burp it. While it did so, she said, 'Well done, *Daisy.*'

Bill looked at Magnus.

'I'll call social services.'

\*　　　\*　　　\*

By mid-morning, a hysterical Geri Taylor had been

340

transferred to hospital along with the baby.

Any attempt Bill had made to question her while he waited for backup had been met with a terrified silence. Even Magnus's soothing tones had brought no response. While they waited, she never let the baby out of her arms.

The arrival of the ambulance, paramedics and a social worker had sent her into a complete breakdown. Screaming and crying, she had begged them not to take her little girl away.

They all kept repeating that they just wanted to check that both she and the baby were well. It was a lie, and she knew it.

By the time they managed to get her in the ambulance, the whole street was twitching net curtains and wanting to know what was happening. Some came out into the street, which made it easy to quiz Geri's neighbours about her pregnancy. As far as they all knew, she had indeed been pregnant, and nine days ago had been seen walking a newborn in a pram. There had been no boyfriend on the scene, as far as Bill could establish, and none recalled by the neighbours during the past nine months.

Bill also discovered that it had been Geri herself who'd informed social services of the pregnancy. A woman from the department had visited her and found her well and happy and looking forward to the new baby. When questioned about the baby's father, Geri had insisted the pregnancy had been the result of a one night stand. She had been drunk at the time and couldn't remember the man's name. It was a common enough story, and the social worker had seen no reason not to accept it. In fact, in her case, the woman from social services had thought it better not to have a man in the picture, since Geri's previous partner had killed her first child.

'We had no idea the child had been born. Normally we get word from the hospital, who would have a health visitor scheduled. We would have followed up with a visit ourselves,' she said worriedly.

Bill reassured her that this was an exceptional case. He didn't tell her that in all likelihood Geri Taylor had never given birth.

He shuddered to think how things might have turned out if Coulter hadn't sought to involve Magnus. If the inmate had carried out his plan without attracting attention to himself, they might never have found the baby. Even now, Coulter would be confident in his belief that he had Magnus and the rest of them fooled.

After the ambulance left, Bill called DS Clark and asked her to check whether Geri Taylor had had prenatal care locally in Partick or had been admitted to any hospital in greater Glasgow to deliver. Before he heard back from her, he had his answer; the doctor examining Geri at the hospital called to confirm that the child couldn't be hers.

'The young woman in question has definitely not given birth recently.'

'How old is the baby?'

'About a week. We're running some tests, but she appears in good health and has been well looked after.'

'I need a blood sample for DNA purposes.'

'No problem.'

Until the baby's DNA was checked against the umbilical cord, they couldn't say for certain—but

Bill was sure it was Kira's child.

Magnus had gone home, professing himself keen to go through the diary again. Maybe there was more to be gleaned from the pages of rambling script. Bill was just grateful for what the professor had already found.

Magnus had been of the opinion that Geri was unlikely to have carried out the foetal theft alone, and Bill agreed. Eventually Geri might reveal how she got the baby, but judging by her current state of mind, it wouldn't be soon.

Bill left a team of SOCOs working the house and headed for his car. He called Rhona before he left.

'It's Kira's child?' She sounded astonished and delighted.

'I'm hoping you'll be the one to prove that. The hospital's sending you a blood sample.'

'How did you find her?'

'Magnus found a repeated reference in Coulter's diary. It said, "I can get her another". He thought Coulter was referring to getting Geri a baby. Not making one for her. I decided it was worth checking his theory out.'

'Thank God you did.'

'I know,' he said. 'The post-mortem on David Murdoch is at one o'clock. Can you make it?'

'I'll be there.'

## CHAPTER FORTY-NINE

When Bill arrived at the station, word was already out that they had found a baby believed to be

343

Kira's, and that Professor Pirie had somehow been involved.

The team were ready and waiting to hang on Bill's every word. He took time surveying the assembled group before he spoke. DC Murphy looked like he hadn't slept for a month, and he wasn't the only one. The grind of a large investigation got to everyone in time. A week ago he'd cancelled all leave until they found the infant, and no one had complained. Well, their commitment and determination were about to be rewarded.

'The hospital has confirmed that Geri Taylor did not give birth recently. They also confirmed that the baby found in her possession is a week-old girl, who she calls Daisy, and who is thriving and healthy.' Bill paused. 'Forensic will shortly confirm if the baby is Kira's, but we are fairly sure of a positive match.'

A cheer went up and Bill grinned. It was the first piece of good news they'd had in some time, and he allowed them their moment of joy.

'Professor Pirie and I believe that Jeff Coulter orchestrated the theft of the baby in order to give it to Geri Taylor, to somehow "replace" the child he killed. However, we still don't know how this was achieved. Even if Geri Taylor was present at the funfair that night, it's more than likely she had help, if only in locating Kira.' He paused. 'David Murdoch's apparent suicide puts him in the frame for both murders, but as yet we have no direct link between him and Coulter. We have been unable to question Geri, who is too distraught at the loss of a baby she thinks is hers.'

Bill allowed time for all that to sink in before

continuing.

'Meanwhile, we concentrate on David Murdoch. The post-mortem should tell us if he did inflict the knife wound himself. The knife is similar, perhaps identical, to the one used on Kira, traces from whose handle were found on Melanie Jones. If David is innocent of both murders, then he is also a victim. I don't have to remind you that Dr Delaney and Ronald Reese-Brandon are still in the frame.'

His brief concluded, Bill asked for anything they'd turned up in the interim. Roy Hunter spoke first.

'The text to Delaney was sent from a pay-as-you-go mobile. Reese-Brandon's text came from the same number. Both Brandon and Delaney admitted in interview with the DI that despite her expensive handset Kira sometimes used pay-as-you-go mobiles for private calls. We haven't linked the number directly with Kira, but both texts originated in the vicinity of the funfair. They were sent within minutes of each other, around ten fifty-two.'

Bill said, 'From what we've learned of Kira, she may well have liked the idea of orchestrating a meeting between the two. Alternatively, her attacker could have been drawing them to the funfair in the hope of implicating them in her murder. Perhaps the perpetrator was aware of the relationship between Kira and Delaney, and summoned her father in order to expose this. The only person we know so far that Kira confided in fully was David Murdoch.'

Bill headed for the post-mortem the moment the strategy meeting was over, cursing the city centre traffic. It wasn't yet rush hour, but it was heavy enough to make him late.

He gowned up quickly and went in to join the rest of the party. Dr Sissons was performing the post-mortem, with Sylvia acting as corroborator. A SOCO was already video-recording the proceedings and a youngish male Fiscal, whom Bill didn't know that well, was on the scene too. His colour above the mask suggested this might be his first attendance at a post-mortem.

Bill met Rhona's eyes and acknowledged her hidden smile of congratulation. He realised he hadn't told her about his brief conversation with Sutherland, and made a note to try and mention it after they'd finished here. When they'd solved this case, he would have more time to spend finding out what SOCA was doing about McNab.

Dr Sissons had not yet removed the knife but David's hands were no longer wrapped around its handle, which was rough and grey and eight inches in length. The angle of entry was photographed and measured. Before Sissons withdrew the blade, Rhona indicated she wanted to speak.

'When I attended the scene, the victim's hands were round the knife handle, although not engaged with it. I subsequently discovered partial prints, which weren't David's, on the surface beneath. I have also checked since then and found that David Murdoch was right-handed. The manner in which his hands were set on the knife suggested he was left-handed.'

\*     \*     \*

After the post-mortem, Bill stripped off his suit

346

and stuffed it in the basket provided.

'So he didn't kill himself?' he said.

'It's unlikely,' replied Rhona.

'What about the partials?'

'I'll run them through the database, but there may not be enough for a match. What about the handwriting on the note?'

'I've sent it to your forensic graphology colleagues with a copy of David's school work for comparison.'

'The note was in capitals.'

'That does make it tricky,' he admitted.

'If David Murdoch didn't commit suicide, then he didn't kill those two girls either,' said Rhona decisively. 'Magnus is right; Coulter is the one in the driving seat. He's controlling someone, someone who knew that Kira was afraid of clowns and who hated her enough to steal her baby.'

They left the mortuary. As the door swung shut behind them, Bill said, 'I spoke to Sutherland about—'

Rhona cut him short.

'It's over, Bill. I'd rather forget about it.'

He watched her walk away, head held high, the sound of her heels sharp in the frosty air. He'd known Dr Rhona MacLeod for a long time. And he knew when she was lying. Rhona had no intention of giving up on Kalinin, but he suspected she wanted him to.

He called DS Clark. 'I'm on my way.'

'OK, Sir. I have some news—a backpack has been found in the River Kelvin by two young boys. It had a clown suit inside.'

'I'll be there in twenty minutes, wait outside for me.'

'Where are we going?' she asked.

'I'll tell you when I see you.'

## CHAPTER FIFTY

The school was so quiet that it was difficult to believe seven hundred girls were inside. Every other school he'd visited had seemed a hive of noisy activity, kids in corridors and crossing the playgrounds, the frantic sounds of a gym lesson in action. At Morvern, quiet study was the status quo. No one was allowed to enter a classroom once a lesson was in progress, as the learning process must never be disturbed. Only the sound of the bell brought activity of sorts: quiet, well-behaved girls moving from class to class.

Bill and DS Clark arrived around three thirty. Morvern's classes ended at four, but various after-school clubs kept many pupils in the building or the nearby playing fields until five thirty. A babysitting service for the wealthy.

Standing in the hushed school, he thought of how Margaret always complained that her afternoon lessons were hell, as the E numbers kicked in from lunch. Some of the children consumed nothing but fizzy drinks and fast food at midday, bought at the nearby shops.

No one here left the premises during the school day. The girls ate healthy lunches in the dining hall, which did not even offer fizzy drinks. You wouldn't find a Coke machine in the corridors here, whatever profit it might make for school funds.

When the Principal arrived to collect them from reception, they were enjoying freshly brewed coffee and chocolate biscuits. DS Clark was experiencing the same first reaction to Morvern he remembered: stunned amazement that this could be a school. Obviously she had not been privately educated.

Diane Porter was dressed as before, chic but casual. He caught her scent, pleasant and unobtrusive. She smiled warmly, although he knew she couldn't be pleased to see him.

'Detective Inspector Wilson. I apologise for keeping you waiting. Prospective parents,' she said. 'I've sent them off round the school with two of my sixth formers.'

'I'm sure they'll be impressed,' he said. His words were genuine and he was pleased to see her acknowledge them with another smile.

'This is Detective Sergeant Clark.'

Ms Porter offered her hand and Janice shook it, almost reverently. She seemed as impressed by the Principal as she had been by the school.

'Shall we go into my study?'

They followed her through the marble entrance hall. As before, the brass plaque on her door was polished to a gleaming brightness. Joan greeted him and asked if they wanted more coffee, or perhaps tea. Bill declined.

The scent of hyacinths still pervaded the room, along with a healthy dose of polish.

Ms Porter offered them a seat. When they were settled, she said, 'How can I help you?'

'Dr Delaney has made a statement regarding his relationship with Kira Reese-Brandon,' said Bill.

His use of the word 'relationship' had clearly

349

caused Ms Porter some consternation, but she made no comment, just waited for him to continue.

'Dr Delaney has in fact confessed to having a sexual relationship with Kira. He also believes he may have been the father of the child she was carrying.'

Her jaw tightened and a spot of colour appeared high on each cheekbone. She knew what that might mean for her as Principal of Morvern, and for the reputation of the school, but she rallied, and he admired her for it.

'I'm very sorry to hear that,' she said evenly.

Bill was sorry to have to make things even more unpleasant for her.

'Dr Delaney has also confessed to being at the funfair the night Kira died.'

She gasped, her eyes wide and her composure gone. This new revelation had truly shocked her; the scandal of a pupil–teacher relationship was small fry compared with the accusation that a Morvern teacher had murdered his star pupil.

'You believe Dr Delaney harmed Kira?' she said in disbelief.

Bill fed her a crumb of comfort. 'We haven't charged anyone yet.'

'I assume you're here because you wish to speak to Dr Delaney? Shall I ask him to come to my study?'

'That won't be necessary.' He paused. 'I'd actually like to speak to Alexandra Stewart-Smith.'

'Sandie?' Her voice rose in apprehension. 'What has this to do with Sandie?'

Bill chose not to answer. 'Can you ask her to come here please?'

Ms Porter took a deep breath and smoothed her

350

skirt, her hands trembling slightly. 'Of course, I'll have her fetched from class.'

'While you do that, may I check her data file again?'

'I'll get Joan to bring it up on-screen for you.'

Bill indicated to a puzzled DS Clark that she should wait in the study while he took a look at the school records. The secretary beckoned him to a seat at the rear of her office, where she retrieved Sandie's record and displayed it on the monitor.

The last time he'd been here, he'd read the details of all the Daisy Chain girls, but hadn't looked at Sandie's as she didn't seem really to be part of the group she longed to join. He'd accepted her story that she was planning to study Medicine at Edinburgh and was worried about passing her exams.

It seemed she was right to be. Based on her current performance, Sandie appeared to have little chance of achieving her goal. Bill was aware, through Lisa, that the exam results required to study Medicine at Edinburgh were high: five As at Higher Level, including all three sciences. Sandie had been nowhere near that by the end of her fifth year at Morvern, although she had gained an A in Biology. Chemistry seemed to be the stumbling block. Her record showed she'd been given extra time in the lab to try and remedy that, and another note on her file made it plain that Sandie was unlikely to gain entry to her chosen university course. Her parents had been loath to accept the school's recommendation that she consider an alternative career.

Bill scanned the remainder of the information, discovering that both parents were doctors and

351

that Sandie was an only child. Extracurricular activities were few—it seemed Sandie was not an all-rounder like the girls in the Daisy Chain gang. Amateur dramatics seemed to be her main interest. He made a few notes in his notebook and closed the file.

'That's Sandie ready for you now,' Joan told him.

He thanked her and made his way back through to the Principal's room. Sandie stood waiting, Ms Porter by her side.

'Sandie has asked me to stay with her this time, if that's all right?'

'Perfectly,' said Bill. Having the Principal witness the interview could prove useful.

Dressed in school uniform and wearing no make-up, Sandie looked youthful again. She politely waited for the Principal to take her seat on the leather couch, then sat beside her. Janice was still seated on one of the armchairs, and Bill took the other.

'How are you, Sandie?' he asked.

'Fine, thank you.'

'How are the studies going?'

She looked taken aback. 'OK,' she said cautiously.

'My daughter, Lisa, wants to be a doctor,' he continued. 'She's trying for Edinburgh. Chemistry's her problem too.' A white lie. 'I see you've been given extra access to the Chemistry lab.'

Sandie said nothing.

'Her middle name's Caroline, like yours.' He put the stress on 'Caroline'.

Just a momentary flicker of her eye and a

thinning of her lips, but he thought Sandie had picked up on his cue.

'I see from your school record that you like amateur dramatics. In fact, you look after make-up and costumes for the group. Have any of the school plays featured a clown costume?'

Ms Porter sat up straighter, clearly aware of the change in atmosphere. Her glance darted from him to Sandie and back again.

'I'm not sure where this is headed, Detective Inspector? I really—'

Sandie interrupted. 'It's OK, Ms Porter. I don't mind.' She addressed Bill. 'Chemistry's going well this term. My teacher thinks I'll get an A. And no, there isn't a clown outfit in the wardrobe department. We do mostly Shakespearean productions.'

Bill was impressed. This seventeen-year-old girl was cool and confident enough to think herself safe. He decided it was time to disabuse her of that belief.

'OK, thanks for clearing that up. The other reason I came here was to bring good news,' he said, smiling broadly. 'We've found Kira's baby.'

Ms Porter's mouth fell open in surprise and delight. 'Really? That's wonderful. It is . . . OK?' she added as a worried afterthought.

Bill was watching Sandie. She was even more surprised than Ms Porter, although not, he thought, quite so pleased.

'She—Daisy—is alive and well, thank God. But you know that already, don't you, Sandie? You know because you gave the baby to Geri Taylor, just as you had been told to do by Jeff Coulter.'

'I don't know what you're talking about,' the girl

353

said, looking puzzled. He had to hand it to her, she was an excellent actress. 'Who are those people?'

'You wrote to Coulter, and the two of you began a correspondence. Kira had rejected you from the Daisy Chain gang, and you were hurt and angry. You told him all about it.'

Sandie still looked confused, yet anxious to help. 'I'm so sorry, but I don't know anyone called Jeff Coulter.'

'He's a psychiatric patient at the State Mental Hospital.'

At this, Ms Porter rose from her seat. 'Detective Inspector, I really think if you are actively questioning Sandie, her parents should be informed.'

Bill took out his warrant card.

'Very well. Please tell them Sandie is at the station, helping us with our enquiries into the deaths of Kira Reese-Brandon and Melanie Jones.'


## CHAPTER FIFTY-ONE

The lab was out of bounds to Petersson, and Rhona thought she'd made that plain. Yet apparently he was in reception now, asking to see her. Rhona tried to keep her expression neutral, because Chrissy was already curious about the phone call.

'I'll be right down,' she said shortly.

'A problem?' Chrissy asked innocently.

'Nothing I can't handle.'

Chrissy wasn't buying it. 'It's that Icelandic guy, isn't it? Must be keen if he's coming here looking for you.'

Rhona ignored the remark. Chrissy was like a shark. Let her scent a single drop of blood and she was in for the kill, your story torn apart and digested in seconds.

Rhona preferred to leave the lab alive and in one piece.

'Can you log the results on the DNA test? Bill wants to know right away if it's Kira's child.'

'Like there was any chance it wasn't.'

Chrissy was well aware what Rhona was doing. 'I'll still be here when you get back,' she promised as Rhona exited.

Rhona took her time disrobing. She wanted to keep him waiting, to show him how inconvenient it was that he should go against her wishes and turn up at her place of work. They were not supposed to know one another. There should have been no obvious connection between them. Her annoyance mounted as she dressed and collected her things, although she knew deep down that he wouldn't have come unless it was important.

A small flame of hope fluttered in her chest, despite her determined attempts to snuff it out. When she saw him, she would tell him she wanted nothing more to do with him or his investigation. But hadn't he suggested—indeed, insisted—on exactly that at their last meeting? And had she not been the one to argue?

She paused at the foot of the stairs and composed herself before opening the door to reception. Petersson was standing with his back to her, wearing a silly puffa jacket that no doubt was all the rage in Iceland but looked overdone for a damp February afternoon in Glasgow. Then he turned and smiled, disarming her.

She hurried over, anxious that he not say her name in any meaningful way. They should appear as professional strangers.

'Mr Petersson?' She reached out to shake his hand, as though they had only just met.

His eyes twinkled, but he played along with the charade. She swept him outside, where he immediately zipped up the puffa jacket while Rhona shivered.

'I have my car,' she said.

'So have I.'

There was a short stand-off before she acquiesced. 'You can drop me back here.'

They walked swiftly to his car and Rhona slid gratefully into its warmth. Once inside, she expected him to tell her why he had come, but instead he started the engine, indicated and took off up University Avenue.

'Where are we going?'

'My flat.'

Rhona opened her mouth to insist she had work to do, then closed it again. Petersson was single-minded, not unlike Rhona herself, and there was obviously something he wanted to show or tell her, something requiring one of the various computers in his flat. If she wanted to know what it was, she would have to go along with him.

The flat was pleasantly warm and messy, as though he had abandoned it minutes before. It smelled as though the coffee machine was on.

'Coffee?' he asked as he took her coat.

She nodded.

'Come through to the kitchen.'

The table was strewn with empty mugs, just as it

356

had been last time she'd seen it. In the corner, three flat screens were lit up and covered in data.

He poured her a coffee and without asking added a measure of whisky. She accepted without remonstration and took a mouthful, which took the damp chill from her bones.

He gave her time to savour it before he said, 'You had a call to your cottage on Skye.'

She almost choked.

'How the hell did—?'

'I made a point of knowing all about you before my first approach. I've seen your bank accounts. I know what direct debits you pay. I can even quote your mortgage payments on your flat here in Glasgow. The property in Skye took a little longer to discover, as it was owned by your parents and transferred to you after your father died.'

She was furious that he should have been able to access her private life to that degree, but at the same time impressed. Petersson seemed to operate like the law, but without the law's knowledge or consent.

'The call to the cottage came from McNab,' he said.

'You don't know that.' Her voice trembled.

'It came from the same mobile as the previous call.'

Even Roy hadn't been able to get that information. Now she knew. 'That doesn't prove anything,' she said.

'The voice said only one word, "Rhona", then hung up. I heard it,' he said.

She felt a flush mount her cheeks.

'So?'

'I compared it to a recording of his voice. It was

357

a ninety-five per cent match.'

Shock was ripping through her, seizing her lungs, stopping her heart.

'Now do you believe he's alive?'

She came back fighting. 'No! He died in my arms.'

'And was revived in the ambulance.'

'He died on the operating table.'

'There was no autopsy.'

'Post-mortem,' she corrected him. 'In Scotland it's called a post-mortem.'

'No post-mortem in Scotland, and no autopsy in England.'

'I don't believe you.'

He ushered her to a seat in front of one of the screens. 'Then who is this?' He clicked and a window opened up. It showed a page of a British passport. The details gave the man's name as William McCartney. He was thirty-six years of age and had been born in Ballymena, County Antrim, Northern Ireland. The photograph was McNab.

She almost laughed. Someone had turned Michael Joseph McNab, a lapsed Catholic, into an Irish Protestant.

'Someone has stolen his identity.'

She could sense Petersson's exasperation.

'Then who did I just speak to, before I came to fetch you?'

She gaped at him.

'I can prove it,' he said.

She waited as Petersson dialled the number, her heart barely beating. He handed her the phone, and the moments during which it tried to connect lasted a lifetime. If McNab were to answer, she thought she might die.

358

The ringing tone carried on. No switch to voicemail, just endless ringing. She lowered the phone and pressed the button to end the call. Petersson looked at her questioningly.

'You bastard!'

She rose, but he caught her arm and pulled her back down on the seat. 'Try again.'

Why she did, she had no idea. Perhaps she had already lost her mind. The ringing tone started again, and crazily she imagined it ringing out in his grave, resounding in the wooden coffin, rising through the six feet of damp black earth that covered him.

The noise stopped. Someone had picked up. Rhona held her breath as she listened to the silence.

'Hello?' she said, finally.

Nothing. No words, no breathing. Nothing.

She hung there, suspended for what seemed like an eternity.

Then someone began to whistle a tune. It was the opening bars of *The Sash My Father Wore*, a Protestant tune played by every flute player on every Orange Order march in the west of Scotland during what was known as 'The Marching Season'. Someone was taking the piss. Please God, it was McNab.

\*     \*     \*

'Stay, I'll make us something to eat.'

The aftermath of shock had set in and she didn't know what to think or how to react. It would be easy to let Petersson take charge. Stay here, eat and relax in the warmth. Savour those moments on

359

the phone.

'I'd rather go home.'

He studied her expression, recognising he was unlikely to change her mind.

'I'll drive you to the lab, you can get your car.'

'No. Just run me home. I'll pick the car up in the morning.'

They set off in silence, then he asked what she had heard on the phone. When she told him about the whistled tune, he looked perturbed.

'What does that mean?'

'Does he know about the passport?'

'I assume so.'

She laughed then, because she was beginning to believe. If she were wrong, the fall back into the abyss would be more terrible than before.

'What happens now?'

'He will contact you again, and we will meet with him. Together, we will catch Kalinin.'

It sounded ludicrous: resurrect a dead man and get him to testify. But wasn't that what SOCA had planned without them?

Another bout of laughter seized her, and Petersson regarded her with concern.

'McNab was a Catholic,' she explained. 'Lapsed, but a left-footer all the same. They resurrected him as an Ulster Protestant.'

Petersson had no idea why she found that so funny. Eventually she regained her composure.

'You said you spoke to him earlier, what did you say?' she asked.

'I didn't exactly speak to him. We exchanged some code words.'

'What code words?'

'I said "Dead Man Walking", then my code

name. He gave his in return.'

'That's it?'

'Yes.'

'I still don't know for certain it was him.' She couldn't bring herself to say his name. 'He never spoke.'

'You said he whistled a tune. He must have thought it would mean something to you?'

'It was a joke of his. He hated the Catholic–Protestant division in the west of Scotland. Always made a point of whistling the wrong tunes in the wrong pubs. It got him into trouble.'

She said goodbye at the door and went up alone. She could tell he'd wanted to come in, perhaps thinking his discovery might be rewarded by sex. Or, to give him more credit, maybe he'd been perturbed by her reaction to the phone call.

The thought of it brought laughter bubbling up inside her again. Was it because the situation was so ridiculous? Or was it joy?

Who else but McNab would make such a call?

## CHAPTER FIFTY-TWO

The teenage girl sitting across the table from Bill could not have looked more innocent. Dressed in school uniform, hair tied neatly back, fresh-faced, Sandie looked as though she would be incapable of squashing a fly without remorse.

But if he was right, this girl had knocked Kira out with chloroform and surgically removed her unborn child, smothered Melanie and stabbed

361

David. It seemed impossible, even ludicrous.

Why then was he so sure it was true?

He recalled Coulter's intensity, the strange magnetism of the man. Could he have influenced this girl enough to make her carry out such crimes? It wouldn't be the first time such a thing had happened—young, impressionable women being in thrall to evil men. Charles Manson was a famous example. But as far as he was aware, Sandie had never met Coulter. He had been incarcerated for the past two years. If they had been in contact at all, it was through letters and an occasional phone call. Was that enough?

'Tell me about that night.'

'I've told you a hundred times.'

'Tell me again.'

She began reciting the same story, but this time, either bored with it or too confident, she seemed to be embellishing slightly. 'David was almost sick on the Waltzers. He'd been drinking and the guy kept spinning the car. After that, he went to look for Kira. I went home.'

'What time was that exactly?'

She shrugged. 'I didn't check.'

'What about Owen?' he said.

'He left when David went.'

Bill consulted his notes again. 'Owen liked you, didn't he?'

She made a face.

'He thought he had a chance.'

She shook her head. 'No way!'

'You rejected him and he left. Owen had kept you back, so you had to hurry.'

She regarded him levelly.

'You had the clown suit in the backpack you

362

were carrying. All you needed to do was put it on. That and the mask.'

She rolled her eyes and said nothing.

'You went to the candyfloss van because that was where Kira was to meet Dr Delaney, all arranged by you.' He waited for a response. When one wasn't forthcoming, he continued. 'I don't think you intended to kill Kira, just take the baby.'

Still she remained silent.

'Geri was waiting. You handed her Kira's bag, which contained the baby. She had no idea who you were because you were still dressed as a clown.' He leaned forward. 'That was the reason why Kira's expensive bag and mobile weren't with her body. After that you had to get rid of the clown suit. Easy. Put it in the backpack. You could have taken it away with you, but it was bloody. That panicked you, so you dumped it instead.'

She twitched in her seat. He could see that he had finally rattled her, and pressed on.

'That's where your luck started to give out. Some kids found the backpack in the Kelvin, jammed against an ironing board. They couldn't believe it when they discovered a mask and clown suit inside.'

Her eyes flickered down to the table. Was she wondering if her DNA was still on a suit that had been submerged in water for days?

'Then the mobile turns up in the park with the Reborn. Coulter couldn't resist it, could he? He'd already sent Professor Magnus Pirie, the criminal psychologist, his diary and asked to meet him. He told the professor you suggested he do that. Did you?'

She opened her mouth to speak, then thought

better of it and shut it again.

'We both know that Coulter is in charge of this game. You're just his pawn.'

Her face was very pale now, but still oddly calm.

'Coulter has nothing to lose. He'll be locked up forever anyway. Maybe you'll end up in there with him.'

At last Bill glimpsed something resembling fear in her eyes. He had done all the talking and he'd learned a lot from it. Sandie hadn't said much; she didn't have to, in the end her face had said it all. He was sure he'd got most of it right, but until he had physical proof, it was all just hearsay.

Sandie glanced at her watch. 'I've been here almost four hours. You can only keep me another two unless you charge me with something.'

Cool as a cucumber. Perhaps Morvern also taught its girls their rights under Scots law.

He left Sandie sitting there and went back to the incident room. A hush fell as he entered, but he went straight to his own room. Sutherland's call came through moments later.

*     *     *

'Do you have enough proof to charge her?'

The hastily assembled team consisted of Bill, Superintendent Sutherland, DS Clark and Roy Hunter. Sutherland had just posed the one question Bill couldn't answer yet. He shook his head.

Roy spoke first. 'Coulter called the same mobile number that had been used to text Delaney and Reese-Brandon, but we can't link that mobile directly to Sandie.'

'What about this alleged correspondence between Coulter and the girl?' Sutherland asked.

'He destroyed the letters.'

'And the PO box?'

'It was registered under Geri Taylor's name.'

'So again, no established connection between Alexandra Stewart-Smith and Jeff Coulter. What does Geri Taylor have to say?'

'That God gave her Daisy to replace her dead baby and that she's never heard of Sandie,' Bill told him.

'And Alexandra?'

'We believe she left the funfair around eleven thirty, which would have given her forty minutes before David found Kira. I think she drew Kira to a supposed meeting with Delaney. Maybe she'd hoped to scare her enough that she would run into the wooded area, but something went wrong. Kira ducked into the maze and she followed.'

Sutherland gave Bill a look that spoke volumes. 'So far, all hearsay.'

'She did it,' said Bill.

'She may well have. But we don't have enough to charge her.'

Bill ground his teeth in frustration. It wasn't the first time he'd known someone was guilty and couldn't prove it, and perhaps it wouldn't be the last. But he wasn't finished yet, not by a long way.

Sandie had been taken home by her very angry father. According to him, Bill would pay for this outrage with his career. He had thrown various important names at Bill to show he meant business, among them the name of the current Lord Advocate.

Once they had left, Bill called Rhona on her

mobile and asked about the backpack.

'I left the lab before it got here,' she said. 'I promise to get back to you in the morning after I've taken a look.'

He ran the Sandie scenario past her. Her initial silence suggested she thought he might be mistaken, then she said, 'The part print on the mobile was a reasonable match for Sandie.'

'She said Kira dropped it and she picked it up.'

'Can you get a warrant for her house? I'd like to take a look at what she was wearing that night, particularly her shoes. In the mobile shot of the clown, it was wearing red shoes or boots which didn't look like part of the costume.'

Bill could imagine what Mr Stewart-Smith would have to say about that.

'And the mirror writing? Is she able to do that? Maybe if we had some of her normal writing we could flip it and check it against the words on the hands. What does Magnus think?'

'I'll give him a call.'

\*　　　\*　　　\*

In fact, he went round there on his way home, thinking it would be interesting to meet the professor on his own turf. Bill liked the flat with its view across the river. They stood for a moment together out on the breezy balcony.

'When I was a teenager, all the opposite bank there was made up of shipyards,' said Bill. 'I still can't believe it's all gone. All those thousands of men. You didn't dare walk past the yard gates when the whistle went. The gates opened and a tide of humanity poured out. Now it's just fancy flats. Like this one, I suppose.'

Magnus had the grace to laugh.

They moved inside. Bill noticed Coulter's diary open on the desk.

'Had any luck with that?'

'A little. Coulter was sent down two years ago?'

Bill nodded.

'I think he met Caroline prior to that. Come and take a look.' He led Bill over and indicated a passage. Even as he read, a tingle went up his spine and he could see Coulter across the table, buzzing with energy, his eyes boring into him.

*Sweet Carolin I make her feel good she wants me all the time*

'There's another passage later on which reads much the same.' He showed Bill.

'But nothing to tell us if this "Caroline" might be Sandie?'

'I'm sorry.' Magnus said it as though he'd failed Bill in some way.

'You found the baby because of the diary. Let's be grateful for that.'

'You've seen the man's charisma. If Sandie met him in the flesh his power would be even greater than through correspondence.'

'She's an intelligent girl. Why would she team up with a man who was barely literate?'

'Sandie sees herself as the misfit. The one not deemed good enough for the Daisy Chain gang. She's clever but not clever enough. Coulter is also intelligent, if unschooled. He would use this weakness to gain her sympathy.'

Bill shrugged. 'It doesn't matter what we think,

unless we get proof.'

'We have Rhona. If it's there, she'll find it.'

## CHAPTER FIFTY-THREE

'Why are you so happy?' Chrissy's eagle eye was upon her.

'Bill picked up a suspect.'

'And let them go again. Apparently her father knows the Lord Advocate. It could be curtains for DI Wilson all over again.'

'Not if he's right.'

'So what do we have?'

'You have the pleasure of the clown suit.'

'No way.' Chrissy shuddered.

'I thought you were joking when you said you were frightened of clowns?'

'You thought wrong.'

Rhona observed her expression and relented.

'You can have the knife,' she said.

'Thanks.'

'I've lifted partial prints from the handle but they're not enough. See what else you can find.'

She led Chrissy to where she had laid it out.

'Wow! That's some knife.'

In a city known for the variety of its stabbing implements, this was a beauty.

'A Kanetsune KB-122 Ten with a leather and shark skin handle. "Ten" in Japanese means both sky and heaven. Blade is eight and a half inches of shiny blue steel minus the bloodstains. The shark skin's bound in criss-cross leather. See what you can find under it.'

'Cut the leather off?'

'Take the whole thing apart. Just find something.'

\* \* \*

The newly dried-out clown costume was red with large white polka-dots. Marked by river silt and darkened by patches of blood, it was simple in shape: baggy round the middle, with tighter cuffs and ankles trimmed with yellow ruffles. It opened at the front by means of a strip of velcro, and down the join were five large yellow pom-pom buttons. At the sides were two deep pockets. A dirty label confirmed it as being sold by 'Razzle', a chain of fancy dress shops. Rhona remembered seeing one on Sauchiehall Street, near the Buchanan Galleries.

She started by identifying, recording and sampling the bloodstains. That done, she gently shook the suit over an inverted metal cone, collecting the debris that fell off in folds of clean paper. Most of it, she suspected, would be residue from the river water. After shaking, she laid the suit on paper spread on the lab table and began brushing, taking care with the folds, ruffles and pom-poms and anything loosely connected to the velcro. She paid particular attention to the pockets and seams.

Then she moved on to taping, concentrating on the neck and wrist areas and sticking the results onto clear plastic sheets. The velcro, as she expected, proved particularly fertile.

When she was satisfied she'd harvested the outside sufficiently, she turned the suit inside out and began again. This was the region which had been closest to the perpetrator's own clothes.

It was a painstaking business and couldn't be rushed. She was searching for broken fragments of fibres, which were often extremely thin—finer than a human hair, and no more than a millimetre or so in length. Using a low-powered microscope and precision forceps, she located two fragments that looked interesting and transferred them directly onto glass slides before examining them through a high-powered microscope.

They looked like silk, probably natural rather than man-made. Synthetic silk fibres were very fine and closely woven, giving the characteristic smooth, 'silky' feel of the fabric, whereas this fragment had a looser look under the microscope. A chemical test would detect nitrogen in the fibre if it was synthetic. Natural silks burned, synthetics melted, although with the increasing addition of lyocell, a synthetic cellulose, it was becoming more difficult to distinguish between natural and man-made silks.

Pleased with her results so far, she turned her attention to the pull-on mask. The mouth opening was wide and framed by large, red, rubbery lips. The nose was bulbous and red with two holes for breathing. The eye sockets were painted in black circles with just slits to see through. A cascade of scarlet curls completed the picture. It was hideous. Chrissy had been deeply discomforted by it, so it must have truly terrified Kira.

Rhona extracted a sample from the wig hair to compare with the strands found under Kira's nails, then began to swab the areas around the mouth and nose openings. After this, she rolled the cap inside out. Her first find was a brown human hair, around two inches in length. A minute examination of the mask also offered up fibres of black mascara around the eye slits and a smear of lipstick from the inside of the mouth, plus, hopefully, enough skin cells to identify the DNA of anyone who'd worn the mask. Satisfied with her harvest, she went to check on Chrissy.

The leather lattice work on the handle had been cut away, exposing the grey shark skin underneath.

'How's it going?'

'Good. There's lots of stuff under the leather. Blood and skin cells included.'

They decided to break for coffee. Chrissy had purchased fresh rolls on her way to work. She warmed them, then split them and lathered them with butter while Rhona poured fresh coffee. She handed a roll to Rhona.

'Magic, by the way.'

The rolls were the Scottish west coast equivalent of a croissant; probably equally unhealthy, but delicious nonetheless.

Chrissy took her time demolishing the roll and savouring the coffee. After this would come the questions about where Rhona had disappeared to the day before. No doubt the girl on reception would have given Chrissy full details of Petersson and their departure together. While she ate, Rhona tried to plan what to say. Lying was pretty futile with Chrissy. Better to stick to the minimal truth.

'You're much cheerier,' Chrissy began.

'I'm sleeping better.' Which wasn't strictly true, although the previous night she had slept like a log.

'That's good. I've stopped phoning you when I'm up with Michael.'

'I noticed.'

'Thought you might be busy.'

'Sleeping.'

Chrissy gave her a beady look. Rhona didn't respond.

'Did you have a nice time yesterday?' Chrissy grinned.

'Yes.'

'Mmmm.' Chrissy toyed with her coffee mug. 'Must be interesting going out with an investigative journalist. Is he working on anything at the moment?'

'Nikolai Kalinin.'

That floored her. Chrissy wasn't often stuck for words, so this was a moment Rhona would cherish.

'Something to do with McNab's murder?'

'Yes.'

'That's why you're seeing him?'

Rhona nodded.

'Well, you should've said.' She sounded peeved.

'I just did.'

'Why is he talking to you?'

Now they were on dangerous ground. She would have to tread carefully. 'He knew I met Kalinin, he wanted to ask me about him.'

Chrissy absorbed that.

'Does SOCA know he's on the case?'

'I don't know.' That was the truth.

'Is he speaking to Bill?'

'No.'

'He just got in touch with you?'

'I was there when McNab died.'

'I was there when they shot him,' Chrissy

372

reminded her sharply. 'Why didn't he speak to me?'

She had put her foot in it. The truth was called for; at least, some of it.

'Petersson suspects someone on the Scottish end of the investigation may be feeding information to Kalinin's group. He wanted to keep his own interest in the case secret.'

'That bastard Slater didn't tell McNab he'd let Kalinin out that night,' Chrissy said with venom. 'Maybe he's the informer.'

'Maybe.'

'What did Petersson ask you to find out?' Chrissy was nothing if not astute.

'The post-mortem results.'

'And?'

'And it wasn't done here.'

'What?'

'The body was taken south.'

'Fucking hell!'

'SOCA *are* in charge of the case against Kalinin,' Rhona reminded her.

'But McNab was shot here. It's under our jurisdiction.'

Rhona shrugged in acknowledgement, hoping Chrissy's anger would quench her curiosity.

'Do you think this Petersson will help nail McNab's killer?'

'He's done things like this before,' she said, non-committally. She wanted desperately to leave the subject, so she conceded on one front. 'I'll tell you if he comes up with anything.' It was her first outright lie, and she felt bad about it. Chrissy would be over the moon if McNab had survived, but she would also be furious if she found out

373

Rhona had suspected this and hadn't told her. However, Rhona knew all too well how corrosive hope could be, so only certainty would persuade her to reveal anything to Chrissy.

## CHAPTER FIFTY-FOUR

Bill was very surprised by the visitor drinking tea in his office. Sandie's father had been so furious at his daughter's detention that they had assumed any further contact would probably involve a lawyer. And yet here was Mrs Stewart-Smith sitting opposite him.

He'd managed to obtain a search warrant for the Stewart-Smith home, but he still wasn't sure if they now had the clothes Sandie had worn at the funfair. Sandie had been distinctly unhelpful. Owen Hegarty had been more co-operative, although Bill suspected the boy, like Bill himself, rarely noticed what women wore.

He took a mouthful of tea and waited for the woman to break the silence.

'My husband told me you thought Sandie was corresponding with a middle-aged man called Coulter.' She paused. 'Have you any proof of that?'

'Why do you ask?'

She hesitated. 'Two years ago, when Sandie wasn't quite sixteen, I discovered she was meeting a man much older than herself. I saw them by chance in town. When I questioned her, she denied it.'

'Can you describe this man?'

'Medium height, with dark hair, in his thirties. Good-looking, I suppose, if you like that type. Around the same time, Sandie's behaviour began to change. At first I thought she was taking drugs. She became secretive, manipulative and prone to lying, often quite blatantly.' She hesitated. 'I also think she became sexually active.'

'And you think she was sleeping with this older man?'

'Probably.'

'Did you discuss this with your husband?'

She shook her head. 'I had no real proof. I tried to raise the subject with Sandie myself.' She winced at the memory. 'She told me to mind my own business.'

'What happened then?'

'I think either she stopped seeing him or he rejected her. She was very low for a while, then she took up with Kira Reese-Brandon and her crowd. At first I was pleased because she seemed happier, but something went wrong between them. Sandie was very upset and very angry.'

'What makes you think Coulter is the man she met back then?'

'Sandie had been very depressed about Kira, but she suddenly cheered up. I found her reading a letter, and when I asked her who it was from, she said she had a pen pal through school. I didn't believe her. I checked her room when she went out and found it.' She paused to collect herself. 'It was very badly written, almost illegible. He called her Caro. Sandie's middle name is Caroline. She preferred it to Alexandra.'

'Was the letter signed?'

'Just initials. JC. There were other letters too. I

375

would find her sitting reading, a funny smile on her face.' She grimaced at the memory.

'I'd like to show you a photograph of Coulter, so you can tell me if it's the man you saw with Sandie.'

She nodded, and he phoned the incident room to ask DS Clark to bring a photo.

When it was put in front of her, Mrs Stewart-Smith stared at it for a long time.

'Yes, that's him,' she said finally. 'That's the man I saw with Sandie.'

So Magnus had been right. Caroline and Sandie were one and the same person, and Coulter had met her when she was underage. No doubt he'd told a good story, charmed her into starting a sexual relationship. Bill recalled what he'd read in the diary. It made sense now.

Mrs Stewart-Smith was watching him with apprehension.

'Did the letters come by post?'

She shook her head. 'There was no stamp on the envelope. That was another thing that worried me. I thought she must be seeing this man again and he was giving her the letters personally.' She was growing more anxious by the second. 'Why are you so concerned about this man Coulter?'

'Two years ago, Jeff Coulter killed the baby of his former partner, Geri Taylor. He was committed to the State Hospital. We know he's been writing to someone on the outside whom he calls Caroline.'

Her hand shot to her mouth. 'My God. And that was Sandie?'

'We suspected it was. What you've just told me suggests we were right.'

'But what does this have to do with Kira's

death?'

'We believe Coulter was manipulating someone on the outside to do his bidding.'

He watched as the meaning behind his words sunk in.

'You think he persuaded *Sandie* to harm Kira?'

'It's a possibility.'

'No.' She shook her head wildly. 'No! My daughter could not have done that.' She stared at him. 'I should never have told you about him. Oh my God, what have I done?'

'Mrs Stewart-Smith, Coulter is a psychopath. If Sandie was under his influence, this would mitigate in her favour.'

'But you let Sandie go. You haven't charged her with anything.'

'If she was present at the scene of crime, forensic will find evidence of that and we will call her back in.'

Her voice sank to a whisper. 'I've betrayed my daughter.'

'No. By telling me about Coulter, you may have saved her.'


# CHAPTER FIFTY-FIVE

Bill and Magnus were both silent and lost in thought for most of the journey across the moorland.

Coulter would know they were coming, as the baby's discovery had been announced on the national news. Initially, Geri's name had been held back, but soon both major Scottish tabloids had declared their own exclusives, stories gleaned from neighbours keen to reveal what they knew about Geri and the arrival of the baby. The only consolation was that, although both papers mentioned the baby Coulter had killed two years ago, neither of them suggested any involvement in this case or mentioned his ongoing relationship with Geri. She'd moved into the flat in Exeter Drive after his incarceration and had apparently kept quiet about him.

That part of the story would no doubt come out in time, and be endlessly discussed. Broadsheets and specially commissioned documentaries would revive the 'is he mad or bad?' debate which had dominated Coulter's trial, and the usual names would be wheeled out as examples of men who persuaded their women to kill. Fred and Rosemary West. Ian Brady and Myra Hindley. Perhaps even Charles Manson, whose mostly female followers had murdered four people including the heavily pregnant Sharon Tate.

The tabloids would denounce Coulter as 'evil' and pass judgement on the immorality of today's teenagers, even the rich and privileged ones. None of the articles, features or programmes would get anywhere near the truth, or an understanding of how Coulter had persuaded Dr Shan, Geri Taylor and Alexandra Stewart-Smith to do his bidding.

Magnus wondered if the current outcome was what Coulter had planned all along and that was why he'd sent the diary in the first place. By exposing it to scrutiny, he was placing himself at the heart of the crime. It had been a game, played out with as much dexterity as a champion chess player. In this case, if attention was the prize,

Coulter was the winner whatever the outcome.

Magnus recalled his feelings after that first interview, his sense that he'd started on a journey with Coulter that he would live to regret. It was strange how the unconscious mind tried to warn us, he thought to himself. Perhaps he should have listened to his intuition. Not read the diary, refused to engage further with Coulter. But Magnus knew that could never have happened. Psychology was driven by the need to know why people act the way they do, and he could never have turned down that challenge from Coulter.

He consoled himself with the thought that if he hadn't answered Coulter's call and interpreted the diary, they might never have found the baby. Less welcome was the thought that their interest had simply driven Coulter to commit more crimes by proxy. Maybe that was why both Melanie and David had died.

On arrival they were met by the same young lady that had greeted Magnus on his first visit.

'You're back,' she said brightly.

Magnus acknowledged her welcome but could think of nothing pleasant to say in return. She didn't seem perturbed by this, merely handed them their badges and rang through for someone to collect them. Magnus wondered if it would be Dr Shan.

Bill read his thoughts. 'Dr Shan is on leave until the investigation into her relationship with Coulter is concluded.'

Magnus wasn't surprised, but he was sorry.

A man met them on the other side of security. He introduced himself as Dr Forth. He was short and balding with dark-rimmed glasses. The only scents Magnus picked up from him were shaving foam and toothpaste.

'This is a terrible business,' he offered as he led them down the corridor.

Magnus wasn't sure if he was referring to Dr Shan's suspension, Coulter's suspected involvement in the funfair killing or both. Whatever it was, Bill chose not to comment and Magnus followed his lead. When they reached the interview room, Dr Forth said, 'I'll have to leave you here, I'm afraid. Orderlies will bring Mr Coulter along shortly.'

They waited in silence, Magnus sensing that Bill didn't want to open a conversation before Coulter's arrival. The plan was for Bill to do the interview with Magnus observing. If Bill wanted him to take over, he would indicate this. As far as they were aware, Coulter knew about the discovery of the baby. He would also know that Sandie had been arrested in connection with the foetal theft.

Magnus could smell the guy when the door opened. A waft of aftershave, sweat and the buzz of adrenalin. Coulter strode in and gave them a wide smile that reached his vivid blue eyes.

'Hi, guys. Back again. How can I help you this time?'

Magnus felt Bill bristle as Coulter took his seat opposite, as though he'd just entered a pub and was joining his mates. Bill had asked that a recording device be set up so the interview could be taped as it would be in a police interview room, and now he set it going and announced the date, time and names of those present. Coulter smiled happily as he did so.

'Pity you're not taking a video. I'd like to have

seen how I do.'

Bill chose to ignore that remark, saying, 'Geri Taylor's in hospital.'

'I heard,' Coulter said in a sympathetic tone. 'Too bad. But it's not the first time she's lost it.'

'The last time being when you killed her baby.'

Coulter shrugged. 'If you ask me, she was better off when the kid died. She couldn't cope with it crying all the time.'

The remark was so devoid of feeling Magnus caught his breath.

'You gave her a replacement,' said Bill.

Coulter smiled at his own generosity. 'Yeah. I made her a Reborn. You saw it, Professor.' He turned to Magnus. 'Little Melanie. Way cute and she doesn't piss, shit or cry.'

'No,' said Bill. 'You gave Geri a real baby.'

Coulter affected amazement. 'How would I have managed to fuck Geri in here?' He waved a hand to indicate the presence of the orderlies, then a smile curled his lips. 'Now Rose Petal, she's a different matter.'

His loaded remark was followed by a tense silence as the two orderlies exchanged brief looks. Coulter continued, enjoying his moment. 'She smells so good. Oil of roses. Rubs it all over.'

'Let's talk about Caroline.'

Coulter appeared momentarily disappointed not to continue down his chosen route, then acquiesced. 'Sweet Caro. What do you want to know?'

'When you met her.'

He assumed a puzzled expression. 'I told you, I haven't met her. She just writes to me. Lovely letters.'

'You met her two years ago, when she was fifteen. Her real name is Alexandra Stewart-Smith.'

He sniggered. 'So I pulled a posh bird. More than one if you count Rose Petal.' He turned to Magnus. 'How do you feel about Rose Petal, Professor, now you know she's been . . . *taken*?' He leered. 'I saw you take a sniff at her.'

Bill continued. 'We know about your involvement in the death of Kira Reese-Brandon and the removal of her unborn infant. We know you ordered Sandie to give the baby to Geri.'

Coulter leaned back in the chair with an exaggerated sigh. 'I'm a prisoner, in case you hadn't noticed. I can fuck my doctor, but I can't touch anyone outside these walls.'

'We know you contacted Sandie using Dr Shan's mobile.'

'Rose Petal was so willing in so many ways. So keen to help me get better.'

'Both Sandie and Geri will testify to your involvement in Kira's death.'

This time Coulter laughed out loud. 'My women don't go against me. They love me. I make them feel special. You two should learn how to do that.'

\* \* \*

The interview had provided them with what they wanted to know. From Coulter's coded replies and heavy innuendo, it was obvious that everything they had thought was true. Coulter had manipulated and controlled Sandie and Geri from inside the hospital. But without a confession from him or the women involved, they had no case against him. It was utterly depressing. To add to it all, Dr Shan had provided Coulter with the means to carry out his plan. Magnus only hoped that what Coulter had said about a sexual relationship between him and Dr Shan wasn't true. The doctor might survive her error in judgment over the mobile, but sex with an inmate could end her career.

## CHAPTER FIFTY-SIX

Rhona was conscious that the only thing that would nail Sandie would be undeniable proof that she was at the crime scene, and that she had cut the baby out of Kira's uterus, leaving her to bleed to death in that tent.

All the work, all the sleepless nights, all the endless thoughts, discussions and arguments, all the evidence they'd uncovered, circumstantial or otherwise, had brought them to this point, but now they needed concrete proof.

She was quietly confident, though, as she flashed the results of her latest investigation onto the overhead screen.

People always forgot their shoes. You couldn't put them through the washing machine or send them to the cleaners. They didn't burn easily. If they didn't throw them away, then most people tried to wash them. But microscopic drops of blood got everywhere; wedged in the spaces between the upper and sole, between the rough grooves on the sole, between heel and sole. Scores of tiny places for it to hide. Much smaller than the human eye could detect, the droplets stayed despite all efforts to get rid of them.

Sandie's red leather boots were no exception. Their quality had probably meant she had to hang onto them to allay suspicion, or maybe she'd thought she'd done a pretty good job of cleaning them. She was wrong.

'I've identified blood from three sources on the accused's boots,' said Rhona. 'They come from Kira, the umbilical cord, and David Murdoch. DNA testing of contact evidence on the cuffs and neck of the clown suit retrieved from the River Kelvin proves that it was worn by the accused. The outfit came from a fancy dress shop called Razzle, and an assistant there has identified the accused as buying it a week prior to the murder. Since the suit has Kira's blood on it, it was the one worn that night. Inside the suit I found microscopic silk fibres, which match a silk scarf that Sandie wore at the funfair, according to Owen Hegarty's account.' The atmosphere in the room was electric, already verging on celebratory, but she wasn't finished yet. 'This trace evidence establishes Sandie was there, but it doesn't prove conclusively that she was the one to operate on Kira. However, the knife retrieved from David Murdoch's body *does*. As you know, the knife has a shark skin handle criss-crossed by leather.' She clicked onto a photo of the knife. 'We found a partial print on the leather, but it was insufficient for a match. However, when the leather was cut away, we found three items of trace evidence lodged beneath. Kira's blood, blood from David Murdoch and—crucially—skin flakes belonging to Sandie Stewart-Smith, linking her directly to the murder weapon.'

It was what they had been waiting for. Bill nodded over at her, beaming. She let the din die down before she continued. 'As to who smothered Melanie, this has proved more difficult. We can link the knife to Melanie's bedroom because we found a dentricle on Melanie's clothes. However, Sandie had visited Melanie's bedroom when she was still friendly with the Daisy Chain gang, so any DNA of hers we turn up isn't admissible. We did identify David Murdoch's DNA on Melanie's mouth and arm, but not her nose, which we would have expected had he tried to smother her by hand. We know David vomited in the bath and it's likely he attempted to wipe away his presence in the room using a hand towel, which is still missing. Forensic evidence, however, throws doubt on David's death being suicide. David Murdoch was right-handed, but his hands were arranged on the shaft as though he were left-handed.'

They moved on to other evidence. CCTV camera footage was shown of Geri Taylor walking along Dumbarton Road towards Exeter Drive just after midnight.

'She was picked up by three successive cameras,' Bill said. 'She was carrying a bag identified as belonging to Kira, which we believe contained the newborn. The bag wasn't in Geri's flat when we searched it, so I would like us to find it if possible. It would provide a link between Sandie, Geri and the baby.' Bill looked to Superintendent Sutherland. 'I believe we have enough to bring Sandie in and charge her.'

'I agree, Detective Inspector.'

\* \* \*

385

This time he had proof that the schoolgirl he was about to interview was a killer. He was satisfied with the outcome, but not happy about it. How could anyone be pleased to discover a seventeen-year-old girl had murdered three people? He recalled Sandie's mother sitting across the desk from him, anxious to help her daughter; her sudden realisation that what she'd told him might have condemned her instead.

He turned in his chair to look out of the window. What would he be feeling now if one of his kids had been murdered? Or had become a murderer? He made a mental note to spend more time at home when this was over, with Margaret and the kids. Except they weren't kids any more, not really, and neither was Sandie.

He drank the last dregs of cold tea and put his mug on the desk, then picked up the phone to call Margaret.

'Is everything OK?' She sounded worried.

'I'll be a bit late. I'm taking the team out for a drink.'

'You're charging someone?'

'Sandie Stewart-Smith.'

There was a moment's silence. 'She's only Robbie's age!'

'I know.'

\*　　　\*　　　\*

The incident room was deserted, only the hum of computers breaking the silence. He'd sent the team to the pub and ordered DC Campbell to tell the barman the drinks were on the boss and that he'd be over later to pay. Only DS Clark remained.

'Ready, Detective Sergeant?'

'Yes, Sir.'

*    *    *

He spread the mortuary photographs out in front of Sandie. First Kira's mutilated body, then Melanie, pale and unmarked, her body swollen by pregnancy. Finally David, a gaping wound in his chest. Sandie kept her gaze averted.

'Look at them!' he shouted.

She jumped, startled, and threw the photos a cursory glance.

'Look at them *properly*.' He spoke slowly this time, his voice low and harsh.

She turned her angry gaze on him, her eyes small and hard, then picked up David's photograph and studied it for a moment, her expression never changing.

'He thought she liked him. I told him the truth.'

'What truth?'

'That she despised him. That she made fun of him all the time in the common room. "My cocksucking disciple". That's what she called him.' Her voice was shrill and bitter, the words clipped and precise.

'When did you tell him that?'

'The night he killed himself. He was drunk, mooning around the Hall of Mirrors. He started on about her, how he missed her. It was sickening. So I told him everything.'

'What exactly?'

'That she was fucking her tutor. That she was fucking her own father. I bet you didn't know that,

387

Detective Inspector? David was the only one she wasn't fucking—that little fag!'

'What happened?'

'He started wailing. Said he couldn't go on. Then I saw the knife and I knew. He was gone forty minutes before he found Kira that night. Plenty of time. He cut out the baby. He killed his precious Kira.'

'Why would he do that?'

She looked at him disdainfully. 'You're all so stupid, I don't know how you ever solve any crimes.'

'You solve it for me then.'

'He killed her because she was leaving him. Then he killed himself because he's an idiot.'

'And how did Geri Taylor get the baby?'

'Have you asked her?'

'She says God gave it to her.'

She laughed. 'There you go, the silly cow's off her head. She went wandering in Kelvingrove Park and found a baby. The baby David left there.' She looked quite pleased with herself.

'Let's have my version now. You bought the costume because you knew Kira was terrified of clowns and you wanted to scare her. You hoped you could force her to leave the funfair. Once she was alone in the park you could do what you planned. But she ran into the mirror maze. You took your chance and followed her in. Then you knocked her out with chloroform that you'd stolen from the chemistry lab at school. You cut her open and removed the baby. You weren't much good at Chemistry, but Biology was your strong point and you knew where to make the incision. You put the baby in Kira's bag and took it to Geri Taylor, then

388

you disposed of the clown costume by putting it in the backpack and throwing it in the river.' He stopped, waiting for a reaction.

She sat back in the chair and folded her arms. Her expression reminded him of Coulter—mocking, arrogant and superior.

'Unfortunately for you the backpack was found by kids, who handed it in. We know the clown costume was bought in Razzle in Sauchiehall Street, and an assistant there remembers you. Your DNA is all over the suit and all over the knife that killed Kira and David. We also found traces from its shark skin handle in Melanie's room. You hated Kira enough to kill her, but why kill Melanie?'

She answered in a bored tone. 'David told Melanie he'd fucked her at the party wearing the mask. She was disgusted. She went mad, screaming at him. He told me he just wanted to shut her up.'

She was good, he had to admit it. What she said made sense. David, mad with jealousy, kills Kira and disposes of the baby in the woods. When he admits to Melanie that he had sex with her, she mocks him like Kira. He puts his hand over her mouth to shut her up and smothers her instead. Without the forensic evidence to say otherwise, a jury might believe her.

'OK. Again, here's my version. You went to see Melanie. You had already killed once and found it easy, and she was the last of the gang still pregnant. You were out of chloroform and you couldn't take any more from the chemistry lab, not after Kira; so you covered her face with a pillow. You had the knife with you, but something happened to stop you using it. I think David turned up and disturbed you.' He saw a flicker of surprise

389

that suggested he might be on the right track. 'You knew David had been at Melanie's and you knew we were looking for him, possibly in connection with her death. That gave you a great idea. Pin both murders on David and get rid of him too. You arranged to meet him that night, and he was so drunk it was easy. You stabbed him, then arranged his hands to make it look like suicide. The note was clever, but he didn't write it—you did.'

Sandie half-smiled. 'You're making this all up. You haven't a clue.'

'What did they do to make you hate them so much? Didn't invite you to their parties? Made fun of you? Wouldn't let you into their gang?'

'I didn't *want* to be in their fucking gang.'

'I bet Kira boasted about being able to do mirror writing. Another thing that pissed you off. That's why you wrote on her hands like that. That's why you drew a daisy on Melanie.'

They had been round the block with this. Even presented with the DNA evidence refuting her version of events, Sandie still sat there in defiance.

'Is that what you told Jeff Coulter? That they were mean to you and wouldn't let you play? What did he say? Screw them? Or kill them?'

She stared pointedly over his shoulder, lips pursed.

'Jeff Coulter. Remember him?'

'I have no idea what you're talking about. I told you already, I don't know him.'

'You met him when you were fifteen. He screwed you. He likes screwing silly wee girls like you. I bet he said you were beautiful and clever. How much he loved you. Then he got fed up listening to his own baby crying and snapped its

390

spine. He was locked up in the State Mental Hospital, and you wrote to him in there, told him your troubles. He gave you the solution. Get the bitch's baby and give it to Geri, because he was sorry for what he'd done to her kid. He was a changed man. If you did that, he would know that you truly loved him.' He paused.

She looked back at him, stony-faced.

'Do you still have those letters, Sandie? I hope you do. Then your lawyer can show how Coulter manipulated you. How he persuaded you to do what you did.'

He watched as the mask slipped to reveal the face of a killer. The cold hatred she directed at him froze the blood in his veins.

'Kira thought she could control everyone. She was wrong,' she spat. 'In the end, I controlled her, and the others. And where are they now?'

\*　　　\*　　　\*

'Good work, Bill. Congratulate the team from me.'

In the old days Sutherland would have produced a bottle of whisky and poured them both a glass. Not any more. Changed times, and not always for the better.

'I will, but that's not why I'm here.'

'There's a problem?'

'DS Michael McNab,' Bill said.

Sutherland eyed him cautiously. 'We have discussed this already. SOCA are handling the case.'

'He isn't dead, is he?'

There was a moment when he knew Sutherland was poised between downright denial and yet another lie, then he went to the door and checked it was properly closed. 'Sit down, Detective Inspector.'

'I prefer to stand.'

'Sit down. That's an order.'

Bill sat. His legs were like water anyway.

'Tell me what you know.'

Bill was surprised he still had a voice. 'Fergus Morrison was shot in a London safe house. Someone had been in there with him. Someone wanted by Kalinin.'

'And that someone is a potential witness against Kalinin and therefore must be protected,' Sutherland said sharply.

A cold fury swept through Bill. 'Bastards! They let us believe he was dead. They made us bloody bury him.'

'The dead are safer than the living.'

They eyeballed one another.

'Has he been in touch?' Sutherland said.

Bill shook his head.

'If he is, I want to know. You will tell me immediately.'

Bill suddenly understood. 'They've lost him, haven't they?'

Sutherland looked peeved. 'He walked out of the safe house.'

'Maybe because it wasn't bloody safe.'

'The *new* safe house. McNab's reckless. None of this would have happened if he hadn't gone to the Poker Club that night.'

'Slater let Kalinin out. He did not inform McNab of that fact.'

They locked eyes once again.

'You will tell no one, I repeat, no one about this

392

conversation, Detective Inspector. And I hope I don't need to remind you that your recent reinstatement is still under review.'

Bill kept his mouth tightly shut, not trusting himself to speak.

'That is all.' Sutherland rose and opened the door. 'As I said, please give your team my congratulations on a job well done.' He pitched the last remark loud enough for anyone within a mile radius to hear, even though there was no one else around.

*      *      *

Bill entered the pub quietly, not wanting to draw attention to himself. The drink had been flowing freely, the talk was loud, the laughter even louder. DC Campbell was doing an impression of the Super. It wasn't half bad. Bill went round the back of the bar and caught the barman's eye, but his offer of money was waved away.

'They set up a kitty. There's plenty in it for you.'

He pushed over a whisky. Bill took it and made his way through the crowd, pausing now and again as someone spotted him and took the drunken liberty of slapping their boss on the back. He found Rhona sitting in an alcove, a glass of white wine on the table in front of her. She slid over to make room for him.

'How'd it go with Sandie?' she said.

'She won't discuss Coulter.'

'She will, when she realises what it means.'

'He's untouchable. He was never coming out anyway. I can't help but think he's the only winner in all of this.'

393

Rhona put her hand on his arm. They sat in silence for a moment as fun and laughter flowed around them.

'I have something to tell you.' Bill spoke quietly. 'It's about Michael.'

She was appraising him, those cool eyes plumbing the depths of his soul. He had made up his mind to do this the minute he'd known for certain, regardless of the consequences. He was ignoring a direct order from his superior officer, but he didn't care. She deserved to know.

She spoke before he could. 'Michael's alive, isn't he?'

He nodded, wondering how much to say. 'SOCA had him under wraps. He was going to testify against Kalinin.' He wondered how on earth she knew, or could even have guessed, that McNab was alive.

'When did you find out?' she said.

'I had a set-to with the Super before I came here. He told me my job's on the line if I say anything.'

'I won't breathe a word.'

DC Campbell, rosy from his comedic exertions and the number of pints he'd downed, spotted them in the corner. He bellowed above the general hubbub. 'Hey, boys! Let's hear it for the boss!'

A circle of happy faces and raised glasses turned towards them. Bill felt Rhona's hand squeeze his arm.

'To the boss,' they shouted.

'To the boss,' Rhona repeated quietly beside him.

# CHAPTER FIFTY-SEVEN

Bill parked in the same place as before and walked along Hamilton Drive, pausing to look over the wall at the Kelvin below. He wondered if the upside-down ironing board was still in place. He'd been angry about it before, now he felt an affection for the item that had stopped the backpack on its way downstream.

Below, two dogs met on the path and had a friendly sniff while their owners exchanged pleasantries. Soon the banks of the river would be green and luscious again, most of the litter covered by foliage. He made a mental note to bring Margaret and the kids here. They could walk as far as Kelvingrove, maybe visit the *Doctor Who* exhibition for Robbie's sake.

He thought briefly of Jeff Coulter. Without the co-operation of Sandie or Geri, they had nothing to charge him with. It was the one fly in the ointment, but there was time yet. Maybe Geri would eventually turn her anger against him instead of blaming herself. Maybe Sandie's parents would make her see sense. Maybe.

He paused at the gate for a moment. The Volkswagen was there so she must be at home. The grass was no longer a carpet of crocuses, but daffodils were nodding in their place. He hesitated at the front door before ringing the bell. Through the glass he saw the outline of a baby buggy in the hall next to the flower-decked table.

When she opened the door she was holding a bottle of milk, just as Geri Taylor had been. Her face lit up when she saw him. From somewhere nearby came the wail of a hungry baby.

'Come in, Detective Inspector,' she said in delight.

He followed her through to the sitting room. The baby had been laid in a Moses basket while she answered the door. Maria scooped the infant up, took a seat on the couch and reinserted the teat in the child's open mouth. Silence quickly descended.

Now that he saw Maria with the baby, Bill could barely register the enormity of what this woman had gone through. She had lost her daughter, first to her husband, then to a killer. The tenacity of the human spirit never failed to amaze him.

Maria planted a kiss on the baby's forehead. 'I decided to keep the name Daisy. It's what Kira wanted.'

Bill wanted to ask about her husband, and as though anticipating this, she said, 'Ronald and I are no longer together. I have custody of Daisy, but he has access to her. He's taken up a new job in London, so he won't be here that often.' She sounded relieved.

He looked up from his study of the baby to find her observing him keenly.

'Kira was extraordinarily gifted, Detective Inspector, but she always needed to control those around her. Maybe it was because she'd been abandoned as a child. She was in a terrible state when social services found her. Perhaps by controlling and manipulating others, she was trying to make sure she would never be abandoned again.'

Bill nodded but didn't comment. If it helped her

396

to believe that, he had no business suggesting otherwise.

A tiny hand found and caught hold of Maria's finger. The expression on her face told Bill that Daisy would be loved whatever happened in the future.

When he took his leave, Maria caught both his hands in hers.

'Thank you for finding Daisy for me. Having her has made my life worth living again.'


## CHAPTER FIFTY-EIGHT

Rhona glanced at her watch. It was almost time. She left the coffee stand and walked towards the exit of the Buchanan Galleries. Adrenalin was pumping through her body and urging her to run down the incline as a child might, in a surge of joy and anticipation. She forced herself to walk even more slowly than usual, as though approaching her execution.

Most of the shoppers were coming in through the double doors from Sauchiehall Street. At eleven o'clock on a Saturday morning, Glaswegians were intent on their favourite pastime. As she slipped out past a mother and teenage girl, both dressed expensively in designer labels, she thought momentarily of Kira. Bill had told her that Daisy had been placed with Kira's mother, Maria, and both were doing well. It was the only good thing to come out of the whole terrible business.

Cold air met her as she emerged. She joined a

crowd gathered at the foot of the steps leading to the concert hall, where a man dressed in a tuxedo was performing 'I Did It My Way' in Italian. At first she barely noticed the light touch on her shoulder, assuming it was just someone pressing close in the enthusiastic audience. Then a hand found hers and clasped it tightly.

'Let's walk.'

He steered her away from the crowd and along Sauchiehall Street. Her heart was beating so loudly and rapidly she could hear nothing but its pounding in her ears. She stole a glance at the man taking long strides beside her. She would never have recognised him.

'Where are we going?'

'Wait and see.'

He led her towards Bath Street. Halfway up the hill he turned in at the entrance to a hotel. The foyer was small and lined in dark paper. He made for a double door on the left. Even out of the view of others he didn't break his silence. They entered a tiny lift and he pressed the button for the eighth floor. Her hand still clasped in his, she could sense his tension. He turned right out of the lift, led her to the far end of the corridor and opened the door to room 803.

He closed it behind them, checked the lock and slipped the card into the slot. When the lights came on, she saw that the outer wall was glass. It rose through two levels and she realised the bedroom was above. The view from the window over Glasgow was extraordinary. Every landmark on this side of the city was identifiable. She could even see as far as the Cathkin Braes to the south.

There was a moment's silence as she registered

398

all of this, realising that he was hiding up here, that seeing the city laid out before him probably made him feel safer. He came to stand behind her, wrapping his arms about her. It didn't matter what he looked like; she could smell the familiar scent of his skin as he placed his cheek against her head. They stood like that for a long time, drinking one another in.

'I cried at your funeral.'

'I knew you would,' he said.

'Chrissy was heartbroken.'

She could hear the pain in his voice as he said, 'I'm sorry about that. I was out of it. I had no idea what the hell they were doing.'

'She organised a funeral mass. We sang hymns.'

He laughed. A glorious sound. 'Good old Chrissy, hedging my bets. I love that lassie.'

'She called the baby Michael after you.'

'No way!'

She wanted to stay like this forever. Not seeing him, she could remember the old McNab. The dark auburn hair, the blue eyes, the scruffy stubble. If she turned round, she would be looking at a stranger.

'What happened?'

'I died. They revived me. When I eventually surfaced, I was in a private room in a hospital in London with SOCA in charge. I was moved to a safe house, which turned out not to be so safe after all.'

'Fergus Morrison?'

'Poor bastard.' He tensed, his arms squeezing her even tighter. 'They moved me to another house, but I decided I was better on my own.'

'What about SOCA?'

'They don't know where I am now. I prefer it that way.'

She wanted to ask what he was going to do, but didn't dare because she feared hearing the answer.

'Einar Petersson?' she asked.

'He helped me. He's OK.'

'I thought he was lying.'

'You buried me. Of course you would think he was lying.'

'And Slater?'

'Who knows? Maybe when it goes to court I'll get some answers.'

He eased her round to face him. For a moment she saw a stranger who merely had McNab's voice. Head shaved, thinner, a short beard dyed black, then she met his eyes and saw the real McNab still in there.

'May I kiss you, Dr MacLeod?'

But it was she who kissed him, tasting the man she had known. When they parted, he said, 'When I woke in the hospital, I vowed I would live long enough to do that again.'

'What happens now?'

'We could go upstairs.'

They undressed in suddenly awkward silence. His body was so much thinner. Taut and wiry like a long distance runner's. She tried not to focus on the bullet wound in his back, but still her eyes were drawn there and she saw him lying on the pavement, the blood pumping out of his body.

'Hey.' He was beside her, bringing her back to the present. 'Come on.' He led her to the bed and threw back the duvet.

They lay facing one another. He traced her cheek, her neck, as though checking that each plane and curve was where it should be. His touch was familiar, but at the same time new. She wondered if his brush with death had changed him, made him calmer and more concentrated.

*     *     *

Afterwards they lay naked and exposed, the duvet thrown to the floor. Warm air from an overhead heater circulated above them, softly brushing their bodies.

'What now?' The same question she'd posed earlier. The one he'd chosen to misinterpret.

'I lie low until the trial begins.'

'They've picked up Kalinin?'

'Soon.'

'How do SOCA know you'll turn up at his trial?'

'They know if I'm alive, I'll be there.'

'Does Kalinin know you're alive?'

'He isn't sure.'

'But he's looking for you?'

She saw it all happening again. The passing car, the shot. He sensed her fear and drew her close.

'Glasgow's my city. I'm safer here.'

'You weren't before.'

'It's different now. I'm dead.' He raised himself on one elbow and grinned down at her. 'You just had sex with a corpse, Dr MacLeod.'

*     *     *

She took a taxi home. He didn't come down with her to the foyer nor would he promise to be back in touch until, as he put it, it was over.

She wondered if it would ever be over. If he did

401

give evidence, what next? A new identity, a new life? She couldn't imagine that, and nothing he'd said suggested that's what McNab had in mind.

'I can't hide from every maniac I've locked up,' he'd grinned.

She asked the taxi driver to drop her on Kelvin Way, deciding to walk home through the park.

Dry, crisp weather had hardened the ground, but the spring flowers were beautiful. Rhona felt absurdly joyful, a feeling she realised she hadn't experienced for a long time.

## CHAPTER FIFTY-NINE

The latest Reborn was almost ready to be shipped. It was going to a couple in London whose own baby had died of meningitis hours after birth. He hadn't copied the photograph they'd sent because it was an ugly little bugger, like a shrivelled raisin. His own version was what he thought the baby boy might have looked like at two months. He'd toned down the redness of the face, filled out the creases and opened the eyes, making them a lovely dark blue. He laid the Reborn in its satin-lined box and put the lid on, then settled down at the table with a sheet of lined prison paper and a pen and began to write.

*Hi Susi*
*Ive finished little Matthew I made him prettier than his picture his mum will luv him I can make you a baby you only have to ask*